This is a story of great ambition and enormous talent met in a colorful personality who —for reasons absorbingly set forth here— failed to gain the ultimate rewards he spent his life in seeking.

At Oxford, George Nathaniel Curzon, eldest son of a baronet, was known as a handsome, charming, and zealous young man, and was widely regarded as a likely future prime minister of England. In the Foreign Ministry his rise was meteoric; in 1899, he became the last great and powerful viceroy of India, perhaps the last true proconsul in world history.

Then, at the height of his early career, he made the mistake of inviting Lord Kitchener to serve as commander in chief of the forces in India. The clash between these two strong-minded, ambitious men sent Curzon into eclipse for ten years.

Leonard Mosley's account of the stresses on Curzon's private life upon his return to England draws on papers that, until now, have been privately held. The death of Curzon's wife—a delightful, naïve Chicago heiress —was followed in time by his earldom and an eight-year affair with the celebrated and lovely novelist Elinor Glyn. Their relationship ended melodramatically when Curzon married his second American heiress.

Following World War I, Curzon became Foreign Secretary, putting himself in direct line for England's highest post—prime minister. But this was not to be. His story—with all its soaring triumph yet profound failure— is told here with a power and authenticity that bring to life a fascinating era through one of its major figures.

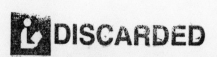

The Glorious Fault

Other books by Leonard Mosley

THE CAT AND THE MICE
THE SEDUCTIVE MIRROR
CASTLEROSSE
GIDEON GOES TO WAR
REPORT FROM GERMANY
DOWN STREAM
WAR LORD
SO FAR SO GOOD
NO MORE REMAINS
SO I KILLED HER

Ambition first sprung from your bless'd abodes;
The glorious fault of angels and of gods.

ALEXANDER POPE, *"Elegy to the Memory
of an Unfortunate Lady"*

The Glorious Fault

THE LIFE OF LORD CURZON

BY

Leonard O. Mosley

HARCOURT, BRACE AND COMPANY

NEW YORK

© 1960 by Leonard Mosley

FIRST EDITION

LIBRARY OF CONGRESS CATALOG CARD NUMBER: 60-9396
PRINTED IN THE UNITED STATES OF AMERICA

Author's Note

GEORGE NATHANIEL, first and last Marquess Curzon of
Kedleston, was almost certainly the most fascinating character
of major importance to have figured in English politics since the
days of Sir George Savile, first Marquess of Halifax (1633–1695).

With Halifax the Trimmer he had, in fact, many qualities in
common. They were both men of great natural gifts and vaulting
political ambition; they were both fine speakers and writers of
remarkable prose, and each loved to hear the sound of his own
voice or read the copious emanations from his own pen; and
neither of them ever hesitated to go back on a solemn pledge
if the contingencies of the political situation made such a reversal
necessary to preserve his advantage.

It was of the Trimmer, it will be remembered, that Dryden
wrote:

> *Jotham of piercing wit and pregnant thought,*
> *Endued by nature, and by learning taught*
> *To move assemblies who but only tried*
> *The worse a while, then chose the better side.*

Halifax opposed the accession of James to the throne of England,
but threw in his lot with him when Charles II died and James

v

succeeded, and while serving him, alternately hated or despised him. Similarly, Curzon swore that he would never support Lloyd George as Prime Minister, but immediately accepted a post in his Cabinet when he became Premier in 1916, meanwhile referring to him privately as "that scurrilous little rascal."

Halifax, sent by James at the head of a delegation to mediate with William of Orange, took the opportunity of making it clear to the invader that he was more than willing to come in on his side. Curzon, having promised Churchill, Austen Chamberlain, and other members of the Lloyd George Coalition that he would stay with them, went secretly to Bonar Law and told him he was with him in his bid for the premiership. Halifax had a plausible explanation for his actions, and as will be seen from these pages, so had Curzon. But of the first, William's General and Commander in Chief subsequently is said to have remarked: "This is the first time I have seen a leader desert his own troops." And of the second, a Coalition Minister said: "So the great proconsul has ratted on us at last."

The parallels continue to present themselves. Both men earned the hatred of the Tories for what was considered their turnabout perfidiousness. Both lived to become the butt of their opponents' spite: half London was invited to the Trimmer's funeral while he was still alive; Curzon was mocked and jeered at in Parliament, from the platform, and across the Cabinet table.

They were each of them remarkable men whose enormous talents failed to earn them the ultimate rewards which they spent their lives in seeking. They each died disappointed.

This biography is an attempt to explain, in the case of George Nathaniel Curzon, the reason why.

This is not, in the ordinary sense of the word, a political biography, although the politics of Britain and the British Empire for the first twenty-five years of the present century play a large part in it. Rather is it the study of a man—and of the epoch in which he lived. It sets out to present Curzon not simply as a public man—a Viceroy, a statesman, a politician—but as a whole human being, complex, temperamental, in sickness and (rarely, in this case) health, in happiness and misery, in moments of private joy and public triumph, in the midst of terrible domestic stress and profound political humiliation.

For the facts I have gone, first of all, to the great mass of papers which Curzon left behind him after his death in 1925. Before he died, he assembled them (each bundle of letters and each file of documents) under periods and subjects, with a note of explanation in his own handwriting attached to every pile. He was one of the most copious as well as one of the most fluently interesting letter-writers of all time, with interests ranging far away from politics. The papers, in boxes, tin trunks, wicker boxes and packing cases, filled two whole rooms. I owe a deep debt of gratitude to the Beaverbrook Foundation for allowing me to have sole access to them for nearly two years.

Curzon destroyed only those letters which, he felt, might throw a light upon his political and private actions of a kind calculated to spoil the picture of himself which he was anxious for posterity to have (and for information about these I have had to go elsewhere). Otherwise he kept everything for his biographers: letters to and from practically all the giants and personalities of his period; scribbled notes; aide memoires and impassioned defences of his actions; secret Cabinet documents; pamphlets, books, bills, notebooks and diaries. There are also hundreds of letters he wrote to and received from his first wife, Mary, and his second wife, Grace, which contain a rich mine of information about his political feelings and personal condition during the great crises of his life.

From these I have taken most of my facts. I have, in addition, consulted most of the books dealing with the epoch in which Curzon lived.

ACKNOWLEDGMENTS

I HAVE ALREADY EXPRESSED my deep gratitude to the Beaverbrook Foundation for allowing me access to the Curzon Papers.

In addition, I wish to thank the following for permission to use letters, diaries, and extracts from books:

The present Earl Baldwin and the executors of the 2nd Earl Baldwin for the use of a letter from Mr. Stanley Baldwin to Curzon

Lord Kitchener for permission to quote his father's letters

Lady Chetwynd for the use of a letter from Sir Arthur Hardinge

Mrs. A. Salvidge and Mrs. A. F. Nicholson for an extract from the diary of the late Sir Archibald Salvidge

The daughters of the late Lord Ribblesdale

Lord Chandos for three extracts from the letters of Miss Laura Tennant

Mr. Murray Lawrence for an extract of a letter from Sir Walter Lawrence

Messrs. Curtis Brown Ltd. for a letter from Thomas Hardy

Lady Florence Spring Rice for a letter from Sir Cecil Spring Rice

Lady Griffith-Boscawen for a letter written by Sir Arthur Griffith-Boscawen

Lord Hankey for a private Minute written to Mr. Stanley Baldwin

Sir Anthony Glyn and Elinor Glyn Ltd. for permission to quote from the diaries of Miss Elinor Glyn

Lord Esher for two extracts from his father's letters

Lord Lansdowne for the extract from a letter from the 5th Marquess

The Hon. Anthony Asquith Esq. for two extracts from letters from his mother, the Countess of Oxford and Asquith

Mr. Francis Noel Baker for a letter from A. J. Balfour

Mr. K. Fitzgerald and Miss Alice McEnery for a letter from Sir John Lavery

S. F. Crowe for a letter from Sir Eyre Crowe

Sir Winston Churchill and Odhams Press for permission to quote from *The World Crisis*

Viscount Davidson for permission to use extracts from his Memorandum

Lady Vansittart for permission to use extracts from *The Mist Procession* (Hutchinson)

Mr. Robert Blake for extracts from *The Unknown Prime Minister*

The Phoenix Assurance Company Ltd. for a letter from Lord George Hamilton

The Public Trustee for extracts from the War Diary of Lord Riddell

Ernest Benn Ltd. and Sir Benjamin Brodie for an extract written by Sir Herbert Warren from Lord Ronaldshay's *Life of Curzon*

Miss Norah Lyttleton for letters from her father, Dr. Edward Lyttleton

Lord Howe for permission to use correspondence with Curzon

Lord Harcourt for a letter from Sir William Harcourt

Lord Salisbury for permission to use and quote from family letters

The literary executors of the late Sir Schomberg McDonnell for permission to quote from letters to Lord Curzon

CONTENTS

xi

The Glorious Fault

CHAPTER ONE

Infancy and Influences

WE KNOW BY NOW that the ends of a man are only too often shaped by his very beginnings; that some men carry, and constantly feel, the marks of their cradles upon them until the day that they die. No one is going to claim that about George Nathaniel Curzon, least of all Curzon himself, for he always stoutly maintained that he was an integrated and completely self-made man. The idea that his ambitions and attitudes were moulded for him in the hour of his birth would have moved him to orotund scorn.

All the same, it is likely that life for Curzon would almost certainly have assumed a different shape, and might well have been happier and less permeated with a sense of failure, had it not been for the fact that when he was born (and for a long time thereafter) his head was too big.

In the late evening of January 10, 1859, the doctor who had been called to Kedleston, the great Adam mansion in Derbyshire, to attend the accouchement of Blanche, wife of the fourth Baron Scarsdale, drew her husband to one side and expressed his doubts about a successful outcome of the struggle in which his patient had already been engaged for several weary and painful hours. Though at first every sign had seemed to show that the cycle of labour and delivery would not be unduly protracted beyond that normally expected in the birth of a first child, something had supervened which had brought the process to a halt and Lady Scarsdale to the verge of collapse.

The supervention was, in fact, the abnormally large head of the Scarsdales' first-born pressing determinedly but so far unavailingly for an entrance into the world. It was not until the morning of January 11 that it was finally drawn clear, dragging a rabbit-sized torso in its wake; by which time both parents were exhausted, the fourth Baron (a clerk in holy orders) from an anguished night of prayer and supplication, and his wife from her more physical ordeal. She was twenty-three years old, and though she lived fourteen years more (and bore ten more children in that time), it was an experience she not only never forgot but also, perhaps, never forgave.

When she was shown her son and heir for the first time she displayed towards him none of the rapture of a mother who has risked death and emerged triumphant, but instead looked at her top-heavy offspring with the cold surprise that was to be the quality of her attitude towards her son for the rest of her life. She handed him back to his wet nurse and asked that he should be brought back for further inspection the following morning. That was to be the pattern in the years to come. She gave no sign that she disliked him or resented him for the pain he had caused her, but neither were there any of those warm gestures and impulsive embraces which might have indicated that she loved him or that he had any real place in her heart. As he grew older and began to yearn for the affection which his nature increasingly needed, George Nathaniel Curzon became slowly aware that beneath the surface his mother's attitude towards him was so detached as to be almost indifferent. It did not stop him from worshipping her, but it had an important effect upon the shaping of his character and outlook, particularly towards women.

Later in life Curzon chose to look back upon the large head which had caused all the trouble as a rather amusing, if freakish, phenomenon, particularly since its size diminished proportionately to his body as he grew older. In a pencilled note of reminiscence which he scribbled under the heading "Baby Days" when he was in his late forties, he wrote:

"I never remember hearing anything remarkable about myself in early days but one thing. It rather reminds me of Sydney Smith to whom a lady once said at dinner by way of paying him a compliment, 'Were you remarkable as a boy, Mr. Smith?' 'Yes, Madam,' was the reply. 'I was a remarkably fat boy.' In the same way, I was a remarkably big-headed boy, and it was considered unsafe to leave me anywhere near the top of a staircase because on one occasion I was over-balanced by the momentum of that article and rolled down from top to bottom."

His body slowly grew up to match the size of his head, but until it did so the mind inside it was rarely unaware of its dimensions. In an earlier note he recalls how once, when still young, he was out shooting with his father and a keeper at Kedleston, and bagged a brace of pheasants with one shot. The keeper began to praise him but was stopped by his father with the words: "That's enough. You'll be giving the boy a swollen head." At that, Curzon recalls, "father turned away and the keeper went red in the face."

When he went to Eton he sulked in shame and fury because the boys called him "Moonface." He wrote in his notebook later: "I could never get hats to fit me. They were always too small and special ones had to be made. The feature of this absurd head was its abnormal breadth from side to side, particularly at the back. I don't know where I got it from because my father has an oval face and head of no extraordinary size. My mother had a small head, and none of the rest of the family have the same feature to anything like the same degree. When I grew up I had to have hats made to 7¼ to 7½ size."

The family into which Curzon had been born looked back with pride on both its Norman ancestry and its close and almost continuous connection with the Church. Both before and after the barony of Scarsdale was created (by patent granted to Sir Nathaniel Curzon in April, 1761) nearly every generation had at least one, and sometimes two, clergymen in the family. They had the gift of the living of the parish of Kedleston, and they almost always handed it to one of their own. What money they possessed, and they were never rich, came to them through the first Baron's grandfather, who married Sarah, the daughter of William Penn of Pennsylvania, and who invested wisely in both the American colonies and the East India Company. It was with the fortune he amassed that the building of Kedleston Hall was begun, subsequently to be taken over by Robert Adam and his brother, who brought in alabaster from the Derbyshire hills and wrought iron from Worcestershire to erect the magnificent mansion which stands today in its parkland outside Derby. "A fine park with old timber, beautiful gateway with lovely iron gate by Adam, a vast house with four wings, of which two only yet built, and magnificently finished and furnished, all designed by Adam in the best of taste but too expensive for his (Scarsdale's) estate," was the way Horace Walpole described it after a visit in September, 1768.

Curzon's father was not only a stern cleric and God-fearing man, he was also fanatically devoted to his house and estates and the barony which they represented. For him the three great rewards of his life were, in order of importance, his peerage and the ancestry behind it, the pulpit of Kedleston Church from which he preached his weekly sermon, and his wife. He loved them all, in diminishing stages, and these, together with his relentless pursuit of the rich game in his parklands, did not leave him much time for his eldest son or the children who followed. His Scarsdale title was for him perhaps even more important than his Curzon name, and he never quite forgave his son for securing a title of his own instead of waiting to inherit his father's coronet.

What may have made Scarsdale important for him was the fact that, at one black moment in his life, there had been a danger that he would not get it. He had always considered himself next in line to his uncle, the third Baron. The third Baron died a bachelor at Kedleston in 1856 at the age of seventy-five. Curzon's father reached for the coronet. But suddenly two other claimants appeared upon the scene, namely Edward Curzon, a captain in the Army, and the Reverend Frederick Emmanuel Hippolite Curzon, the vicar of Mickleover in Derbyshire. It seemed that there was a skeleton in the Curzon cupboard, and these two had come to rattle it. In the 1780's, the second Baron had departed for the Continent after the death of his wife at the age of twenty-four. He left behind a son, his heir, and a daughter. In Brussels he met and fell in love with a beautiful young Belgian girl named Félicité Anne Josèphe. They went to live at Altona, a suburb of Hamburg, and there six children (five sons and a daughter) were born to them, all, unfortunately for them, out of wedlock. It was not until 1798 that the second Baron and Félicité were legally married before the British consul in Hamburg. Soon their seventh (and first legitimate) child, Alfred, was born, followed at intervals by three others. Alfred was therefore, legitimately speaking, the second Baron's second son, and after his father died and his half-brother assumed the title, he was the heir to the title and estates. In fact, he predeceased his half-brother, but he left behind a son, Curzon's father, the third Baron's nephew. When the third Baron died a bachelor, Curzon's father naturally expected to succeed. But now here were his two illegitimate uncles hot upon the scene loudly asserting that perhaps they were not illegitimate at all. They had reason to believe, they said, that their father and mother had gone through a form of marriage in Hamburg before the birth of one or other of them. (They were not entirely sure which one.) They told Curzon's father that they were determined to take legal action to secure the succession for whichever of them could prove his legitimacy.

There was consternation at Kedleston Hall and a great flurry of family lawyers. It was not until Curzon's father promised to continue paying them the substantial pensions they had been receiving from the third Baron that they reluctantly agreed to retire their suit, and Curzon's father came into what he had always considered his own. Thereafter the barony of Scarsdale was more precious to him than ever. "It was just as well that the two claimants retired," wrote Curzon to his wife Grace many years later. "Their suit would certainly never have succeeded." And, meticulous as always in the illumination of transgressions other than his own, he went carefully through the parchments containing his family tree, clearly separating his natural great-uncles and aunt from his legitimate ones. Where one of them had somehow got herself into the right, instead of the wrong, branch of the family, he put his pen through her name from right to left and wrote firmly at the side: "This lady was not legitimate."

It would be wrong to say that the Scarsdales were not dutiful parents. So far as creature comforts were concerned, they were not remiss. Sir Harold Nicolson, in a sketch of Curzon's early life, has suggested that there was hardship in the house and that life at Kedleston was run on the lines of a country vicarage. It all depends upon the standpoint from which you look at it. An estate with an agent and scores of tenants, plus a shoot over which the Reverend Lord Scarsdale often shot thirty brace of pheasants in an afternoon does not exactly hint at privation. The regime was, in truth, sometimes harsh; economies in the kitchen, over whose fire was the sign "Spare not but waste not;" thrice daily attendances in the family chapel; tiptoeing and silence in the house. But Curzon had his own pony to ride when he was five. The family trekked each year to Broadstairs or

Llandudno, where they took a house with their servants. One of Curzon's first memories is "the burnished reflectors of the lighthouse on the Great Orme, and the wallflowers on the parapet of the banqueting hall at Conway Castle." He was taken on regular trips to London to be fitted for suits at Swears and Wells, then known as the Lilliputian Warehouse. The suits were of velvet, Little Lord Fauntleroy kind, and his mother must have imagined him as such, for Curzon writes in one of his scribbled memories: "My hair was kept in corkscrew ringlets brushed round the finger with a hairbrush, and falling upon the shoulders. I remember I cried very bitterly when it was cut off." (There is a lock of his hair in an envelope among his papers; two other envelopes contain the hair of his two wives, and a third a cutting from the head of another woman who, for a time, figured importantly in his life.) The Scarsdales always stayed at the Burlington Hotel, next to the Arcade, where Curzon liked to hang around and watch the parade of the dandies. Each Sunday he was walked to Rotten Row "to have pointed out to me the celebrities, statesmen, generals, ecclesiastics and men of fashion, who used to ride there. I always myself regarded it with a mournful interest, for one of my uncles had been killed there by a fall from his horse while nodding to the girl whom he had hoped to marry. She had broken it off. . . . His horse reared as he took off his hat and he fell against the curb." From there the family group went on to the Zoological Gardens, which he hated. "I always thought, and still think, that with the exception of the lions and tigers and other big mammals the animals were shamefully huddled together, and that the management was painfully old-fashioned and unintelligent." But his favourite outing was to Madame Tussaud's, where he would stand in long and rapt contemplation of the reclining lady "whose bosom rose and fell." He never told his mother that the figure reminded him of her on those occasions when he sometimes stole into her bedroom at Kedleston and watched her while she was asleep.

Such, until the age of seven or eight, was the life of George Nathaniel Curzon—a rigid, disciplined life in which the main contact with his parents was either on these holiday outings or at morning prayers.

For companionship he had his pony, on which he lolloped around the park, or his younger sister Sophy, with whom he played hide-and-seek in the bushes. Except that it was barren of affection, however, Curzon's childhood was that of a normal child; and then into his life came a phenomenon that had a lifelong effect upon his character and his emotional construction. That phenomenon was a formidable individual known as Miss E. M. Paraman.

There is no photograph of Miss Paraman among Curzon's records and no account of her physical appearance except a mention by Curzon in passing that she had "grey eyes, thin hair and a large thin mouth." But there is ample evidence of her character.

She was hired by Lady Scarsdale in 1866–67 as a governess for Curzon and Sophy, and once she was established in the household, she became the dominant element in their lives. She had made it a condition of her employment that there should be no interference with her management, a condition to which Blanche Scarsdale was only too glad to give her consent. It is doubtful whether even the most indifferent mother would have handed over such blanket control of her children to another had she known what type of person was receiving it; but in this case the dutiful Scarsdale parents appear to have made no deep or prolonged inquiries into the character of Miss Paraman. Otherwise they would have discovered that she was, in all the long and colourful history of English governesses, the most remarkable of them all.

One of the more comforting qualities of the human make-up is its power to forget painful experiences, or, if forgetfulness is not possible, to wrap them around in a protective cocoon of nostalgia so that even great suffering, when looked back upon over the years, can be remembered without a cringe or a shudder. The mind of the average human being can digest almost any pain and any fear if given enough time. The damage may well have been done but the act which caused it loses its power to hurt with the passing of time.

That Curzon was permanently damaged by the treatment he received at the hands of Miss Paraman there is no doubt at all. It does not need a professional psychiatrist to see in many of his subsequent actions and attitudes both as a statesman and as a man the harsh hand of Miss Paraman pushing him inexorably in the direction he knows in his heart he should not be following. She came into his life at a moment in his childhood when he desperately needed a parent or parent-figure, and the fact that the vacuum was filled by this ogress—for such Miss Paraman undoubtedly was—had devastating results. It is a measure of her profound effect upon him that he was even able to look back upon her with affection, indeed with love, added to an almost masochistic pride in what she made him endure.

"This remarkable woman," he noted many years afterwards in one of his loose-leaf diaries, "controlled the first five of our family for over ten years and left on all of us a mark which has never been effaced. She was a good teacher, even for subjects such as French or music, of which she knew nothing herself. In her ordinary and sensible moments she was devoutly attached to us, and continued to be so until she died in 1892, when I went and stood by her grave. She taught us good habits, economy, neatness, method, and a dislike of anything vulgar or fast. But in her savage moments she was a brutal and vindictive tyrant and I have often thought since that she must have been insane."

If Curzon's parents had been more approachable, he and his sister might easily have sought protection from them. But Miss Paraman's system of terrorism was so complete that "not

one of us ever mustered up the courage to go upstairs and tell
our father and mother. . . . She spanked us with the sole of her
slipper on the bare back, beat us with her brushes, tied us for
long hours in chairs in uncomfortable positions with our hands
holding a pole or a blackboard behind our backs."

Perhaps because she sensed in Curzon the one most eager
for attention, even if it was of the painful kind, she singled him
out for the more severe humiliations.

"She shut us up in darkness," he recalled, "practised upon
us every kind of petty persecution, wounded our pride by dressing us (me in particular) in red shining calico petticoats (I was
obliged to make my own) with an immense conical cap on our
heads round which, as well as on our breasts and back, were
sewn strips of paper bearing in enormous characters written by
ourselves the words Liar Sneak Coward Lubber and the like.
In this guise she compelled us to go into the pleasure ground
and show ourselves to the gardeners. She forced us to go through
the park at even distances, never communicating with each
other—to the village to show ourselves to the villagers. It never
occurred to us that these good folk sympathised with us and
regarded her as a fiend. Our pride was much too deeply hurt."

One of the humiliations Curzon remembered most clearly
was the occasion when Miss Paraman forced him to write to
the butler asking him to make a birch with which he (Curzon)
was to be punished for lying. The butler had always been the
member of the domestic household for whose respect he had
striven. "When he came one day with a letter and saw me standing in my red petticoat with my face against the wall of the
schoolroom and said, 'Why, you look like a Cardinal,' I could
have died of shame."

As Curzon recalls the blacker moments of these childhood
ordeals, his writing grows larger and less controlled, as if his
pencil had begun to race across the page, and the indignities
pile up, line upon line: "She made us trundle our hoops all

alone up and down a place near the hermitage where w
black firtrees and a general air of gloom of which w
intensely afraid. She forced us to confess to lies we ha
told, to sins which we had never committed, and then punished
us savagely as being self-condemned. For weeks we were not
allowed to speak to each other or a living soul. At meals she
took all the dainties for herself and gave us nothing but tapioca
and rice. I suppose no children so well born or so well placed
ever cried so much, or so justly."

Yet he could add, after such a catalogue of unhappiness:
"That the good woman was devoted to us I believe there can
be no doubt. She was especially proud of me and was always
wanting me to go and see her during her illness in later life. . . .
I look back on her as one of the most extraordinary phenomena
I ever encountered. She represented a class of governess and a
method of tuition (in entire independence of the parents) which
have both disappeared. With children who are constantly with
their parents such a system would be incapable of concealment.
I must say for all of us that I believe we honestly forgave her
for the misery she had caused us."

In Curzon's case, it was not so much the misery she caused
him at the time as the long-term effect of her dominating and
domineering character upon a young, bright, eager but unusually
pliant boy. Thereafter, it could almost be said that he spent
his life looking for stronger, more ruthless, and more egoistic
characters upon whom he could bruise himself, and he found
them at every stage and in every place he went, at school, in
politics, and in his own home. "There is only one thing that
Curzon likes more than hurting others," Kitchener once said,
"and that is to persuade others to humiliate him." He was to put
himself in such a position that there was no lack of such opportunities in the years to come.

Had Curzon succeeded in going on to a normal boyhood in
school, once he had escaped from Miss Paraman's evil clutches,

the emotional wounds caused by her ministrations might have
healed and left upon him only minor scars. But once more the
fates (plus the laxity of his parents) thrust him into the orbit
of someone who, though far from being another Miss Paraman,
was to exert a most baleful influence upon his character. This
was a man called Archibald James Campbell Dunbar, who was
second master of Wixenford School, to which Curzon was sent
in May, 1869, when he was ten years old. Wixenford was a
preparatory school in Hampshire which was ostensibly run by
the Reverend Cowler Powler, a close friend of Charles Kingsley
and rector of the adjoining parish of Eversley. But Powler left
the practical running of the school to Dunbar, and Dunbar was,
in the words of Curzon, "the most remarkable feature of Wixenford life and one of the most curious characters I have ever met."

Curzon was fascinated by him, as he had been by Miss
Paraman, and fell beneath his spell with the same reluctant
Schadenfreude of a rabbit which, having broken away from the
toils of a rattlesnake in one glade in the forest, finds himself
transfixed by the gaze of a cobra waiting for him in the next.

"He was a man of very passionate, proud and imperious
temperament," he confided to his notes in later life, "and he
could brook no superiority or control. He was always on the
lookout for insults and fancied that people were deliberately
outraging his feelings. . . . As a master he was for the most
part detested by the boys to whom he was savage and cruel.
On the other hand, he made great favourites—of whom I was
one—and though he never spared us one jot or tittle of his
displeasure or punishment if we had provoked either, he could
be extremely nice to us when he was in a gracious mood."

Favourite or not, life at Wixenford for Curzon was once
more a series of punishments, though psychologists may be interested to note that by this time he resents them far less. "He
executed all or nearly all the punishments whether by spanking
on the bare buttocks or by caning on the palm of the hand or

by swishing* on the posterior. I remember well all three experiences. He was a master of spanking, though he used to say that it hurt him nearly as much as it did us. I remember that it was at about the fifteenth blow that it really began to hurt, and from thence the pain increased in geometrical progression. The largest number of smacks I ever received was, I think, forty-two. But comic to relate, I still remember the delicious feeling of warmth that ensued five to ten minutes later when the circulation had been thoroughly restored and the surface pain had subsided."

Far from turning Curzon against Dunbar, the regime of the rod seems to have heightened his admiration for his master, and he worked hard to please him. He mentions with pride that though some of the boys "had hands covered with weals" and others suffered even more severely, "with the birch he never gave me beyond ten or twelve strokes—and that for some peculiarly grave offense—in his bedroom at night." In his three years at Wixenford, Curzon rose to be head of the school and in his last term carried off five prizes. (Later on, when he was Foreign Secretary, Curzon's associates used to marvel at his extraordinary habit of using the breaks between important international conferences to wrestle with the household accounts of his many homes in England; he would never allow his wife to do them. This passion for domestic finance he may well have acquired at Wixenford, for he recalls: "I also kept the school accounts. I still have the tin cashbox in which I kept the money and the account books. I believe I was never out a penny at the end of the term.")

By the time he left Wixenford, Curzon's association with his strange and moody master had grown so close that even his departure did not bring it to an end. They kept up a frequent correspondence with each other until after Curzon entered Parliament, and their friendship was terminated only because Dun-

* British school slang for "flogging."

bar imagined a slight (none was intended) on Curzon's part and indicated that he wished to hear no more of or from him. Curzon notes with regret that he never saw or heard from him again.

So far as Curzon's character was concerned, that made little difference. Dunbar had been the third great influence in the shaping and moulding of Curzon's formative years. There had been first the impact of his mother's cold indifference (she who "was dearer to me than anyone in the world"), followed by the dedicated and sadistic domination of the vivid Miss Paraman, and now, to give the final twist, there was this pain-and-pleasure relationship with Dunbar, the Saturnine Scottish *gruppenfuehrer.*

The boy who went back to Kedleston in the spring of 1872 before going on to Eton, was the product of these three. He was a puny, pale child of thirteen, much given to spots, boils, and colds. Inside his brain was packed a great deal of knowledge, for, whatever else they had done to him, his two dark tutors had at least taught him to read and learn.

But emotionally, he was as unstable and unpredictable as a half-trained greyhound. As many a statesman and politician was to find him in later life, the masters at Eton (with one exception) found him insufferable.

CHAPTER TWO

A Most Superior Person

ETON COLLEGE in the eighteen-seventies and eighteen-eighties was a vast incubator dedicatedly engaged in the task of hatching out the future rulers of the greatest Empire the world has ever known. From the headmaster down to the youngest fag in the school, everyone was serenely aware that the cachet of an Eton education would, in future life, put every scholar two jumps ahead of the rest in the race for the choice positions in politics, the Church, diplomacy, and the more rewarding branches of the Civil Service. It was the most exclusive and the most influential club in the world; and any boy who did well could be sure that at the head of practically every department of the State there was an Old Member waiting with a helping hand and promise of preferment. The time would come (as it came with a shattering shock to Curzon in his lifetime) when the Eton tie round a man's neck would not be enough, when the upstarts from outside, with more worldly ability if less breeding, would push their way into the privileged positions of power. But when George Nathaniel Curzon came to Eton, the possibility of such a revolution seemed remote. Let the "outsiders" scramble for the lesser jobs. In the fight for the

great and vital offices of the Empire, particularly the higher
posts of Government, the boys of Eton were conscious of the
need to compete only among themselves. They had an almost
predestined sense of future greatness for the best among them;
and every Old Etonian who visited them—great Liberal leaders
and great Tory chieftains alike—hammered home the conviction
that from Eton would come the leaders of the future. (It must
be admitted that another Old Etonian, Gladstone, did several
times warn them that there were other boys from humbler
schools who were coming along to challenge them. The boys
of Eton retorted by taking Gladstone's picture in "Pop"* and
turning it to the wall.)

Curzon was well aware, from the start, of the privilege of
an Eton education, and he set out to get the most from it. For
the first year he was a quiet little mouse of a pupil, working
hard at his lessons and doing as he was told. He was also
miserable because, unlike the other boys, he never received
visits from his parents, not even on Eton's great day, the Fourth
of June. "It is a big day here and everyone's father and mother
come, so I suppose you will come," he wrote just before the
event in 1872. But on June 5 he wrote again to his father:
"Many thanks for your letter yesterday saying you couldn't come.
I was very sorry as I was all alone and everybody else's people
came. Your loving boy, George."

By the end of his first year, however, he had made a discovery. Not all tutors, he realised, were ogresses like Miss Paraman or tyrants like Dunbar. His tutor at Eton, Rev. Wolley Dod,
was in fact a weak man, and soon Curzon's attitude towards
him was "I rather despised the old gentleman's capacity to
impart instruction or maintain order." Since there was no one
around to dominate him, Curzon began to see the possibilities
of doing a little dominating himself. Soon he was at loggerheads
not only with Wolley Dod but with his other masters as well.

* Exclusive debating society.

"I was a confirmed cutter of names in desks and if an opportunity came to make a joke at the expense of one of the masters
I was always a leader." Curzon's insubordination, begun carefully in case he was salutarily checked, surged into open rebellion when he found that there was no one powerful enough, or
harsh enough, to cut him down to size.

"Looking back at Eton days," he wrote in his notes later on,
"I recall distinctly how little I was in harmony with many of
the masters, and how completely they misunderstood me, or
was it that I misunderstood them? I was one of the most undis-
ciplined boys in Wolley Dod's house, but I was one of the most
studious because I yearned to excel. I was one of the rowdiest
because I had high animal spirits and liked to respect myself
as not wholly a sap. . . . But I never neglected my lessons and
a sudden challenge from an indignant master invariably found
my answer ready and right, my work well done, my sums and
problems beautifully worked out. Thus I was always among the
first in class, though one of its apparently least satisfactory
members."

Such behaviour would have galvanised Paraman or Dunbar
into acts of awful reprisal, and even the average run of school-
masters might have been expected to visit it with the salutary
punishment it deserved. But with the appropriately named
Wolley Dod he got away with it every time. Having made a
lumbar probe and found his housemaster and assistants woefully
lacking in spine, Curzon became almost intoxicated with the
pleasures of independence and embarked on a career of way-
wardness and wilfulness that must have aroused their ire but,
apparently, never any positive reaction. The posterior which had
been whacked so unjustly and so often in the first eight years
of his schooling remained unwarmed during the whole of his
time at Eton.

"Out of school," he recalls, "I carried my indiscipline or independence to a pitch that was never suspected of so hard-

working and orthodox a student as I was. I made it a point of honour to attend Ascot Races every year, not because I cared in the least for racing but because it was forbidden and therefore dangerous. . . . Another of my somewhat daring eccentricities was that I had a zinc lining made for the bottom drawer of my oak bureau, in which I used to keep a stock of claret and champagne. It was not that I cared for drinking but that I enjoyed the supreme cheek, as an Eton boy, of giving wine parties in my room."

When a master checked him in class, he would lapse into a sulk from which nothing would rouse him. His Italian tutor once made the mistake of calling him "a brainless ass with no talent and no sense of the beauty of the language." That was enough for Curzon. Thereafter he cut both his French and Italian classes, a departure which was regarded with a certain smug satisfaction by the sorely tried masters of both, for they could already taste the sweetness of revenge when the examination results were announced at the end of the year, and the arrogant George Nathaniel's name would be among those at the bottom. But they were no match for the guile of their devious pupil. He studied in secret. He won the Prince Consort's prize for French by a larger percentage of marks than had ever been done before. To the mortification of the Italian tutor, whose pet pupil was a half-Italian boy who had lived most of his life in Florence, Curzon carried off the Italian prize, too, by a wide margin. The history master, Mr. Cornish, rebuked him one day for inattention. Curzon dashed from the classroom, tears coursing down his face, and did not return for the rest of the term; but he won the history prize.

He revelled in these triumphs, and not only at the time. When he recalled them in later life, he never gave any indication that such subterfuges as he had adopted might perhaps have had their reprehensible side. "Looking back, I think I must have had an extraordinary gift for assimilating the contents of books, committing to memory what was wanted, and writing just what was required. I won the Holiday Task Prize, never looking at the books during the vacation but spending the week before the examination in a savage effort which fixed everything in my mind and left me no time to forget. In this way I won more prizes than had ever been carried off before."

With each year his contempt for his masters increased and his boldness became more pronounced; and though the frustration of the faculty mounted, so did the admiration of the scholars. He was made captain of Oppidans (the society of Eton boys who lived outside the College), president of the Literary Society, and auditor of Pop, Eton's most exclusive society. By the time he was eighteen years old the feelings of destiny were beginning to swell in his breast, and his friends were already saluting him as a future Foreign Secretary or Prime Minister. He took pen to paper and began what was, in future, to be one of his principal activities, the writing of long letters. Later in life he could begin a new missive with the words: "This is my thirty-ninth letter today." Lord Esher recalls the dinner party at which the first Lady Curzon mentioned that she had received a letter that day from her husband, then Viceroy of India. A guest rashly asked if she might read it and it was handed over—a letter more than one hundred pages long.

At Eton, Curzon kept his output down to a round dozen letters a day, and he sent them to anyone who struck his fancy— Ruskin, Tennyson, Asquith, and Gladstone. To Gladstone he wrote an invitation to come and address the Literary Society, and to his delight received an acceptance. In his Eton diary there is an entry marked Ascension Day, May 30, 1878:

"Being in London for the day, called on the Rt. Hon. W. E. Gladstone (at 10, Downing Street) with reference to his coming visit to Eton to lecture on Homer. He was at breakfast with a large party of ladies and gentlemen but came out at once, shook hands most kindly, and took me into a small side room where he told me he looked upon the visit as a bargain which was certainly to be kept. Said he considered himself bound to do anything for Eton. Called again June 20. Introduced me to Mrs. G., young G. (like a sleepy assistant behind a silk-master's counter), Albert Gray and others. Everything arranged."

Only two events marred the intoxicating success of his life at Eton. The first was the death of his mother, which shattered him for a whole term. He had written to her at least once every day while he was at Eton, and among his letters to her are still to be found the strips of purple cloth or chintz covering with which, with her approval, he proposed to curtain his study windows and cover his furnishings. She replied infrequently, and she came to see him only once.

The other blow was the lack of interest in his victories by his father, the Reverend Lord Scarsdale. He never came to Eton at all. One of his letters to his son reads: "I congratulate you on your success, but for goodness' sake do not get too puffed up. And do not celebrate your success by wearing your hair long and wrapped round your ears. You know what I mean and I do detest long hair."

For all his show of independence, it would have been out of character for Curzon to have failed to find someone to dominate him as he was now dominating others. The individual who, perhaps inevitably though certainly not in the same baleful way, took the place of Miss Paraman and Dunbar was an Eton master named Oscar Browning. Curzon first came into contact with this cultured, sensitive, and attractive personality through his association with the Eton Literary Society, which Browning had founded in 1871. He was one of those masters, to be found in every school, who seems to have that special quality which brings boys clustering around him. He was a good talker, a passionate devotee of learning, a man of taste and discrimination, and he and Curzon took to each other at once. Their friendship was soon to cause trouble for both of them. Browning encouraged Curzon in his extra-curricular activities, and, one suspects, took a vicarious delight in the discomfiture of Wolley Dod. Only too often when he cut his classes, Curzon spent his time walking or studying with Browning, and the closeness of their association was not lost upon Curzon's "dame"* at Eton, Mrs. Wolley Dod. She sat down and wrote a letter to Lord Scarsdale warning him of the "unhealthy association" that was growing between master and boy. Scarsdale wrote to Oscar Browning asking for an explanation, and got a long and most eloquent reply in which Browning angrily insisted that his interest in George Nathaniel was but that of a friendly uncle towards a nephew in need of help, advice, and guidance. Lord Scarsdale, on July 14, 1874, wrote gruffly back:

"Exceedingly regret this extremely unpleasant complaint from Mrs. Wolley Dod with ref. to your conduct towards my son George. I am fully aware of your desire that he should grow up a clean and pure-minded lad, and know that it is possible that your notice of him may have served to annoy his tutor. I give you full credit for acting from the purest motives and I do not wish the kindly relations between you and the boy to fall through. I quite believe that you were instrumental in rescuing George from companions of more than doubtful repute, and that your sole desire and object has been to elevate and improve his character. I have a kind letter from Mr. Hugessen on this matter, for he too takes a warm interest in George, and I can only hope that no further unpleasantness will occur. Thanking you for so full an explanation of the circumstances."

In spite of this letter and its hope that the friendship between master and boy should continue, action appears to have been taken behind the scenes to see that it did not. By order of the headmaster, all communication between the two, either in per-

* Matron in charge of a boarding house.

son or by letter, was forbidden, and shortly afterwards Browning left the school. Curzon wrote to him in great distress on July 20, 1874:

"I must write a parting letter to you and I do hope that we may soon be permitted to communicate with each other again. I cannot say how distressed I am that I am prevented from seeing you, all through the unkind and ungentlemanly and obstinate conduct of my tutor, whom I detest the more I see him. But I must thank you with my whole heart for all the inestimable good you have done me, for you have always been open to me as the best of counsellors, and you have warned me against evil companionship. I do not know how I shall get on without being even allowed to see you. I am so very sorry I have been the innocent cause of all this trouble for you, but I attribute it all to my tutor. Please thank Mrs. Browning and Miss B. for all their kindness to me. And you know how grateful I am to you for yours. I wrote a very long letter to my father yesterday evening, who I am sure takes the right view of the case, asking him to write at once to the headmaster calling upon the latter to revoke his urgent decision, as he cannot know how much he is doing by separating you from me. At any rate, even if we are prevented from intercourse, I hope there will be no obstacle to our communication in the holidays. I return to you today the books you so kindly lent me. Again I must say how distressed I am about this, as it has put me in very low spirits as this is the last letter I must write you unless my father affects our reunion. . . . I send you this under-cover through Morris."

There was to be no reunion between them so long as he remained at Eton, but there were to be more letters. Browning wrote frequently to him from Italy, inviting him to join him and his family at San Remo for a holiday, and afterwards at Spezia. Curzon replied that he would ask permission of his father, but whether he got it or not, he never went. "I saw you on the street

today but did not dare to cross over and accost you," Curzon
writes in 1876. And in 1877: "Thank you for yet one more gift.
I shall treasure it. Please do not acknowledge this letter in any
way." It was not until he was at Oxford that he made a trip with
Browning to Italy.

Browning's place in Curzon's affections (and despite Mrs.
Dod's accusations, it was probably no more than a strong avuncu-
lar interest on Browning's part, made extravagant by Curzon's
emotional reaction) was taken by a fellow Eton scholar, Edward
Lyttleton, who was later to become headmaster of Haileybury
and of Eton. Curzon preferred to worship Edward's elder brother,
Alfred, who was captain of the school, an all-round sportsman
(he was afterwards a famous M.C.C. cricketer) and, in Curzon's
words "one of the most delightful and lovable characters." But it
was Edward who made the first approach. Edward was a senior
Eton scholar who had taken an interest in Curzon almost from
the moment he entered the school. He wrote him and asked for
a photograph, and after it was received sent Curzon a letter of
thanks in which he warned him of the dangers of mixing with
the wrong circles at Eton and regretted that he himself had
dared not seek a closer acquaintance in case it might be mis-
construed.

The sentiments of his letter, which would seem exaggerated
today, but were not unusual in communications among men in
the Victorian and Edwardian eras, produced a swift reaction on
Curzon's part. The friendship with Edward, and with Alfred too,
continued long after Eton days were over, and both brothers
were always potent influences in Curzon's life during his early
manhood. Unlike the early influences, they were for good, and
they did something, if not perhaps enough, to sober and solidify
a character which found far too many opportunities at Eton for
indulging in heady bouts of self-esteem.

One thing, however, is certain about Curzon's days at Eton:

he greatly enjoyed them. He kept a desultory diary of his life there between the ages of fourteen and nineteen, and upon the fly-leaf he wrote the following:

"This book contains fragmentary scraps, all relating to my life at Eton from 1872. . . . They are the contemporaneous record of what was to me a happy and glorious time, perhaps the happiest and most glorious that it will ever be given me to enjoy."

The final item in the book is dated June 4, 1878, and is headed: "This is decidedly egotistical." Underneath he writes: "The proudest, *I expect*, day of my life. Speeches in the morning. Remarks overheard by S. B. (his sister Sophy) and Co. 'Where is C.? I heard him last year and liked him so much.' 'Isn't he splendid? What wouldn't I give to be his sister!' As soon as they were over, gents I have never seen seized me by the hand and 'Well done, you were the best of all.' There was a French lady, tremendously voluble, with 'Je vous félicite, Monsieur.' In the evening, tent dinner at Surly. Toast Queen and royal family. At eleven Ladies and Floreat Etona. Ponsonby, my great friend, rose to propose the Captain of Oppidans. Later on my health proposed by Dod! Such fun! All the above is pure and unadulterated conceit, but as the truthful moments of a successful day may suffice in after years to recall the pleasurable emotions which at the time excited G. N. C."

IF THE ORDINARILY SUCCESSFUL Eton boy of the eighteen-seventies and eighteen-eighties went out into the world confident of his future, Curzon did so with his sense of destiny bolstered by the frequently expressed conviction of all his friends that he was marching forth to undoubted, and imminent, eminence. Not that Curzon needed any bolstering from outside, for he was already convinced in his own heart and head that the most precious prizes in public life would soon be within his grasp. Soon after he went up to Balliol, he wrote to his friend Reginald Brett (later Lord Esher): "I do not know that I build any castles in the air specially for Oxford. My castles come later on in life." He was so supremely confident, and so obviously directing his energies towards speedy promotion, that some of the wiser friends felt it necessary to urge him to make his ambitions less nakedly obvious. Brett wrote to him in 1878:

"Love and respect humble folks, dear George, if you wish to be great and good. There are so many people ready to worship success. You are very ambitious, I know: and right ambition is very noble and wholesome, but it must be directed to some altruistic not egotistic end." And he added, shortly afterwards: "You know that you have been accused—as I believe so wrongly—of a general superficiality of heart and mind. I believe it to be untrue, but at the same time it is harmful that such a belief should hold for a moment in the minds of your contemporaries and of observant outsiders. There is only way to guard against the damage which such a view taken of you—and affecting you through the bearing of such persons towards you—can do you: and it is by allowing yourself to feel strongly and deeply, even passionately, about your friends. Superficiality means plenty of intellect and not enough heart. Dear George, let your feelings have full play, and you will get round everybody as you have got round me."

But worldly success was just what Curzon wanted, and he saw no reason either to abate his ambitions or conceal them. His attitude to life was no different at Oxford from what it had been at Eton when he wrote about his masters: "They never realised that I was bent on being first in what I undertook, but that I meant to do it in my own way and not theirs." Work in his own way was what he undoubtedly did at Balliol, and it was very different from the routine of the average undergraduate. His university life had begun with a blow that might easily have shattered a less determined young man. In 1874, while on holiday from school, he took a tumble from his horse when riding in the woods near Kedleston and injured his back. He was in severe pain for several days and was laid up in bed. But the pain passed off and he forgot about it until just before the university year began in 1878. He was on holiday in France and was suddenly struck down by a most violent and continuous pain in his back, and his alarm was increased when he noticed that his right hip had become malformed. He hurried back to London and consulted a physician, who told him that he had curvature of the spine and that he must give up any idea of going up to Oxford and, instead, take to his bed for a prolonged rest.

Curzon had no intention of doing any such thing. He took a cab to Harley Street and saw a bone specialist. To his mental, if not physical, relief this expert told him that there was no reason why he should not pursue his studies at Oxford so long as he wore a harness round his waist, to keep the spine supported, and refrained from any violent exercise. It was in harness that Curzon arrived at Balliol in 1878 at the age of nineteen. He was to continue wearing a harness (and feeling almost constant pain) for the rest of his life. From this moment onwards, any study of the life of George Nathaniel Curzon must take note not only of the strange and evil influences of his childhood but also of the dolorous ache in his back which plagued him unto his deathbed, robbing him of sleep by night and patience by day, forcing him to take drugs, and often, at some of the most vital moments in his career and in the affairs of the Empire, turning him into a fractious and unbalanced semi-invalid. On the other hand, it also acted as a constant challenge, goading him into extraordinary feats of physical and mental exercise and endurance from which some of his most remarkable achievements emerged.

At Oxford the trouble with his back enabled Curzon to invent for himself, without any adverse comment from his tutors, a regime of work which was unorthodox in the extreme. Unless he was particularly interested in a lecturer, he rarely attended lectures. His plea of pain or weakness was invariably accepted. On the other hand, he rarely missed a meeting of the Oxford Union and was soon among the speakers. In his last year at Eton he had begun cultivating an orotund delivery, crammed like a currant-cake with classical quotations, and in the Union debates his oratory was rich to the point of indigestibility. The sentences rolled off his tongue like great waves on their way to the beach, foaming with literary allusions and metaphorical comparisons, bubbling with little spurts of incidental wit until with slow, majestic inexorability, they crashed down upon the cowering heads of his opponents. What added piquancy to Curzon's periods of purple prose—"painfully conscious examples of Balliol scholarship," according to the *Undergraduate Journal*—was the sonority of his delivery and the way in which, mixed with his otherwise genteel delivery, he used the short Derbyshire "a," with much the same salutary effect as Winston Churchill achieved in 1940 by his insistent pronunciation of "the Nazis" as "the Natzies." He spent so much time studying for his speeches to the Union, the Canning Club, and other Oxford political societies that one suspects he neglected the scholarly curriculum that would earn him his degree. He was, in any case, so overconfident of success that he had no qualms about the outcome of the examinations, and waited for the results with quiet anticipation of his success. For once, however, his method of studying "in my own way, and not theirs" failed him. When he scanned the results in *The Times* in 1882, he saw to his horror that he had won not the First which he had come to expect as his own, but a mere Second. At first he could not believe it and telegraphed Oxford from Kedleston for confirmation. When he was informed that it was indeed so, he burst into uncontrollable sobbing and afterwards wrote in his diary: "I cannot believe it. I suspect skulduggery."

So did quite a few of his friends. From all over Britain and from many British embassies abroad, where his older friends were now learning the diplomatic trade, came letters in which furious anger and consternation were mixed with condolence. It was his friend Alfred Lyttleton, now a member of the Tory Government, who put the disaster into its proper context and brought the aggrieved Curzon back to a sense of proportion by writing on July 4, 1882:

"I who know you well do not think the less highly of you because an unkind fate has robbed you of the glittering spoils of your labour. In the reputation you already have in the political world you have, even now, got those spoils to a very high degree. Of course you could have got the first class for certain had you denied yourself the Union, the Canning, and those other literary, social and political enterprises which have earned you the name of the most famous Oxonian in my knowledge of Oxford that I can remember. After the annoyance and vexation have passed you will be able to think that you have a substantial consideration to show for your *academic* loss."

This was comfort and compensation, but Curzon's was not the sort of character to be wholly consoled by such letters. To have come out second to others, to have been found inferior to undergraduates upon whom he looked down, to be declared unworthy of the topmost prize, all these things mortified him, no matter how warm the sympathy of his friends. The humiliation, for such he considered it, rankled in his mind from the moment the results were made public.

That summer he had made an arrangement to travel to Greece, Egypt, and Palestine with one of his older Etonian friends, R. R. Farrer. But Farrer, who was to die soon afterwards of tuberculosis, was taken ill in Italy and could not keep the rendezvous they had arranged in Alexandria. Curzon was not displeased by his friend's defection, for he had a project to carry out and he needed isolation and concentration in which to do it. By day, as he wandered around the Parthenon in Athens, or ex-

amined the smashed fortifications of Alexandria, or looked contemptuously down on the Armenian priests touting for alms
outside the Church of the Holy Sepulchre, he was just another
English milord ploughing his way through the Grand Tour. But
whenever he boarded a train or boat, or whenever he was in the
privacy of his room, out came his books and papers, and he wrote
and wrote and wrote. His onslaught of letters to his friends continued unchecked, and none of them gave any hint of his secret
activities. To Farrer a letter written from the Levant on March
24, 1883, said: "Had an affair with a baroness (in Cairo). Got to
know her most intimately. This is for your private ear only. Ah,
seductive Cairo!" He goes on to mention that he has explored
inside the pyramids and climbed to the top of one of them, and
that he found the Sphinx a most dreary and disappointing lady.
But he makes no mention at all of his nocturnal labours. The
first his friends knew about them was when they opened *The
Times* and saw the announcement that the Lothian Prize, Oxford's highest academic award to an undergraduate, had been
won by George Nathaniel Curzon for his essay on Justinian. More
than anything else, it was the surprised pleasure of his friends,
plus the ad hoc methods under which he had achieved his essay,
that mollified him and provided the anodyne he needed for the
pain of his earlier failure. He could once more look at the world
and say: "You see, I am better than you, after all." His self-
confidence came back to him with a rush, and whatever doubts
he had previously entertained about himself retreated into his
subconscious. He came back to Oxford full of such buoyant and
obvious belief in himself that he was not even hurt by a satirical
verse about him, which was in circulation among the colleges
about this time. The verse was, in fact, destined to yap at his
heels and cause him great distress in his future life, and when he
was in his sixties and engaged in a mortal fight for his political
future he wrote to his wife: "Never has more harm been done to

one single individual than that accursed doggerel has done to me." But that was in 1920. In 1883, when he heard it for the first time, he laughed it off.

> *My name is George Nathaniel Curzon,*
> *I am a most superior person,*
> *My cheek is pink, my hair is sleek,*
> *I dine at Blenheim once a week.*

Who wrote it? Some say that it was J. W. Mackaill, afterwards Professor of Ancient Literature to the Royal Academy, and others, that it was H. C. Beeching, afterwards Dean of Norwich. But it was almost certainly penned by one he counted among his most intimate and admiring friends, Cecil Spring-Rice, who later, when Ambassador to the United States in Washington, was suspected by Curzon of trying to wreck his engagement to the girl, Mary Leiter, who subsequently became the first Mrs. (and afterwards Lady) Curzon.*

He was now twenty-four years old. The pictures of him at this period of his life make it obvious why his friends frequently mention in their letters "I long to see your shapely profile again,"

---

* The lines first appeared in the *Balliol Masque*, a collection of rhymes by Mackaill and Beeching and others about Oxford personalities of the day. Mackaill afterwards presented the collection to the college library. In this version the verse went as follows:

> I am a most superior person, Mary,
>   My name is George N-th-n-l C-r-z-n, Mary,
> I'll make a speech on any political question
>   of the day, Mary,
>   Provided you'll not say me nay, Mary.

This first version was undoubtedly a parody of a song written by Curzon himself for *Waifs and Strays*, a magazine of Oxford poetry started by Rennell Rodd in 1879. He wrote:

> When I was a little lady, Mary,
>   And thou wert a little lass,
> Ere ever we knew what we had, Mary,
>   To make us together life pass.

and why he was so popular with the ladies at the country house parties which he began to attend so frequently. He was tall, and because of the leather harness he wore for his back, erect to the point of ramrod stiffness. He took infinite pains over his clothes, and affected a bowler hat with a curved brim that showed off his thick curly brown hair. ("My hair was quite straight as a child and boy," he wrote in one of his notes about himself. "It was only after leaving Eton in my nineteenth year that it began to curl. For a time it curled extraordinarily in front, but after ten years this began to abate and it became wavy rather than curly.") His face was lean, sensitive, and handsome, the brown eyes bright and piercing, and the aquiline nose above the full, rather sensual mouth gave him the impression of always wearing a delicate sneer. But when he laughed, this expression disappeared to be replaced by a boyish look that moved one of his friends at this period, Laura Tennant, to write: "Oh, George, how I do love your rosy pink and laughing face! You must laugh more often." Laura Tennant was probably the first love of Curzon's grown-up life, a passion he shared with several of his friends, including Rennell Rodd, St. John Brodrick, and Alfred Lyttleton. She was just the type to stir the poetic emotions of the Victorian young men of Curzon's class—lovely of face, with a touch of evanescent, gossamer-like frailty about her that seemed to hint that she was not long for this world. As indeed was the case.

Laura Tennant was one of the famous Tennant sisters, of whom the eldest, Margot, was to become the most famous. It was Margot who several years later, after rejecting a proposal from Alfred Lord Milner, wrote to Curzon "as my oldest and most treasured friend" to ask him which she should choose of two suitors who were pressing her: young Evan Charteris or the

---

I used in those days to say, Mary,
   That the girl I should claim as my own,
Provided she'd not say me nay, Mary,
   Would be one that I had not then known.

Liberal leader, the Rt. Hon. H. H. Asquith (later Lord Oxford and Asquith), a man considerably older than herself. Curzon advised her to take Asquith. Charteris "gives her the elan and fascination of youth, looks and physical charm, things that will last a maximum of ten years," Curzon wrote to a friend. "The other will give her devotion, strength, influence, a great position, things that last and grow. Therefore I said take him, for though you will miss the fugitive you will gain the permanent." Margot took his advice and married Asquith (he was never to know that Curzon turned his trick for him), and if she never experienced the idylls of romantic love, she found compensation in becoming the most famous political hostess of her day.

If the truth be told, when she wrote for Curzon's counsel she was harking back to the time when his suit would have been the most favourably received of all. Like her sisters, she was secretly in love with him. But of them Curzon preferred the fairy-like Laura, and she, in turn, adored him. She wrote him a series of letters which, even when read many years afterwards, still give out the warm glow of her sweet and lovable nature, and in every turn of phrase seem to be imbued with the fey-like quality of one sensate with the knowledge of mortality. That she too would have welcomed Curzon's overtures seems more than probable, for the heat of her emotion towards him is tangible in every paragraph; but Curzon's affection for her was one thing, and his attitude towards marriage was something else again. The advice he had given Margot was the advice he was resolved to act upon himself, to wed only when his career was established and then only to someone who would help him in furthering it. So Laura (in 1885) married Alfred Lyttleton. Curzon heard the news of her engagement while at a house party with Mr. Gladstone and Alfred Lord Tennyson, the Poet Laureate, and between them they sent her a joint felicitation. A year later she was dead, after an abortive childbirth.

Work was the passion which most interested Curzon at the

moment. He was resolved to leave Oxford and enter politics with as many academic prizes as possible hung, like scalps, around his belt. The winning of the Lothian Prize was not enough; that had merely effaced a humiliating defeat. He was now out for bigger trophies. "I will always look back on the winter of 1883–4 as the hardest working time of my life," he writes in his notes. "In the spring of 1883 I had won the Lothian Prize . . . and in the autumn of the same year I had been elected a fellow of All Souls. I had not then thought of entering for any other history prize, the more so since I was only a private student and had never passed through the historical schools."

In December, 1883, however, he happened to encounter a distant cousin of his in the Bodleian Library at Oxford. Curzon's attitude towards his relative was one of cool, patronising superiority, for he knew that the young man had taken an honours degree in history and had still only come second to him in the competition for the Lothian. The cousin unwisely remarked that he was about to enter for the Arnold Essay, the senior historical prize in the university open to graduates of several years' standing. The subject for the year was to be Sir Thomas More. Curzon's fierce competitive instincts were immediately aroused, and he determined once more to do his cousin down.

"I had no idea of the tables being reversed," he writes, "and I resolved to enter and spare no effort to repeat my former success. But the undertaking was no light one, for I knew nothing about Sir Thomas More. I was only aware that a successful Arnold Essay required to be of the dimensions of a book, witness Bryce's Holy Roman Empire, and that the period of More's life was one of the most written about and contested in world history."

It was December, and the rules laid down that the essay must be handed in by midnight, March 31, 1884. Curzon took the train to London and buckled down to work as never before. "For the next three months my daily routine was the same. My father owned a house, No. 34 Wimpole Street. There I lived alone, the only other inmate being an old housemaid who bitterly complained to my father of the late hours which I used to work and in which I used to require refreshment. 'Tea in the morning, tea in the afternoon, tea in the evening, tea at night, tea after midnight,' was the language of her quite legitimate complaint. My day was spent as following: I rose at ten in the morning and breakfasted before 11. At 11-15 to 11-30 I was in my seat in the Reading Room of the British Museum. At 2-30 I took half an hour's interval for lunch and went for a stroll through some of the galleries. At 5-30 fifteen minutes were allowed for a cup of tea."

He left the Museum at eight in the evening and walked to the Horseshoe Tavern, where he bought himself one of the hostelry's famous two-and-sixpenny dinners. "Leaving there at 9 I looked into the Oxford Music Hall, which was close by, for half-an-hour's relaxation, and then walked back to Wimpole Street. At ten, or soon after, I was in my chair from which I did not rise again until 4-30 or 5-30 in the morning. During the day at the Museum I studied, or arranged my material. At night I wrote the book. I have it now, a big MS. volume of many pages filled with small writing. So fine did I run the business that I had not completed writing the MS. on the day on which the essay was to be handed in."

On March 31 he took the evening train to Oxford, writing in his carriage and continuing in his study until just before midnight. Then, with a gesture of typical Curzonian theatricality, he put the MS. in a cover and walked over to the Old School. As the clock in the tower above began striking twelve, he hammered on the door until the custodian opened it.

"I apologised for my intrusion on the grounds that I was incommoding him in the interests of the prize-winning essay," he writes.

That was how it came out, too. A few months later the

results were published, and George Nathaniel Curzon was declared the winner. His cousin, who had not been told that Curzon was competing, once more had the humiliating experience of seeing his own name in second place. His fury (he never spoke to Curzon again) only added to Curzon's jubilation, and he added a contemptuous footnote to the incident in these words: "My cousin subsequently published his essay as a volume, but I never did the same with mine. I was so conscious of the conditions under which it had been composed, and painfully aware of its imperfections, either as a literary or historical work."

Once more he could look with satisfaction at his fellowmen, and feel superior.

CHAPTER THREE

Politician and World Tourist

W HAT DID George Nathaniel Curzon really want from
life at this period of his career?

That he was consumed with ambition and inter-
ested passionately in his own advancement goes without saying.
He made no bones about it. In his Oxford days he had joined
every club and spoken at every debate likely to bring him to the
attention of the political leaders of the Tory Party, knowing
only too well that they (like the Liberals) regularly scouted the
universities in those days for promising material. He used his
friends and his family connections without scruple to get him
close to the men of the party caucus who could give him preferment in his ambitions; and if it was a question of charming an
influential lady, he did not hesitate to do that too. "I went to
Eaton [Hall] not long ago and made great friends with Lady
Grosvenor," wrote Alfred Lyttleton in April, 1883, "upon whose
table I saw a photograph of you." Lady Grosvenor had the ear
of some of the highest in the land.

But it was not only his greed for personal eminence which
goaded him now but also his sense of mission. In the years

since leaving Eton, he had become an ardent Imperialist imbued
with a feeling of personal responsibility for the future happiness
of the vast Empire over which Britain in the eighties exercised
her control. He looked around him and became convinced that
he was surrounded by influences that, if they were not checked,
would wreck and ruin the great concept of Empire as it had
been built up by the visionary statesmen who had gone before.
Though he admired Gladstone and Asquith as men, he despised
them as statesmen. Their view of the imperial destiny as an
eventual association of equal millions was anathema to him. His
attitude towards the common people was that of a benevolent
patrician. He did not even believe that Englishmen, let alone
Scotsmen, Welshmen, Irishmen, Indians, and other lesser breeds,
had earned the right to equality with those who had spent their
lives and their brains in learning to rule them. To the masses
whom he was fitting himself to control and direct he determined
to bring food sufficient for their needs, the opportunity of living
healthy and decent lives, and every freedom they desired except
the freedom which, he believed, would be fatal for them—the
freedom to rule themselves. To Balfour's dictum that "people
only too often prefer self-government to good government" he
had only one reply: "More fools they! They should not be
encouraged to encompass their own doom." Convinced Tory
that he was from the age of fifteen, solidly certain of the divine
rightness of his class to rule, he despised the sentimentality (as
he saw it) of the Liberals in their tendency to hand the sacred
powers of government down to inferiors fitted neither by race
nor tradition to control the destinies of Empire. Edward Lyttleton, although himself a Liberal, expressed something of what
Curzon felt when he wrote to him about this time:

"What is wanted of you now is that you should make politics
something more than a vulgar ladder to notoriety, viz. the opportunity of keeping the image of true patriotism before your very

ignorant fellow countrymen. They are ignorant of many things. If you can show with simple sincerity that you are working for Great Britain and not for yourself, we shall owe you a big debt."

Lyttleton had about the same level of contempt for the Tories as Curzon had for the Liberals. He realised that aspirant politicians must make the rounds of the great ones in the party, and understood why Curzon had now begun to engage himself in a campaign to bring himself (by social contact) to the attention of the Tory leaders. When Curzon wrote an exuberant letter about a weekend he had spent at Hatfield, the ancestral home of the all-influential Salisburys, he replied:

"It is a capital thing to be doing. No better field could be chosen than Hatfield, I take it. But Lord Salisbury will not manage to secure the leadership [of the Tory Party] will he? These staunch Tories here talk about him rather as Canaan was talked about by Jacob: able but unstable. And this leads me, rambling, to an answer to your question on politics. Why, oh why are you not a Liberal, George?"

Curzon was not a Liberal because his was not a liberal mind, but a feudal one. His own idea of himself is perhaps best expressed in a letter which he received shortly after he entered Parliament. He wrote on it: "This I shall treasure." It came from a young American Rhodes scholar who had been at Oxford in Curzon's time and had written (as did many another of his fellow undergraduates) asking for his photograph. "I attended the Union debates at Oxford," he wrote. "You were the only young man who fulfilled my ideal of what a specimen of the Conservative, and especially the aristocratic, party should be. It was the aristocratic turn of your disposition which forcibly struck me, for which, indeed, I had been abundantly prepared in works of fiction, but had never seen exemplified."

By aristocracy, Curzon did not necessarily mean a member of the House of Lords, but a member of that body of men who by breeding, tradition, and education were born to be rulers of their fellows. His contempt for the bourgeoisie or the proletariat when they attempted to become great political leaders was such that later on, in the privacy of his notes, he would have some malignant things to say about many of them, particularly Lloyd George, who were to come to the fore in the years that lay ahead; and even in 1901, in a letter to the Edwardian novelist Ouida, he could say of Joseph Chamberlain: "An unlovable man . . . but not, I think, animated by base or petty motives. His lack of the finer finish must be attributed to his origin and education, both narrow, municipal and a little sordid." The House of Lords as part of the machine of government he considered an archaic institution. He wished to make his career, and reach the heights, in the House of Commons, and the knowledge that his father's death and his own assumption of the Scarsdale title would automatically expel him from the House caused him to band with a number of young men similarly placed to campaign for its reform. Later on, however, he gave up the struggle and went to the Lords of his own accord, without waiting for his father's title; and he ended his life with a thundering and embittered denunciation on his deathbed of the institution which had (or so he convinced himself) cheated him in the end of his right to the highest office in the land.

Meanwhile, he was a proud and confident peacock busily engaged in cleaning his quills and polishing his feathers in preparation for his entry into the political arena. He cultivated the Party chieftains and haunted the political clubs. " 'Tis done, and you will be elected at the first committee meeting," wrote A. J. Balfour to him around this time. "The Carlton is a beastly club, infested by the worst of his species, the bore political, but you were quite right to belong to it." The Tory leaders gave him a recommendation to the local association of the South Derby division, and, after some protracted discussion over his financial contribution to both the campaign and the divisional coffers, he was adopted as the official candidate. (The local Tory leaders, thinking him a rich man's son, had asked him for a contribution of £250 a year; he replied that, on the allowance his father gave him, that would leave him only £200 a year for fares and food.) Almost at once he realised that he had made a mistake in accepting the division of South Derby, a constituency which he had imagined filled with good, pliant, and solidly Tory countryfolk. Instead, as he wrote to St. John Brodrick: "My electorate is 11,500, over 7,000 new voters. Of these between 4,000 and 5,000 are colliers and manufacturers (factory workers) and I haven't a chance with them. They won't even hear me."

In his speechmaking tour around the division, he ran for the first time into the more merciless kind of heckling, the kind which tries to drown a speaker rather than interrupt him, silence him rather than stimulate the discussion. The effect upon him was rather as if he had received—only it was too expensive for his audience—an egg in his face. He did not like it a bit. He liked it so little, in fact, that at first, much to the embarrassment of his supporters, he attempted to raise the cry of: "Sabotage!" and "Conspiracy!" He wrote to St. John Brodrick:

"I have been for three days canvassing among the collieries and potteries of my worst district. You have no conception of the tyranny which prevails. No shopkeeper dare admit he is a Conservative for fear of losing his custom. Even the publicans have to pretend that they are Radicals."

He was abashed, ashamed, and abysmally depressed by the reception of his carefully planned speeches, which he delivered—in his best and most florid Union style—with hardly a mention of domestic affairs but always with the destiny of Empire as his theme. He could not understand why no one listened to him, and why his opponent, who could hardly string a couple of paragraphs together, should be so much more popular. "The other man dwells, in speech after speech, on the same points, and they are so trivial and domestic," he wrote. He himself had decided to campaign on a platform almost entirely devoted to

foreign affairs, and on the disastrous pass to which the Liberals
under Gladstone had brought the Empire. He certainly had the
material for a devastating indictment. Britain had suffered humiliating setbacks on the northwest frontiers of India. There had
been the cowardly abandonment by the Government, and by
Gladstone in particular, of General Gordon, murdered by the
fanatical warriors of the Mahdi at Khartoum. There was the
sorry situation in Egypt and the disintegrating situation in South
Africa. All these crimes of default, inefficiency, or lack of courage
he could quite justly lay at Gladstone's door. But when he raised
his vibrant voice in ringing condemnation, and appealed to the
voters to send him to Westminster "so that strong men can once
more take the reins of our great Empire's affairs from the hands
of the spineless little Englanders" he was listened to with jeers
or in stony silence. He was abashed, ashamed, and abysmally
depressed, and in the quietness of his room he wept. "I wept
less for myself than for the ignorance and backwardness of the
voters," he wrote.

Curzon had not yet learned the lesson—and, in fact, he never
did learn it—that the way to a voter's heart at election time is
through his stomach or his pocket, and that in South Derby they
did not care a fig what was happening in India and the Middle
East but were desperately concerned at the fact that income tax
had recently gone up from sixpence to eightpence. When the
results were known, Curzon found himself second in the poll
by a wide margin of votes. He had been so sure of his own
defeat that, three days before the poll, he began making preparations for a voyage around the world; and by the time the declar-
ation was made he had recovered his spirits sufficiently to turn
to his successful opponent and wager him £5 that, in spite of
the result, he (Curzon) would be first to make his maiden speech
in the House. He won his bet.

It was unfortunate for his future career, however, and even
more unfortunate for his future understanding of the minds of

those he was so anxious to serve, that the only moral he drew from his abortive struggle was that the electorate had proved itself unworthy of him. In this belief he was encouraged by friends like his old tutor at Oxford, Raper, who wrote urging him to get himself a new constituency without delay, "this time, I hope, a town one where I think you would be better appreciated because they are generally more intelligent." He was surprised and hurt when Lord Randolph Churchill, whom he admired as one of the giants of the Tory Party, tartly told him that he was entirely responsible for his own defeat and that a wiser and more wily politician could easily have won the seat. The idol toppled at once in Curzon's estimation. "Since he has become a swell he will scarcely look at his subordinates," he wrote, "and the barest civility is all that one can expect from him."

And he immediately transferred his admiration to the Tory leader, Lord Salisbury, for whom he spent much time doing research and assembling facts for his patron's speeches. In return, Salisbury commended him to the Tory divisional leaders in Southport as a potential candidate, and when they insisted—as in the case of South Derby—that he should pay his own electoral expenses and also contribute annually £300 to the local funds, it was the Tory chief who persuaded them to waive this condition in Curzon's case. The local association reluctantly agreed to assume the whole of the financial burden. In the General Election of 1886, George Nathaniel Curzon became an M.P. for the first time.

He was, however, never to forgive Lord Randolph for his snub, and the opportunity for a gesture of reprisal—he was not yet important enough for it to be called revenge—came not long afterwards. In the new Tory Government Lord Randolph was appointed Chancellor of the Exchequer. He had for some time been preaching the doctrine of what came to be called "Democratic Conservatism," and had gathered around him a group of young Tory supporters, of whom Curzon was one. But Curzon soon learned that Lord Randolph's ideas, which were merely those of encouraging younger members of the Party and of bringing the Government into terms of closer contact with the electorate, were anathema to Salisbury, and his enthusiasm cooled with the rapidity of a thermometer dipped in a bath of icy water. When Lord Randolph realised that the rest of the Cabinet were against the reforms he was proposing, he resigned, and naturally expected his young supporters to rally round him. So far as Curzon was concerned, he got no sympathy at all.

"I was at Hatfield when it all came out," he wrote to St. John Brodrick, "and I happen to know that Randolph Churchill did it [i.e., resigned] not of premeditation, and therefore from a passing burst of temper." And he added gleefully that his new patron, far from being appalled by the resignation, was "only too pleased to get rid of him. I was at Hatfield that night and only too well remember the thanksgiving and hosannas that went up."

When Lord Randolph made his resignation speech, Curzon followed, and in what The Times called "a brilliant maiden speech" found time to score several times off the recent object of his respect and admiration. In Parliamentary life, he was never to be one who stayed to get his feet wet before deciding that a ship was sinking.

Not long afterwards he abandoned his Parliamentary duties and, with the permission of Lord Salisbury, set off on a journey round the world, a voyage which he considered "as necessary to the education of a statesman as the Grand Tour was to a gentleman of culture in the last century." He kept a catalogue of the countries he visited with the same care as he kept an account of his expenses: "5 days Tonking £4-5-0. . . . 31,500 miles at a cost of £336.5.0 or £1.15.0 a day."

To Asia he had come armed with letters of introduction from Salisbury, Gladstone, and Balfour; as an M.P., he expected to be regally received by Her Majesty's diplomatic and consular representatives. They did him well and saw to it that the kings, princes, emirs, and other potentates to whose courts they were attached received him with due pomp and circumstance. In truth, they were all without exception delighted to have Curzon among them, for in appearance and manner he exactly filled the picture of milord Englishman which they had in mind, and they heaped him with compliments and presents, some of the latter embarrassingly human in character. "Judge to my surprise," he wrote to St. John Brodrick, "when, having passed through the arch, I was told by the Sultan that I was now his brother, and entitled to share with him the rights and privileges of his family. What these entailed I only discovered when I retired to my chambers late in the evening, replete after a long banquet, and found an exquisite little creature waiting for me beside my couch, sent there by my 'brother' for my pleasure. It took all the strength of my character to send her on her way, and all my charm and tact to persuade her to go without hurting the sweet child's feelings. I may say that we allowed a time to lapse before her departure, so that she would not be blamed for having failed to please me." To which St. John Brodrick wrote back: "I can imagine that the experience was, at first, something of an affront to your decent feelings, but I am sure you have since decided that, as an upstanding Englishman, aware of the reputation of his country in foreign parts, you will resign yourself to your duty from now on."

His tour was not solely confined to such esoteric and hedonistic routines. He kept his eyes open and his ears cocked, and he took copious notes. The results of his researches he reproduced in a series of articles which he wrote for the newspapers, the fortnightlies, and the quarterlies. He also kept a full diary in which, among other things, he recorded his impressions of some of those he met on his journeys. Among them was H. M. Stanley, the rescuer of Livingstone, whom he encountered at an Embassy luncheon party in Cairo. He wrote of him: "A short and solid, almost podgy man, a figure the reverse of elegant. He was very shy when he came in and did not thaw until well into lunch. I asked him what was the first question he had asked when he first got back to civilisation from the African jungle. He replied: 'Does the Queen of England still reign?' and the answer came: 'Yes.' And the second question: 'Is the Conservative Government still in?' and the answer came from every mouth: 'Yes.' Stanley said: 'Thank God.' Gladstone he regarded as the most dangerous and incompetent of statesmen. 'Has he ever visited Egypt? Has he ever come out further afield than the Ionian Isles? No. Then how can such a man be competent to rule the British Empire? There are two qualifications that should be required of every member of the British Parliament:— 1). That he should be under 70 years of age, and 2). that he should have travelled the British Empire.' With his snowy crown of hair, clean-shaven face, save for a small grey moustache, and his resolute features, Stanley's is a noticeable head. The expression is one that seems to know no passion or excitement, but is eloquent only with a great reserve. There is very little play of movement of his features in talking. He gives the impression of preferring to be left alone. People have talked about his eyes. They are not large, but a big black iris blazes in the middle of a grey pupil, and seems to fix your soul. He is 46."

Curzon's first world tour was to be but one of many voyages to distant places. The Asian bug had bitten him, and it kept him in its thrall for the rest of his life, so that nothing else was ever more important. After his return to England and another short flirtation with politics at Westminster, he was off to Asia again, this time to Persia. From this prolonged and intensive visit emerged his famous two-volume, thirteen-hundred-page book, *Persia and the Persian Question*, which Curzon was always afterwards to regard as his literary chef d'oeuvre. It was the fruit of some of the most concentrated labours of his life. To write it he neglected his constituency and the House of Commons, and instead took rooms in the outer suburb of Norwood, where he worked on his MS. with fanatic application. His only relaxations were two. Twice a week he went back to his beloved British Museum, "that haven of Elysian study and intellectual delight." It was in this period that "I got to know almost every row of books on the shelves of the Reference Library, and on my way to the refreshment room I became familiar with every bust of the Caesars and the great marble pieces of the sculpture of Greece, Egypt, Assyria and Rome. I can still hear the tinkle of the great arc light as it was lit towards evening in the centre of the big glass dome of the Reading Room." His other break with routine was to go into nearby Crystal Palace. "I saw and respected it. It seemed to be the final resting place of all sorts of objects which had attracted the general interest, but had now ceased to be popular. Around some of the ponds were models of the huge prehistoric lizards and other monsters whose discovery had startled the world during the middle of the nineteenth century. One of the main courts contained a reproduction of the Moorish Alhambra Palace, which always caused me much delight." In a characteristic footnote to this entry, he has added the remark: "At any rate, until I saw the original."

It was a lonely life, but it enabled Curzon to finish his MS. in less than nine months. In between its completion and publication, Lord Salisbury, who had shown himself remarkably indulgent over Curzon's "absentee membership" of the House, called him into his office and offered him his first major step up the ladder of political advancement. It was also the first fruit of his travel in Asia and his intensive study of Asiatic affairs. Salisbury wrote to him on November 10, 1891:

"Gorst's migration to the Treasury has left vacant the Under-Secretaryship for India. Are you disposed to undertake it? It concerns matters in which, without any official obligation, you have shown great interest in a very practical way, and it carries with it in the House of Commons duties which sometimes involve important questions."

Curzon leaped at the opportunity. It was one for which he had been working ever since he had become an M.P. Every article he had written, and every social contact he had carefully made, had been directed towards this target. He did not even mind when Salisbury insisted that he censor his book on Persia in order not to involve the Government, of which he would now be part, in controversy over his views of the Persia situation, which came at that time within the purview of the India Office. He cheerfully excised all the harsh criticisms he had previously put in about the Shah and his administration.

Persia and the Persian Question, when it was published the following year, was described by the friendly press (like the *St. James's Gazette*) as "a standard work on the subject," and by the opposition press (like the *Daily Chronicle*) as "nearly seven pounds weight of solid print." Curzon treasured most a letter written to him about it by the novelist Thomas Hardy, who said, in a moment of unaccustomed humility:

"You have been much in my mind since we met. I had not then seen your monumental work on Persia—which I have done since. The amount of labour and enterprise it represents and the value to investigators of the facts acquired put some of us scribblers to shame."

Curzon's own opinion of it he expressed in a verse he wrote for the Crabbet Club, a society of young men in politics, literature, and the arts which had been founded some years before by Wilfred Blunt:

Stanley in Darkest Africa may mix with dusky broods;
  Give me the mystery of the East, the Asian solitudes;
Ten thousand readers fall to sleep o'er Stanley's turgid pages,
  Mine, tho uncut, will light a fire for unbegotten ages.

In truth, the effort it had taken to write *Persia and the Persian Question* all but ruined Curzon's health for good. His back gave him more severe and constant pain during this period than any time before, and he was so run down and generally debilitated that his family doctor insisted that he take a holiday in Switzerland before taking over his new job with the India Office. Once more, Salisbury indulgently gave him leave of absence.

He went to St. Moritz. There his principal preoccupation was not Asia and not politics, but money and marriage.

CHAPTER FOUR

Mary Leiter

I HAVE SAID that George Nathaniel Curzon's family was far from being a poor one, but it was not a rich one either. His father relied mainly upon his rent-roll and the production of his tenant farmers to provide the money with which to run the estates at Kedleston and to clothe, feed, and educate his ten sons and daughters. There was money coming in from investments in India, but it was no great fortune. The Reverend Lord Scarsdale had upped his son's allowance, by the time he took up the under-secretaryship for India, to £1,000 a year but made it clear to him that he could not expect any more until he came into the inheritance itself. As an M.P. he received, of course, no salary whatsoever. Members in those days were unpaid, a harsh fact with which Curzon entirely agreed. He had voted against a Liberal M.P.'s attempt to bring in a private bill to give Members a small salary on the grounds that "it will bring into the House shallow and ambitious careerists bent on making a *business* of the duties and obligations of Government." The only additional form of income to which he could turn was that from the writing of articles and books. From this he had, over the past two or three years, been making some £400-500 a year. But now that he was about to take an official position, he would have neither the time nor the permission to write— not on the Asiatic subjects, anyway, upon which he had made himself an expert.

From a financial point of view, therefore, the outlook was bleak for him. It was, of course, easily possible in those days to live a civilised and satisfying life on £1,000 a year. But Curzon had extravagant tastes, and the circles in which he moved— circles which he considered necessary not only for his pleasure, but also for his social and political advancement—were composed mostly of people considerably richer than he was. Now that he was coming to the front in politics, it would be a constantly nagging problem how to keep up with his peers.

In Switzerland, while "gay young things go careering down- hill on toboggans all around me," he spent many an anxious hour trying to work out a solution to his financial needs. He was ill- fitted for a career in business, and, in any case, he would have no time for it. For a rising young politician of more than thirty years of age, what was the answer? Was it contained in a remark made to him in one of the letters frequently exchanged between himself and Oscar Wilde, a fellow member of the all-male Crabbet Club? "You should marry, dear George," Wilde had written. "Espouse some beautiful female worthy of your talents. You are eminently suited to such husbandry, and your career demands it." Wilde was, at the same time, seeking some aid for himself. "I want to be one of Her Majesty's Inspector of Schools," he wrote to Curzon from Tite Street, Chelsea, in 1885. "This is ambition—however, I want it, and I want it very much, and I hope you will help me."

On the other hand, Cecil Spring-Rice, another Oxford friend now in the diplomatic service, wrote to him decrying marriage: "I hope to see the next announcement not of your marriage but of your entry into the Government. So many of our friends seem bent on making their families not so much great as numerous.

When you are Secretary of State for Foreign Affairs I hope you will restore the vanished glory of England, lead the European concert, decide the fate of nations, and give me three months' leave instead of two."

There had been plenty of opportunities for Curzon to marry already, for with his handsome appearance, his charm, and his undoubted talent and future, he was a more than eligible young man. And it would certainly not be true to say that his strange experiences in childhood had done anything to turn him against women as a sex, so long as they kept to their rightful place, that is. He firmly believed that women should confine their activities to the drawing room, the boudoir, the bedroom, and the kitchen. When they began to obtrude into public life, their charms faded for him and he fought them bitterly. He had kept up a warm and close association with the surviving Tennant sisters, and Margot adored him. (She did not marry Asquith until 1893.) But Curzon regarded her as rather too forthright, intelligent, and independent of mind to accept the subordinate position which he would expect his wife to assume. He preferred the outright, worshipping admiration of another sister, Charity, the beautiful Lady Ribblesdale, but she, alas, was already married.

Curzon at this period belonged to a group of young aristocrats who had formed themselves into a society which came to be known as "the Souls." Its membership was confined to a charmed circle of "personages distinguished for their beauty, breeding, delicacy and discrimination of mind," as the St. James's Gazette afterwards described them, and its female members— all of whom had to be married—included some of the most lovely and intelligent women in the high society of the day. They held dinners in London or gathered at some country house for the weekend to talk of literature and the arts, to play charades, and to write poetry or plays, which they acted on the lawns. They were a genteel Victorian version of the intellectual coffee-bar coteries of today (though such a comparison is calculated to make them spin in their graves), serenely aware of their superiority to the common herd and the mundane activities of the day. Curzon's favourite party-piece at these gatherings was his famous imitation of the Poet Laureate, Alfred Tennyson, reading "Come into the Garden, Maud," a performance he liked to repeat, when he was in a good humour, to the end of his life.

As an eligible bachelor, he was naturally the target for the matchmaking proclivities of the female members of "the Souls," who went out of their way to introduce him to their unmarried sisters, cousins, and friends. For a long time, however, these sirens did not tempt him, and the fear began to grow among his friends that he was destined to become a lifelong bachelor. He was thirty-one years of age, and in many ways he was beginning to mellow. He had even begun to cultivate a sense of humour about himself (though it was never there to sustain him in the crises of his life), and the vein of self-mockery, as well as his attitude towards marriage, is demonstrated in a verse he wrote at this time for a privately circulated pamphlet of the Crabbet Club:

> For me no mean ignoble stage—give me the wide whole world,
>> The seas of either hemisphere must see my sails unfurled.
> I have seen the houris of Tom Moore in the streets of Ispahan,
>> There has trembled on my lips the kiss of the maidens of Japan.
> My looks are of that useful type—I say it with elation—
>> That qualify me well for almost any situation—
> I've sometimes been mistaken for a parson, and at others
>> Have recognised in butlers and in waiters long lost brothers.
> Perchance with all these gifts you'll say, it's strange I am not wedded,

And preach a sermon on the woes of life when single-
    bedded,
But if Clarissa I adore, and rashly go and marry her,
    To Chloe's subsequent embrace it may erect a barrier.

He went on, in another privately circulated piece of doggerel, to hymn the praises of a life of celibate sin, urging his fellow members of the Crabbet Club to further and further excesses in these words:

The juvenile and tender,
    Without regard to gender,
Shall be handed up to Godfrey's indiscriminate embrace,
    And Oscar shall embellish
    In a play that all will relish
The gradual and glorious declension of the race.
    To us will be the glory
    That shall never fade in story,
Of reviving the old axiom that all the world's akin,
    That the true link of union
    Which holds men in communion
Is frank and systematic and premeditated sin.

The motto of the Crabbet Club, coined by Wilfred Blunt, was, incidentally: *Mens insana in corpors sana*, though it is highly unlikely that the majority of the members took it seriously. Like "the Souls," they were merely rebelling against the rigid dictates of stuffy Victorian morality.

Such was George Nathaniel Curzon's state of mind at the beginning of the nineties when a young girl of twenty, named Mary Victoria Leiter, came into his life. It was, on her part, a case of love at first sight.

So far as Curzon was concerned, it began as no more than another casual flirtation, rather more pleasant than most, and the idea that it might develop into something more permanent hardly entered his mind. He had first met Miss Leiter at a garden party given by Lady Ribblesdale, and he was at once struck by her high spirits and great beauty. She had a complexion of most delicate pink-and-white, and her long hair was a shade of auburn with Titian glints. He was always partial to women with red hair (each lock of hair he kept among his papers was of that colour), and he quickly secured himself an introduction. They got on splendidly together, and henceforward, though she was having a gay time at balls in London, trips to the Continent, and cruises in the Scandinavian fiords, Mary Victoria Leiter's impressionable mind was monopolised by thoughts and dreams about Curzon. He was, from the first glance they exchanged, "the most wonderful, the most charming, the most handsome, the most clever of all the men I have met. I almost died when he touched my hand."

It was typical of Curzon that, having discovered she was an American on her first trip to Europe, he immediately wrote to his friend Cecil Spring-Rice in Washington, asking him to inform him in all possible detail of her background and family. (He was to regret this later on, for Spring-Rice, who fell in love with Mary Leiter himself, subsequently told her what Curzon had done.) The news he got back was that her father was the famous Chicago millionaire, Levi Leiter, who had vast stakes in Middle West real estate, and was, in spite of his German-Jewish background, a convert to the Episcopalian church and a pronounced Anglophile. His daughter had been baptised a Protestant and named Mary Victoria after the English royal family. Curzon received this intelligence with no qualms at all at the beginning, but when more serious intentions began to kindle in his mind he began to have doubts, for he knew his father well enough to know that the Reverend Lord Scarsdale would still consider the Leiters Jewish, no matter what acts of conversion they had undertaken.

For the moment, however, this did not trouble him. He was charmed and flattered by Mary Victoria's obvious hero worship of him. He wrote his first letter to her on July 31, 1890, replying

to one from her, and saying: "It is a pleasure for me to have
met and known you here. I shall think of you while you are
away, and beg both of you [her mother had come with her] to
come back and not wholly expel me from your memory in the
interval. . . . I wish you a happy season at Washington and
American men whose wiles will just fall short of making you
forget that Englishmen can also be charming. God bless you,
Mary Victoria."

Twenty-four hours later he wrote again: "After my letter
had gone, and when I came back to dress for dinner, I found
your second and the blessed keepsake therewith. Thank you for
it, my dear. I wore it in my shirt last night. I have it in my tie
now, and many times in the coming nine months till you are
back again, I shall wear it in memory of the dearest girl I have
met for long. That girl is Mary Victoria. All unworthy even of
her regard is the man whom indulgent friends address as
GEORGE."

In the next two years, it was Mary Leiter who kept the
correspondence going, sending him at least three letters for each
one he wrote back. And in practically every letter was a keepsake, or, by special parcel, a gift. He sent back, at her urgent
request, a better photograph of himself than the one she had
purloined from his rooms—and wrapped it up in three of his
latest political speeches. "You need not look at them, but if you
do, make allowance for any number of reporters' errors, which
always occur in provincial newspapers."

When she sent back her own portrait, describing it with
some misgivings as "a horror," he replied: "You are quite right.
The photograph is a caricature. It is not nearly good enough for
you. It makes you stern, contemplative, severe. A woman should
be tender, yielding, gentle. Again the manner of the hair spoils
that which is one of a woman's fairest gifts, the outline of the
head. Why will women sacrifice that delicate and artistic curve?
And yet they do, to my eternal sorrow."

For her twenty-first birthday, he sent her a flattering little homily along with his gift:

"When a man attains his majority, it is customary to wish him good fortune in the career of achieved manhood which he is supposed not till then to have entered upon. No such particular wish is necessary in your case, since in my judgment, before attaining your majority, you have reached the measure of complete and (what is far less usual) sensible womanhood. The little box I send you is from Canton in China. It is not a bad specimen of their art of enamelling on china. It pleased me when I got it from there, and I hope it may strike your fancy."

He broke off his work on the book on Persia for a few days to be with her when she passed through London in the following year, and it was obvious that this time her presence made much more of an impact upon him. His regard for her was now much more serious than the indulgent affection of a sophisticated milord for a worshipping visitor from overseas. "Thank you for writing me such a nice farewell letter," he told her when she left. "I prophecied a year ago that you would come back, and even if you do not do so again, we may meet elsewhere. The little gem of a *Horace* is a delicate and eloquent reminder of you. There is a line in it well suited to you in your present plight. 'O fortes peioraque passi, Cras ingens iterabimus aequor.' 'Brave heart who have vanquished greater toils before, Tomorrow we put out again upon the mighty deep.' And now back to old Persia, with his panorama of mingled splendour and squalor, the superb oriental medley of dignity and decay. God bless you always, dear Mary."

But he still had to be stimulated by Mary Leiter into keeping up the correspondence. She was by this time so enamoured of him that, as she wrote to a friend, "I will have him, because I believe he needs me. I have no shame." And the letters came winging across the Atlantic and continued whether there was any reply or not. She beseeched him to send her news of his

political progress, and the next time he wrote was to tell her
that a possible Parliamentary promotion which had been in the
offing for him had not come to fruit. "When Ferguson was made
Postmaster General, all the papers with one accord appointed
me Undersecretary for Foreign Affairs, and the matter was looked
upon as so certain that I kept getting letters and telegrams about
it every day. Lord Salisbury, however, appointed another man.
It is a bore to lose one of the things for which I have combined
taste and qualifications, as the chance may not recur. But if I
do not leave J. W. Lowther (who got the job) standing as still
as a church steeple, I am not your obedient servant."

Mary wrote back a message of condolence and sympathy in
which she angrily asserted that, in any case, a job as second, or
under-secretary, to any man was unworthy of such a talent as
his, and that he should be patient and wait until his genius was
recognised and the top job was offered to him. She chose an
unfortunate moment for this sop to his pride, for he accepted
the under-secretaryship for India at almost the same moment.
He wrote back:

"I have just received your letter, and though this is about
the *321st* letter that I have written during the last nine days,
yet I will write it. It is only upon accepting office that you learn
both how many friends you have, and what good they think of
you. You see, all your complimentary remarks about not being
second have been knocked on the head by the indiscretion of
Lord Salisbury in wishing to make me Under Secretary for India,
and my folly in accepting it." He added, with a touch of characteristic Curzonian disingenuity: "I have a lot of meetings, and
I shall retail such rubbish with a solemnity that will make the
people think it all very grand and fine. One of the greatest
delusions is that I can speak. I know one person who knows
very well the reverse, and that is your affectionate George."

The Government fell, and Curzon, though returned to Parliament at the subsequent election, found himself out of office. He

immediately departed once more on his travels, this time to the Far East. And the correspondence continued. It could get no warmer on Mary Leiter's part. She was head over heels and irrevocably in love. George, too, appears to have done some thinking, about himself, about his future, and about Mary while he was away. The letters he sent back to her began slowly to take fire. He wrote to her from Saigon:

"Of course you will come to London this year [1893]. Then we can talk over lots of things. We are both getting old. I struck 34 three days ago, and you must be 23 or 24, I think. Are we more wise? I retain an unconquerable frivolity, which, after being repressed during these six months of travel, will need some early outlet."

On March 3, 1893, they met again, after a separation lasting two years and a correspondence lasting three. The meeting took place in London. Mary, who was travelling with her father and mother, stole away for a rendezvous in Curzon's rooms in St. James's, and when she came away in the early hours of the morning, her dearest wish had come true. Curzon had proposed, and Mary Victoria Leiter and George Nathaniel Curzon were engaged to be married. There was only one small cloud of doubt to mar the clear blue sky above her, and that was conjured up by certain sentences in a letter which her beloved sent her the following morning. He wrote:

"You were very sweet last night, Mary, and I do not think I deserved such consideration. While I ask you, and while you consent to wait, you must trust me, Mary, wholly, even as I trust you, and all will be right in the end. I will not breathe a word of it to a human soul. And since that is the line we take, it will be well that I should not write too frequently for fear of exciting suspicions. You need not fear that I shall not think of you, and rely upon your fidelity as upon a rock. You will let me hear how you are going on, Mary, won't you, and sometimes, if you are down in your luck, you will remember that my kiss of love has rested upon your lips. God bless you, my darling child."

She left London that day with her parents, deliriously happy, and yet puzzled too. For, at Curzon's urgent request, the engagement was to remain secret and she had sworn to tell no one, not even her father and mother. She did not quite understand why, for she wanted to shout the glad news to the world.

What she did not know was that, for the moment, Curzon was afraid to tell his father.

IF IT HAD BEEN a curious and vicarious courtship, it was an even stranger betrothal: love at long distance and by correspondence only. The patience she had shown in waiting for Curzon's proposal had to be exercised even more firmly by Mary Leiter after he had asked the question and secured her answer. It was indeed a strange man with whom she had fallen so hopelessly and yet so willingly in love. He had explained to her about his back early in their acquaintance, and mentioned the pain it gave him in practically every letter thereafter; yet such was his gluttony for self-punishment that he seemed deliberately to choose projects that would make the suffering worse. "Long hard rides all the day," he wrote her from the Far East; "vile, sleepless, comfortless nights; excursions by sea boat, by river boat, on horse back, pony back and elephant back; in chairs, hammocks and palanquins." He professed his love for her was as great as hers for him, but he would never put a date on their marriage. He, who still wrote seven days a week to some of his school and college friends, sometimes let a fortnight go by without writing to Mary. He let three weeks go by after their secret engagement before sending her a letter. "I have had so many letters to write, I have had no time to write you," he told her on March 23, 1893. She answered that she well understood and that he was not to worry; her letters at least would keep the bond firm between them. And she sent, along with her letter, a beautiful silver inkstand whose magnificent workmanship warmed Curzon's heart. He used it for the rest of his life. *

Mary Leiter was a most intelligent and cultivated young woman: she spoke and read French and German easily; she appreciated the arts; she sang, played the piano, and loved literature. Though her adoration of Curzon made her completely uncritical of him, she was not entirely without feminine guile. Her letters to her beloved during the two years between secret engagement and marriage, passionately affectionate though they were, still managed to be masterpieces in the art of keeping him intrigued, stimulated, and just a little jealous. She never neglected an opportunity to point out that, wherever she went, young men spent their time trying to rush her to the altar (including his own friend, Cecil Spring-Rice). There were so many of them that Curzon began to refer to them somewhat ruefully as "the Thirty;" and when he hinted that she might show a little more fervour in repulsing their advances, she gently pointed out that she could hardly do that without revealing her engagement; and he did not want that yet, did he? One thing she made clear to him in her letters, and that was her complete and happy agreement in his view of the place of women in society. About her, at least, she convinced him, he would never need to have qualms;

* When Curzon arrived at the Foreign Office in 1919 to take over the office of Secretary of State, his reaction to Sir Gilbert Scott's Etrusco-Byzantine decor was one of extreme distaste. "How ghastly," he murmured, "how positively ghastly!" On the table behind which he would henceforth sit in judgment on the actions of His Majesty's plenipotentiaries stood a standard Foreign Office inkstand. The thought that he would be expected to dip his pen in this unremarkable receptacle was too much for him. "Is this the inkstand of a Secretary of State?" he asked the underling beside him. "It must be removed immediately. When I was at the Privy Council I was furnished with an inkstand of crystal and silver. This contraption, if I may say so, is merely brass and glass." And until a replacement arrived of which he approved, he used Mary's silver inkstand.

she was perfectly content with the inequality of the sexes. So, without fear (or so he thought) of offending her, he let himself go on one of his favourite subjects at this time: the "unnatural" intrusion of females into public life.

"The terrace of the House is as crowded with women as the Royal Enclosure at Ascot," he wrote her on June 21, 1893, "and the intrusions of the sex fill me with an indignation that no blandishments can allay. Give me a girl that knows a woman's place and does not yearn for trousers. Give me, in fact, Mary."

He was infuriated at a proposal that women should be allowed to become members of the Royal Geographical Society. It was bad enough, in his view, that females should be allowed to wander over the uncharted tracts of the world and make discoveries; but that they should be accorded recognition for their "unladylike activities" by being elected to the Royal Geographical Society was too much. He campaigned and lobbied the members against such a revolution with a fervour that turned the whole affair into a national controversy. He was caricatured approaching the peak of a Lebanese mountain, with the shade of Lady Hester Stanhope awaiting him at the top. "You see, I was here before you were, Mr. Curzon," says Lady Hester. To which Curzon replies: "Yes, milady, but not with my approval." The controversy concluded in a debate at the Royal Society which was eagerly reported in all the newspapers, and when it was over Curzon gleefully reported to Mary: "I have pulled off my combination against the ladies at the Royal Geographical Society successfully, having won, at the second and final meeting, by 172 to 158. All the papers are very down on me, since 'woman's emancipation' is the fashionable tomfoolery of the day. The funny thing is that I won it by argument, as I made a sensible speech, while the people with far the easier case to defend, failed deplorably."

He added a footnote which throws light on a different facet of the same subject: "There came today the little enamel Jeypore ring which has now attached itself to the end of my watch chain. I was half afraid you would want me to wear it, which not even you would have made me, not because it is not beautiful—which it is—but because a ring on a man's finger seems to me not less absurd than a hoop through a woman's nose." The memories of Miss Paraman were still in his mind, and he was determined that no other woman—by activity or symbol—would henceforth play a dominating role in his private life, or, if he could help it, in public life either. (He was to suffer a humiliating defeat in both spheres in the years to come.)

The correspondence went on, week after week, month after month, and still Curzon would give Mary no sign of when the marriage would take place. Into his letters to her, he packed everything—his views on politics, Asia, the Russian question, the theatre—except the wedding date. They quarrelled briefly because Mary had seen Eleonora Duse perform and did not like her. "I do not think I agree with you about Duse," he replied frigidly. "I am no lover of the theatre, and I rate acting low among the artistic faculties, but I think she is more than you state and is profoundly artistic because she has no art." And he also let himself go on a subject about which he had lifelong prejudices—the French. "They are a wonderful people. Children afflicted with delirium tremens before they have left the cradle. There is no people in the world I so heartily despise."

All this time, he moved through London society as if he were still a free and independent bachelor. At the country house parties, the young unmarried girls of good family were still gently, but obviously, put in his way for him to dally with, and to no one did he give any hint that he was not so detached as he pretended to be. From his long-standing friendships with the opposite sex, he began slowly disentangling himself, but in his relationships with women Curzon was always a man who was reluctant to make the swift and brutal snapping-off that an emotional situation sometimes demands, and this was not to be the only occasion in his life when the eventual announcement of a *fait accompli* produced profound shock and unhappiness among his intimate female friends. Meanwhile, he wrote to Mary: "Be patient, we will be happy together someday," but did nothing to assure her that such a prospect was imminent. Far from it, in fact. In a letter dated September 3, 1893, he said:

"I like to think of you. It is tranquilising. I have often said that when engaged, if ever, I should frequently long to be out of the thing and should curse instead of hugging my chains. Not for one second have I had such a feeling. No, the fact that you have given yourself to me is a source of great pride and most serene happiness. I am spared all the anxiety of what is called a great courtship, and I have merely, when the hour strikes, to enter into possession of my own."

To all but the infatuated Mary, this might well have touched a faint chord of resentment. She was, however, stirred and pleased by the increasing ardency of his letters, and they seem to have done much to assuage the pain of separation. For now it was Curzon's turn to pour endearments into his letters. "Graceful, tall, dark girl, bend over me and kiss me on the brow, the cheek, the lips, pour your soul on to the lips of your loving George," he wrote from the House of Commons Library on July 17, 1893. And, a year later: "Your loving letter received. Blessings for it. It contains one mistake only. You speak of *a* loving kiss. Why the singular number? Surely that would be criminal. I positively cannot let you off with one. There will be a number, a crowd, a bewildering sequence, an ardent succession, an ecstatic pell-mell."

These endearments enabled her to receive the news with fortitude, if not with pleasure, that her fiancé, far from making plans for marriage, was principally engaged in trying to persuade Salisbury to let him go off on a long and complicated journey back to India, where he hoped to climb the Pamirs and visit the Amir of Afghanistan. He would like to go at once, he told her, but "if the Government stay in, as it looks, through the impending season, then I shall try and work the Pamirs next summer." He added: "It will be the last wild cry of freedom, and then I shall come for you when it is over."

It was now 1894, and they had been engaged more than a year. Mary told him that she had persuaded her parents to make another trip to Europe in the summer, and there is no doubt that even her patience was beginning to fray at the edges, for she wrote Curzon that before they arrived—they would spend forty-eight hours in London—she planned to tell her father that they were engaged. This caused him some alarm.

"How good it is that so soon I shall see you, kiss you, take you on my knee, hold you in my arms," he replied. "I will think over what you say about taking Adolphus [which is the name by which he and Mary called Mr. Levi Leiter] into our confidence, and will discuss it when you come."

His eagerness to see his "black-browed queen," however, was such that, as her ship approached England, his qualms were drowned in a turbulent sea of pleasurable anticipation. To her fears that his love for her might have cooled, he replied: "I do not think I shall have to do much shamming to appear glad to see you. I never shammed well and you would detect me in a moment. No, wide open and eager with delight will be the lover's arms into which (given a reasonable seclusion) you will spring, and already in anticipation are being formed the kisses that lips will leave on lips. . . . I shall hold myself free the whole two days, and we will cram into them a century of emotion. I am very hard at work here, but this is a moment's interlude of bliss."

So indeed it seems to have been. He was so overjoyed to see her again, and so confirmed in the wisdom of his choice of a future wife, that he reluctantly consented that she should break the news to her father and mother, so long as they kept it a secret. He still did not inform his own father or his friends, but wrote to Mary: "How nice of your mother to be so enthusiastic about our marrying. It is delightful to think that neither of them mind." And with a calmness that must have been received by Mary with mixed feelings, he added: "I don't suppose when we marry that a couple engaged for so long will ever have seen less of each other during the engagement. That is one of the quaint anomalies of the situation."

They parted with renewed pledges of deep, even passionate, affection, she to tour the Continent, he to go off on his "last adventure" to the Pamirs. As her farewell gift, Mary sent him a touching letter in which she pledged herself to lifelong "widow-hood" if he did not return; and Curzon made a will, to be opened only if he should die, in which he set forth "so all the world shall know" his great and abiding love for her. The bitter-sweet note of parting had, however, changed to something more complacent by the time he got to Kabul, from which he wrote: "Think of the oceans that separate us. And yet, dear heart, we are tranquil in the mutual confidence of absolute and long-tested trust, and in the hope of early fruition. Put up your lips to kiss and be kissed, Mary, and sway your lissom body in your lover's arms."

It is a measure of Mary Leiter's steadfastness that she found this letter consoling. It was only several months later that Curzon at last got down to discussing hard-and-fast plans for their marriage; and she did not even complain when he inferred that it was she who had been dilatory. He wrote to her on January 2, 1895:

"Now, darling, apply yourself. I want to talk business, and ask your views and your plans. There are practically only two times when I can come out from England and marry you. One is Easter and the other is Whitsun. I shall want at least 3 weeks' leave, one to get out, one to wed you and find out what a darling you are (or what a mistake I have made), and one to get back again (or to bolt)." He goes on to discuss the Parliamentary calls on his time which might interfere with his freedom of movement, and then proceeds: "My own idea about the announcement would be as follows. When I get back to England, I shall *privately* tell my father, and him only, of our engagement, but I do not think he will announce it publicly till seven or eight weeks before the marriage." To this he adds, with no sense of irony: "Long engagements, particularly when the two parties are separated, are a nuisance."

In this letter he reveals that even now he has not yet talked formally to her father on the subject of marriage. "Of course, when I hear your opinion, I shall at once write to your father, to whom as yet I have neither spoken nor written on the subject, and formally ask him to allow you to marry me."

This letter was written as he was returning to England from India, and forty-eight hours after his arrival he journeyed to Kedleston for the all-important interview with the Reverend Lord Scarsdale. To what may seem, in this day and age, his exaggerated joy and relief, he found his parent completely lacking in hostility to his project.

"Blessed Mary," he wrote on February 5, 1895. "I have been home and told my father. I had to make none of the apologies or explanations or defences that you imagined. He said: 'So long as you love her and she loves you—that is all. You are not likely to make a mistake at your age, and she is old enough to know her own mind.'"

George Nathaniel Curzon was thirty-six years old, and an Under-Secretary of State in Her Majesty's Government. Yet he went on: "Of course, I did not tell him of previous events, or long engagements, but gave him to understand that only now was I going to *propose* (odious word), but from what I knew that a favourable answer was not improbable! I also told him I was writing to your father. He thought that all this was right and proper, and a sight of your lovely face on the smaller Miss Hughes photo (profile, white dress, hand behind back) completely convinced him. It is certainly one of the sweetest pictures ever taken."

So everything was arranged; or so it seemed. Mary had closeted herself with her father and gone into Curzon's financial status in some detail; and made it clear that if she and her future husband were to live in the state to which she was accustomed— and if they were to have the means necessary to move in circles where Curzon could secure political advancement—a substantial parental subsidy would be required. The old millionaire agreed to provide an annual stipend of £6,000, and said he would also instruct his legal advisers to draw up a marriage settlement. It was a little less than Curzon had hoped for, but he wrote her cheerfully enough: "Of course we will get on with whatever your father is generous enough to give us, and can easily cut our coat according to our cloth. I shall bring £1,000 a year (a paltry sum, I fear, but my family is poor), which will make up £7,000, and then when I get into office we shall have something more. You said last summer that to do all we wanted to do we ought to have £10,000, but I have no doubt that we can get on perfectly well with less."

The date was fixed. It looked as if the bonds of matrimony were to be tied at last, for good and all. And then first Curzon and then Mary began to waver, he about the exact date, she about his love and constancy. He wrote to her on February 22, 1895: "I have wired you concerning previous letters about dates. Darling, I am run to death just now. My youngest brother is very dangerously ill, with pleuro-pneumonia. He nearly died the day before yesterday, and until Sunday is past we cannot know if he will pull through. This is the only obstacle that might delay the announcement (about which I should, of course, wire), or, if the poor boy dies, that might have to postpone our marriage."

He alarmed her by telling her that he, too, was in bed with his back, "which aches terribly and I am scarcely fit to move about. . . . My back, which you will learn is the weak part of me, aches and gives me a good deal of pain. This is when I am overworked or fatigued, and I have merely to take to bed and lie there until it ceases to trouble. This is the third day. . . . I am rather a crock, and have led a hard-working, exhausting life which has taken it out of me. I want to be looked after, and to have a little comfort and some repose. It will be so sweet if you will help me to this. I think you will."

But he wired her next day to tell her all was well again. His brother had turned the corner. His back was better. And, in reply to a letter he had just received from her, he said: "Sweet child, you ask whether I am prepared for a somewhat demonstrative affection! Darling, I should be miserable if I did not get it. Perhaps also I shall show a creditable capacity for returning it; when you are lying in my arms, you will not think me too phlegmatic. I will cover not your lips but all your limbs with kisses!"

The sun was shining for Curzon once more. Not, however, for Mary. Her next letter was full of doubts and hesitations. His friend, Cecil Spring-Rice had, it appeared, been telling her things about him of such a nature that she wrote offering, even at this late hour, to break things off, as perhaps, after all "you do not love me, but are devoted to another, and I am, in any case, completely unworthy of you."

Curzon was furious. He wired her a pledge of undying devotion, and followed it up with a letter: "You must not let Springy talk nonsense to you, darling. So far from my people or my friends objecting to my marrying, they are one and all delighted, and so far from their daring to object to you (which is a childish idea) they are all simply enchanted. . . . I am so glad you spoke out to me so frankly about him. He has *said* disloyal things about both you and me. He writes me the most charming letters and I know he has a great regard for me. But he cannot forget that he loves you and he cannot get the better of his jealousy. I think we should be lenient, darling, I do not understand jealousy myself, but I would not for that reason condemn it hardly in others.

As to the Miss Morten story, darling it is simply grotesque. I
met her twice and thought her a charming, unaffected, simple-
minded girl, as I told you. I paid her not the least attention. The
story would be annoying were it not ridiculous. As for you being
a drawback to me, how could any sensible man talk such fustian.
Why, you are going to be the making of me! I have been drifting
about for years, and you are going to anchor me safely in port.
Don't listen to any such nonsense. A man can never do his best
till he is married, and you are going to make my life happy. Then,
about your beauty (oh, that man is black with jealousy, that is
it), why, it is going to be not merely my heart's treasure, my
arms' possession, but my glory and my crown."

It took several more letters, and a month of time, before Mary
was completely satisfied. Having leapt so serenely over all the
craggy obstacles in the past, she was obviously determined to
jib emotionally at the last fence, and it took all Curzon's sweet
persuasion to coax her over it. "Of course I agree that we should
spend the time before the wedding going over everything with
Adolphus," he wrote. "When I come I shall be ready to see anybody, talk with anybody, do exactly what you like, darling."

He brushed off the fact that some of the Chicago newspapers
had begun sneering at the origins of her family. "Let them invent
what they like about professions and businesses and pedigrees.
That does not affect our happiness."

So it came to pass at last. On Monday, April 22, 1895, at
11:30 in the morning, Mary Victoria Leiter and George Nathaniel
Curzon were married at St. John's Church, Washington, D.C. His
father gave the bride a gift of family diamonds and rubies. His
sister, Evey, brought a ring and a bracelet. He himself gave her
a turquoise belt from Cairo, a silver brooch and clasp from
Bagdad, and a little silver box from Siam—"quite a cosmopolitan
collection, I think." And Mary in return presented him with a
rubber-tyred brougham.

The gift from old Levi Leiter was even more considerable.

In addition to the £6,000 a year, he settled $1,000,000 upon his daughter, and rather more than that upon any children which might result from the marriage. It was, however, a settlement that was to give Curzon as much worry and litigation as financial security in the days to come.

But, for the moment, he was content. In his own strange fashion, he had settled his personal affairs. He need not worry now about the financial side of his career. He was securely in possession of a lovely, talented, and besottedly adoring wife.

Now he could turn his attention back to the dedicated pursuit of his political career.

As if to confirm the conviction in his mind that this was a turning point in his life, he came back from his honeymoon to find a letter from Lord Salisbury offering him a position upon which he had set his heart—a position which, he believed, was a stepping stone to the eminence he coveted, the premiership. It was the job as Under-Secretary of State for Foreign Affairs.

"I have accepted the Foreign Office somewhat against my will," Salisbury wrote. "I had much rather that Devonshire had taken it. But he would not do so. And now having to undertake it at a time when much difficulty seems to impend, I am naturally trying to secure the best assistance that I can. Therefore I venture to turn to you. You are more familiar with Eastern questions than any man on our side and your ability and position in the House of Commons will enable you to fight a good battle for us if our policy is attacked in the House. I hope therefore you will not refuse to accept the Under Secretaryship of Foreign Affairs."

Curzon paused before accepting, and then wrote back to Salisbury and indicated that he would take the office only if it were accompanied by an offer of a privy-councilship. He moiled in doubt and frustration after the dispatch of the letter, wondering whether he had been too reckless in making conditions—particularly since he wanted the job so much.

His gamble paid off. On June 28, 1895, Salisbury wrote to

tell him that it was Queen Victoria's desire that he should attend Windsor Castle the following day to be sworn of the Privy Council. Salisbury rubbed home the fact that he realised that Curzon had been trying it on by remarking: "It may be a satisfaction to you to remember that (so far as I know) there has been no instance of any one holding a political office at your age having received the office in living memory."

Curzon was content. He had a wife, an income, a fortune in the offing, and the secure knowledge that his Party needed him enough to be willingly blackmailed.

He settled back to prepare for the next phase of his career—the phase that would, he confidently believed, take him soaring to the highest office in the land.

CHAPTER FIVE

The Statesman Emerges

A CHARACTER DOES NOT CHANGE very easily, if it can change at all, at the age of thirty-six. Yet the triple crown of success which he achieved in the year 1895—important political office, a happy marriage, and financial security—did give some resilience and pliability to a nature which had hitherto been almost as rigid as his malformed spine. There are those who will say that what the assumption of the office of Under-Secretary of State for Foreign Affairs added to Curzon's character was not flexibility but deviousness; and certainly, under a chief with an outlook such as Lord Salisbury's, a subordinate needed to learn how to twist and turn if he was to make anything of his office. In the year 1895, when the Tories came back to effective power and Curzon was given his job, the British Empire, which had for so long been pre-eminent and unchallenged, was beginning to feel the cold wind of competition, and the envy and jealousy of other nations was changing, in places, to overt hostility. The race was on to mop up the last puddles in Africa and Asia, and for the four great European powers (Britain, Russia, France, Germany), the game of poker was in progress, with small nations as the stakes and rich new colonies and markets as the jackpot.

"The world is unquiet," said Curzon at a speech at Derby on November 6, 1895. "Uneasy symptoms are abroad. We hear the moaning of sick nations on their couches. . . . If we would guard against the perils of the future, we must lift our eyes across our island seas to the greater world beyond." It was a world in which, as he had seen for himself, the Russians were glowering over the mountain peaks at India; the French were engaged in colonialism of the most sordid kind in Siam and Indo-China; the Germans were infiltrating into China and Manchuria, long considered by Britain to be England's spheres of interest.

Curzon had not much doubt that, if properly played, the game could still be won by Britain, for in his view she had two invulnerable aces in the hole: the untarnished nature of a colonial mission, and the military and naval muscle in a strong right arm.

He soon discovered, however, that Lord Salisbury was not at all anxious to get involved in the game; and that when circumstances did force him to play, he did so with an untroubled lack of application that seemed to Curzon monstrous and dangerous. In the struggles for new markets, new spheres of interest, new colonies, Curzon did not believe in giving an inch to the rival powers because he believed that they would then be encouraged to snatch a mile. Salisbury, on the other hand, was all for a quiet life; he liked to sweep international rivalries under the carpet, where he could not see them. He did his best, at first, to keep back Foreign Office reports and developments from his subordinate, so that he would not be able to see them either, and Curzon had to use every kind of strategem to find out what was going on. Several times, he appealed to his chief direct.

"I have to be the mouthpiece of the office here, and it would, I think, be an easier task if I knew always what was going on," he wrote to Salisbury in 1896. "I hope I am not making an improper request. It is certainly not actuated by curiosity, and if you tell me that it is undesirable that I should know and see more I shall be content. But I do feel the difficulty of having to speak here as if I knew all, whereas I only know part; and I am sure you will exonerate me for mentioning it."

This from the chief spokesman of the Foreign Office in the House of Commons!

His appeal had so little result that, later in the year, he wrote again: "I do not know how it is, and no one in the office seems able to explain, but I have never once since I have been in the office heard of any intended deputation to you until after it has been and gone. I should very much like, for instance, to have been present at the deputation about Indo-Chinese railways, a subject which I have long studied and in which I take a great interest. But the first I heard of it or saw of it was your speech in *The Times* next morning."

Salisbury temporarily mollified him by giving odd scraps of information, but he also made it very clear to Curzon that, so far as Foreign Affairs were concerned, he was nothing more than his master's voice in another place; and Curzon found himself repeatedly mouthing sentiments and policies to the Commons with which he was diametrically opposed, policies which were, moreover, as he believed, perilous to the future of the Empire. He did not like it a bit. But the office, and the advancement it promised, was too precious; and not for the first time in his life, he put principle second to expediency—and did not resign. Instead, he blew off steam by writing letters to his wife or his friends complaining. In one, to Lord Selborne, he set out the different attitudes of himself and his chief in these words:

"I never spend five minutes in inquiring if we are unpopular. The answer is written in red ink on the map of the globe. Neither would I ever adopt Lord Salisbury's plan of throwing bones to keep the various dogs quiet (Madagascar, Tunis, Heligoland, Samoa, Siam). They devour your bone and then turn round and snarl for more. No; I would count everywhere on the individual hostility of all the great Powers, but would endeavour so to arrange things that they were not *united* against us. And the first condition of success in such a policy, in my opinion, would be the exact inverse of your present policy; for I would be as strong in small things as in big."*

What particularly irked him was Salisbury's complacence in face of what he believed to be the cunning and unscrupulous plottings of the French in Africa and Asia. His mixture of hatred and contempt for the French waxed rather than waned with the years, and he was furious at the way they were behaving in the Far East. "Shuffling little stubble-bearded Frenchmen of the most unattractive sort," he wrote of the Gallic colonialists he had met. "How tired I get of the type. All civil on the lip and smirk in the address, but no real bonhomie or frankness, and a desperate and jealous hatred of the English at the bottom."

He added, in a letter to his wife, Mary: "Why do we *allow* the French to take a leading part in the affairs of the world?"

But these were his private sentiments, and he was careful that they did not reach Salisbury's ears; or, when they did, he hastily repudiated any disloyalty to his chief. He was on his feet constantly, in the House or on public platforms, passionately justifying (in those rich and fruity perorations for which he had now become so famous) policies in which he did not believe; and this improved neither his health nor his temper. The pain in his back was such that he was forced to take to his bed at every opportunity, and Mary Curzon came to know what life was like with a man who worked all day, read or wrote practically the whole of the night, and rarely slept. Not that she complained. Far from it. "I find him the most indefatigable of husbands," she wrote to her sister, and it was definitely meant to indicate that she was pleased with her situation. True, she took a little time to get used to the fact that she must not only keep him in touch with all the domestic details but also let him

---

* This letter was, in fact, written a few years later, when he was Viceroy of India, but it is a succinct expression of his opinion and feelings at the time.

take complete charge of the household whenever the spirit moved him. He would never let her choose the staff for the house they had taken at 1 Carlton House Terrace in London, but would sweep the red Foreign Office boxes from his bed, strap himself into his leather harness, and descend to interview the applicants for the jobs as butler, footmen, cooks, and betweenmaids. He was, in fact, a chronic chooser of domestic helpers. His diary of his public life is interspersed with anguished private yelps of dismay at the inefficiency, insobriety, insolence, or incontinence of the servants he chose to serve him; but never for a moment would he accept the fact that his wife might be a better judge than he was. She had to learn, too, to keep the household accounts up to date, and present them to him in detail every Friday night, and be prepared for a long lecture on carelessness or extravagance if she was a shilling or two over her budget. ("I always cheat a little," Mary confessed.) Otherwise, his wife found him a gentle husband and certainly not lacking in the "extravagance of affection" which, on her part, she had once felt he might resent. If there was one thing stable in Curzon's life in the ten years from 1895, it was his marriage. Even he admitted that he had been lucky in his choice and that Mary Victoria was a paragon among women. She soon made their marriage fruitful by bearing him a daughter, Irene; and next time, she promised, she would give him the son he so passionately wanted. (It was one of the few things in which Mary Curzon let him down.) She was always much more of a prop upon which he could lean than ever he realised during her lifetime; an intelligent and sympathetic hostess, a shoulder upon which he could weep his tears of mortification, quick to sense his moods and respond to them, and always submissive to his opinions or prejudices. Though she must often have longed to argue or discuss with him, she allowed him to become master not only of her body but of her mind as well. So far as she was concerned, it was a case of "L'état, c'est lui."

But even Mary Curzon's all-consuming patience and sympathy could not quieten him when he was in one of his moods. The legacy from boyhood was still with him, and he was just as quick as ever to take genuine disagreement as a personal slight or insult. He had been a strong supporter of an entente with Germany until he went to Berlin and asked for a personal interview with the Emperor. When it was curtly refused he told Salisbury that the rebuff was obviously not directed at himself but at England and her policy; but in private, he was humiliated and chagrined. His enthusiasm for the Emperor quickly dissipated, and when he spoke of Germany in future the note of hostility crept into his voice. Sir William Harcourt, the leader of the Liberal Opposition, took him to task for his increasing references to Germany, "which he is so constantly making and which, coming from the Foreign Office, are singularly impolitic." Harcourt had always been a friendly patron of Curzon's despite the fact that they sat on opposite sides of the House, and he had meant the rebuke in a purely political sense. But Curzon took it personally, and he rushed home to Carlton House Terrace and wrote a furious letter.

"Your words, whether read in this country or in Germany, cannot fail to convey a damaging impression, which I am now powerless to remove," he told Harcourt. "I should have had no cause for complaint if this criticism had been merely part of the ordinary cut and thrust of Parliamentary warfare, still less if the rebuke had been justly earned. But I feel it is rather different when a charge that I believe to be wholly groundless is publicly brought against me as Under Secretary by the Leader of the Opposition, and I am the more hurt that it should have come from one whose friendship I have always regarded it a privilege to claim."

Sir William Harcourt sent a note back immediately, disclaiming any intention of attacking Curzon personally and telling him gently, between every line, not to be a fool. But Curzon was far from being mollified. Perhaps he was afraid that Salisbury would get a wrong impression.

"What vexed me was not your criticism of my remark about the German railway," he wrote back, "but your suggestion that it was only one of a series of similar affronts from my lips to that country. If the feeling that you complain of exists in the Foreign Office or elsewhere, it certainly is not shared by me, since I may confess that I have always been an ardent advocate of the entente cordiale with Germany, which no one rejoices more than myself that Lord Salisbury has successfully re-established."

It was not the last time in his life that he failed to understand that those who got up to criticise him were men who also had deep and fervently held beliefs. So long as he was up on his feet in the House of Commons, speaking his brief, he felt proud and arrogantly sure; but he was never to get the feel of politics (and perhaps not even of statesmanship) sufficiently to realise that opposition, attack, and the fisticuffs of debate are the very stuff of democratic government, and were not always meant as an assault on his *amour-propre*. As the months went by, he became increasingly touchy. He could not hit back publicly at the gad-flies who, he became increasingly convinced, were interested only in stinging him, for that would have aroused the deep displeasure of his patron, Lord Salisbury. So he let the frustration curdle inside him until it was rancorous.

The result was, as any psychologist could have foreseen, that his back became worse. It was always to be most difficult to endure physically in those moments when he was mentally distressed. It became so troublesome about this time (1898) that he consulted a specialist about it. He kept the report among his private papers, and it reads as follows:

"There is nothing to suggest the least possibility of the presence of organic disease. In fact, it may definitely be said that none exists. Nor is there ground for fear that any will develop. There is strong reason to expect that the increase of curvature of the spine—which, no doubt, so far as any has occurred, was due to overwork—will be corrected under the favourable conditions which can now be secured. The best course will be to rest as much as possible in bed or on a couch till the pain of the present attack has subsided, and for the next few weeks to avoid muscular fatigue. There is strong ground for believing that the rest which can now be secured will lead to such improvement that, in future, the trouble will be much less than has been recently the case."

Rest. It was the one thing Curzon would never allow himself. It was almost as if he used his colossal and fanatic energy as a goad to make his back ache, so that the resultant pain would whip him into further bouts of ferocious activity. As if, in fact, he *needed* his curvature of the spine.

THERE WAS, of course, always one unfailing anodyne for Curzon's dolour, and that was public recognition of his talents. And in 1898 there came an announcement from Lord Salisbury that quickly restored him to reasonable health and enabled him to rise from his bed of pain—the announcement that he was to succeed Lord Elgin as Viceroy of the Indian Empire. If the goal on the far horizon of Curzon's ambition was always the premiership, the office of Viceroy was an interim target upon which he had set his sights; and while he was Under-Secretary at the Foreign Office he had done quite a little lobbying and intriguing in order to get it, making sure that the leading statesmen of both parties, Tories and Liberals alike, were aware of his knowledge of India and his passionate interest in the welfare of the sub-Continent. One of his stratagems had been to get himself elected to an exclusive dining club, the Grillions, "a famous old club," he wrote to Mary, "with only sixty members, men like Gladstone, Chamberlain, Morley, Goschen, Balfour, Leighton, Derby, etc. Rather nice as I am by ten years the youngest member." And he never neglected an opportunity to buttonhole an influential member and expound his theories about Asia. With Lord Salisbury he was even more direct, and wrote to him as early as 1897, long before Lord Elgin's term of office was at an end, pointing out that what India needed now was a young man to take over its direction. He asked his chief to bear him in mind when the new appointment was made; and thereafter, every time he supported a Salisbury policy with which he disagreed, he followed it up with a reminder that he would like to go to India. Not, he hastened to point out, because he was personally ambitious. "My strongest impulse, I can honestly say," he told Salisbury, "is not a personal one at all. It is the desire, while one is still in the hey day of life, to do some strenuous work in a position of responsibility and in a cause for which previous study and training may have rendered one in some measure less unfit for the effort."

He was happy and triumphant when Salisbury at last informed him, in June, 1898, that the great position was his. He was even more ecstatic when he discovered that practically everyone in public life—after a preliminary gulp of astonishment that one so young (for he was still only thirty-nine) should be given such imperial power—welcomed his appointment. True, *The Times* rather frigidly called it "an interesting experiment." There were those, particularly in the Liberal Party, who feared he would use his new position to exploit his predilection towards "gunboat diplomacy" and would start glowering back at the Russians shadow-boxing just across the Afghanistan frontier. In his letter of congratulation, his old friend Sir William Harcourt ended with the words: "Let me beg as a personal favour that you will not make war on Russia in my lifetime."

But on the whole there was a general recognition that for once the play-safe Lord Salisbury had made a bold and intelligent appointment. The president of the Crabbet Club, Wilfred Blunt, wrote him the usual cynical letter of congratulation, reminding him that all members were dedicated to irresponsibility and hoping that he would prove both the most frivolous and the last of the Viceroys, but for once this humorous approach fell on stony ground. Curzon took his new position too seriously to be amused at jokes about it.

For the rest of the year, he scurried to and fro with an energy and freneticism that was unusual even for him. He had two long talks with Queen Victoria, who was charmed with his serious demeanour and sense of dedication, and classed him, along with Kitchener, at that moment wiping out the humiliations of defeat in the Sudan, as one of her two most loyal, worthy, and promising servants. His own impressions of Victoria he described in a letter to Mary, who was staying at that time at the Priory in Reigate, which they had leased while she awaited the birth of her second child. "After lunch sent for to Queen," he wrote, "in upstairs sitting room. She bade me sit and kept me in conversation for 25 mins. She was surprisingly better in appearance and more alert in conversation than when we were at Windsor: talked incessantly and with great animation about you and baby, about Elgin, Lockhart, Warburton, Indian Civil Service, natives, etc. etc. She is said to be very nearly blind but you would never gather it. In the face she looked marvellously well. Dress cut very open over her neck and shoulders, so that one could see her well-padded body. . . . After dinner we all stood about in tartan-stuffed drawing room and were sent for by the Queen in turns."

It was just at the moment when Curzon was once more seated with the Queen that a telegram arrived from Kitchener announcing his victory in the Sudan and the fall of the Dervishes. Victoria, who was well aware of Curzon's throbbing voice and sense of the dramatic, handed it to him.

"Read it to them, Mr. Curzon," she said. "And do it justice."

He rose to his feet "and did so amid breathless silence. A glorious victory. . . . At 7 P.M. today the Queen sent for me again and talked about India. She said we must both hold ourselves with dignity and appear on public occasions only in carriages or on horseback. . . . Will write again. Take every care of yourself, precious Kinkie, and send pappy some blue socks (that he ordinarily wears) if back from the wash."

In the course of the next few months, while still carrying out various Parliamentary duties, correcting the proofs of his new book, *The Frontiers of India*, interviewing prospective A.D.C.'s, he made long farewell speeches to his constituents in Southport, to his father's tenants at Kedleston (who gave him an illuminated address), and at several celebration dinners.

He was also deeply immersed in financial calculations, for he was determined that he would do his position justice ("We shall be the images of the Empress to our new subjects, and our life must live up to what they expect from a ruler and his consort"), and it seemed certain to him that his income and allowances would not be sufficient for the majesty and panoply that would be expected of him. In this matter, however, Mary had once more come to the rescue by writing to old Levi Leiter in Chicago, and her father did not let his daughter down.

"Keep his [her father's] letter very carefully," wrote Curzon, on September 6, 1898. "When he speaks of his bond to you of $1,000,000 payable on his death, I presume he is alluding to the sum provided for in the marriage settlement over and above what we now have. If I remember right, the two sums together will give us about £16,000 a year then. Anything else that you get will be, I imagine, your share with this deducted. He speaks very generously about our requirements in going out to India, and his present to you of £600 in addition to your own £1,400 will be a great help towards the tiara."

But would all this be sufficient? "I hope that our income up to the end of the year may enable us to get along and pay for our Indian requisites without applying to him for more," he added, with no sense of the piquancy of the situation—a Chicago millionaire providing the wherewithal for a British Viceroy to keep up appearances.

There was also the question of a house in London to which Mary could come back when she needed a rest from India. Curzon was anxious to buy 1 Carlton House Terrace, but the asking price was well over £20,000.

"I have no objection," he wrote to Mary, "to your asking him [Mr. Leiter] about your desire to borrow the money for the house. I have no idea at what rate we could borrow, for I don't know what security we can give beyond the house when we have bought it. But of course we cannot do it unless he accepts the repayment of the loan, as an obligation upon himself, as soon as he can, at an early date, find the ready money. . . . We must have the promise from him before we can proceed in the matter. For otherwise consider our position. We shall be paying about £1,000 a year in interest on the loan, and £500 a year in rates and taxes on the house."

He sounded a little more cheerful in a subsequent letter, when his agent informed him that the American publisher Harper & Brothers had given him a £1,500 advance on his new book; and his worries cleared when Mary informed him that her father had promised to produce the money to purchase 1 Carlton House Terrace, and that he wasn't to worry about the interest.

After this, he got down to his next task, that of engaging a nurse for his children (his second daughter, "our skinny little yellow horror, Cynthia" had meanwhile been born), and to this he devoted endless hours of interviewing applicants and reporting back in detail to Mary. "She is ladylike yet not quite a lady," he wrote about one of them, "neatly dressed, shows acres of gum and files of artificial teeth. She asked 1) Might she take out her bicycle with her? I said I would enquire, but thought that if the roads permitted it, there would be no objection; 2) Would she have to ride? I said No. 3) What exactly would be her social position. I replied that she would be nurse to the children of the Viceroy, and what position could be more defined than that?"

It must have seemed to George Nathaniel Curzon that suddenly the golden clouds of glory were gathering around his head. Even his father unbent enough to express pleasure at his son's advancement, and wrote to him:

"I begin to realise what a splendid position you have deservedly won. Congrats pour in from every quarter, and the county generally are as proud of you as I, your Father, am, and more I cannot say."

This, from a parent who hitherto had kept his hands firmly in his pocket when everyone else was patting his son on the back, was such an overwhelming development that Curzon broke down when he received the letter and burst into tears. "It was not the first time I had seen dear George cry," wrote Mary to her sister, "but this time it was different, the happy sobs of a son who has been recognised at last by his own—a prophet at last honoured in his own country."

There was more to his joy than this, though it was not to give his father quite so much pleasure. Queen Victoria had indicated at his first audience with her at Windsor that she wished to give him a title, and she came back to the subject when he stayed with her at Balmoral.

He determined to choose an Irish title, since this would not qualify him for the House of Lords and would thus enable him, when he returned from India, to go back to the House of Commons. But what title should he choose? His instinct was to choose one that would carry the family name of Curzon; especially as, while this very subject was being discussed, Mary was about to bear his second child, and both of them fervently wished it to be a son to carry on the line. But so far as a Curzon title was concerned there were difficulties. His friend Sir Schomberg McDonnell, who was at this time in liaison between the Queen and the Government, wrote to him on August 22, 1898:

"I hope that the great event has taken place, and that it is a son. Lord Salisbury wants me to see you and talk to you about your title, as the Queen seems to wish the matter to be settled, and agrees to it being an Irish peerage. Lord Salisbury however adds that I am to beg you to avoid, if possible, the choice of the title of Curzon of Kedleston, as this will probably lead to delays and discussion."

For there was (and still is) another family with the name Curzon as part of their remainder. The Earl of Howe's son has the title of Viscount Curzon. McDonnell added that he did not himself see that there would be any difficulty in Curzon's choosing his own name for his peerage "if you will take immediate steps to see Lord Howe or George Curzon [Lord Howe's son] and send me their consent in writing to their doing so. But it is absolutely useless and a waste of time to propose this without Lord Howe's consent. I am sure the Queen would never allow it, and I am sure that, if Lord Howe discovered, as he certainly would, your intention, he would protest strenuously and successfully. So pray square him as soon as you can."

Curzon decided to move with great care. He was determined to have his own name in his title, and in this he was thinking more of the future than the present. By the normal process of inheritance, he would automatically, upon his father's death, become Lord Scarsdale. But he was far from being unaware that it was customary to award a successful Viceroy, at the end of his term of office, with something much more distinguished than a mere barony, which was his father's rank. An earldom would put him level with Howe, and a marquisate (the title he believed his efforts would win him) would put him ahead and make him the first Curzon in the land. It was, however, essential not to show the Howes that he was banking on this possibility, and the letter he wrote to George, Viscount Curzon, merely asked him to use his good offices with his father to allow him to use the family name in his forthcoming Irish barony.

The Howes were not such fools as to be unaware of which way the winds of aristocratic preferment were blowing, however, and Viscount Curzon wrote back on September 4, 1898:

"I think I had better tell you what my father says: 'I cannot see any possible objection to George Curzon taking the name of Curzon of Kedleston. After all, it is a question which concerns us, and if we do not object, I don't see that anybody can possibly object. So far do I think that any objection can be made that, as I feel quite confident his reign in India seems certain to be a success in every way, it may be the means of perpetuating the name of Curzon, and I think that it will be a great gain and revive the glories of a name which has already done something to ensure the respect of the country to which we belong.'"

But after this amiable opening, came the flick of the seigniorial whip:

"'You will see,'" Earl Howe went on, "'that I can have no possible objection to George Curzon's taking the name of Curzon of Kedleston, but I think that the title should cease whenever he succeeds his father, and that it should not be revived even if he was made an Earl. This I feel sure he will consent to.' So now, old boy, you know my father's opinion, and I will only for myself send you my heartfelt wishes that health, happiness and success may ever be yours. By whatever name you may be called, we shall always be 'Both George, both Curzon, both agreed,' etc.!!"

The Howes settled back, convinced that they had fended off any permanent encroachment upon their prior right to have the family name in their title. But they reckoned without the adeptness of their distant cousin. He wrote back just as warmly and accommodatingly as they had done.

"You have been very good about telegraphing, and I have received all your wires and now your letter," he wrote on September 7, 1898. "I am very pleased to learn that your father has written with such kindly generosity about the proposal which I mentioned to you both; and that his attitude is reflected in yours. Please express to him my sincere sense of obligation and the hopes that the old name may not suffer any discredit in its revived form. The Queen spoke to me about the matter at Balmoral and agreed in preferring the proposed form of title."

After which Curzon himself added a baited afterthought: "I think, however, that it would be invidious, and that she might be offended, if I were to anticipate what, after all, may never happen in the future, and to pre-judge the possibility of her future favour by saying anything about an earldom now, or the form that, if ever granted, it should take. The only point that has been raised is the very restricted one of this Irish title which will drop off from me of its own accord [he crossed out the last ten words and substituted] which I shall cease to wear when I succeed, if I ever do, to the higher English title of my father."

The Howes swallowed the bait and were mollified. (For the time being, anyway; there was to be much more trouble in the years to come.) Curzon wrote immediately to McDonnell to tell him that he had the necessary consent, and received the reply:

"I think you were most wise not to discuss the future with Lord Howe. I enclose the form of announcement."

On September 21, 1898, the following announcement appeared in the *London Gazette*:

> "The Queen has been pleased to confer the dignity of a Peerage upon the Rt. Hon. George Nathaniel Curzon by the name style and title of Baron Curzon of Kedleston in the Peerage of Ireland."

What Curzon thought about the apprehensions of the Howes over the sanctity of their title could well have been summed up in the motto he asked the Ulster King of Arms to put on his coat of arms: "Let Curzon Holde what Curzon Helde."

Now all the preparations were made, and Curzon's eyes turned East towards the Himalayas and the opportunities, rich with promise, that lay beneath their shadows. He signed the last reply to "more than 1,000 letters" of congratulation he had received; and with Mary and her new tiara, their two daughters, a

nurse, a butler, a new landau, two hack horses and a pony, set
sail for India, imbued as never before with a sense of civilis-
ing mission.

Just before the boat left Tilbury, he was handed a letter from
Margot Asquith, the close and adoring friend from his youth,
now married to the man about to become Leader of the Liberal
party. She wrote:

"Most dear George, You will have more letters than you can
read. It is a great position and a *fine* tribute—and you deserve
everything you get. To us who love you it is with a deep innate
joy we watch you move in whatsoever direction you will. *I* am
sorry for myself that you are going so far and so long. . . . God
bless you and keep you strong, and prosper your work. I am at
whatever distance away from you, both your most loving and
only girl."

But from Asquith himself, though they were old friends, there
was no message. Later, when Curzon was in trouble and would
have appreciated Asquith's sympathy and help—and it was not
forthcoming—he remembered this.

CHAPTER SIX

Journey to Heaven

GEORGE NATHANIEL CURZON was, at thirty-nine, the youngest Viceroy of India in history.

His was, as Lord Beaverbrook has remarked in his book, *Men and Power*, an "office filled with pomp and ceremony. . . . In his train followed long strings of elephants and retinues of gaily colourful servants. . . . For all the rest of his life Curzon was influenced by his sudden journey to heaven at the age of 39, and then by his return to earth seven years later, for the remainder of his mortal existence."

To a man even of Curzon's boundless confidence in his own legislative ability, here was a position awesome in its power, confusing in its complexities, daunting in its responsibilities, and yet, at the same time, compulsively fascinating in the omnific influence it gave to its holder over the destinies of millions of men, women, and children. To Queen Victoria, the Indian Empire was the most treasured jewel in her Crown. To the legislators at Westminster, it was at once a source of trade and wealth, a bulwark against Britain's rivals in the pursuit of their Asiatic ambitions, and a perennially well-stocked granary from which could be drawn the soldiers to defend the outposts of the Empire. To the man and woman in the street at home, India was perhaps the proudest red spot of all on the map of the Victorian world.

But seen from in its midst, India could not be quite so easily docketed. From 5,000 miles away, it might look like one vast and viable satellite of Great Britain. What became apparent immediately one plunged among its heaving, palpitating millions was that here indeed was not just one country or one people, but an Empire of a hundred different races and many different religions and ways of life. Its subjects spoke so many different languages that English was (as it still is) the lingua franca. It was racked by internecine feuds and antipathies, by poverty, disease, and prejudice. At any moment its moiling hatreds and frustrations might come to the boil—setting one sect or race against another, or all of them against the British Raj, which held this teeming slice of earth under its benevolent thrall.

If Curzon needed a reminder of the immensity of his inheritance, he got it on the afternoon of January 3, 1899, when the State carriage containing himself and his wife drew up at Government House in Calcutta. All around him in the streets and squares, his subjects, their brown bodies jammed together like a colony of ants, were squeaking and shrieking a welcome to the newly arrived overlord. From the reviewing stand at the top of Government House steps, he watched his armies marching before him: soldiers from every regiment in India, men from the hills and the plains, the deserts and the jungles, wiry little Ghurkas and Pathans, majestic Punjabis and Mahrattis; soldiers on foot, soldiers on horseback, soldiers on lumbering painted elephants. The tears that were never far away on emotional occasions welled into Curzon's eyes. "I suddenly saw what had come into my hands, and what prodigies of energy and inspiration would be needed on my part to guide them," he wrote later.

That night he dressed himself in the court dress of a Viceroy, smoothing the silken tights over his shapely legs, donning the gallant gold-and-crimson jacket, and over it the jewelled sky-blue

cloak and sashes of his office, and, with Mary in her vivid peacock dress and new tiara, descended to the great hall for the
banquet held in his honour.

"Never before," wrote Mary to her sister, "has George looked
so beautiful."

One by one his vassals came forward to be presented: the
governors and the lieutenant-governors of his provinces, the
maharajahs and rajahs from his princely states, Hindus and Mos-
lems, Christians, Buddhists and Sikhs. To Curzon's impressionable nature, it was glory, glory on all sides, and "all was novelty,
brave hopes and high aspirations."

For a time, at least, it remained that way. When Lord Salisbury had taken the revolutionary step of appointing one so young
to be Viceroy of India, he had done so because he believed that
Curzon was an amenable subordinate and would make no major
moves without securing the consent of the Government at home.
But a change came over him the moment he felt the warmth of
the viceregal throne on his breeches. The servile junior minister
who had so often stifled his principles in the interests of office
now felt himself strong enough, and far enough away, to act
alone, and, if need be, in defiance of Westminster. He viewed his
position as similar to that of a Roman proconsul in Britain or
Gaul during the time of the Caesars. He had time and distance
on his side. And as the Government became increasingly involved
with the difficulties and disasters of the Boer War, Curzon became less heedful of any advice they might offer him.

One of his first acts was to make it clear, to both his governors
and his princes, that in future they must bend the knee of authority to him. Hitherto, a provincial governor had usually been
so much a master of his own affairs that he took a decision first,
and only afterwards informed the Viceroy and his Council. Curzon put an end to all that. Henceforward, no one could make a
move without securing his permission. He sent out an order chid-
ing high officials for their solvenliness in dress. "Some of them

have been known to attend official functions in trousers," he pointed out, and reminded them that the Lord Chamberlain had laid down that their dress should include breeches. Knee breeches and stockings would be worn, he said. He drafted an order informing the princes that in future they should visit Europe only after asking his personal permission, but was persuaded that such discipline would turn them into a band of rebellious schoolboys; and he substituted a less peremptory message merely asking them to inform him first before they left the country. He wiped out the cherished independence of the City Council of Calcutta with a stroke of a pen, handing control of affairs over to his own subordinates; and, in face of opposition from British and Indians alike, gradually ended the decentralised forms of administration and brought them under his personal control.

News of his autocratic methods caused something of a stir in England, and one newspaper published a rumour that the Viceroy's military secretary had resigned because Curzon insisted that the secretary should stand behind his chair during meals. This he furiously denied in a telegram to the newspaper concerned.

In all these activities, Curzon never had any doubt of the high motives which inspired them. What always seemed to others (friends and enemies alike) to be his worst fault—his complete inability to delegate authority—seemed to him a supreme virtue. He was so conscious of the inferiority of others that he had to do everything himself; and this weakness (which he considered a strength) turned him into a slave, performing unnecessary labours for which there were hundreds of competent subordinates. All through the intense Indian heat, he worked a twelve-or fourteen-hour day. He made speeches. He drafted bills. He listened to complaints and petitions. He wrote those copious notes to his friends. He conceived and drew up a constitution for a new northwest frontier province, and he wrote it out in his own hand, all 250,000 words of it. (He also permanently offended the lieutenant-governor of Punjab, part of whose province would be swallowed up by the new state, by neglecting to inform him about it beforehand.) He hired and inspected the servants. He oversaw the family expenditure. And constantly he complained about the inefficiency of his underlings, the pressure of his work, and the pain in his back. He could not understand that others might be offended by his attitude; that what to him was dedicated labour was to others—particularly the talented and equally dedicated higher ranks of the Indian Civil Service—pure arrogance. And it was not without a certain relish that the old-stagers among them waited for him to make his first mistake. He did it within the first year of his assumption of office.

In Rangoon, the capital of Burma, which came within Curzon's Indian dominion at that time, a small group of soldiers, out on the town for an evening's entertainment, emerged drunk from an illegal liquor-den and surprised a Burmese woman on her way home to her family. They dragged her off to a nearby open space and raped her in turn. Her screams brought a number of natives to the scene, and eventually the soldiers made off, leaving the woman more dead than alive.

The local governor's inclination was to hush up the whole affair, so long as the men were found and punished; but at the subsequent court-martial, the native witnesses were either persuaded to withdraw their evidence or cajoled into so doing, and the accused soldiers were acquitted. There the matter might have rested if rumours of the outrage had not reached Curzon's ears. He at once called for a full summary of the evidence of all concerned.

He was rightly appalled and outraged. From the first he had made it clear that he considered that the prime duty of a Viceroy was to see that justice was impartial for all, no matter what their race or creed. The idea that British soldiers had so grossly abused the hospitality of the country in which they were stationed and then had evaded punishment by a trick, whipped him into a fury.

He sent a peremptory order to the colonel in command of the regiment to which the soldiers belonged telling him that the accused men were to be dismissed from the Army and sent back to England in disgrace.

This was no more than rough justice. But after he had thought about it for another forty-eight hours, Curzon decided to go further. He sent telegrams and letters to London. He demanded urgent and ruthless reprisals against the regiment and made it clear that if his demands were not obeyed, he would resign and put his case to both the Indian public and the people at home. And though Salisbury and his friend St. John Brodrick, who was then Minister for War, counselled caution, he refused to heed them. So they gave in, and the reprisals were taken. The regiment was shipped, at a moment's notice, to Aden and there deprived of all leave and privileges for a year. Its colonel was sacked. The sergeant-major from whose squad the accused men came was reduced to the ranks.

Curzon was satisfied. He allowed the news to leak out to the native Indian Press and basked in the praise they lavished upon him for his determined defence of the inviolability of their women. But he also won for himself the embittered resentment of the whole of the British Army in India; and he would need the help of their more influential officers in the days to come. . . .

In 1900 he informed Queen Victoria that he was leaving on a tour of India's provinces and princely states, which would, he hoped, bring before all races and creeds a reminder of the blessings of her benevolent and enlightened rule. To India's millions, however, the monarch they recognised and accepted was the monarch they saw or whose presence they felt, and it was Curzon rather than Victoria who drew credit from the visit. It proved to be a tour in which triumph mounted upon triumph. The people abased themselves in their millions when he and Mary drove through Bombay. Everywhere else he went, he was treated as if a god had come down to earth.

Mary Curzon kept a copious diary of the tour, and almost every page contains some mention of the almost overwhelming panoply and ceremonial that attended them. Books were printed setting out the programme of their visits. Stationmasters were wired to hold up traffic while their royal train chugged by. Herds of elephants were brought in and given new paint and canopies. Coolies were set to building and clearing. Tigers and bears were rounded up for the Viceroy's sport.

"I think that our miserable luck at shooting so far," wrote Mary from Baghi, "is that the preparations for the Viceroy's camp entail such hundreds of coolies and mules, and a general turning upside down of the whole country. Miles of paths are cut on any hill the great Sahib may walk on, and underbrush cut down and a grand clean-up made of the country. This is done in each small state we go through, and as crowds follow us everywhere every bird and beast flies before this invading army."

From Patiala she wrote: "George arrived in his special train at 3 o'clock from Bhawalpur, where he had been installing the young Nawab, and I arrived half an hour later in my special. . . . At Patiala the Chief is only ten. The beautiful camp which had been weeks preparing to receive the Viceroy, burned to the ground three days before he was to arrive, and the splendid hangings and carpets, valued it is said at £150,000, were all destroyed, and a camp had to be hastily borrowed from the Rajah of Kapurthala and put up to receive George. . . . A broad avenue led to his tents, and the mustard and cress plots of green before the tents were adorned with immense glass bowls of gold-fish and gigantic coloured chandeliers sitting on the ground."

They went on in H. M. S. *Hardinge,* accompanied by ships of the fleet, to visit the Sultan of Muscat, who, Curzon had heard, was thinking of accepting a large bribe from the Russians to allow them to establish a coaling station in the area. Salisbury would have accepted a Russian *fait accompli* of this kind with a shrug of the shoulders; but not Curzon. In his book on Persia

he had said that any Briton who allowed a foreign power to infil-
trate into the Persian Gulf should be impeached and hanged as a
traitor, and he was personally determined to see that his old
patron did not finish his career at the end of a rope.

With the guns of the *Argonaut* and the *Hardinge* trained
upon them, the Viceroy and his lady, and the Sultan and his
aides sipped sherbet in the heavy heated shade. The Sultan in
his speech referred to Mary Curzon as "a pearl." Curzon replied
by saying that the Persian Gulf was also a pearl, and, with a
certain emphasis in his voice, that it was a pearl which Britain
considered beyond price. The point was taken and more sherbet
was drunk.

When Salisbury heard of Curzon's action he protested feebly
that the Viceroy had seen fit to go over his head, but Curzon
soothed him by saying that he had merely anticipated the intelligent move the Premier would undoubtedly have made himself
had he not been so occupied with more important matters.

"The morning after we left Muscat," wrote Mary in her
diary, "we cruised all day among the islands and fiords of the
most barren description. The land is uninhabited save for a few
fishermen, and its main interest is a strategic one, as the bays
and inlets afford anchorage for a fleet, and as the land is No
Man's, Russia or France could take advantage of the harbourage
in the event of war. . . . At sunset we pursued our way towards
Shargah, where the fleet was waiting for us, and we formed a
procession. A sea got up in the night and was running quite high
when we got to Shargah, where George was to hold a durbar for
the Arabian sheikhs. It will remain unique for sick sheikhs, high
sea, and pea-green staff."

It was on this tour that Curzon saw, for the first time, the
famous tomb of Taj Mahal and embarked upon one of the most
energetic hobbies of his viceroyalty: the restoration and recognition of India's famous monuments. It was Mary who first drew
him to it and excited his enthusiasm. "No word of mine can give

any idea of the Taj," she wrote to Curzon. "It is the most divine creation of a building in the whole world. You will never be able to satisfy your eyes by seeing it enough." What Curzon did see, when he went over it for the second time, were signs of decay and neglect, and he forthwith issued decrees for its restoration, for which he pledged the Government of India's financial backing. Meanwhile, Mary was receiving a visit from the Rani. "Her sedan chair was brought in, and the Rani popped into the drawing room, wearing huge Turkish trousers of bright pink, a white jacket, and at least 60 yards of bright blue gauze wound about and dragging behind her. On her hair was a very quaint silver ornament, four arms of a Dutch windmill 8 inches across fastened on her forehead, and two wreaths of silver flowers forming a kind of hat. Her hair was parted up the back, and hunched amidst the silver roses on the top of her head. She spoke a little English and she explained that her health was poor. Lady McDonnell asked her from what she was suffering. She replied: 'Me inside out.' The trial of looking grave was terrific, and as soon as she had gone I laughed till I cried. I forgot to say that she had white gloves on, with rings on each finger over the glove."

If Mary Curzon kept her girlish sense of humour during the tour, her husband remained conscious of the majesty of his position throughout, and found little to amuse him but much to inflate his pride in the resources of his Empire. When the viceregal party arrived at the Portuguese territory of Goa, and the visit became almost a farce, owing to the effeteness of his hosts and the lack of training of the Goanese soldiers, he was at the same time happy that this was not British India and contemptuous of the way these "lesser-breeds of European" ran their dependency.

"The Governor's wife met us," wrote Mary in her diary; "she was a Portuguese from Shanghai and she spoke English, looked Chinese, and fanned herself like a Spaniard. A band played 'God Save the Queen' with the Army performing feats on the bugle, and we then started to walk through the town on foot. . . . All the brilliant staff and the Portuguese marquises straggled along behind until we reached the palace. The army in the meantime had passed us at a quick march, and was again playing The Queen when we reached the door. We stopped only for a moment there, and then proceeded to the Fort. The Army again passed us at a quick march, and as we entered the ruined fortress bugles brayed, dogs howled, and the tired ranks presented arms with shaking knees."

Curzon had meanwhile become so hot that his collar had gone, his back was aching, and his contempt was mounting. Then the Governor came along and explained that the Army had intended to give the Viceroy a royal salute, but that it was in such a state of collapse from its exertions ("Our whole walk had not been three-quarters of a mile!" wrote Mary Curzon) that it could not do so.

The Viceroy looked at the Portuguese Governor for a long moment with contemptuous eyes, and then he said:

"I am so sorry, your Excellency. How very ghastly for you."

THE TOUR WENT ON with a fervour that mounted with each new state they visited. At Hyderabad, Mary wrote, "Again we went forth in the yellow chariot with the escort of the 4th Hussars, and drove through brilliantly illuminated streets packed with people. . . . We drove under triumphal arches on which gigantic portraits of George and me were painted and illuminated from behind, so we shone forth in red-nosed radiance. . . . Dinner was short and beautifully served, and ended with little pies being served from which flew little live birds as you cut open the lid. They flew wildly about and lit on my tiara and one rested comfortably on George's head."

In Peshawar, Curzon held a great Durbar to which all the tribesmen of the frontier, Afghans, Afridis, Central Asians, Mahsuds, Mohmands, Orakzais, and Swatis had been invited, and

3,000 vermilion-bearded warriors crouched on the racecourse while "George's 31 guns boomed, and George made a speech which was very thrilling, as it told all these wild fanatics what the policy of the Government was towards them."

And then back they came through Calcutta, where every arch they passed under "opened just at the right moment and dropped rose petals on our heads, while on every side cheering crowds waved signs saying: 'Hail to the Indefatigable Viceroy' and 'Please, sir, Reduce our Taxes.'"

Through it all, Curzon, in his robes of state, majestically acknowledged the plaudits of the multitude, received delegations, listened to petitions, made long speeches; and, like the one-man band he was determined to be, used up every nonpublic moment in continuing to direct the affairs of his Empire. "Our life here is the same," he wrote from one remote province, "strenuous, unceasing, exhausting, an endless typhoon of duty." He complained constantly of overwork, exhaustion, and pain. But when he had a day free, he used it for work. "I will not detain you at length today," he told the Secretary of State, St. John Brodrick, "because even if I had the material to do so I am much too tired. With the exception of three quarters of an hour for lunch, I have sat for eight hours in succession in this chair, engaged for the greater part of this time in composing my famine speech for Council on Friday. I have not therefore much vitality left in me."

He came back from what he himself called "my triumphal march through India" with the draft of a new bill to alter the labour laws on the tea-plantations of Assam and in the mines in the North; with a scheme to reduce the hold of the rascally money-lenders on the Indian peasant farmers; and with a plan to create a Department of Archaeology through which the ancient temples and monuments of India would henceforth be kept in a state of preservation. On his tour he had found many a shrine woefully neglected, and in Gwalior he had given the local railway office twenty-four hours to clear its books and records out of a shrine "which is peeling with decay, and over which the babus crawl like mice." The restoration of India's treasures from the past was, in fact, to be one of Curzon's greatest and most lasting works. He had always been a great lover of art.

"I regard the stately or beautiful or historic fabrics of a bygone age as a priceless heirloom, to be tenderly and almost religiously guarded by succeeding generations," he wrote; "and during my administration of the Government of India no one shall find me niggardly or grudging in the practical realisation of this aim."

Nor was he. In the years to come, no ancient monument was remote or insignificant enough to escape his attention, and he started an enthusiastic crusade to make the Indian people appreciate their treasures. "I was talking to an authority who has just been visiting Agra," he wrote to one of his governors, "and he told me that the custodians of the tomb at the Taj still wear very dingy garments—he thought they should wear the traditional garb of Moghul days—and what is worse, they still carry those abominable lamps. Do you remember that when once we were there together I drew attention to these and orders were given that a new design was to be prepared. Nothing has apparently been done."

He was not satisfied until his desires were carried out. He was determined to restore the Taj Mahal to its original beauty, and he carried on a correspondence for six months with Lord Cromer, then Governor-General of Egypt, to find him "a silver hanging lamp of Saracenic design" to put in the temple. Eventually he went to Egypt and found it himself, and it hangs in the Taj today—out of place, some purists say. Curzon paid for it out of his own pocket.

In spite of the overwhelming amount of work which he insisted upon undertaking, with the inevitable effect upon the state of his back, there is no doubt that Curzon's first two years of office as Viceroy of India made him a proud and happy man. True, he was not content; contentedness was not in his nature. But he could look around his Indian Empire and feel that, at long last, he was fulfilling the role in life for which he fundamentally believed he was predestined—that of the great patrician overlord bringing the benefits of his training, knowledge, and instinctive superiority to the guidance of lesser and more fallible multitudes.

The crusading zeal with which he imbued every one of his acts in India did not, in any degree, include the importation of the ideals of democracy to the Indian sub-Continent. He did not, in his heart, believe in democracy and equality even for his fellow countrymen in Britain; and he was certain that liberty, equality, and fraternity were definitely not for the Indians. He was, of course, aware that there were stirrings of nationalism and independence afoot in his realm, but he scoffed at them as the "vapourings of a few misguided idealists." He had no hesitation in telling the members of the Indian Congress—the same Congress which was, one day, to produce Gandhi and Nehru and an independent India—that they were a mixed-up minority completely out of touch with the feelings of their fellow Indians. And when some of his more advanced subordinates suggested that Congress had come to stay, and should be treated as a serious body, he sneered.

"My own belief is that Congress is tottering to its fall," he said in one of his speeches, "and one of my ambitions while in India is to assist it to a peaceful demise." He added that while he was "sensible of the desirability of consulting and conciliating public opinion in India, the composition of the Congress, at any rate in recent years, has deprived them of any right to pose as the representatives of more than a small section of the community."

No, his task, Curzon asserted, was to ameliorate the lot of the masses, while at the same time encouraging the middle classes to take over the minor chores of Government for which, as a race, they were fitted. There was no thought in his mind that even the "educated Indians" should some day take their place at the head of the Empire. That would always remain the dedicated duty of the British. "If I thought that it were all for nothing," he said in a speech to the British community in Calcutta, "and that you and I, Englishmen, and Scotchmen, and Irishmen, in this country were merely writing inscriptions in the sand to be wiped out by the next tide; if I felt that we were not working here for the good of India in obedience to a higher law and a nobler aim, then I would see the link that holds England and India together severed without a sigh. But it is because I believe in the future of this country and the capacity of our own race to guide it to goals that it has never hitherto attained, that I keep courage and press forward."

He put down any nationalistic fervour with rigid discipline and reprisal. And when he was attacked for trying to "improve the lot of these toiling masses, against their very will," he would sometimes break down and write, with tears dropping over the page:

"Grind, grind, grind, with never a word of encouragement: on, on, on, till the collar breaks and the poor beast stumbles and dies. I suppose it is all right and it doesn't matter. But sometimes, when I think of myself spending my heart's blood here and no one caring a little damn, the spirit goes out of me and I feel like giving in. You don't know—or perhaps you do—what my isolation has been this summer. I am crying now so that I can scarcely see the page."

This letter was written to Mary, at home in England. For Mary, expecting a third child, had gone home in a weakened condition, her health steadily ground down by the Indian heat and her husband's constant and demanding indefatigability. She had left unwillingly but in great hopes. This time, both she and her husband were sure, the child would be the son they had prayed for, the son who would carry on Curzon's title and name. "Surely the world would not be the same," Mary wrote to her sister, "if there were not to be another George, to grow up in his image and example."

But it was not to be. On the voyage home she was taken so desperately ill that she called friends to her cabin and dictated her will, convinced that she was dying. What died instead was the child; and whether it was the son they both desired we shall never know.

For a time Mary kept the news from Curzon, well knowing that, in the mood in which she had left him, he would have been driven frantic. "I fear he would have followed me home," she wrote afterwards. And to her husband, all she could say as comfort was: "Never mind, my husband, next time, next time." She was down in spirits to a depth that was unusual in one so normally cheerful and sweet natured.

Whether, in fact, for all his love for her, Curzon would have followed Mary home is a question. He had reached a stage by this time when the viceroyalty had become not so much a task as an obsession with him. For the moment, even the visions of high political office at home paled before his Asiatic ambitions.

The Government was changing in Britain. The premiership of Lord Salisbury was giving way to that of A. J. Balfour, and there were rumours in both the British and the Indian Press that Curzon was to be offered the post of Secretary of State for Foreign Affairs. In fact, Balfour never made the offer; his opinion of Curzon's capabilities was always much less than Curzon's own. But Curzon was immediately assailed by exhortations from the Indian newspapers beseeching him not to go home, but to remain in India and finish "the great task which you have begun." He stayed behind, to press on with his task, convinced more than ever now that he was India's only hope, the fulcrum of her present, the keystone of her future. He now had no doubt at all in his mind that he would reach the heights and be remembered through history as the greatest Viceroy of them all; and he settled down to his desk, writing away steadily through the hours, almost welcoming the blood and tears which lay ahead, convinced that they would result in greater glory for himself and India.

He had no inkling, at this moment, that what lay ahead was disaster, humiliation, and tragedy.

CHAPTER SEVEN

Clash with Kitchener

IN WRITING OF THE TRAGEDY which, for a time, all but broke
up his career, and certainly broke his heart, I must once more
make some reference to the strange defects in Curzon's
nature. It must have become clear by this time that he could
show himself, when the occasion demanded, extraordinarily skil-
ful (or, as his enemies would say, devious) in navigating his
career through the shoals that threatened it. But there were
times—and they usually occurred at the most vital moments of
his life—when he would set his course and insist upon holding
it even though every friend around him warned him that there
were rocks ahead. It was not even that he could not see the
rocks himself. A demon stubbornness or, more likely, a perverted
sense of pride would not let him alter a decision once he had
taken it, and he plunged on straight ahead, hand rigid on the
rudder, convinced until the leaks sprang all around him that he
was unsinkable.

This tendency to act like King Canute was undoubtedly
responsible for his downfall in India, though Curzon was afterwards to blame everyone but himself—especially his close friend,
St. John Brodrick—for the shabby end to his glorious career. All

107

through the crisis with which these chapters will deal, there was always an opportunity, even up to the eleventh hour, for Curzon to save the situation by the exercise of a little tact or diplomacy; but these were qualities which were not in his make-up.

The rock upon which he foundered was Lord Kitchener of Khartoum. And the irony of the tragedy is that it was Curzon himself who insisted on planting the rock in his own path.

By 1901, when Curzon had served two-thirds of his term as Viceroy, he had achieved such power and secured such popularity among the Indian people that he considered his position impregnable. Not every move he made secured him plaudits. His partition of Bengal infuriated the powerful Hindu community. But the masses admired him. He gave them circuses, but he also gave them bread. His court glittered with pomp and panoply, but most of his legislation was immaculate and far-sighted. When, to commemorate the reign and death of Queen Victoria, he proposed the building of the great Victoria Memorial Hall at Calcutta the princes and merchants contributed their thousands, and millions of the masses gave their annas. And when later in the year he held a great Durbar, with tens of thousands of troops and hundreds of elephants, to celebrate the accession of Edward VII, the grumbles of the few over its great cost were drowned in the cheers of the vast crowds over what was undoubtedly a scene of bizarre and barbaric splendour. And all the time, he pushed through his agrarian reforms and tax reductions.

There were, however, those who maintained that success had gone to his head. He was increasingly liable to act on his own, as an independent monarch, and ignore the advice sent to him by the Government at home. He despised the supine premiership of Lord Salisbury—not without reason, for Salisbury was dodderingly inefficient—and he was equally contemptuous of the Cabinet of A. J. Balfour, Salisbury's cousin, who took over the

office from him. Balfour had filled the Cabinet with his own and
Salisbury's relatives, and they took over the Board of Trade,
Foreign Affairs, and the Admiralty. Curzon wrote a doggerel
verse about it:

> *In Trade's keen lists, no alien herald*
> *His trumpet blows, but Brother Gerald;*
> *Foreign Affairs have Cousin Cranborne*
> *To hint that ne'er was greater man born;*
> *While Cousin Selborne rules the Fleet,*
> *Even the sea is "Arthur's Seat."*

And when the Government objected to one of his plans, such
as a reduction in Indian taxation to celebrate the Durbar or the
number of princes he planned to send to the Coronation in
London, he would go over their heads and telegraph furious
protests to King Edward. He was so confident of the strength
of his popularity that his letters were constantly full of threats
of resignation if he did not get his way.

In his relations with his subordinates in India, his attitude
had also tended to become more and more arrogant. He made
it quite clear to his subordinates that he despised them as lesser
men. He irked them by taking decisions without consulting
them, and by garnering to himself all the work which they had
hitherto been used to doing. He humiliated them by criticising
them in public. "The trouble with that man," he said, audibly,
when one of his governors was making a long speech, "is that
he is an unabashed and indefatigable windbag." And if his popularity with the Indian masses increased, so did the resentment
of the higher ranks of the Indian Civil Service. "Going to a
reception nowadays," wrote one of them, "is rather like making
a pilgrimage to the Oracle at Delphi."

St. John Brodrick wrote a long letter beseeching his arrogant
friend to proceed with care. He seemed to have sensed that the
letter was a dangerous one to have written to Curzon in his

present mood, for he ended it by hoping he had not been too bold.

He was, in fact, too bold so far as his friendship with Curzon was concerned. Far from paying heed to his obviously deeply felt and affectionate convictions, Curzon never forgave St. John Brodrick for them. He put the strictures down to jealousy. And he wrote in his diary, later:

"St. John Brodrick was, in some respects, my closest friend in public life—until, in an evil hour, he became Secretary of State for India while I was Viceroy. In two years, he succeeded in destroying entirely my affection and my confidence. Burning to distinguish himself at the India Office, as the real ruler of India, as distinct from the Viceroy, egged on by counsellors bitterly hostile to me, in a position to gratify a certain latent jealousy of my superior successes in public life—a feeling of which all our friends were cognisant—phenomenally deficient in tact, and tortuous and mean in his actual procedure—he rendered my period of service under him one of incessant irritation and pain, and finally drove me to resignation."

Now this is nonsense. St. John Brodrick was, like Curzon, a hard-driving and ambitious man, and wanted to make a success of his job. But if anyone dug Curzon's grave in India it was Curzon himself.

We come back to the rock on which he foundered. Curzon, once he felt himself secure in his viceroyalty, took upon himself more and more the rights of an autocratic ruler. He was particularly determined to work independently of the Government at home over India's relations with her neighbours. There had been so much bungling and so many disasters in the war in South Africa that all of Britain's rivals—especially Russia, France, and Germany—were beginning to blow themselves out and make threatening gestures of hostility; and nowhere more than in the Persian Gulf, which Curzon considered to be (and he was undoubtedly right) a sphere of Indian interest which must be kept inviolate. To all his pleas to the Government at home to back him in protecting Persia and Afghanistan, the other main bulwark against Russia, with powerful military forces, he was apt to receive messages from the Cabinet saying: "The Empire must cut its coat according to its cloth" or "We are more interested in the economics than the ethics of the situation." So he made his own foreign policy so far as Persia and Afghanistan were concerned, and mounted his military forces to meet the minor encroachments from France and Germany and the major military threat from Russia which he was convinced were coming. When London telegraphed him in pained protest, he threatened to "end my work in India" in order to bring them to heel, meanwhile leaking news of his independence to the Indian Press so that he had local public opinion on his side.

In answer to Curzon's military moves in Persia, Afghanistan and Tibet ("the outposts of my Empire," as Curzon called them), the home Government, having at length given way to his independent action, asked him to take some of the money from India's Treasury to finance the extra military establishments he was creating. This Curzon peremptorily refused to do, as it would cut into the funds he was accumulating for a further popular programme of Indian tax reduction. This further infuriated the Cabinet, and poor St. John Brodrick was once more thrown into the conflict, and filed a protest with Curzon.

Curzon replied by ignoring the protest, merely saying that his most anxious problem at the moment was the question of who, now he had brought the Indian Army up to strength, should be its new Commander in Chief. It was generally agreed that the outgoing Commander in Chief, Sir Power Palmer, had been weak and incompetent. To meet the dangers which might have to be faced, Curzon and the Government at home were for once in agreement in recognising that a big man was needed. But who?

Balfour and Lord Lansdowne suggested the Duke of Connaught. His suit had also been strongly canvassed in royal circles, and King Edward (while still Prince of Wales) wrote Curzon that "he is much more able than appears on the surface." There were others who favoured Lord Roberts, the Commander in South Africa.

Curzon, however, was after much bigger game than this. The position of Commander in Chief in India was second only in protocol and prestige to that of the Viceroy himself. Why not, for this important subordinate position, secure the services of the most widely hailed hero of the day—Lord Kitchener of Khartoum, the soldier who had avenged Gordon, who had slain the Mahdi, who had saved the situation in South Africa, whose name was on everyone's lips as the greatest British soldier of them all? How wonderful to have him in India—as Curzon's deputy!

He wrote first to Kitchener early in 1900 and found him more than willing to take on the job (for Kitchener had ideas and ambitions of his own with regard to India). He then told the Government at home that Kitchener was the man he wanted.

At once all his sincere friends raised their hands in dismay and wrote posthaste to warn him against what they felt sure was a foolhardy action.

Lord Esher wrote: "I find him an uncouth and ruthless man."

Lord Lansdowne wrote: "I do not myself think that it would be safe to put him there. He is a great organiser and a strong administrator, but I distrust his judgment and I am told that in S. Africa he is not regarded as a good commander of troops in the field. He apparently drove the Egyptian army very nearly into mutiny, and I shudder at the thought of turning him loose without previous apprenticeship in India."

And Lord George Hamilton conveyed the news that Kitchener had, indeed, been given the job in these words:

"After some communications with my colleagues, your opinion carried the day and it was determined to select Kitchener for C in C in India. I look with some apprehension upon this appointment, as I fear the effect of his rough and unsympathetic manner and strong economic hand upon the native army. You will have carefully to watch him."

Curzon was to remember that last sentence in the days to come. But meantime, he was overjoyed that his personal selection had won the day. The most famous soldier in the world would shortly be arriving to join his staff. And though everyone warned him that Kitchener was arrogant, ambitious, unscrupulous, and a bully, he had no doubt in his own mind that he could handle him.

With supreme confidence, he sent a telegram of congratulation and welcome to Kitchener, and blandly ignored any hints from his friends that he was taking a viper to his bosom.

IT HAD BEEN SETTLED that Kitchener should not take over the position of Commander in Chief in India until the war in South Africa was finished, and that took rather longer than the experts had calculated. As a result, nearly two years passed between his appointment and his assumption of office.

In the meantime, Curzon succeeded in getting himself hopelessly embroiled with the British Army in India. They had never forgiven him for the furious reprisals he had insisted be taken against them after the raping incident in Rangoon; and now he turned their resentment into a deep and abiding hatred by once more inflicting upon one of their regiments punishment which they considered harsh and unjust.

As in the Rangoon case, Curzon was right in principle (he almost always was), but tactless and impetuous in applying it. This time, too, he made the diplomatic error of venting his horror and outraged indignation upon a crack regiment which was regarded by the public at home as an especially gallant and heroic body of men. The regiment was the Ninth Lancers, which had been shipped to India to reinforce his army after winning several famous victories in the South African war. Shortly after their arrival, two of their troopers quarrelled with an Indian cook and beat him up so badly that he had to be taken to hospital, where he died. The commander of the Ninth Lancers then made the mistake of trying to hush up the scandal. The troopers concerned were given drastic regimental punishment, but they were never arraigned before a formal court-martial. Two months passed by, and the regiment, sighing with relief, thought that nothing more would be heard of it. Nor would it have been had not a relative of the dead man written to the Viceroy.

Curzon at once had an independent inquiry made, and when he had satisfied himself that the Indian cook had, indeed, been brutally beaten to death, his wrath was volcanic. Once more British soldiers had abused India's hospitality and misused one of the very citizens they had been sent to protect. Not only that—the commander of the regiment and his officers had connived at and compounded the crime by trying to conceal it. Here was a case (he was convinced) where only the most condign punishment could fit the crime, and he announced at once that he was determined to hit the Ninth Lancers where it hurt most. He cancelled the leave of all officers for a year (no mean punishment in a hot country). He ordered special and drastic regimental drills and duties for the troops. And he decided to humiliate the Ninth Lancers publicly by telling the people and Press exactly what he had done.

There were those who tried to suggest that perhaps Curzon was going a little too far, and there were others who pointed out the danger of throwing mud on so famous a regiment. The Viceroy, however, was adamant. Having once made up his mind, he determined not to retreat "even though these things give me sleepless nights and days of misery." He wrote to Sir Ian Malcolm: "Anyone who dares to touch a crack British regiment—even though it contains two murderers—is looked upon as though he laid hands on the Ark of the Covenant." And with almost masochistic emotion, he waited, a willing martyr, for the attacks upon him which he knew would result from his drastic reprisals.

They were not long in coming. At home, the Ninth Lancers' case was taken up in the newspapers and in Parliament, and in almost every case Curzon was made the villain of the piece. He was condemned not only for the harshness of his punishment but also for his foolhardiness in sullying the name of a famous regiment and tarnishing the reputation of the British Army.

If Curzon had been consistent in his actions against the Ninth Lancers, the whole affair might have been an overnight scandal—at least so far as the public were concerned—which could soon have been forgotten. But his love of ceremonial trapped him into a tactical error. In the plans he had drawn up for the great Durbar to celebrate Edward VII's accession, the gallant horsemen of the Ninth Lancers were pencilled-in to take a leading role. Curzon's military secretary suggested to him that, in the circumstances, it might be better to leave them out.

"My dear fellow," retorted the Viceroy, "have you taken leave of your senses? The two things are not in any way connected. I need all the cavalrymen I can get for the procession."

So the Ninth Lancers were informed that, despite the Viceroy's wrath, they would indeed take part in the Durbar. Neither officers nor men neglected the opportunity thus presented for rehabilitating themselves in the eyes of the public. They used every moment of their isolation in their barracks to polish up their drills and skills and ceremonials. They were determined that no body of troops in the forthcoming Durbar would shine more brightly. And when the great day came, they were successful in administering to their by now hated persecutor a resounding slap-in-the-face. They rode by, impeccable, majestic, splendid, their horses groomed to the last hair and prancing like the steeds of kings, their buttons and breastplates gleaming, their helmets in place on heads held high. And if the native population watched them in sullen silence, the reaction of the European members of the crowd was fervent to the point of hysteria. Wave after wave of cheering greeted them every yard of the way, and even the Viceroy's own guests decided to risk the wrath of their host and wildly waved their hats.

Curzon was mortified. Later, in reporting the incident back to London, he claimed that he viewed the demonstration with the contempt he felt it deserved.

"One interesting event happened," he wrote. "The 9th Lancers rode by amid a storm of cheering; I say nothing of the bad taste of the demonstration. On such an occasion and before such a crowd (for of course every European in India is on the side of the Army in the matter) nothing better could be expected. But as I sat alone and unmoved on my horse, conscious of the implication of the cheers, I could not help being struck by the irony of the situation. I do not suppose that anybody in that vast crowd was less disturbed by the demonstration than myself. On the contrary, I felt a certain gloomy pride in having dared to do the right. But I also felt that if it could be truthfully claimed for me that I have (in these cases) loved righteousness and hated iniquity—no one could add that in return I have been annointed with the oil of gladness above my fellows."

In private, however, he was truly cast down, once more filled with gloomy conviction that no one understood him or his mission, that he was one man battling alone against the ignorance, rancour, and malevolence of lesser men.

As for the Army, though it had won a toothsome revenge for what it considered an unjustifiable slur upon its honor, that did not mean that it was prepared to forget. In any crisis which might arise in the future, it now knew which side it would be on.

THE BATTLE ROYAL which raged between Curzon and Kitchener in India in the years 1902–5 was, on the face of it, brought about by a simple fact of military establishment and administration. In the past, a Commander in Chief of the Indian Army had often had to lead his martial campaigns far away from his base and, for long periods, almost completely out of touch with the Viceroy and his Council. So, for convenience, the control of the Army had been split up into two parts—the operational and the administrative. The Commander in Chief decided how he would fight, what he would need for his campaigns, and what tactics he would use in battle. The job of keeping him supplied and satisfied was given to a Military Member whose job it would be to provide a link between the Commander in Chief and the Viceroy's Council. The Military Member was always inferior in rank to the Commander in Chief, who ranked second only to the Viceroy. He was intended to be no more than an efficient errand boy between the two, though he did have permanent access to the Viceroy and to his Council, which the Commander in Chief did not.

But during Curzon's reign as Viceroy, the position of Military Member had been allowed (in fact, encouraged) to grow in power and prestige. Curzon had shown himself deeply interested in Indian military affairs, as we have seen earlier, and he had used the Military Member frequently as a "front" behind which he interfered with the strategy, and even the tactics, of the Army. Kitchener's predecessor, General Sir Power Palmer, being neither a great soldier nor a strong personality, had not complained too audibly about this. Therefore, as Curzon's nominee and obedient servant, the Military Member (Major-General Sir Edmund Elles) found himself frequently controlling those activities in the Army which were never intended for his department. Elles was an amiable and efficient soldier, and he did what he was told to do with an admirable skill and dispatch; but to anyone except Curzon, it must have been obvious from the start that Kitchener would find him an intolerable thorn in his side. Kitchener did not even accept the principle (for which there was much justification) of having a Military Member at all, and when he arrived in India and found him in the position of being all but a rival commander in chief, with, moreover, easier access to the Viceroy than he had, he determined to get rid of him.

It is an amazing example of how naive, ingenuous, and lacking in perception of character Curzon was that he did not realise how dangerous a character he had taken on even when he met Kitchener face to face. Mary Curzon was much more acute, and, as if sensing the tragic struggle that was looming, she tried to fend it off with warm-hearted words.

"Do please take the army and all the military straight into your heart!" she wrote, in a welcoming letter to Kitchener. "It will be a wonderful load off George. . . . I suppose you know that the prayer of the soldiers has been that the two giants would fall out, and it will be a great grief for them to see you work in harmony, and to know the intense satisfaction it is to George to know that you are here at last."

Curzon, on the other hand, obviously considered his future adversary a quaint, rather wild character who could be managed in the same way as an unruly boy by a wise father.

"He seems to think that the military government of India is to be conducted by concordats between him and me," he wrote patronisingly, a month after Kitchener's arrival. "Accordingly he comes and pours out to me all sorts of schemes to which he asks my consent. It is all so frank and honest and good tempered that one cannot meet these advances with a rebuff. Here and there I head him off or steer him into more orthodox channels. But as yet of course he does not know the ropes."

To apply the adjectives "frank" and "honest" and "good-tempered" to Kitchener was naivety indeed. He was, if anything, even more tortuous of character than Curzon. But the Viceroy continued to be enamoured of his new Commander in Chief, and took to writing home about him as if he were a new, and rather snappish, dog.

"He stands aloof and alone," he wrote to Lord George Hamilton, "a molten mass of devouring energy and burning ambitions without anybody to control or guide him in the right direction."

Curzon had no doubt that he could be the Svengali of this restless military Trilby. "Now the Viceroy, as long as he is a personal friend of this remarkable phenomenon, is the only man who can supply the want; and therefore it is that during the remainder of my time here I shall endeavour, as far as possible, to avoid the dangers that otherwise lie ahead."

He was, of course, aware that there were dangers; even pet dogs sometimes bite, but not if a strong and superior master remains in control at the end of the lead. It is not surprising, therefore, with these self-confident notions running through his head, that subsequent developments were going to give Curzon a salutary shock.

For the first few months of their association, however, Kitchener gave every outward sign of being an amenable deputy. True, he made it quite clear what he thought about the Military Member, and had already begun writing to London to intrigue against him. But otherwise he wrote, "Curzon is all that one could wish, and as kind as possible."

He was well aware that Curzon was determined, at all costs, to keep his pre-eminent position as head of the Indian Empire. "The system by which a Member of the Council is made responsible for the administration of the Army, independent of the C. in C. while the latter has only executive functions is extraordinary," he wrote. "I asked Curzon why he liked to keep up such a farce, and his answer was, 'If the C. in C. had anything to do with the machinery, he would become too powerful.'"

Still, Kitchener promised that he would give the system a year's trial—a promise which, it soon became apparent, he had no intention of keeping.

Meanwhile, he humoured the Viceroy. Hitherto, Curzon had signed his official documents "Curzon of Kedleston," but he quickly realised that this would look very tame beside the Commander in Chief's documents if he, in turn, signed himself "Kitchener of Khartoum," with its reminder of an historic military victory. So he wrote to Kitchener to say that he had to put his signature to so many papers that he would in future use only the name "Curzon" and would Kitchener do likewise. Kitchener, confident that everyone knew who he was, title or no, amiably agreed. (There was to be a great row about this later. The Howe family, hearing about it, protested, and Curzon got a peremptory note from Buckingham Palace telling him, on the King's orders, that he was to use his full title in future.)

Curzon had described his new Commander in Chief as "aloof and alone," but he was far from being so. Unlike the Viceroy, he had surrounded himself with several able, loyal, and trustworthy subordinates who were ready to die for him, if necessary, and were certainly willing to help him in his intrigues. He had also, before leaving London, established a channel of communication through which he could always get the ear of the Government. This channel was his adoring admirer, Lady Salisbury, daughter-in-law of Curzon's former patron. To her he wrote his innermost thoughts and opinions, and she immediately rushed across to her husband or to the Prime Minister, A. J. Balfour, to canvass their support. The influence of the Salisbury family in English political life was such that her advocacy of Kitchener's case had, probably, more influence upon the final result than did anything else.

Slowly, while the Viceroy relaxed in complacent self-confidence, Kitchener began to flex his muscles. He decided that the time for shadow-boxing was over. He had taken the measure of Curzon, and decided that he was a temperamental titan with feet of clay. He forthwith took the first kick at the Viceroy's underpinnings by telling him that henceforward he must keep his feet out of Army affairs, particularly those concerned with the disposition of the troops along the frontiers of India. Under Sir Power Palmer, it had been Curzon who toured the frontier area, rallied the troops, and made recommendations for their disposition. Now Kitchener told him to keep out and stop meddling. When Curzon protested that he was, after all, still the first man of the realm, Kitchener did something which gave Curzon his first appalling realisation that he had, perhaps, invited a cuckoo into his nest. Kitchener threatened to resign. Resignation had always been the weapon Curzon had used to browbeat the Government at home, but he was shrewd enough to see that, from now onwards, it was a threat he would have to abandon. Kitchener had usurped it. If it came to a question of whose resignation should be accepted, his own or his Commander in Chief's, there was no doubt, even in his mind, which sacrifice would be accepted. Curzon's reputation as a Viceroy might be high, but Kitchener's reputation and prestige were even higher among the masses at home, and they would rise against any Government that attempted to humiliate him.

He gave way with what graciousness he could muster, and from that moment onwards Kitchener became undisputed lord of the frontier. He rubbed home his victory by making a triumphant tour of the area, and he was hailed as a conquering hero wherever he went.

His next move was to outdo the Viceroy in the pomp and circumstance of his daily life. He tore the innards out of great houses and turned them into palaces stuffed with art treasures and the trappings of majesty. He clothed his servants in ornate silken uniforms. Curzon had no taste for elaborate foods, but Kitchener was something of a gourmet and a gourmand, and he gave great banquets at which rich foods and wines were served; and if the Curzons dined off silver plate, Kitchener saw to it that his guests ate off gold.

And all the time he schemed to force the resignation of Sir Edmund Elles, the Military Member, and make himself the all-powerful Commander in Chief whom Curzon most feared. Kitchener's ambitions were given an extra goad by two incidents of a personal nature, which strained relations between him and the Viceroy. The first happened at a viceregal banquet at which, when the Curzons sat in state at the end of the dinner, Mary inadvertently forgot to set a chair beside them for Kitchener. He decided that he had been insulted, and departed in a dudgeon; and not even the gift of two antique gold mustard pots from the Vicereine mollified him. Shortly afterwards, one of his aides came to him in great distress over an affair of the heart. Mary Curzon's sister had been staying at the Viceregal Lodge, and the aide had fallen in love with her; he proposed and they became engaged. And then without warning the engagement was broken off. Kitchener's aide was so brokenhearted that he asked to be sent back to England immediately, and the Commander in Chief came to conclusion that it had all happened because the Curzons did not want one of their relatives to marry into the opposition camp.

By the beginning of 1904 there was no longer any suggestion that here were a Viceroy and his deputy working together for the good of India. What Mary Curzon had feared had come to pass, and the two giants were squaring off for conflict.

The first news Curzon got that Kitchener had broken his promise, and was scheming against the Military Member, came when he was told by Lord George Hamilton that the Commander in Chief had been sending secret letters—sometimes taken home personally by his staff—to Lord Roberts at the War Office. He was not seriously alarmed at first and sent Kitchener a mild rebuke:

"In his letter which came by yesterday's mail, the Secretary of State mentioned that he had heard from members of the Imperial Defence Committee of 'schemes of wide reform and of great alteration' being put forward by you—as he assumed in private letters to the War Office or C. in C.; and he asked me to warn you that 'although communication between the two C. in C.s are always recognised, any changes of an important character must be referred through the Indian Government here. Otherwise

we shall have a double set of communications which will be a
source of great embarrassment and personal friction.' "

Kitchener promised to be a good boy in future. What he did,
instead, was to increase his correspondence with Lady Salisbury,
warning her to be "very careful that everything I write is *quite
private*," and to send off his criticisms to his friends in the War
Office by telegraph in code.

If it be thought, however, that he was being an underhanded
cad, it should be pointed out that Curzon—now he realised the
nature of his adversary—was not entirely abiding by the Queens-
berry Rules either. He did not read Lady Salisbury's letters, for
he did not realise that they were being sent. That was his gerat
miscalculation. But he did use his position as Viceroy to call for
the Army codebook, and he had Kitchener's telegrams intercepted, and he personally deciphered them before letting them
go forward to their destination. (He was to adopt this tactic, with
salutary results, later on in his struggles with an even wilier
adversary, Lloyd George.)

At home, too, he had his own private channel of communication with powerful influences. His particular confidant was Sir
Schomberg McDonnell, who had the ear of King Edward VII,
though it must be admitted that what he asked from McDonnell
was not backing in his quarrel with Kitchener (he still did not
believe he needed it) but influence in securing for himself the
reward he believed he now deserved for his exertions in India—
the Order of the Garter. McDonnell maintained in his letters that
he was constant in putting Curzon's name before the King, but
somehow the honour was never forthcoming.

At this time Curzon was still supremely confident that if it
did come to a struggle between himself and his Commander in
Chief, victory would be his. He had no doubts either about the
rightness of his case or of his own superiority in any conflict
which might be coming. He had now changed his mind about
Kitchener to the extent that he no longer regarded him as a pet

dog, but rather as "a caged lion dashing its bruised head against the bars." He was well aware now that Kitchener was more than ready to use the ultimate threat of resignation to get his way, and he let the Government at home know that he saw the danger of this possibility.

"I want you clearly to recognise," he wrote to the Secretary of State, "that no effort on my part shall be wanting to prevent such a disaster as the loss of Kitchener's services. I am not looking at it from the point of view of public opinion alone, although I know well that however trumpery the issue upon which he might elect to go, public opinion in England (though certainly not in India) would side with him, and say he was driven out by me, or by the bureaucracy, or by anything but the real cause."

But Curzon was sure his superior tactics would win the day. He could not believe that a man "who cannot even express himself in public, or write a literate letter" could best an aristocrat whose whole life had been spent in learning how to rule. He made repeated efforts to get the relationship between him and his opponent back on the basis of friendship and understanding, and by the middle of 1903 he was foolish enough to believe he had succeeded. He took Kitchener into the mountains with him on a shooting expedition, in circumstances which, Curzon hoped, would enable them to talk things over quietly, uninterrupted by the demands of day-to-day office work.

"He is out with me here in camp at this moment, and not a cloud flecks the sky," he wrote. "Though he most surely must have known that I pressed for his appointment to India and did everything to smooth his advent, he confesses to having started with the idea that I was opposed to him. He now realises his mistake and is aware that I am his best friend."

The "silly quarrel" over "a trivial matter" had blown over, Curzon believed. "Kitchener . . . commenced by trying to destroy the Military Department and to concentrate the administrative and financial, as well as executive, work of the Indian

Army in his own hands. This I declined to allow, and he has now settled down to his work, in which he is introducing a timely zeal and efficiency."

Since this was a moment when Kitchener's intrigues were bubbling most furiously, the complacency such a note displays makes one marvel at Curzon's capacity to see a situation as he wished it, rather than as it was. So confident was he, indeed, that he let the public announcement go forward that he had accepted an extension of his term as Viceroy. Sir Schomberg McDonnell wrote him in some perturbation about this:

"Now to leave minor matters and revert to the refrain of my song. Don't be ridiculous and pooh-pooh viceregally my counsel. I have been for so long 'head lad' of the P. M.'s string that, to continue the racing jargon, I know the *stayers* in the field. And, my dear George, you are the only stayer of the lot. I speak with the brutality of friendship, you are a street ahead of all your contemporaries in ability. You suffer from the instincts of the great ruler and the great gentleman, and you are going to sacrifice the certainty of being Prime Minister to the splendid ambition of being India's greatest Viceroy. Believe me, you have no business to go back to India. You *must* stay here. . . . You have made your reputation as a great Viceroy, and the time has come for you to direct other viceroys. Your successor, if run by you from home, cannot go wrong. Of what use is it for you to go back when the situation demands you here? You have got to train now (I lapse again into racing slang) for P. M. When you win the race you will dictate the policy of the Empire—India included—but you won't win it if you remain away much longer."

It was wise advice, and Curzon should have taken it. From McDonnell's subsequent letters it is clear that he was well aware of the storm that was brewing between the Viceroy and his Commander in Chief and was doing his diplomatic best to persuade his friend to opt out of the struggle. But Curzon was in no mood to give up his power and privileges in India. He was convinced

he had a mission to finish. He still did not believe that the challenge of Kitchener was something he could not meet and overcome.

He had informed the Government that before embarking on
his further term of office he intended to take a leave in England.
While there he planned, among other things, to settle the differences with Kitchener once and for all. He also expected to receive the Garter from the King, and he wrote to McDonnell to
ask how the situation stood.

"As to the Garter," McDonnell wrote back, "I think you ought
to have the next vacancy and said so to His Majesty with the
audacity of an Old Private Secretary." He did not add, however,
that Edward VII had heard about the differences with Kitchener
and, not wishing to become involved in the quarrel, was holding
back his preferment. Instead, McDonnell offered Curzon a sop
by saying: "The Office of Lord Warden of the Cinque Ports is
vacant. Surely it would suit you, and you it?"

Curzon indicated that it would. He sent Mary (who had
rejoined him after her illness) back to England ahead of him,
because she was not only deathly sick from the murderous Indian
heat but was also expecting another child. This time Curzon
knew it would be a son to carry on the line. They had decided to
call him Dorian.

He called in Kitchener and told him he was sailing for England for six months' leave, and he suggested that they should
both endeavour, in his absence, to cement their re-established
friendship. Kitchener warmly agreed and they shook hands. But
in fact he was furious. He was convinced that Curzon was going
home chiefly to outwit him by putting his side of the case to the
Cabinet at first hand, and he made an attempt to secure leave for
himself. When this was not forthcoming, he redoubled his correspondence with Lady Salisbury and made it quite clear that
if his views of the position of the Military Member did not
prevail this time, he would really resign and create a public

scandal. His adoring friend immediately raced round to the Cabinet with his letter.

Curzon sailed for home. He still had no inkling of the extent of the conspiracy that was going on behind his back. He had no doubt that, once confronted by his unassailable arguments and the magic of his advocacy, the Cabinet would give him its fullest backing against his "upstart" Commander in Chief and put Kitchener permanently back in his subordinate position.

There was only one small cloud on his horizon. Mary had given birth to her third child, and it was once more a daughter. Yet, for the son he yearned for, there was still time, still time.

He forgot the torment of work, the grinding Indian heat, the trials and travails of office, and even, for a time, the pain in his back. He lifted his head proudly in preparation for what he was convinced was to be his apotheosis. The hero was on his way home.

CHAPTER EIGHT

Ill Omen at Walmer

C URZON ARRIVED BACK in England in mid-May, 1904, to a welcome home that was not only much less fervent than he expected but rather less than he deserved. After all, his achievements in India had been great. He had sacrificed his health and his peace of mind to his task. It might have been expected that the Government of the day would have given adequate recognition to his efforts.

Seen from this distance in time, however, it seems clear that Great Britain in 1904 was ruled by not much more than a shoddy clique of short-sighted and mean-minded men. The Prime Minister, A. J. Balfour, though of a complex character was, on the surface, a lackadaisical and easy-going person who did not in the least mind being under the thumb of his powerful relatives, the Salisburys, who, of course, viewed Curzon merely as a thorn in the side of their friend Kitchener, and therefore were against him. Curzon himself summed up Balfour's attitude well when he wrote to Mary:

"You will have had your talk with Arthur long long ago, and I have no doubt you will have found him as gentle and as attractive as ever—sitting down at once to write the letter that is never penned, and pouring out the appreciation that fades away so quickly in absence."

Balfour was never very anxious to exert himself on anyone's behalf (not even on behalf of himself), and now that Curzon had got himself involved in a controversy that might cause political repercussions at home, he was certainly not going to side with him by giving him a lavish homecoming. So the delegation that greeted the returning Viceroy was just about adequate, but certainly no more.

Writing about it before he arrived, Curzon had said to Mary:

"My idea is to arrive in London about May 18-20. But I don't suppose, darling, from the public point of view it makes much difference. I do not suppose for one moment that anyone will come down to meet me, or that the slightest notice will be taken of my arrival. Who cares for India? Did anyone greet Dalhousie on his return, or Warren Hastings, and why should I be more favoured? No, I am quite ready to slip in unnoticed—though it will be a different tale in history."

He was depressed by the absence of distinguished officialdom. Nor did his spirits revive overmuch at the sudden spate of invitations which began arriving as soon as the newspapers announced that he was back in London. He accepted engagements to address a Lord Mayor's luncheon and several other important occasions, but for once in his life personal anxieties took precedence over his career.

He was cast down over the condition of his beloved Mary. He found her in low spirits and in poor health. Her mental state was aggravated by the knowledge that she had grievously disappointed her husband in failing to produce a son for him, and she was resolved to remedy the omission as soon as possible. Curzon had professed to make light of it.

"Darling, it doesn't a bit matter if sweet Naldera [she was later christened Alexandra at the request of the Queen] is a girl. Don't fuss about that. Girls are very lovable and we have no reason to be anything but proud of ours. Perhaps too a boy might be thought to be filling the cup of good fortune to overflowing. So we will take whatever it is with gratitude and without repining. We will be content with our little Naldera and postpone Orien-Dorian until some future date. . . . After all, what does the sex matter as long as you are all right?"

But Mary Curzon was not all right. The beautiful, glowing young woman who had gone so eagerly to India was, Curzon found, thin, yellow, frail. True, she made light of her own condition and insisted upon accompanying him on his round of social engagements. She refused to be treated as an invalid, and in her heart she cherished a secret ambition which she determined to bring to fruition with the least possible delay. The light had gone out of her eyes, however, and the freshness of springtime from her spirit.

It may seem ironic that someone who was heiress to a fortune of over a million dollars should have financial worries, but she was in fact greatly perturbed over the state of their bank balance; and in this Curzon was hardly a comfort. He had embarked on great and extravagant plans for refurnishing 1 Carlton House Terrace, their London home, and at the same time had wrung his hands over the expense of it all. By the terms of her father's will, Mary was not allowed to realise on her capital (it was held in trust for the children), but she resolved as soon as she was well to go to America and try to persuade the trustees to give her an advance on her income.

Meanwhile, Curzon did nothing to ease her anxieties by forecasting the dire poverty in which they might find themselves at any moment. To his dismay, he had discovered that the acceptance of the office of Lord Warden of the Cinque Ports would involve him in an outlay of some £2,000 to make Walmer Castle, his official residence, habitable. There would be the cost of the uniform of his office, plus at least another £600 per annum for the upkeep of the establishment.

Curzon as a pensive scholar
Eton, 1878

Curzon *(center)* and two Oxford friends, Hon. W. W. Palmer *(left)* and E. K. Douglas *(right)*

Colonel N. Chamberlain, Curzon, H. Lennard, and P. V. Lake in Gilgit, North India, 1894

Curzon Papers

Mary Leiter, of Chicago, who became the first Lady Curzon in 1895

Curzon Papers

Lord Curzon in his House of Lords robes, 1920

Prime Minister Stanley Baldwin and Curzon, his Foreign
Secretary, 1924

"As you say," he wrote to Mary, just before his arrival in England, "we shall not get on with present income. Our income will only be £7,600 a year, and we shall be living at the rate of £11,000–12,000."

He was nevertheless eager to take on the job of Lord Warden, and not only because it appealed to his sense of the dramatic. He was well aware of the famous men who had preceded him— the Younger Pitt, Wellington, Dalhousie, and his former patron, the late Lord Salisbury—and he felt that the prestige of the position would help his popularity with the English people.

That summer, in a lavish ceremony held in Dover Castle, he was duly installed. His friend George Wyndham, who was M.P. for Dover, made the speech of welcome. Though the weather was cold and wet and windy, a large concourse heard Curzon's inaugural speech, in which he dwelt in his most organ-like tones on the devotion to, duties of, and faith in the task of Empire in India. His commanding figure, strapped erect in its leather harness, carried the robes of office with majestic effect.

The same evening he and his wife moved into Walmer Castle and gave a celebratory dinner party. It was noticed by his guests that he was in a mood of bubbling gaiety. He took them on a tour of the fortress, expatiating on its history, pointing out the canvas couch on which Wellington had died, the desk at which Pitt had written, the bed in which Queen Victoria and the Prince Consort had slept (they departed within twenty-four hours because Victoria found the bed damp and Albert got a streaming cold). He insisted that the gentlemen should take their port on the battlements overlooking the English Channel, but though he afterwards allowed some of the ladies to join them there, he would not let Mary come out. "The poor chick is too delicate, and we must take special care," he remarked, and as he said it, he smiled at her fondly. What the guests did not know was that Mary, as a pleasant surprise to make his big day complete, had confessed to him that she was pregnant yet again.

The period of rejoicing was brief. On the morning of September 12, Mary awoke to the sound of a great beating of wings in her room and saw that a robin had flown through the window. Soon it alighted on a chair beside her bed. Mary was not normally a superstitious woman, but she believed that the appearance of the bird was an ill-omen and that "I fear someone will die," she wrote to her sister.

From that moment, her feelings for Walmer Castle underwent a change. "Our very own fortress, safe from the world," suddenly seemed to her like a frightening prison. She slept badly. She was always looking over her shoulder as she walked the corridors, and she began to have delusions that she heard moans and shufflings in the night. Curzon became so worried over her gloomy spirits that he pleaded with her to leave the place, saying that he would resign his position. But she would not let him.

In the early hours of September 22, she woke her husband and told him to call the doctor, but before he could arrive it was all over—at least so far as the baby was concerned. What chiefly concerned the doctor was not the miscarriage but its aftermath, for it soon became apparent that Mary was gravely ill, and the long struggle began to save her life. They tried to keep from her the knowledge that her baby was dead, that she had once more failed her beloved husband, but she was not deceived and the fight went out of her. She became convinced that she was going to die, and her certainty communicated itself to her husband. The thought of it drove him into a frenzy of fear and panic. As the years had gone by, he had come to rely upon Mary as a rock, not so much because she was his faithful wife and mistress and the mother of his children, but because she had been so solidly his ally in all he had tried to achieve. "I am so proud when I see you run after, admired and adored," he had written to her. "What woman in London combines great beauty with exceptional intelligence, as well as a tact which is an inspiration? The combination is wholly unique, and there is no

limit to the influence which you can exercise at home, as you
have done in India, smoothing down those whom I ignore or
offend, and creating our own atmosphere of refinement and
devotion."

He could not bear the thought of losing her. For five days
and nights he sat beside her bed during the crisis of her illness.
While she slept, he wandered onto the battlements, weeping in
misery and desolation. When she woke and began to ramble, he
took pencil and paper and carefully scribbled down every word
she said.

Among his papers is a great sheaf of foolscap, covered with
stains and candlegrease, to which he has attached an explanatory
paragraph saying:

"These are the notes made by me at Walmer Castle in September 1904 when My Darling was dying and when she gave
me her last instructions and bade me farewell."

It is a curious and pathetic document, for it is a minute-by-
minute account of someone about to die, and it records every
pain, every groan, every rambling and incoherent murmur. Yet
its cumulative effect is curiously moving, and nothing more
clearly illuminates the sweet wholesomeness of Mary Curzon's
nature nor the tormented state of her husband.

"At one time, when she thought she was going," he wrote,
"she asked me to read through our favourite Psalm 'Lord who
shall dwell in Thy Holy tabernacle or who shall rest upon Thy
Holy hill' and I read it through in floods of tears. She repeated
the first two sentences after me, then she asked me to repeat
Tennyson's Crossing of the Bar and I repeated the first verse. She
said 'But you must not moan for me' at one moment when she
thought she was nearly going she said repeat the Lord's Prayer
and I repeated it and she after me. . . . At intervals when she
asked to be alone with me she said Bless you and 'Sweet Pappy'
and 'I love you dearly.' About 5-30 she asked to see the sea and
the outer shutters were unbarred and the inner shutters folded

back and she looked out upon it. Then she said I always had a presentiment about Walmer from the first I knew it would bring misfortune I knew it again when a little robin came in at the window and settled on the back of the chair."

But though both of them were sure that death was coming, this illness was not to be the occasion. Curzon went on scribbling. He took down a list of Mary's bequests, and it covers three closely written pages. They discussed the design of the tomb in which they would lie side by side, and she asked if it might be "a marble effigy over each of us looking towards each other so that we might one day be reunited." (This was later faithfully carried out by Curzon, and they lie there together today.) But as they continued to talk, she slipped away not into death but into a deep sleep, and soon began slowly to recover. A few days later she was well enough to dictate a message of thanks to all those who had prayed for her recovery, and at the end of the month she was well enough to get up.

They left Walmer Castle as soon as Mary Curzon was in a condition to be moved, and they left it with Curzon hating every stone in the old fortress. His thankfulness at his wife's recovery was tempered by the news the doctors had given him that she would henceforward be a permanent semi-invalid, and would certainly never be able to bear a child again. He was depressed and unhappy as never before in his life. He blamed Walmer Castle for his misery. He was afterwards to maintain that Mary's miscarriage had been brought on by the bad drains in the castle. "I curse the name of the place," he wrote. And he forthwith resigned as Lord Warden of the Cinque Ports and resolved (although he changed his mind later) never to go near the place again.

NOW WAS THE TIME for him to put in train a much more important resignation. All his friends (with one exception) rallied

round him and urged him to give up the idea of going back to
India. He had every excuse for throwing his hand in. Mary would
be convalescent for some time and would not be able to accompany him. The worries of the past few weeks had exacerbated the
condition of his back, and he was in great pain. From his interviews with Balfour, he must have gained some insight into the
extent to which Kitchener's conspiracies had succeeded and been
made aware of the storms which would confront him upon his
return.

Balfour made it quite plain, in fact, that he inclined to
Kitchener's view over the question of the Military Member, and
there is little doubt that if Curzon had elected to remain at home
Balfour would have appeased him with the Garter or even the
earldom which he coveted. He listened to Curzon's impassioned
advocacy of his case with every evidence of sympathetic attention, but the moment Curzon had gone from the room Balfour
threw up his hands and said: "Why does the man get so worked
up?" If ever there was a statesman upon whose gravestone should
be written the epitaph: "Anything for a quiet life," it was A. J.
Balfour. And he was certainly not going to support anyone who
seemed bent on disturbing it.

Not entirely to his surprise, but certainly to his fury and distress, Curzon discovered that his old friend St. John Brodrick
had also gone over to the enemy. Brodrick's personality was not
unlike that of Curzon in that he was ambitious, indefatigable,
emotional, and temperamental, but there is no reason to believe
that, as Secretary of State for India, he judged the case of the
Military Member on anything but its merits. Curzon was ever
afterwards to believe that Brodrick decided in favour of Kitchener
because he was jealous of his lifelong friend; but Brodrick's own
papers give ample evidence that the decisions he took cost him
much soul searching and unhappiness.

But there it was. The facts were plain. If Curzon went back
to India, he would go in the knowledge that in the subsequent

battle—if he stuck to his guns—all the ammunition from home would be reinforcing his enemy. "Don't go," pleaded Schomberg McDonnell. And even Mary Curzon herself begged him to reconsider and stay at home. Indeed, there were political reasons why he should do so. Balfour's Cabinet was of poor repute. Curzon was one of the few Tories whose reputation remained untarnished. When the Government fell, as it inevitably soon would, he would be able to come forward with clean hands.

To none of the arguments of his wife and friends, however, would he give way. It was almost as if he saw the great disaster ahead of him and, in his misery, was determined to charge, bull-headed, towards it. Of course he rationalised it into a sense of duty and maintained that he was returning only because he had a mission to complete.

"I was aware that a severe struggle lay before me," he wrote afterwards. "I felt it a duty however to the Government of which I had been the head for so long not to desert it in the hour of trial, but to sacrifice all personal considerations to the necessity of fighting its battles."

At the end of November he sat down and wrote a letter to Mary. "It is with a sad and miserable heart," he wrote, "that I go leaving all that makes life worth living behind me, and going out to toil and isolation and often worse. But it seems to be destiny; and God who has smitten us so hard must have better things in store."

On the morning of his departure he pinned the verses he had written to her on Mary's pillow:

I would have torn the stars from the Heavens for your Necklace,
 I would have stripped the rose-leaves for your couch from all the trees,
 I would have spoiled the East of its spices for your perfume,
The West of all its wonders to endower you with these.

*I would have drained the ocean to find its rarest pearl-
drops,*
 *And melt them for your lightest thirst in ruby draughts
 of wine,*
 *I would have dug for gold till the earth was void of
 treasure,*
*That since you had no riches you might freely take of
mine.*

*I would have drilled the sunbeams to guard you through
the daytime,*
 *I would have caged the nightingales to lull you to your
 rest,*
 *But love was all you asked for in waking and in
 sleeping,*
*And love I give you, Sweetest, at my side and on my
breast.*

He arrived back in India on December 9, 1904. Almost from
the moment of his return, the tragedy began to quicken. In his
absence, Kitchener had been consolidating his forces and was
now quite confident of victory.

"The thing to do," Curzon had once written about a pig-
sticking expedition, "is once you have the poor brute cornered
to give him no quarter. Press him, press him, until he cannot turn,
and then thrust in and kill."

Such were Kitchener's tactics. He realised from the moment
he saw the Viceroy upon his return that he was winded, uncertain, and on the run. Not that Curzon would have accepted such
a summary of his condition. Against all the signs, he was still
confident that victory would yet be his.

He had promised Balfour before leaving home to give
Kitchener's arguments a further consideration. His interpretation
of this promise was that both of them should put their case to
the Viceroy's Council, and that they should abide by the vote of
that body. After a conversation with Kitchener, he was convinced

that his Commander in Chief would be content to accept the verdict. Nothing, in fact, was further from Kitchener's intentions.

The vote of the Council was taken. Its all-British membership (for the Indians themselves had no part in the quarrel) sided with the Viceroy. It was almost the overwhelming support that Curzon had expected, and he immediately sat down and penned a dispatch to St. John Brodrick at the India Office asking for the Cabinet's endorsement of the Council's views. He asked Kitchener to append his own view, and was delighted when all the Commander in Chief did was to write out a paragraph making clear his adamant view that the office of Military Member should be abolished and his own position strengthened.

In fact, Kitchener did not bother to expand his argument because he had already dispatched one of his aides to London with a full statement of his case. He had written a long letter to Lady Salisbury. And he had also secured support which, he believed, would decisively weight the argument in his favour in London: he had secretly canvassed the opinion of high officers of the Army in India. Now indeed, for Curzon the chickens were coming home to roost. With one exception, every single officer in the Army sided with Kitchener against the Viceroy who had insulted them. It was a moment when Britain feared war with Russia and relied upon the support of her Army Command for her protection, and there is no doubt of the influence this opinion had upon subsequent decisions.

Not that Curzon was slow in indulging in some rabbit punches of his own. He too had sent secret messages back to London, and was exerting every effort to get his way. He played his final card by sending a private letter to A. J. Balfour, pleading the bonds of old friendship and telling him that if the Cabinet refused to stand by the decision of his Council, he would resign his office, convinced that (on this critical occasion at least) the threat would be effective.

Judge then his astonishment and mortification when a deci-

sion arrived from London. It was unfortunate that the dispatch
which brought the news to Curzon was written by St. John Brodrick in a mood which was not exactly friendly. He had been told
by some of Kitchener's friends of Curzon's criticisms of his ability
and sneers at his competence (and certainly the Viceroy had
been free with contemptuous references to his onetime friend).
His dispatch, therefore, was not so diplomatically written as it
might have been, and included some acid references to the
Viceroy. But the kernel of its content was a compromise. It went
halfway to mollifying Kitchener by putting the Military Member
into civilian clothes and calling his office the Military Supply
Department, by giving the Commander in Chief direct access to
the Viceroy, and by demanding the resignation of Sir Edmund
Elles, who had clashed sharply with Kitchener on several occasions. On the other hand, it preserved the Military Member's
department and gave him power to control the political and
financial side of the Army.

What more could Curzon possibly hope to gain? Kitchener
himself considered the dispatch a considerable defeat for his own
view, and was considering resigning over it, when, to his astonishment, he received a visit from the Viceroy. Curzon was in a
great emotional state. He said he considered St. John Brodrick's
dispatch a profound insult. He told him that unless the department was allowed to retain its old name, and its head allowed to
continue operations as a soldier in uniform, he would resign. He
then pleaded with Kitchener to support him in this, and then,
to the Commander in Chief's amazement and contempt, crumpled
up and burst into tears.

Kitchener was horrified at the collapse of this man who had
hitherto always been so cold, superior, and aloof. He was so
taken aback that, for once, his conscience was pricked and he
heard himself—to his later fury—promising to back up the Viceroy
in what he afterwards called "his puerile requests." He added:
"I could have bitten my tongue out for making such a stupid

remark. I suppose I was rather excited by the discussion. I was prancing up and down the room, talking to him very straight on the subject. I told him if he insisted on the title, everyone would know what he meant by it, and that he did not intend to loyally carry out the decision of the Government—and when he collapsed I rather lost my head."

But if Kitchener's acquiescence was intended as a pat on the back for a defeated opponent, Curzon did not take it that way. His tears dried immediately. He was infused with new confidence. Once more he was convinced that he had won a great battle and that all was coming out right for him in the end. He determined to make it quite clear to the world that he considered victory was his.

Forty-eight hours later, in a speech before the Legislative Assembly, he attacked the Cabinet's action in giving him instructions contrary to the advice which his Council had all but unanimously sent them. He went on to say that thanks to his efforts, however, the damage done had been repaired. He had secured important concessions which would make the Military Member's department as powerful as before. And when the Cabinet, astonished at the speech, asked him what on earth he thought he was doing, he sent back an angry telegram saying that he insisted Sir Edmund Elles retain the post of Military Member, or alternatively, if this was not possible, Major General Sir Edmund Barrow be appointed in his place. He suggested this latter name well knowing (as the Cabinet well knew) that Barrow was an old enemy of Kitchener's and was the only high-ranking officer who had sided with the Viceroy when the Commander in Chief had canvassed military opinion.

Kitchener, when he heard of the development, could hardly believe his ears. His patronising pity for Curzon quickly turned into furious rage when he learned that the Viceroy had (like himself) been sending secret telegrams to London. And when a few days later he got a letter from Curzon which practically called him a liar, his reaction was to write to Lady Salisbury:

"In the old days I should have called him out on it and shot him like a dog for his grossly insulting letter."

He did no such thing, however, for he realised that he did not need to do so. Curzon was busy shooting down himself. Right until the last moment he could not believe that he could lose the battle. He did not even see defeat in view when St. John Brodrick replied that under no circumstances could the Cabinet accept concessions or allow the appointment of General Barrow. He knew that the letter was in Balfour's pocket in which he threatened, if rejected, to resign. "The Government will never allow me to," he told Mary. So he telegraphed to Balfour telling him that the new plan must be modified or he would go.

From Curzon's subsequent explanations it seems certain that he did not mean it as a serious ultimatum. He was relying upon his previous letter to make it clear that all he wanted was an arrangement that would not humiliate him. But Balfour had forgotten about the letter ("he only half read it at the time, and it slipped his facile memory afterwards," Curzon wrote bitterly), and he took the telegram at its face value; or at least he professed to do so.

On the morning of August 16, 1905, George Nathaniel Lord Curzon, Viceroy of India, was at breakfast when a bearer brought him an important dispatch from London. He opened it. It was from the King, and it said:

"With deep regret I have no other alternative but to accept your resignation at your urgent request. Most warmly do I thank you for your invaluable services to your Sovereign and your Country and especially to the Indian Empire."

It was all over. The great edifice which he had so painfully and so painstakingly built for himself had collapsed overnight, and lay all around him in miserable ruin.

CHAPTER NINE

Humiliation, Tragedy, and Recovery

THE DRAMAS OF LIFE, unlike those of a play, are seldom conveniently divided into clean-cut scenes and acts, and when the curtain came down on Curzon, on the morning of August 16, 1905, it was far from being the end of this particular drama.

For one thing, Curzon would not believe at first that it really was all over, and that his resignation had actually been accepted. "How could I announce that I had resigned?" he had written to Mary, only a short time before. "What would be my excuse? I could not give your health as the reason, for you are returning. I could not give mine—weak as it is—in the face of all that I am doing. . . . I could never hold up my head again. What is more, even if I made the announcement now, I do not believe that I should be able to carry it out later on. The public would not like swopping horses if we found ourselves in midstream."

He telegraphed home (and followed up his telegrams with long letters) trying to hint, without saying it outright, that perhaps even at this hour the resignation might be withdrawn. "I am not in the least worried or defeated," he wrote to Mary, "being supremely conscious of having done the right thing. So Kinkie [his pet name for his wife] must not worry either." Even at this hour, he was still relying upon his "long private letter" to Balfour. But whether Balfour had, as Curzon afterwards stated, by "inhuman carelessness . . . either never even read or completely forgotten about it," he was certainly making sure that Curzon should have no opportunity of changing his mind. He followed the announcement of the resignation almost immediately with the news that Lord Minto had been appointed Viceroy in his place. The deed was done, and Curzon as Viceroy was definitely dead.

If he had returned to England at once, which a greater tactician almost certainly would have done, Curzon might have had the satisfaction, if not of restoring his position, at least of firing off a few salvos while the public at home still remembered the tremendous battle which had taken place. The British public can be very kind towards a gallant loser—especially if he can persuade them that he was robbed of the verdict—and their reaction to the appearance of a defeated hero might well have ameliorated some of this sourness of the Cabinet towards him. But Curzon, having been counted out, would not climb out of the ring. He wrote to King Edward telling him that the particular sorrow of his "enforced resignation" was the fact that it would prevent him from personally conducting the Prince of Wales on his forthcoming tour of India. To the Prince of Wales himself he sent an even broader hint, saying: "I own I shall feel rather bitterly when I think of someone else doing the honours of Government House at Calcutta."

King Edward thereupon made a kindly and thoughtful gesture. He asked his officials to allow the retiring Viceroy to remain behind and do the honours for his son. Their reaction was one of embarrassment and perplexity, for they had already pencilled-in this ceremony for Minto. St. John Brodrick now felt so malevolent towards his onetime friend that he even suggested that Curzon should stay on at Bombay until the Prince of Wales came, but that—since Minto would by this time have arrived—he be received by the royal visitor merely as "a private individual." It was Sir Walter Lawrence who saved him from this rather callous snub by writing to Lord Knollys at Buckingham Palace warning him that Curzon was in a sick and highly temperamental state, and was on the verge of "what I rather dread, the public breakdown of Lord Curzon. He is ill and cannot control his feelings, and a scene might be very painful to Their Royal Highnesses and cast a gloom over their arrival."

In the end, Lord Minto's arrival was postponed. Curzon greeted the Prince and Princess of Wales at Bombay in his capacity as Viceroy. When Lord and Lady Minto arrived shortly afterwards, they were practically smuggled off the ship and taken to Calcutta—without any formal welcome—in order to salve Curzon's feelings and give him his last taste of viceregal ceremonial.

But it was to cost him dear, for it meant that he hung on in India long after interest in the controversy had died. Its effect was to turn Curzon into that most pathetic of all political figures, a lame-duck Viceroy who, everyone knows, is on his way out, his prestige gone, his authority weakened, and surrounded on all sides by career-conscious officials only too well aware that he can do them no more good.

Kitchener was not speaking to him. (He was only persuaded "with the greatest reluctance" to shake Curzon's hand when he eventually did depart.) He spent his long, sleepless nights writing long screeds justifying the attitude he had taken, bitterly attacking Kitchener and the by now hated St. John Brodrick, and waiting for the news from home that would be at least some comfort in his misery and humiliation—the news that his great work for India had been recognised by the earldom he believed he deserved. His friends, in their letters of sympathy, continued to assure him that he would get it, but the comforting kick upstairs did not come. All he could discover from London was that perhaps Balfour was deferring the recognition until he actually landed on English shores.

As Curzon looked out into the Indian sky from the balcony of the Viceregal Lodge, the sky must have seemed even more full of vultures than usual. For to add to his troubles, Mary was far from well. When she rejoined him in India at the beginning of 1905 she had come because, she had assured him, she was completely recovered from the miscarriage which had all but killed her. But this was a subterfuge on Mary's part. She was well aware of the fact that she had not long to live, though she did not confide this calamitous news to her husband, and she had come back to India well knowing that it would speed up the processes of mortality. "Some day, though, the bell will go and I shall not appear," she had once written, "as India, I know, slowly but surely murders women. But I suppose many humble and inconsequent lives must always go into the foundations of all great works and buildings and great achievements." She was sacrificing her humble and inconsequent life to the task which she considered more important than anything else in the world, the propping up of her husband. She was his leaning-post through all the crisis of the resignation and its distressing aftermath, but she found the weight almost more than she could bear.

The anti-climactic weeks slowly passed. At long last, Curzon was able to sign his final signature, hold his final levee, and give place to his successor, Lord Minto. The outgoing Viceroy and his wife sailed for England expecting that by the time they reached home some gesture might be made to them by the Government. In one of his more petulant letters, Curzon had indicated that he did not desire any honours from a Government that had treated him so badly as had Balfour's. But he also made it plain, in subsequent letters, that he did not mean this irritation to be taken literally; he still preferred to believe, anyway, that some recognition of his work was not a matter of party politics, as indeed it was not. One might have thought that even personal jealousies and antipathies could, in this case, have been submerged in a gesture of magnanimity, and that Balfour might for once have opened up his heart. An earldom, a Garter, a viscountcy even, would have been welcome to Curzon at this moment, even though he so strenuously maintained that he was not "a dog hungrily waiting for bones to be thrown." A little friendly insistence on Balfour's part would have overcome all his sulky pride. But what waited for him at the end of his long and melancholy journey was nothing. Balfour once more found a wonderful excuse for doing what he was most capable of—nothing. Curzon arrived back in England on December 3, 1905. On December 4, the Tory Government gave up the ghost, and Balfour handed in its resignation to the King. The Tories were swept out of power by the Liberals.

Would the Liberals, then, be big enough to give what the Tories had been so small in withholding? It was not a mere matter of political preferment. Great public servants do not usually have to be of the same complexion as the Party in power to be recognised for their services. And with Curzon's position, there was a strong Liberal measure of sympathy, not only for his achievements as Viceroy but also for his stand over the position of the Military Member. The *Daily News* had written that "by irony, which will awaken sympathy for Curzon, he has been censured not for his mistakes but for a rare exhibition of wise statesmanship." And the other Liberal organ, the *Daily Chronicle*, had maintained that "he was really fighting an attempt to establish a military autocracy."

There was, however, something in the personality of George Nathaniel Curzon which seemed to goad the powers-that-be into pricking him, and the friendly, forgiving, all-embracing gesture was not forthcoming. The King suggested through his advisers that a promotion for his ex-Viceroy might be not unfitting. "Dammit," he is said to have remarked, "when you compare him with some of the fellows they want me to elevate, the man stands out on merit alone." But he did not feel strongly enough about the situation to go over their heads (or at least was not willing to go against his Government so early in the day). And the Liberals proved strangely stubborn. The other proconsuls of the day had been honoured—Milner for his work in South Africa and Crowe for his rule in Egypt. But not Curzon. Was it his onetime friend and admirer, Asquith, husband of Margot, himself now a power in the Government, who scotched him by suggesting to the new Prime Minister, Sir Henry Campbell-Bannerman, that the elevation of Curzon would be a dangerous move because it would send Curzon to the House of Lords and strengthen the Tory Opposition? That was what Curzon afterwards suspected.

Whatever the reasoning of the Liberals, the result was to turn a melancholy homecoming into something unnecessarily shabby. Rarely have politicians shown themselves to be so meanminded and unimaginative. Bannerman looked calmly upon the wounded and bleeding lion and said: "If his own party wouldn't honour him, why should I?"

The effect upon Curzon was, for the future, to be important and unfortunate. It not only made him bitter. It also made him cynical. For all his faults, he had always hitherto regarded his career as a mission in idealistic statesmanship. He determined, from now on, to shake off the idealism and become a careerist pure and simple—a politician like the rest of them. It might not have been so tragic if his deliberate transformation had turned him into a good politician. Unfortunately, he did not have the equipment, the temperament, or the experience for that.

In fact, from the catastrophe of India he took to heart only one lesson, and it was to be a mistaken one. He decided that henceforth, no matter what the pressure, no matter what the principle involved, he would never again resign a public office. It was a disastrous decision.

Meanwhile, he retired to the south of France, to write new pamphlets about his Indian administration (they were sour and

sterile, and his friends fortunately persuaded him to suppress
them), and to moil in his misery. Once again he could take a
certain masochistic pleasure in the thought that the whole world
was against him.

"One wonders when the hail storm that rains upon us is going
to stop," he wrote to his wife that spring. "We are nearly beaten
into the ground."

His only consolation now was the love, admiration, sympathy
and understanding of Mary Curzon. But in the summer of 1906
even that was taken from him.

In truth, Mary Curzon had never really recovered from her
illness at Walmer and her last miscarriage. She had gone back
to India against all medical advice and well knowing that her
life would be shortened by her decision. She knew the risk and
yet she took it, and it was done because she felt George Curzon
needed her and she loved him beyond her own life. "There is no
happiness so great to a woman as the admiration she can feel
to the depths of her heart for her Belovedest," she once wrote.

After Curzon's return to England, Mary tried desperately to
distract him and stop him from brooding over his disastrous
defeat, but her health became increasingly uncertain, and by the
summer of 1906 she was bedridden. On July 22, after four days
of crisis during which, as before, Curzon never moved from her
side, Mary Curzon died.

"I have seen it coming, and dared not avow it to her or even
to myself," he wrote to Sir Ian Malcolm. The blow was no less
painful because it had been expected. Curzon hid himself away
with his grief, and though he knew that thousands of her friends
and admirers shared something of his sorrow, he insisted on a
private funeral at which only a handful of relatives and retainers
were present. He wrote to Ian Malcolm from Kedleston:

"We lay her to rest peacefully, no one here, no show. This
is as she would have wished."

Now Curzon really did feel defeated, abandoned, alone. He

stayed at Kedleston all through the summer and autumn "hiding my head," he wrote, "in loneliest misery."

IT WILL HAVE BEEN SEEN from what has been related so far that in such circumstances as these, George Nathaniel Curzon always reacted in the same way, with the same defensive tactics. If he did not bay defiance at the world, neither did he cower like a beaten dog. When his masters snubbed him in class at Eton, he went off to the haven of his own study and laboured in seething isolation until the moment came when he could emerge and calmly snatch all the most important prizes from their favourite pupils. When Oxford failed to give him the First he felt he had merited, he avenged the humiliation by secretly writing the essay that gained him an even greater award.

But how could he hit back at his tormentors now?

To do so he needed to get back into Parliament, where he would have a platform from which he could excoriate, denounce, and outmanoeuvre those who had laid him low. But for the moment Parliament was barred for him. The General Election had taken place too soon and his physical condition was too poor to give him the opportunity of standing. And though he was a peer, he had deliberately chosen an Irish peerage so that he should not be debarred from sitting in the Commons, for only a selected number of Irish peers were elected to the Lords. True, he could have asked the Tories to put him up as their candidate at the first by-election, but that would mean asking favours from egregious Balfour and even risking a refusal from him. Relations between them were such that the rumour had spread through the political world that at their first meeting after Curzon's return to England they had refused to shake hands with each other. Curzon had felt it necessary to deny this, but there is no doubt that Lord Ribblesdale summed up his feelings towards the Tory leader when he wrote: "It must obviously have been difficult for you both to meet quite as the G. N. C. and A. J. B. of old days. I daresay you felt more inclined to be carefully courteous rather than spontaneously cordial."

So what was he to do? The Liberal majority was such that a General Election was obviously years away. He who had once campaigned for the right of the elder sons of peers to remain M.P.'s even after their fathers died seemed to have only one possibility before him now—his own elevation to the Lords through the inheritance of his father's title. That was certainly no immediate prospect, for the Reverend Lord Scarsdale was very much alive.

It was nearly two years after his return to England from India that a solution was found for his dilemma. One of the representative Irish peers, Lord Kilmaine, died and thus created a vacancy among the Irish contingent in the Lords. Curzon's name was put forward, at the suggestion of Lord Lansdowne, as being a suitable replacement. The nomination was hardly given a warm welcome by the rest of the Irish peers, and they had solid grounds for their objections. For one thing, Curzon was not an Irishman and had no interest in Irish affairs. For another, if elected he would hold the seat in the Lords for life, not being able to relinquish it even upon the death of his father and his assumption of the Scarsdale title. "Why should we diminish our representation," asked the Irish contingent, "just because an Englishman wants to get into the Lords?" They refused to allow Curzon a walkover, but put up two rival candidates. Curzon wrote a fighting address in which he appealed to their sense of patriotism and pleaded with them to forget "narrow-minded and domestic matters," and all his coroneted friends rallied round to lobby for him. But the election was a close thing, and Curzon scraped into the Lords by only two votes.

The victory was a hollow one, anyway. The bitterness over his Indian humiliation still burned in his breast, but it burned in his breast alone. To everyone else it was a stale quarrel, and no one wanted to hear about it. He made occasional appearances in the Lords and spoke when there was a Foreign Affairs debate. When the question of India or Asia or the Persian Gulf came up, his remarks were listened to with attention and respect, though they could hardly be said to have had much effect upon the actions of the Government, whose policy was diametrically opposed to his ideas of an assertive, almost belligerent, Imperial line. He found much more satisfaction in writing long letters to the Press, sometimes almost two columns in length, about the problems which took his fancy; and here his habit of signing himself merely "Curzon" (which he had persisted with in India, despite the protest from the King) once more got him into trouble with the Howe family.

"My dear George," wrote Earl Howe from Curzon House, Mayfair, on February 28, 1908, "My attention has been called to a letter from you in the Morning Post of today which is signed Curzon. It will I am sure be in your recollection that before her late Majesty granted you the title of Curzon of Kedleston, my father and I were consulted and we raised no opposition on condition that the title was Curzon of Kedleston and not Curzon only, and a grant was made in that way. You have now taken your seat under the title and signed the roll as Curzon of Kedleston, and I feel certain that it was by inadvertence that you signed the letter in this morning's paper, and that it is enough for me to call your attention to the matter to ensure that you will add the words 'of Kedleston' on future occasions! I write on behalf of my son and myself and I am sure you will meet our wishes in that respect."

Curzon was furious. With his papers dealing with his title he has penned a note saying "for years I was pursued by this trivial but irritating question," and he wrote back to Howe to say:

"I hardly know why you have revived the question of the signature now. It was all thrashed out years ago. Moreover, when your mother raised it again at Wynward in September last I wrote her a long letter, to be shown to you, of which I have never even had an acknowledgement. My title is Curzon of Kedleston and as such on official and formal occasions I sign myself. But I often abbreviate the full signature in ordinary practise, as the papers do for me, and as many other peers who have territorial suffixes to their names do likewise, and I really could not bring myself never to do so in the future."

But Earl Howe was not going to let him get away with that. Though Curzon had not received the expected earldom on his return from India, Howe was well aware of his ambition to make George Nathaniel the best known of the Curzons; and Howe was determined not to allow him to do so unless he attached the extra handle to his name. Howe wrote back:

"I quite understand that there are occasions when it is natural that you should use the abbreviated signature, and I appreciate your willingness to comply with my request that you should make use of your full signature in public documents—including letters to the papers!"

Then he added the gentle threat: "I can assure you that, apart from the arrangement we made when you took the title of Curzon of Kedleston, there is a strong feeling, *which is by no means confined to my family,* on the subject, and as I hope and believe my son will more and more take an interest in public matters, the inconvenience of the same signature would be a serious one. I hope we may meet and talk as of old!"

The answer to that which Curzon would like to have sent was "a plague on your side of the house!" But he stifled his irritation and was more careful with his signature in future.

so far as his political career was concerned, this was Curzon's period of rustication. His dreams of future grandeur and eminence did not fade. The goal was still always before him of the premiership which, he felt, was less a necessary fulfilment of his own ambitions than a logical conclusion—no matter how long delayed—to the inexorable demands of destiny. Curzon was a man of temperament, of moods, of frenetic impatience, but for this he was content to work and wait, wait and work, and make himself ready for the moment when the hour would strike. Cheated of an immediate vindication of his Indian administration, he was more than ever convinced that only by attaining the premiership would he be able to show the world his real mettle. To get it he was prepared henceforward to devote every waking hour of his life.

But his setbacks and humiliations had taught him caution. The years between 1905 and 1914 were not propitious even for the most ambitious Tory, and he decided to expend them wisely in consolidating himself with the public. Let the other members of the Party tilt at the Liberal windmill and waste their energies on the domestic quarrels which, to his mind, were sterile and uninteresting (for he was never able to persuade himself that Home Affairs were matters for anyone above the level of a municipal councillor).

He set his cap, instead, at those nonpolitical offices best calculated to keep him in the public eye. He allowed his name to go forward for the eminent office of Chancellor of Oxford University, and secured it by a substantial majority over the rival candidacy of Lord Rosebery. To the astonishment of the heads of the colleges, he made it clear that he did not intend to regard his new post as a sinecure. At the end of his ceremony of installation (over which he spent many hours choosing the most cherubic page-boys to carry his train) he indicated that he was taking the word at its face value, and was in fact installing himself. And those who began by sneering at his interference soon changed their tune. His passion for administration and his zeal for reform found all the scope they needed. He took in hand the finances of the colleges. He sent begging letters all over India for treasures for the Bodleian. He organised appeals for funds. The masters (whom he was apt to treat in the same way he had treated his subordinates in the Indian Civil Service) spent their time complaining of his bullying over day-to-day affairs at the same time they blessed his foresight in putting Oxford on a solid basis such as she had not known for a hundred years.

"As it chanced," wrote his Vice-Chancellor, Sir Herbert Warren, afterwards, "it was a case of the hour and the man. He was called upon to save as well as to preserve Oxford and he welcomed the opportunity in the spirit of the 'Happy Warrior.' That he loved Oxford there can be no doubt. Whether loved or not in return, he should certainly be highly esteemed by her."

Most other men would have found a resident and active chancellorship of a great university a fulltime job, but not Curzon. He wrote an average of twenty-four letters a day in connection with university affairs. He brought world statesmen like Theodore Roosevelt to Oxford and presided at their addresses. Only when illness or absence abroad kept him away did he miss the ceremonies at which distinguished personages were awarded the doctorates he had suggested for them.

But he had other irons in the fire. Shortly after he was installed at Oxford, he was asked to stand for election as Lord Rector of Glasgow University. He hesitated about this until he learned that Sir Henry Campbell-Bannerman would be the Liberal candidate. At once he changed his mind and accepted; for here at last was the opportunity for partial revenge. Bannerman was the Liberal leader who had refused him the earldom he felt he had earned from India. To defeat him at the University poll would, indeed, be a sweet retaliation. He sat down to write a scorching address that would make the electors aware of the contempt he felt for Liberalism and its leaders, and he was about to send it to the printers when news reached him of Bannerman's death. "Damn the fellow," wrote Curzon to Sir Ian Malcolm, "he has done it deliberately!"

In Bannerman's place the name of a new and fiery meteorite

of the Liberal Party, David Lloyd George, was substituted. It was the first clash between two men who were destined to strike sparks off each other in the future, and though this was not the sort of contest in which they could exchange personalities, both of them worked hard to score off each other in their addresses and both of them knew that it would be a close contest.

"I have not heard anything about the election on Saturday," Curzon wrote to one of his friends. "The candidates seem to be the last people informed or concerned, and for all I know the little Welsh bruiser may leave me a mangled and eviscerated corpse."

But though the lord rectorship had previously been a Liberal office (the retiring Rector was Asquith) Curzon limped home with a majority of 12 over Lloyd George, with the doughty Socialist, Keir Hardie, a bad third. If Curzon expected Lloyd George to be cast down by his defeat, he was quick to learn the resilient nature of his future adversary.

"I met the little Welshman shortly afterwards," he wrote, "and half expected him to direct that angular elbow towards my eye. To my astonishment, all he did was cackle with laughter and say: 'Trust the Gaels to choose a Lord. They're even more snobbish than the Welsh!'"

Curzon's attitude towards the rectorship of Glasgow was rather different from the one he had displayed at Oxford. He did not have the same love for the university. He thought the students "rather a wild and uncouth lot." There would not be the same opportunities for solemn and well-publicized ceremonial. And in any case, he had really only entered the contest in order to spite Bannerman.

He therefore found repeated excuses for failing to turn up for the official ceremony of installation. He wrote that his back was bad. He was confined to his bed after a motor accident. He was forced to sail for South Africa for the benefit of his health. The students of Glasgow, who have never been the most equable members of the fraternity of learning, became increasingly restive over his procrastinations; and when, as a final excuse, Curzon pleaded that a Governmental crisis forced him to stay in London after he had faithfully promised to appear in Glasgow, their irritation erupted into a public procession in which they pilloried their Lord Rector as Rostand's chanticleer who believed that the sun could not rise without his vocal encouragement. Much to Curzon's annoyance (he was always infuriated at seeing himself lampooned) the political cartoonists took up the theme, and he was portrayed as a ridiculous over-puffed cockerel for some time to come.

"Really," he remarked, "it is intolerable that they should lecture and hector a Lord Rector in this fashion."

But it taught him a lesson. He made a hard-and-fast arrangement to go to Glasgow and make his address, and he delivered it nine months before his three-year term was up. He gave the students full value, and made one of his most emotionally effective speeches on Britain's imperial role in Asiatic affairs.

SLOWLY THE PAIN of Mary Curzon's death subsided. The days were filled with more and more activities. He added the presidency of the Royal Geographical Society to his list of offices, and promptly made himself popular by putting the finances of that body in order and by sponsoring a resolution to allow women to join, thus reversing his previous stand. So far as this last reversal was concerned, he was careful to point out that "they will have only a limited voice" in the affairs of the society, and he did not budge one inch from his antagonism to the intrusion of females into public affairs. "Trousers, trousers, why do women—with the lovely shape which God has given them—want to wear trousers?" was still his attitude.

He accepted an invitation, also, to become an Honorary Fellow of the Royal Institute of British Architects, and he began making the first serious purchases towards what was afterwards to become one of the extracurricular passions of his life—the collecting of art treasures and old buildings. He had always been interested in painting, sculpture, and architecture. At Eton he decorated his study with old prints he found in Windsor, and carved ivory elephants he discovered one day in a Derby antique shop (they came from India and may well have sparked his first interest in the sub-Continent). "Monuments in London have always been objects of my fancy," he wrote of his student days. "In the majority of cases, I have felt that they were dingy and inadequate, and I used to gaze with a sense of melancholy at the figures of defunct Russells and Cavendishes and Graftons that presided over the fortunes of the less favoured squares. . . . When I was a lad, I always wondered at the designation of the Marble Arch gateway, originally intended, I believe, for Buckingham Palace, for it always presented the blackest and most funereal appearance. Somewhere in the nineties however it received an unexpected cleaning and re-emerged in its pristine beauty. Then for the first time I realised it was of bona fide marble."

His taste was, if anything, in advance of his time, though not perhaps always quite so discriminating as he believed. As a young man, while most of his contemporaries were gushing over Landseer, he was transfixed by the colours of Constable. But he also wrote: "I recollect the opening of the Albert Memorial. Of the storm of criticism it then aroused, I do not share the unfavourable views that have been so widely disseminated about this monument. So far from regarding it as fantastic and absurd, I have always thought it one of the sights of London."

He hung 1 Carlton House Terrace with tigers' heads and mementos from India. But his sense of colour was unerring, and he did up the curving corridors of Kedleston with some exquisitely lovely Eastern embroideries and hangings.

Curzon now had the money to indulge his zealous crusade

to preserve and restore England's old buildings. It is true that Mary's death had not left him the dollar millionaire he had once expected to be. In the last weeks of her life, when she found herself too ill to make the journey to America, she had written to the trustees in Chicago to clarify some details in her father's will. She discovered that, except for her jewellery and pictures, she had nothing to leave him; in terms of actual cash, that is. "The property is thus pretty safely tied up," the lawyers told her. "Poor pappy," she said to her husband on her deathbed, "I have nothing to give you."

It was hardly as grim as that. What Curzon received was some £4,000 a year, being his share of the income from the $1,000,000 marriage settlement, plus his daughters' share (amounting to approximately £10,000 a year) until they came of age. The girls had also been left a considerable fortune by their grandfather Levi Leiter, to be held in trust for them, and because of this the American trustees insisted that they be made wards of Court. Curzon was officially designated their guardian and had to appear before a judge each year to get permission to use any part of this further income (which amounted to another £15,000 a year) for their housing, upkeep, and education.

There were to be tremendous rows with his daughters later on about the way in which he used the allowance the Court awarded him, and four years before he died he wrote a long and impassioned justification of his expenditure. "I was given by the court full discretion as to the expenditure of the allowance made to me," he wrote. "I might have spent it, if I had chosen, on betting or gambling or racing or on any form of extravagance. I did not. The only extravagance in which I indulged was the erection of the Memorial Chapel and the restoration of the Church at Kedleston at a cost of nearly £20,000 in memory of my first wife. This was done by permission of the courts to whom the figures were submitted."

The troubles over the money from the will were, however,

to come later, when his daughters reached their majority. For the moment he had from this source an income amounting to something over £20,000 a year. He had insured Mary's life for £100,000 and drew another annual £4,000 from that sum. While he had been in India he had made some shrewd investments which brought him in another £2,000. He had the considerable royalties from his books. And he still had the £1,000 a year from his father.

No, he was far from being a poor man—though he was certainly always in need of money—and he was certainly able to buy the pictures, restore the old buildings, and lease the houses that took his fancy. In 1911 he bought his first castle.

Tattershall Castle came into the public eye in that year because its owner had announced that he was ripping out its magnificent fourteenth-century mantelpieces (from which Pugin is reputed to have modelled those in the Houses of Parliament) and selling them to America. This was followed by a rumour that the magnificent keep of the castle was to be taken down and shipped piece by piece across the Atlantic. (This seems unlikely, for the keep is made of tens of thousands of small bricks and is, in fact, one of the finest survivals of fortified brick dwellings in Britain.) A public cry went up. Appeals were made to the National Trust to save Tattershall from the Yankees, and a local resident offered £5,000 to anyone who would raise a similar sum for the purchase of the castle. But support for Tattershall was vocal rather than financial, and no benefactor showed any willingness to come forward.

And then Curzon saw a picture of it in *Country Life,* and at once his interest and enthusiasm were fired. He journeyed to Woodhall Spa from Kedleston, and then drove the three miles across the Lincolnshire flats to Tattershall. Long before he arrived there, his imagination was stimulated by the sight of the great, solid wedge of dull red brick looming over the Lincolnshire plain. It was one of the days when his back was paining him, but he tramped up the stone steps from floor to floor, pottered around the vast rooms, and all but burst into tears at the sight of the rubble in the fireplaces where the great mantelpieces had been. For he had arrived too late to save them; they had been taken out and shipped away, and no one could tell him where they were. It was cold and raining slightly by the time he reached the battlements, but he bared his head as he looked down upon the river and the fields below him, and what he said was:

"The vandals shall not have it."

That night he returned to London and sent an offer by telegram of £12,000 for the purchase of the castle. It was accepted. Tattershall was his. At once he set to work to track down the missing mantelpieces, but it took him many months before he found them in a Bayswater antique dealer's. They were packed, ready to be shipped to America. Then began a great haggling match (for Curzon was a shrewd buyer) in which he used everything from threats of adverse publicity to stirring appeals to patriotism in order to get them at a price he felt he could afford to pay. He got them at his price. The following year he marched proudly at the head of a great procession, the mantelpieces on carriages behind him, to a formal ceremonial in which they were restored to their original positions. It was not without a certain relish that he left the restored Tattershall Castle in his will to the National Trust, which had been unable to save it.

These were the activities that filled his days. His nights, which were more sleepless than ever, he consumed in long bouts of letter writing. To one bunch of letters among his papers is attached the note: "These are a selection from the 1,350 letters of sympathy and condolence I received when my darling Mary died. I answered more than 900 of them in my own hand." An announcement was made that he was suffering from sciatica, and from all parts of the country and from scores of places abroad, the victims of lumbago and other aches of the back wrote in, sending pills and ointments, recommending doctors, masseurs, and homeopaths. He answered them all.

To one of his correspondents, whom he never actually met,

he wrote regularly for nearly seven years. This was the famous Victorian novelist, Ouida (Miss de la Ramée), and for her— though she was much older—it developed almost into a love affair by letter. Curzon had first written to her while he was still a young M.P. to ask her to autograph one of her novels for him, adding an awful pun in the postscript by describing himself as being "one of your constant Ouidas." Later she wrote him almost weekly, in purple ink on mauve paper, in such enormous writing that there was room for only two words to a line. She gave her heart to him when she read, in a Press report from India, that he had condemned the habit in some famine-ridden villages of eating dogs. "It is a monstrous thing," she wrote, "and how magnificent of you to denounce it. It is as cruel as eating babies." For Ouida was a dog-lover to the point of mania, and she filled the house in Leghorn, to which she had retired, with great colonies of abandoned dogs. She was also an Imperialist of the most blimpish kind, and suspected even the most right-wing Tories of plots to give away the Empire. "That scurvy no-gentleman, Chamberlain" was her particular bête noire.

Curzon treated this eccentric old lady with gentle good humour and never failed to answer her letters. His heart warmed to her when she wrote to him after his resignation as Viceroy:

"I cannot resist sending a word to you of my sympathy and indignation. It is odious that you should be lost to India through a brute like Kitchener and a nonentity like Brodrick, and it must be so grievous to you to have to leave all the good seed you have planted unharvested. You will have a great career in England before you, but that will not wholly console you for leaving your work undone in the East."

In 1907 Ouida fell on bad times. She had spent all her money on her work for animal welfare. What money she had for food went to her beloved dogs. The sight of one eye had gone and the other was failing. In desperation, she had written to her friend for help. He replied:

"I have not much money because my wife's fortune belongs

to the children, and is administered under the Court of Chancery. But I am sorry that you should be in need and if any aid of mine can at all alleviate this condition, I gladly give it. I ask you therefore to accept the accompanying cheque, but only on condition that it is treated not as a loan but as a gift, for I have never made a loan in my life. The circumstances however to which I have alluded will of course [last two words were crossed out] prevent me from repeating it. I will of course respect your confidence and not mention the matter to anyone. Indeed I have destroyed your letter."

He did not, of course, destroy the letter (he never destroyed any paper he wished the world to see) but kept it in his file of Ouida correspondence. Over it he has written: "I sent her £50." And to her biographer, he later wrote: "In the declining years of her life, when she was destitute and all but deserted, I was able to give her some help. But I think she wasted most of it upon her colony of dogs." She died in poverty in Leghorn in 1908.

IT WOULD BE MISTAKEN to presume from all this that Curzon had only a public life in these years, and that his personal activities were confined to letter writing. For a time after Mary Curzon's death he did, indeed, become something of a hermit. But when he emerged from his shell, he once more indulged himself in one of his most cherished social activities—country house parties at which he could surround himself with the leading political figures of the day, plus the most lively and decorative ladies. He confined his opposition to the female sex to their obtrusions into public affairs, and he was so far from being misogynistic in his attitude towards them otherwise that he once wrote: "A dinner-party without a woman present is nothing more than a meeting of masticating and chunnering males."

For a time after Mary's death he took a new lease on a house

in which they had lived before going to India, the Priory at
Reigate, but he soon decided that it was not grand enough for
his purpose. During a visit to Basingstoke to make a speech, he
was taken to luncheon at Hackwood House, a few miles away,
and its splendid setting in a great wooded parkland took his
fancy at once. He leased it in 1907, and soon began to give great
house parties that became features of the Edwardian and pre-
World War I period. Once more all his female married friends
decided that what dear George needed was a wife, and they
brought down their prettiest friends and relatives to entertain,
and perhaps entice, him. The Hackwood estate was rich in game,
and he gave great shooting parties. When the Parliamentary ses-
sions came to an end, he filled the house with a gay throng of
the most prominent personalities of the day. At a typical Whitsuntide house party (this one took place in 1911) his guests
included the Asquiths, the Balfours (he had made his peace with
A. J. B.), Winston Churchill, Viscount Haldane, the Salisburys,
Lord Ribblesdale, Viscount Milner, Lady Edward Cecil, Mrs. J.
J. Astor, the Countess of Dudley, the Duchess of Rutland, Lady
Diana Manners, H. A. L. Fisher, Mr. and Mrs. St. Loe Strachey,
the Hon. Mrs. George Keppel, Lady Kenmare, and Prince and
Princess Pierre Troubetzkoy. They played croquet and tennis on
the lawns by day. The tables groaned with good food and wine
in the evening, and then they talked, or played charades, or
watched firework displays in the park. And they flirted and
intrigued.

Acting as host to a gay throng of distinguished people was
one of the things Curzon did best. When he relaxed, he could
be a most charming companion, witty, amusing, fond of rather
risqué stories. At Hackwood he was at his most easygoing, broad-
minded, tolerant, and worldly. There were occasions when he
could whip himself into a fury of puritanical indignation over
those who transgressed the moral codes—but these strictures he
reserved for the lower orders. Once he discovered that one of

his housemaids at Carlton House Terrace had allowed a footman to spend the night with her, and "I put the wretched little slut out into the street at a moment's notice," he wrote to his wife. He argued fiercely that Edith Thompson, the woman in the famous Thompson–Bywaters murder case, should hang, not because he considered her guilty of murder but because of her "flagrant and outrageous adultery."

But this was not a standard to which he felt either he or members of his own class should be expected to adhere. For them, provided they were discreet and did not get involved in public scandal, everything was allowed, and he loved to gossip or write to his friends about the latest society liaisons.

At the Hackwood house parties the eligible young ladies vied with each other to please and tantalise their host, and the activity can surely have caused them (or him) no pain whatsoever. He was just past fifty years of age, but he carried his years lightly and all that they had done for him was to dust his luxuriant hair with enough grey to add to his distinction. On his polished, handsome face a romantic female could detect the look of bravely borne *tristesse* brought on by the tragedies and disappointments through which he had so recently passed. He was rich, intelligent, gallant—and a widower. He was, in fact, a catch for any girl who could attract him.

George Nathaniel Curzon was, however, not so easily caught. At this period of his life he was not looking for a new wife—not consciously, anyway—even though he was not averse to a temporary amorous adventure. His heart was locked up with Mary's in the tomb beneath the marble guardian angel in the memorial chapel at Kedleston, and he did not wish it anywhere else.

So it certainly was not love that stirred him one evening in London, in 1908, when he saw a lovely woman at a ball given by Consuela, Duchess of Manchester, and voiced his ardent admiration. She had glowing, blue-grey eyes, a skin of wondrous whiteness, and long, luxuriant red hair. She was talking animatedly to Alfred Lord Milner.

"Who," he asked, "is that with Alfred?"

In this case, he was behind in his gossip, and he was quickly enlightened. He was told that the woman in question was none other than the famous Mrs. Glyn, the Elinor Glyn who had written the *succès de scandale* of the moment, the novel *Three Weeks*, which, mainly because of its amorous tussling on a tiger skin, had become a worldwide best-seller. Mrs. Glyn was widely reputed to share the passionate inclinations of her palpitating heroines, and going around London at the time was a verse about her which Curzon must undoubtedly have heard at his clubs:

> *Would you like to sin*
> *with Elinor Glyn*
> *on a tiger skin?*
>
> *Or would you prefer*
> *to err with her*
> *on some other fur?*

Curzon's admiration for her might well have remained a vicarious one had it not been for another item of gossip which was speedily passed on to him—that Milner was madly in love with her and that there was a deep and abiding friendship between them. His competitive instincts were immediately aroused.

A few weeks later he went to a matinee at the Adelphi Theatre where a dramatised version of *Three Weeks* was being performed, with Elinor Glyn herself in the leading role. He was entranced at the sight of this lovely, voluptuous redhead throbbing through the transports of violent emotion as she lay on her tiger skin in the centre of the stage, and when he got back to Carlton House Terrace he went immediately to his trunks, filled with his Indian mementos, and took out the skin of a tiger he himself had shot on a hunt in Gwalior. He wrapped it up and sent it to Mrs. Glyn with a letter full of warm admiration.

He was furious when he discovered, a few days later, that Milner had had the same idea and had sent her a tiger skin himself. But he was mollified by Elinor Glyn's reply, which expressed her undisguised pleasure at the gift and went on, moreover, to mention her own deep admiration for him and her extensive knowledge of his work in India.

A meeting was arranged. Curzon went to it prepared to meet a rather shallow beauty with a flair for writing love stories; another Ouida, in fact. But his amused contempt changed to delighted surprise when he discovered that Elinor Glyn was not only a great beauty but also a cultivated and well-read woman who had taken the trouble, before they met, to acquaint herself with every detail of his life and career.

He came away already half-bemused by this remarkable and attractive woman. As for Elinor Glyn, it was a case of love at first sight. Curzon seemed to her to be the epitome of every quality and attraction she sought to give the heroes of her novels —stern, strong, masterful, tall and handsome as a god, a simmering human volcano only waiting for the love of the right woman to rouse him. She resolved there and then to have him for her own.

IN WRITING about Curzon's relations with Elinor Glyn (and also of her friendship with Milner), the papers left behind by both men are of no great help. Neither of them appears to have wished the world to know about his association with her. Just before he married for a second time, Curzon destroyed the bulk of the letters she wrote to him, an action which he must have taken under urgent compulsion, for he very rarely got rid of any scrap of paper dealing with his own activities. His trunks and packing cases are filled with thousands of letters, bills, menus, scribbled notes, drawings, and photographs, records of every man and woman he ever met. Yet though it is known that she wrote him long and passionate love letters, they have all gone. What were left after his marriage were torn up and burned by his orders just before he died; and what odd notes were left after that were destroyed by his wife. The name of Mrs. Glyn has even been excised from the lists of guests he entertained at Hackwood and Montacute (where she stayed several times), although the initials "E. G." have once or twice been overlooked.

Curzon wrote nearly five hundred letters to Elinor Glyn, but in a moment of heartbreak, sorrow, and sense of abandonment, these "she burnt herself," according to her grandson and biographer, Anthony Glyn, "the funeral pyre of her last and greatest love."

Milner's letters to Elinor also seem to have disappeared, and his biographer, Sir Evelyn Wrench, is able to make only scanty references to her. In this case there is even a tendency to suggest that Milner hardly knew Mrs. Glyn at all. It is, however, easy enough to prove the facts from other sources.

They met for the first time in 1903 in Carlsbad, where Elinor was holidaying and Milner was recuperating after his work as Governor-General in South Africa. It was a meeting of minds (at least on her part) rather than bodies and emotions. "I always thought that he must be the re-incarnation of Socrates," she wrote afterwards. They shared a mutual love for Greek literature, and Milner read Plato to her in between their walks through the Bohemian woods.

Her husband at this time held that position in name only. He had squandered his fortune and was hell-bent on killing himself, as his doctors continually warned him, by a life of over-eating, overdrinking, and all-night gambling. He was not expected to live long.

Curzon, however, moved in and ousted Milner from the pre-eminent place in Elinor Glyn's heart. Of Milner she was soon writing:

"I have seen him, my old friend. I wonder why in the past I never loved him. He loved me and he loves me still. His stern face grew soft when his eyes rested on me. We talked for hours in the firelight and he forgot his duties and his dinner. We visited past scenes—Stephaniewartz and the new moon! I gave him a new moon out of the tiniest diamonds—Cartier I remember designed it and made it into a pin—he wears it still! We spoke of Nuremberg and our joyous day there; of pine woods; of forests; of walks high up in the mountains where, gay as children, we used to wander; and he reminded me of our playful afternoon when we got lost and I was childish and pretended there were bears coming out of the dark trees to eat us! and how I held his hand and made him run down into the open early moonlight. I had forgotten it all."

But Milner wanted not only to remember the past, but also to think about the future. She had to tell him.

"His face at last was full of wistful pain," she wrote in her diary. "And at last he went away and I fear he will not come again. I cannot love him—I love only one. But even though he will not see me, we shall write. That side of me he can safely have, the intellectual. He shall be the friend of my ideals."

She had been seeing Curzon regularly now for two years, and though he too read the Greek philosophers to her and wrote her sonnets, the association was far from being simply intellectual. So far as Elinor Glyn was concerned, Curzon was now the most important thing in her life.

"How dark! how cold!" she wrote in her diary. "Leaden skies and damp lawns. Glorious roses spoilt, tears in the air, a wild rebellion in me. Day after day, the same life, incomplete, hungry, with no aim nor end, only to get through with it. There is a magnet here in England and I am a needle, and between the two are all sorts of paltry obstacles and some great ones, and I feel I could scream to the night: 'Tear me a path, sweep them aside, let me be free to follow my bent.'"

For Mrs. Glyn, when she gave her heart, gave it in a great gusher of emotion, and Curzon found it overwhelming. She wanted to tell the whole world about her tremendous love, but he counselled discretion. She opened her arms wide and bade him come into them, but he reminded her gently that it might not be fair to her husband.

She accepted his caution with a humility unusual in one of such tearing and tempestuous temperament, but she confided to her diary:

"O thou great one, calm and wise, accept this my cry of worship. Know that for me thou canst do no wrong. Thou art the mainspring of my life, for whom I would die, for whom I would change my character, curb my instincts, subjugate every wish, give my body and soul, worship blindly. Maimed or sick, well or strong, thou art adored, thy arms for my comfort, my soul for thy assuagement."

As the heat increased, and as the tempest of passion roared more and more fiercely through Elinor's body, Curzon began to think that perhaps the affair was going too far. He made tentative attempts to disentangle himself, but it was not only the red of her hair that flamed in his face on these occasions. She wept, she raged, she clung and would not let him go. He decided that his best policy was to surrender to her wild embraces (which, indeed, he found pleasant enough), but if the truth be told, after the first stormy encounters were over, and his conquest made, Curzon, while he dallied in Elinor's adoring arms, always kept a slightly pensive eye upon the door leading from the boudoir.

It would do Mrs. Glyn an injustice to suggest that she was entirely unaware of the flaws in the character of her lover. To some extent it was his very elusiveness which attracted her. She not only adored him; he represented a constant challenge to the potent influence of her love, and to hold him against all comers became the battle of her life. So far as the more intimate side of their relationship was concerned, she had no qualms about her supremacy over her rivals. But for that she needed propinquity, the opportunity to exercise the tactile magic with which she never failed to galvanise him; and Curzon could be evasive. When he was away from her, his eyes were only too often straying towards less tasty but far more practical fruit.

The love of a beautiful woman was all very well, but there were other things to be considered, his political ambitions above all. By 1912, when their liaison was four years old, Curzon sniffed the air and decided that the scent of political preferment was once more blowing his way. The world situation and the political situation were both restless. The Government couldn't last forever, and he was determined to heighten the prestige he once more enjoyed in the Tory Party in readiness for the high office which would one day be his. To some extent, the wounds left behind by the humiliation of India had been healed, especially since even the Liberals were now beginning to think that he had been right and Kitchener and St. John Brodrick wrong, after all. What bleeding there was left had been satisfactorily bandaged-up by a gesture from King George V, who did what his father had not dared or bothered to do, and made him an earl.

But if the heights were beginning to beckon him again, he realised that he must begin making some practical plans to prepare himself. His daughters were growing up and soon they would be on their way, taking their fortunes along with them. The effect upon his income would be serious. To live in the manner to which he had now become accustomed, to keep his fine houses, give his great parties, restore his castles, and buy his pictures, he would need far more money than he seemed likely to have a few years hence.

He began to think seriously of marrying again. He did not expect to find anyone to take the place of Mary in his heart, nor did he wish it. But whomsoever he chose would obviously have to be someone who, like Mary, would be able to fortify the financial needs of his career.

As if she knew what calculations were passing through his mind, Elinor Glyn chose this moment to produce a new novel, which she called *Halcyone*. Its heroine was a beautiful girl who loved Greek literature and sculpture but who had few worldly goods. Its hero was a rising young politician named John Derringham, who was wooing a rich American widow named Mrs. Cricklander in the hope of marrying her and securing the financial stability he needed to fulfil his statesmanlike ambitions. Mrs. Cricklander was the villainess of the piece—readers were left in no doubt about that. She was interested in marrying only if it made her the wife of a Cabinet Minister and the hostess of great society parties; and when the Tories went out of power, she dropped Derringham at once and went off and married a rising young Radical instead. So Halcyone got her man after all.

There are too many coincidences in the story for it to have been a work of pure imagination. The person of Halcyone was modelled on Mrs. Glyn even to the extent of having red hair. John Derringham was tall, handsome, and the scion of an aristocratic house, though poor; and he had, like Curzon, been captain of Oppidans at Eton. As to Mrs. Cricklander, it can be surely no accident that just about this time a certain American millionairess, Mrs. Alfred Duggan, appeared in London, though she was not, unfortunately for Elinor Glyn, to prove such a political and marital turncoat as is Mrs. Cricklander in the novel.

No one will ever know now what Curzon thought about *Halcyone*. It seems doubtful that he could have enjoyed it, for the hero is a vain, petulant, selfish, and sometimes quite unscrupulous man. But the record of his opinion has been destroyed.

Not that their association had come anywhere near to the breaking-point—yet. In any case, though he sometimes struggled in the coils of affection with which Elinor enfolded him, he saw no real danger in the situation so long as she could be persuaded to remain discreet, so long as she did not make too many demands upon him, and so long as her husband remained alive.

Mrs. Glyn summed up her own attitude about this time by writing in her diary about Curzon:

"He is too busy over his own great aims to care for your worship. Cease brooding for hours if his little finger aches. Cease praying for his glory and happiness and health from morning to night, and instead be joyous when you do see him, and between whiles concentrate upon your affairs for the benefit of your sweet ones and those dependent on you."

But when he wrote her, her spirits soared, for "the writing always makes my heart beat. Why are we such slaves to emotion, that the sight of the traced words on paper causes sudden physical sensation of thumping pulse, of heat and cold? Alas, the power of the Loved One, even at a distance!"

Though she was now very careful, at Curzon's urgent behest, not to tell all and sundry about the way she felt, she did pour out her heart in letters to a firm friend who was the wife of a Swiss diplomat in London, and the words of adoration have a temperature even higher than was usual in Mrs. Glyn's feverish purple prose. She called Curzon "my King and I his grovelling slave, ever ready to kiss his hands, lick his beloved toes." And she did get a certain triumphant amusement when she heard people referring to the two men in her life, Curzon and Milner, as cold, remote, and autocratic men. "How different are your personalities, both so great, both true and noble and splendid, and yet the sight of one picture moves every passionate emotion and the other stirs a gentle admiration. And you are both counted as cold and stern and indifferent. Women, they say, are things of naught in both your lives!"

She and her daughter Margot stayed with Curzon in Derbyshire and at Hackwood. Curzon crossed to Paris to share, for a time, a house she had taken there. And then, in 1916, her husband, Clayton Glyn, who had been doggedly drinking himself to death, finally did it. Now it seemed at last possible for the dream of her life to come true, and she telegraphed the news to Curzon in a fever of expectation over the nature of his reaction. He merely replied by sending her his deepest condolences.

It is not unfair to presume, from what was to follow, that in fact his reaction was one of alarm and panic. The possession of the married Mrs. Glyn was one thing, but the thought that she was now free was something else again. Honour demanded that, after a decent interval, he should offer her his hand. But did he want it? Would such a marriage, to such a tempestuous and unpredictable woman, further his career? The prospect of her red head presiding permanently over his dinner tables and his garden parties, as well as lying on his pillow for the rest of his life, made him pale.

If she had expected a proposal, it certainly did not come. The only comfort she could take from his silence was to hope that he was doing the gentlemanly thing and restraining himself until a decent period of mourning was over. But from this moment on she began to detect a cooling of their relationship. Not that she suspected (consciously, at any rate) that another woman had come between them. "Sometimes, I have felt it [the coolness] can only be because you have grown to love some other woman," she wrote in her diary. "But you yourself, when I asked you, have told me it was not so, and you would never lie to me or deceive me."

She did not, however, know men quite as acutely as she imagined.

That winter and the following spring, she spent much of her time at Montacute, a house which Curzon had leased in Somerset. At his request, she put herself in charge of the decoration and furnishing of the great house, braving all the rigours of winter in order to make it worthy of her King—and, perhaps, dreaming of the time to come when she would queen it there herself.

She was at Montacute one morning in 1916 when the *Times* arrived. She opened it at the society page, and there she read that the engagement was announced of Earl Curzon of Kedleston and a widowed American millionairess, Mrs. Alfred Duggan.

Curzon had not written to prepare her. According to her

biographer, he did not write her afterwards, either. "Their faithful, passionate friendship had lasted for eight and a half years, and now it was severed by one public blow of the axe," he writes.

Elinor Glyn burned her lover's letters. She never wrote or spoke to him again. Instead, to her friend, the Swiss diplomat's wife, she poured out her misery and stupefaction. "Oh, that he whom I adored, whose nobility I treasured, whose probity I worshipped, could prove so faithless and so vile!"

IT IS PERHAPS as well for her peace of mind that she never learned the whole story of Curzon's engagement. It was bad enough to have been thrown aside with such savage suddenness. But in actual fact it was even worse.

Curzon had been planning his marriage to Mrs. Duggan long before the public announcement had been made, and (as in the case of Mary) they had been secretly engaged for many months. The official announcement was made on December 11, 1916. But on September 25, 1916, he was writing to his future mother-in-law, Mrs. Hinds:

"Grace told you, with my consent, that we are to be married on her return from the Argentine. You and your other daughter are the only people who know, since we did not think it right to make any announcement before a year had elapsed from the death of her husband. . . . Many people in the past year have striven to prevent it, but we know our own minds."

The strain of the double life must have been a telling one, even for a character of such indefatigability as George Nathaniel Curzon's. Elinor Glyn, in her sorrow, wrote:

"Oh, my dear Lover, the day may come when you will wish to give of all your honours for my deep love."

But almost simultaneously, Curzon was writing to Grace Duggan:

"While you are away, Gracie, you need have no fear that I shall have thought, wish, fancy or hope for anyone but you. My life will be one of willing solitude, with a good deal of hard work, until you come back; and then I shall be yours, and you mine, and the sun will be shining in the heavens. Our dates hold good. December 11, announcement in the Press. December 16, your return. December 21, Event!"

He wrote this twenty-four hours after spending a weekend with Elinor Glyn at Montacute.

CHAPTER TEN

Cabinet Minister

A S IT HAPPENED, the marriage between Curzon and Mrs. Grace Duggan did not actually take place on December 21, 1916; it was postponed until January 2, 1917, because of a happy event which meant much for both of them. This was the appointment of Curzon to the office of Lord Privy Seal in the new Coalition administration which had just been formed by Lloyd George. This appointment, unlike his first Lord Privy Seal post under Asquith, carried with it a seat in the War Cabinet. It marked the return of Curzon to an influential role in the affairs of the British Empire for the first time in more than ten years.

For him it had been a thirsty decade of wandering in the political desert, and it is little to be wondered at that he gulped greedily at the waters of the oasis to which Lloyd George now led him. He had been waiting for a long time, and his parched state had not been eased by the sight of the lesser men who had been supping at the waters before him.

In 1914, upon the outbreak of war, his desperate eagerness to get back into office had, in fact, tempted him into performing a typical Curzonian manoeuvre. The Conservative Party had decided that while Balfour (as chairman of the Imperial Defence Committee) should continue to collaborate with the Government, other members of the Party should not help the Liberals by giving them strong support in the conduct of the war. But the prospects offered by the emergency were too strong for Curzon to resist. Without telling anyone in the Conservative Party, he wrote a letter to the Prime Minister, H. H. Asquith, offering his services. Asquith not only turned him down, but also slyly let it be known that once more Curzon was secretly planning to betray a pledge to his Party.

Mortified as well as rebuffed, the ex-Viceroy wrote bitterly: "Pitiful that at 39 one was thought fit to rule 300 millions of people, and at 55 is not wanted to do anything in an emergency in which our whole national existence is at stake."

The Conservatives eventually agreed to join the Government in 1915, and when Asquith formed the first Coalition administration in that year Curzon was offered, and swiftly accepted, the job of Lord Privy Seal. But he was given no say in major matters of policy, and when the first War Cabinet was formed towards the end of the year, he was not included in it. It was almost as if he had been hanging around too long, waiting for a nod and a beckoning finger, and Asquith's attitude towards him was tinged with the patronising contempt of one who suspected that Curzon would accept any snub in order to hold on to his job.

So, for nearly eighteen months, he glowed dimly and gloomily from the front bench of the House of Lords, while all around him played the brighter searchlights of flashier men. True, he had his seat in the Cabinet at last, and that had always been one of his dreams; but it was far down the line at the end of the queue. Though he was by far the senior peer, in experience at least, he was not even Leader in the House of Lords, for that position was held by Lord Crewe. He had hoped to get his hands upon some important department whose tasks and problems would be worthy of his mettle, and for this reason he worked hard to pilot the bill through the Lords whereby a Ministry of Munitions was created. On January 6, 1916, he had written to Crewe:

"As regards munitions, as you know, I was invited by the Prime Minister and Lloyd George to go into the Department and represent it in the House of Lords. Since the Committee meetings at which you and I were present, I have never once been invited inside the place or been made party to the proceedings. I offered at the beginning to go there and work if they would give me a room. No notice was taken of the offer, and I have never received a single paper or item of information about the work."

He felt snubbed, underemployed and frustrated. "Indeed," he wrote, "I often wonder why I was invited to join or am in the Government at all. . . . Twenty years ago I was thought good enough by Lord Salisbury to represent the Foreign Office singlehanded in the House of Commons; but now apparently I am not qualified to represent the Government in any debate on any subject whatsoever. I have accepted the position without a murmur and have been content to sit in silence for seven months. But now I have decided to speak, since I can really find no ground for continuing to be a member of a Government to which I am not permitted to render any service, all the more that I am excluded from the Committee which deals daily with questions and countries to a study of which I have devoted thirty years of my life."

It was a threat of resignation which, however, he had no intention of carrying out. Better to be a privileged servant inside the house than someone once more on the street, looking enviously through the window. And though his efforts were not adequately recognised by the majority of his Cabinet colleagues, the fact remains that he did some extremely valuable and constructive work towards the war effort while a member of Asquith's administration. He became head of the Shipping Control Board

at a time when the U-Boat war upon the British merchant fleet
was beginning to make its disastrous inroads upon British ton-
nage, and his organising skill was such that members of the Board
registered officially and publicly their appreciation of his work.
He fought a maddeningly frustrating war with that urbane
flâneur, Balfour (a statesman with "the mind of a marshmallow,"
Curzon said), over the creation of an Air Board to control the
slowly expanding Air Force and cope with the Zeppelin raids
now beginning over London. Balfour was First Lord of the Admiralty, which had the Air Force in its grip at this time, and he
fought Curzon's plans to wrest its control from the Navy more
as a dialectical exercise than as a firmly felt policy. It was only
one of the many occasions in his life when Curzon clashed with
Balfour, who disliked him; and Curzon was wrong in thinking
of his antagonist as a marshmallow. He was to act in future more
like a jellyfish with a considerable sting.

Curzon used his still considerable influence with the rank-
and-file members of the Tory Party to campaign for the introduction of compulsory military service. He had advocated this
step even before the war, much to the fury of the Liberals, and
once in the Cabinet he felt so strongly about it that he even
contemplated refusing Asquith's offer of the Order of the Garter
if a Bill for Compulsory Service did not receive the vote of the
Commons. That is surely a measure of his violent conviction on
the subject, for the splendid robes of the Order of the Garter
had always attracted him as a jewel does a jackdaw; besides
which, the award of the Garter would be yet one more vindication of his Indian regime. (The bill passed and Curzon got his
Garter.)

But all this work, sterling though it might be, was to Curzon
as unsatisfactory as a three-course dinner. Nothing that he did
carried the position, prestige, and power he craved. Neither his
state of mind nor his pride was improved when he held out
strongly for the retention of British troops in Gallipoli—on the

grounds that the Dardanelles would be dyed red with their blood if they withdrew—only to be contemptuously informed by his old enemy, Kitchener (who was Minister for War), that they had been withdrawn with hardly a casualty.

All around him, Curzon saw men he considered his inferiors making a muddle and a mess of the war. The casualties overseas were mounting. There had been disasters at sea. The mistakes at home were monstrous. Asquith seemed to have lost his grip and turned the wheels of the war machine with loose and even inattentive fingers. Curzon was certainly not alone in his disquiet. Bonar Law, too, as Leader of the Tory Party, was gravely concerned with the dismal and deteriorating situation. Among the more far-sighted, there was a growing conviction that the situation could be saved only if the day-to-day direction of the war were taken out of Asquith's hands and put into the grip of someone more dynamic.*

The part played by Curzon in it was that of a politician desperately engaged in hedging his bets and playing both sides, so as to come up with a win no matter which of the two contenders

---

* This biography is concerned with George Nathaniel Curzon and does not deal with the events, other than those which concerned him personally, of the political crisis of 1916. The full story of how a movement to strengthen Asquith's administration eventually brought about his overthrow and replacement as Prime Minister by Lloyd George has already been given by Sir Max Aitken (now Lord Beaverbrook) in his classic study of English politics, *Politicians and the War*. This masterly account of the machinations and intrigues, the dinner parties and secret meetings which preceded the change has now become the stuff of history. At least a dozen writers on the period have quoted, paraphrased, or rewritten him. Yet the original retains the authentic flavour of acute and accurate observation, and its superb sense of drama cannot be improved upon. As the actors move across the political stage, at one moment crying their innocence, at the next slipping their daggers from under their cloaks, Aitken stands in the wings, a cynical, worldly, and yet not unsympathetic observer; and politics come to life with almost Shakespearian impact. This, future generations will say, is how it happened—and what wonderful theatre it all was.

for the premiership—Lloyd George or Asquith—passed the post first.

Having made his return from the wilderness to public affairs, he was determined, at any price, to keep to the centre of the stage, no matter what solemn pledges he may have made to his colleagues. And when Robert Blake, in his biography of Bonar Law, *The Unknown Prime Minister,* says of Curzon's part in the political crisis: "It is difficult to acquit Curzon of a considerable measure of sharp practise in all these transactions," he is writing no more than the truth.

Not that Asquith suspected him, until the last, of double-dealing. From the moment that Curzon had joined the first Coalition Government, he had always been one of Asquith's most outwardly loyal supporters, more loyal to him as a Tory than were some of his Liberal colleagues. When the crisis of December, 1916, came it was generally concluded by both Tories and Liberals that Curzon would be behind Asquith and against Lloyd George in the struggle for power. Asquith himself counted upon him.

But on December 3, 1916, he wrote a letter to Lord Lansdowne saying, in effect, that he was against Asquith. Twenty-four hours later, he wrote to Asquith assuring him that he was still with him. On December 3 the Unionist Party had met and had instructed Bonar Law to tell the Prime Minister that an internal reconstruction of the Government was no longer possible and that Asquith should hand in his resignation to the King. Should he refuse, the Tory members of the Cabinet would resign en bloc.

Curzon informed Lansdowne that he was fully in agreement with this decision. "Had one felt," he wrote, "that reconstitution by and under the present Prime Minister was possible, we should all have preferred to try it. But we know that with him as Chairman, either of the Cabinet or the War Committee, it is absolutely impossible to win the war, and it will be for himself and Lloyd George to determine whether he goes out altogether or becomes Lord Chancellor or Chancellor of the Exchequer in a new Government, a nominal Premiership being a protean compromise which, in our view, could have no endurance."

Yet the following day, December 4, 1916, he wrote to Asquith:

"My dear Henry,—Lansdowne has, I think, explained to you that my resignation yesterday was far from having the sinister purport which I believe you were inclined to attribute to it. However, I have not written to emphasise that but to strike a note of gaiety in a world of gloom. Just now I recalled these lines of Matthew Arnold—I cannot remember in what poem:

> 'We in some unknown Power's employ
> Move in a rigorous line;
> Can neither when we will enjoy
> Nor when we will resign.'

"We are hourly expecting you to facilitate the process of asking for our seals. Yours ever, Curzon."

This letter could be interpreted in only one way, and Asquith so interpreted it. He believed that Curzon and his colleagues were still behind him, and that they were merely handing over their seals to him so that he could go ahead with the reconstruction of his Government.

Having dispatched two such diametrically opposed letters in the space of a few hours, it is little wonder that Asquith's biographers later remarked of them: "If the two letters were not in evidence, it would scarcely seem possible that they were written in the same hand."

Curzon continued to play his devious game. Having reassured Asquith with a letter, he then went on to convince him in person. For, the same day that he posted his note to Asquith, he went to 10 Downing Street with Cecil and Austen Chamberlain (though Chamberlain denied afterwards that he was present) to confer with the Prime Minister. Curzon acted as spokesman. He pointed out that he and his colleagues had consented to the Unionist resolution calling upon him to resign not in a desire to force him into retirement. Just the opposite. They did not believe, Curzon said, that anybody else could form a Government, certainly not Lloyd George. The result of their action, he assured the Prime Minister, would be the return of Asquith with a stronger Government and a greatly enhanced position. He also went on to affirm with great vigour that neither he nor the Tory Ministers for whom he was acting would take office under Lloyd George or Bonar Law should they attempt to form, or succeed in forming, a Government.

This was balm to Asquith's soul and grist to his mill. He was not only lulled into a sense of security. He was suffused with new strength, convinced that he would emerge victorious from the struggle after all.

Yet, a few days later he was out of office. He went to the King and resigned, and sat back to await his recall. Confident that Curzon and his colleagues were behind him, he was sure that Lloyd George would not succeed in forming a Government. It was just a question of patience and time; and then he would be back again.

But Lloyd George worked quickly and astutely. He turned his attention first to A. J. Balfour, the sly Tory jellyfish. Balfour had been lying low in the country all through the crisis, not intriguing like Curzon but lurking in the background, watching the way the fish were jumping. Lloyd George sent Bonar Law to talk to him as one Tory to another, and Bonar Law was dry but persuasive. After half an hour's conversation, the Tory leader said to Balfour:

"Of course you understand that I have come from Lloyd George to ask you on his behalf to become Foreign Minister."

Balfour smoothly replied:

"That is indeed putting a pistol at my head, but I at once say yes."

In fact, Balfour would have wanted to use the pistol himself had he not been given the offer. He was determined to be in the Government, and made a show of reluctance only to preserve his *amour propre.*

This was Lloyd George's first great triumph, for Balfour, as an ex-Premier and Tory leader, carried great influence. With Balfour on his side, Lloyd George was halfway home.

Soon, as Asquith's biographer remarked, there were not enough pistols to go round. Lloyd George knew that Curzon, Chamberlain, Cecil, and Long had told Asquith that they would never serve under him (Lloyd George). He also knew that they had agreed among themselves not to accept office individually without consulting each other. It was no use, therefore, taking out the pistol and attempting to press it to the head of one of them while the others were present. It would have been wrested from his hands. Austen Chamberlain, for one, was an upright, honest, and straightforward man who believed that once a promise was made it should be kept. His example alone would have prevented the others from accepting the loaded ultimatum, no matter how acceptable.

So Lloyd George decided to see the members of the quadrumvirate separately. His main target was Curzon. He knew that Curzon, so far as politics were concerned, would never say no to a shotgun wedding, provided that a powerful dowry came with it. And Lloyd George had a rich dowry to offer.

In Curzon's case, he sent a prominent Conservative, Lord Edmund Talbot, as his emissary. Talbot handled the pistol with delicacy and skill, gently stroking Curzon's ambition with the barrel. "Espouse Lloyd George," he said in effect, "and you will not only be given a seat in the Cabinet, but in the War Cabinet too, with a large say in the direction of the war."

Curzon did not hesitate. Ignoring his pledge to his colleagues, whom he did not consult, and his promise to Asquith, whom he did not inform, he at once said yes. Confronted by his unilateral decision, the others decided at once to join him in the Lloyd George administration. It was the swiftest political *volte-face* since the days of Halifax the Trimmer.

It may well be said, to change the metaphor, that Lloyd George's offer was that of a carrot to a donkey, and that the donkey swallowed it a little too swiftly for decency. True, Curzon made a show of presenting conditions to Lloyd George before accepting office. He asked for an interview, and he and his colleagues were ushered in to see the new Prime Minister. "Ushered," as one of the observers of these events remarked afterwards, "was indeed the word. Curzon was leading the sheep into Lloyd George's pasture. There they were shorn."

They made two conditions. One was that Lloyd George should not ask Winston Churchill to join the Ministry. There was no danger that this ultimatum would be rejected, as Curzon well knew. Lloyd George was depending upon the Tories for support in his new administration, and the Tories would never have accepted Churchill at this time. He had no difficulty whatsoever in agreeing to say No to Churchill.

Next, the sheep demanded that Lord Northcliffe should be excluded from the administration. Once more, Lloyd George fell in with their wishes. He knew the Tories would not accept Northcliffe.

So the Lloyd George Coalition Government of 1916, which was to win the war, came into being. Curzon was a member of it. Asquith, whom he had pledged to support, was out in the political wilderness once and for all.

Of his own part in this game of cut-and-thrust, Curzon, not surprisingly perhaps, says little in his papers. The author of the three-volume life of Curzon, Lord Ronaldshay (now Lord Zetland), was writing to an authorised brief and he completely ignores the intrigues of this period, merely contenting himself with remarking that Curzon was included in the new Lloyd George administration. A careful search of Curzon's papers has failed to discover any reference to the circumstances in which he took office. His "Notes for my Biographer" are covered with long and perfervid justifications of every move he made with the exception of this one. So far as Curzon was concerned, the attainment of a seat in the War Cabinet was enough—and the intrigues which preceded it best forgotten.

No wonder Curzon was happy, that morning of January 2, 1917, when he married Grace Duggan. Once more his financial status was secure. Once more he had a rich and beautiful wife. And in politics he felt strong, strong, strong.

In truth, though Lloyd George had enticed Curzon with a carrot, the new Prime Minister genuinely wanted him (at this time, anyway) in his new administration. He had seen him at work under Asquith and admired his capacity for organisation. It was a moment when expediency could be married comfortably with conviction, and Lloyd George was able to say, with more sincerity than usual, that he was happy that Curzon was a member of his team.

"Why Curzon? Is he valuable?" asked Lord Riddell of him afterwards.

"Yes, he is," replied Lloyd George. "He has travelled a lot. He has read a lot. He is full of knowledge which none of us possesses. He is useful in council. He is not a good executant and he has no tact, but he is valuable for the reasons stated."

It is perhaps not too much to call the first quarter of 1917 a honeymoon for George Nathaniel Curzon in every phase of his life, politically, socially, and domestically. That is not to say that everything went smoothly—what honeymoons do?—but the difficulties and problems he encountered were new and exciting, and he never failed to be aware that, after so long in the doldrums, he had wind in his sails, and his ship was once more on its way. What did it matter, then, if sometimes the weather got a little rough?

In the Cabinet at this time, he was never in doubt as to his ability to handle any squall that came up. His relationship with Lloyd George was, for the moment, cordial in the extreme. On questions concerning Asia or Asia Minor, the Premier never failed to defer to his superior knowledge; and though he often made fun of Curzon's pomposity and loved to give his friends hilarious imitations of Curzon's manner of speaking ("He always feels he is sitting on a golden throne, and must speak accordingly," he told Lord Riddell), Lloyd George valued his presence in the Cabinet and could not understand why others thought him "tricky." To Riddell he repeatedly praised Curzon because he possessed "information of a sort which is uncommon in British politicians. He knows foreign countries; he has travelled widely. He is dogmatic and often unreasonable, but he brings something to the general stock which is very valuable."

Curzon's antipathy towards his colleagues in the Cabinet, during the honeymoon period, was confined to Balfour, who was Secretary of State for Foreign Affairs—and not merely because he knew he could do the job better himself. He did not like the circumstances in which Balfour had entered the Cabinet. (He had accepted the invitation with even greater alacrity than Curzon himself.) He had never forgiven Balfour for his abandonment of him in India. But his hostility towards him now was much more than personal. At such a moment in history, with the gravest crisis in Britain's history looming over the nation, he genuinely believed that Balfour was the wrong man in a vital place. He was too amiable, easygoing, and amenable. He was too inclined to allow himself to be dominated in Foreign Affairs by Lloyd George and his clique of private secretaries in the "Garden Suburb" of huts which now surrounded 10 Downing Street. His acts of commission, Curzon considered, were calamitous, and his acts of omission were disastrous.

He fought him strenuously, but vainly, "in his unfortunate insistence upon the Jewish National Home in Palestine, in which, ignorant of the facts and regardless of the future, he forced his pledge upon the Cabinet in order to placate the Jews and bring them in on our side in the war." But what principally irked Curzon in Balfour's behaviour as Foreign Minister was "his passion for surrender on the altruistic ground that 'What did it matter?' It was only due to the fierce opposition of Milner, Long and myself that he was prevented, together with Lloyd George, from giving up Cyprus to Greece during the war."

The future of the nation's relations with her Allies and the neutrals boded ill if Balfour continued to control them; and the cauldron of Curzon's resentment simmered all the more because he realised that the Foreign Secretary was firmly entrenched. Lloyd George liked him ("he does what he is told"). He would not go until he decided to do so himself. And yet, Curzon complained, he was a failure and a danger.

"The characteristics that made him a failure, even a danger, as Foreign Minister were the same characteristics that made him a failure as prime minister," he wrote later. "It was not lack of courage—he had shown that in abundance in the Boer War—nor lack of ability—he had that in a superlative degree—nor one-sidedness—he would always listen to an argument. It was sheer intellectual indolence, a never-knowing-his-case, an instinctive love of compromise, and a trust in the mental agility which would enable him at the last moment to extricate himself from any complication, however embarrassing."

And he added the bitter final denunciation:

"The truth is that Balfour, with all his scintillating intellectual exterior, had no depth of feeling, no profound convictions, and strange to say (in spite of his fascination of manner), no real affection. We all knew this. When the emergencies came, he would drop or desert or sacrifice any one of us without a pang, as he did me in India, as he did George Wyndham over Ireland. Were any one of us to die suddenly, he would dine out that night with undisturbed complacency, and in the intervals of conversation on bridge would be heard to murmur 'Poor old George.'"

It is one of the ironies of the situation that Balfour, if called upon to sum up Curzon's character, might have written something very similar himself.

There was no love between them as they faced each other, Curzon smoulderingly hostile, Balfour coolly contemptuous, across the Cabinet Room table at 10 Downing Street in 1917. Later, Curzon's feelings were to curdle into fury and hatred.

IT WAS PROBABLY the circumstances in which Winston Churchill entered Lloyd George's Cabinet in 1917 that made Curzon realise that the honeymoon was over; and made him realise, too, that henceforward he would be dealing with rather sharper and smarter men than he had been accustomed to in previous administrations.

The Prime Minister had wanted Churchill in his administration from the start, for he admired his brains, ability, and Parliamentary skill, and feared to have these qualities pitted against him in opposition. Churchill was his friend, but Churchill was also determined to rise high in the political firmament, and if Lloyd George would not give him airspace he would find someone else to help him put his star into orbit.

But as a price for their entry into the Cabinet, Curzon and his friends had extracted a promise from the Premier that he would not, in any circumstances, offer Churchill a job. "They would not have Winston at any price," he told Riddell. "Had I insisted, the new Ministry would have been wrecked."

Amid all his other worries, for the war was going badly, the problem of Churchill preyed on Lloyd George's mind. He profoundly wished to have him working by his side. There, he would be an immense asset. Outside, fretting and frustrated, he was a potential danger. There was a move afoot, among the Government's opponents, to throw out Lloyd George and his colleagues and substitute a quasi-military administration in which the Army would be given full control of the direction of the war. There were rumours that Lloyd George's predecessor, still smouldering resentfully over his defeat, would be willing to become the titular head of what became known as the "Asquith–Brass Hat Alliance." The Premier was confident that he could, for the moment, hold it at bay. But what if Churchill, champing in the foreground, lent his considerable talents to the movement? The possibility almost made Lloyd George's leonine locks curl in alarm.

"Here was a man of extraordinary abilities," wrote Beaverbrook of Churchill in *Men and Power*, "of adroit debating strength, of originality and resourcefulness. At the height of the war he was out of employment. Yet the greater part of his career had been occupied with problems of a military kind. . . . He rightly felt he had special talents to offer in the crisis of world war. Instead he was extruded from the centre of action by men of lesser ability and initiative, and his knowledge and his inventiveness of mind—all were wasted."

Beaverbrook, who was moving between the two and knew what was passing through their minds, added:

"Lloyd George's position while the war continued to go badly was therefore immensely precarious. A great speech by Churchill, a direct thrust by the Asquith group—each of these or all together —might carry the day against the Government. . . . Churchill, although hated by the Tories, and mistrusted by half the Liberals and all of the Socialists, would be the linchpin in a coalition that might and could drive Lloyd George from the seat of power. Seeing the whole picture with the eye of a master of political tactics, Lloyd George was frightened."

Aware of, only too well aware of, his pledge to Curzon and the other Tories in his Cabinet, the Premier held his hand until word reached him from his friends in the Lobby that Asquith had made definite approaches to Churchill. He immediately wrote to Bonar Law, leader of the Tory Party:

"My dear Bonar, I think you ought to know that Asquith told Winston that, if he came in, he would put him in the Admiralty."

To Lloyd George this was a danger signal as bright and as baleful as a ball of fire. When it was followed by an eloquent speech from Winston in Secret Session strongly attacking the Government's policy, the Prime Minister decided that the time had come to act. "Churchill could not be left out of the Government," writes Beaverbrook. "He must be fenced in, and that forthwith. What could not be squashed must be squared, and what could not be squared must be squashed."

He asked Sir Max Aitken (as Beaverbrook then was) to come and see him, and gave him an awkward, almost indelicate, mission. Would he go across to his friend Bonar Law, and try to "square" him into accepting Churchill in the Cabinet? For Lloyd George knew that if Bonar Law—who had a cool contempt for Churchill's temperament, and no warm admiration for his abilities—could be persuaded to swallow the Churchill pill, his Tory colleagues might be expected to find it less distasteful than they were indicating at the moment.

Curzon particularly was beginning to howl with the alarm of a small boy who has seen the nurse go to the cupboard and take out the bottle of castor oil.

He had heard the rumours of Churchill's impending triumph, and he was furious. He had, in the past, tended to regard Churchill with the faintly contemptuous patronage of an elder and superior statesman for a loud and upstart careerist. In the old days, when Curzon was Viceroy, Churchill had treated him with the deference and respect he felt he deserved. Churchill sent him autographed copies of his books (Curzon thought the title "The River War" a very poor one), and thanked him warmly for his advice on political tactics. ("I think it most kind of you to find time to write to me," Churchill said in a letter of June 3, 1901. "You advise me to be sincere. Thank heavens I have tempered my sincerity with some prudence, but even as it is I have got

into trouble. . . . Luckily for me, it has all passed off very well
—thanks chiefly to my father's many friends and admirers—and
I have, I think, secured a position difficult to win, difficult to
hold, but on the whole perhaps more difficult to win than to
hold.")

This was the deferential, nephew-to-uncle missive that Curzon liked to receive, full of proper respect. But on the whole, his
opinion of Churchill could be summed up in the remark quoted
by Schomberg McDonnell to him: "He is an ill-educated man
with a great natural power of writing English. He has much
confidence in himself and none at all in anyone else. He has no
sense at all, and a minimum of manners."

This opinion was reinforced when in April, 1917, Churchill
had got up in the Commons and dared to criticise Curzon's
activities as Lord Privy Seal. No, no, no, he would *not* have this
loud-mouthed orator in the Cabinet. And he sat down to write
letters to prevent it.

To Lloyd George he wrote on June 8, 1917:

"My dear Prime Minister, May I again and for the last time
urge you to think well before you make the appointment
(W. Ch.) which we have more than once discussed? It will be
an appointment intensely unpopular with many of your chief
colleagues—in the opinion of some of whom it will lead to the
disruption of the Government at an early date—even if it does
not lead *as it may well do* [author's italics] to resignations now.
Derby, who opened the subject to me of his own accord this
evening and who has spoken to you, tells me that it will be
intensely unpopular in the Army. I have reason to believe the
same of the Navy. Is it worthwhile to incur all these risks and
to over-ride some of those who are your most faithful colleagues
and allies, merely in order to silence a possible tribunal of the
people whom in my judgment the people will absolutely decline
to follow? He is a potential danger in opposition. In the opinion

of all of us he will as a member of the Government be an active danger in our midst. Yours sincerely, Curzon."

A few days before, Curzon had written to Bonar Law in a determined effort to head off any tendency to compromise:

"Confidential. 4th June, 1917. My dear Bonar, Possibly there may be no truth in what we read in the papers as to Govt. reconstruction, e.g. Addison in the War Cabinet! Churchill at Air Board and so on. I just write to say that I hope none of these steps if contemplated will be done behind our backs. As you know, some of us myself included only joined LL.G. as on distinct understanding that W. Ch. was not to be a member of the Govt.—It is on record and to the pledge I, and I think all my colleagues, adhere. . . . Yours ever, Curzon."

There were other protests, too, notably one from Sir George Younger, chairman of the Unionist Party. Nobody wanted Churchill—except Churchill and Lloyd George.

It was in these circumstances that the Prime Minister asked Sir Max Aitken, as a friend of them both, to act as go-between in the "squaring" of Bonar Law.

"It was on 17th July, 1917 [writes Beaverbrook in *Men and Power*], that I was summoned to No. 10 Downing Street. As I walked through Whitehall my unfailing measure of optimism prompted me to believe that I would be offered at last a place in the Government dealing with war issues. My confidence was strengthened by the veiled sunshine and the warmth, with dry exhilarating air. When I was shown into the Cabinet room, Lloyd George was genial and talkative. But he did not say the words I expected him to speak."

Instead, he asked Aitken to undertake the "difficult and tiresome" task of telling Bonar Law that Churchill was coming into the Government, as Minister of Munitions, and persuading him to accept it.

Bonar Law proved just as indignant as Aitken had feared—

particularly because the Prime Minister had taken the decision without consulting him, and had thus presented him with a *fait accompli* of the most irritating kind.

"His pipe was lighted," Beaverbrook recalls. "It flashed through my mind: 'This will put his pipe out.' And it did."

But fortunately for Lloyd George, Bonar Law realised that there were only two alternatives before him—to accept the *fait accompli* or resign. And unlike Curzon, he was never the sort of man to use resignation as a threat unless he meant to carry it out. Nor was he anxious to break up the Coalition. He made a wry face and swallowed the Churchill pill. But he said: "Lloyd George's throne will shake."

For a time, at least, it seemed about to totter. The Tory Press screamed with rage. "That dangerous and uncertain quantity, Mr. Winston Churchill—a floating kidney in the body politic—is back again in Westminster," wrote the *Morning Post*. Walter Long spoke for his colleagues in the Cabinet when he wrote to Bonar Law: "The real effect [of the appointment] has been to destroy all confidence in LL.G. It is widely held that for purposes of his own, quite apart from the war, he has deceived and 'jockeyed' us."

But he did not resign. Nor, in spite of his strong threats earlier on, did Curzon. He raged against Lloyd George too. "He has gone back on his solemn pledge," he wrote. But after one shrill cry of what Lloyd George afterwards called "insensate fury," he accepted the apotheosis of "the ill-educated man."

It would not be long before he would be referring to Churchill by an even stronger term—"an evil genius."

IT WAS ALL VERY WELL for Curzon to gnash his teeth over Lloyd George's treatment of solemn pledges, but on two occasions in 1917 he demonstrated that he himself had not lost his facility for dodging around previously stated positions when they got in his way. In his case the plea of expediency was rather more difficult to accept, and his actions persuaded at least one of his colleagues in the Cabinet to regard him as not so much "tricky" as downright treacherous.

Austen Chamberlain had resigned as Secretary of State for India over the failure of the India Army's campaign in Mesopotamia, and his place had been taken by E. W. Montagu. It was Montagu who now had the task of bringing to fruition the long-planned and far-reaching scheme for the reform of the administration of Government in India. In this he had the collaboration of Lord Chelmsford, but Curzon, not surprisingly in view of his immense experience of India affairs, had been constantly consulted and his views incorporated in the draft scheme of reform. In fact, he wrote several paragraphs of the draft himself, striking out those written by Montagu. When Montagu proposed:

"His Majesty's Government and the Government of India have in view the gradual development of free institutions in India with a view to ultimate self-government within the Empire, . . ."

Curzon struck this out and substituted:

"The Policy of His Majesty's Government, with which the Government of India are in complete accord, is that of the increasing association of Indians in every branch of the Administration, and the gradual development of self-governing institutions, with a view to the progressive realisation of responsible Government in India as an integral part of the British Empire."

If this substitution, with its emphasis on the eventual emergence of *responsible Government* in India did not mean the eventual emergence of *parliamentary* Government there, what did it mean? Surely, Curzon could not be woolly-minded over, of all things, India? Surely he realised what he was saying?

But to Montagu's astonishment and dismay, when the completed draft was sent to him, Curzon completely reversed his previous stand. He had decided, for reasons of his own, to change his mind and now insisted that he did not want "self-governing institutions" or its corollary "responsible government" at all, and that the reforms envisaged would take India along the path to democracy far too fast.

Montagu wrote to him: "I am sure you will not resent it when I say that your Note on my Report comes to me as a great shock and a surprise. From our conversation together, I had ventured to hope that your criticism would be mainly directed to detail, and I notice with extreme regret your very weighty word of doubt about the principles on which the Report is based."

But Curzon, having decided to face the other way, would not turn round again.

Montagu wrote him again: "I want very much to make an appeal to you. Controversy with you distresses me very much. You talk in your letter of my hopes and aspirations. My hope and aspiration is to carry forward a continuous Indian policy; that is the only one I have. . . . Will you not let me help you while you are making up your mind? If you see points for criticism why will you not let me try to answer them? I seek for nothing but to act as a colleague."

For Montagu was now seriously alarmed that a clash of opinions between himself and Curzon would mean that one or other of them would have to resign. And what chance would he have against the weighty experience of the great Indian panjandrum?

As it turned out, he did not need to worry. Curzon continued to voice his opposition. He forecast disaster ahead if the reforms went through. But he did not vote against them. And all that the clash served to demonstrate to his Cabinet colleagues was that, even on the subject of India, Curzon did not always know his own mind. Why else had he changed so drastically? It was one more fascinating glimpse of the strange working of the great man's mind.

WHAT WAS THIS peculiar tendency of Curzon to switch his horses so inexplicably—to wait until the last moment, when everyone thought he was with them, and then to refuse to recognise his most solemn pledges?

It is possible to understand his motives when he did it in order to secure political office, when the observance of his solemn word of honour to his colleagues would have meant depriving his country of the services he felt patriotically bound to give. And, of course, as in the case of India, he was right to change his mind if he thought it was for the good of the Empire. But there were other occasions when he reversed himself in circumstances that were almost shockingly wilful.

The case of women's suffrage, which came up for discussion in 1917, is to the point. It must be obvious by now that Curzon was a vehement opponent of any move which might take women out of the kitchen (or the boudoir) and give them the rights and privileges of men. He was not only against "women in trousers;" he was so determined to protect "their gentle contours from the eroding influences of the storms of public life" that he had enthusiastically accepted the presidency of the Anti-Suffrage League. This was by no means an all-male organisation. Some quite influential women of the day, convinced that emancipation would ruin the sex, were leading figures in the league, including Lady Cromer and the novelist Mrs. Humphrey Ward. They worshipped Lord Curzon as the leader of their crusade against the vote, and never so much as during the year 1912, when he campaigned for support with such eloquent enthusiasm that he enticed £20,000 into the League's kitty.

In 1917, the attitude of both Parliament (still an all-male institution) and the nation (still exercising an all-male franchise) underwent a profound change of front. The female sex had proved itself valiant, capable, and efficient in carrying out the duties to which it had been called, many of them previously regarded as the prerogatives of the male. The majority of mem-

bers in the House of Commons yearned to reward them for their
courage and ability by giving them the privilege they had so
manifestly earned—a vote and a say in the affairs of the nation.*

The Anti-Suffrage League was alarmed and aroused. They
realised that the defences were in danger of collapsing, and the
petticoat revolution about to sweep down upon them, when a
clause was inserted into the Representation of the People Bill
providing for a considerable broadening of the existing franchise.
The Commons voted through the measure by a large majority,
with only fifty-five diehards voting against it.

In these grave circumstances, the only hope was the House
of Lords and the influence of Curzon to stem the tide. A meeting
was called. New hope flowed into the veins of the reactionaries
among the female sex when Curzon made it clear that he was
as fervidly against "this biological mistake" as ever. The Committee came away convinced that he would not only rally the
House of Lords against the bill, but would help to vote it down.

What went on in Curzon's mind between this meeting and
the subsequent vote in the Lords remains a mystery, for Curzon
destroyed many of his papers about this phase of his activities.
What happened is in Hansard, the official report of the proceedings of Parliament.

It seems that Curzon must suddenly have remembered that
the Representation of the People Bill was, if not a Government

---

* Women had already, in 1917, been allowed to receive awards
making them members of the Order of the British Empire, and
Curzon had the task of deciding what title should be given to those
receiving the first two classes of the Order. The title of Dame was
suggested. Curzon strenuously objected on the grounds that the term
suggested "a housemistress." He was overruled and Ponsonby wrote
to him from Buckingham Palace on May 24, 1917: "With regard
to the precedence of women, the King has reluctantly come to the
conclusion that women who receive the first two classes of the
Order of the British Empire should be allowed to receive the title
of Dame. His Majesty shared your dislike of this appellation but
without some handle to the name it is impossible to give any satisfactory precedence. . . ."

measure, at least one approved by them, and that, as a member of the Cabinet, he could hardly vote against it. The obvious thing, then, was for him to resign his position as president of the Anti-Suffrage League.

He not only did not do this. He did not even acquaint the League with the doubts that were passing through his mind. Instead, he urged them to lobby the undecided peers in the Lords and engage their support in opposing the bill. He then got up and made a speech ridiculing the measures planned and expressing his unwavering opposition to the suffrage of women. "May I congratulate you on your speech?" wrote Mrs. Humphrey Ward. "It was most important to us to have it laid down that the Bill is not a Government Bill and that there will be absolute freedom of speaking and voting upon it."

With Curzon's full approval, the League had persuaded Lord Loreburn to move the rejection of the clause in the bill extending the franchise to women, and the members crammed the galleries and got ready to cheer when Curzon rose to support it. He was as ringingly passionate in his denunciation of the measure as they had hoped.

"If your Lordships pass this part of the Bill," he declared, "you are doing more than crossing the Rubicon—you are opening the floodgates to a stream which for good or evil will submerge many landmarks we have known."

It was enough. The dowagers turned and almost embraced themselves with glee. The battle was won. The sex was suppressed. Through Curzon's efforts, they could now turn once more upon their daughters and their serving-maids and say: "Back to the boudoir—back to the kitchen!"

But Curzon was not finished. Having roused the House to vote against the clause, he added a rider:

"Logically, the direct consequence of everything I have said is that I should support the amendment." He paused, and then as the faces paled in the Strangers' Gallery, he went on: "I do not intend to do so." And then he launched into an impassioned explanation of why—since the Commons had already voted the clause—he did not intend to support its deletion. The effect upon the House was immediate. The amendment was defeated and the clause went through.

Curzon behaved as if he were genuinely bewildered when the members of the Anti-Suffrage League descended upon him in all their fury. He was sincerely hurt by the letters of abuse which poured in upon him, and even went to the extent of complaining to the Committee. "I suspect," he wrote to his wife, "that they come mostly from outraged spinsters." Since spinsters were getting the vote as a result of the passing of the disputed clause, this could hardly have been the case, but Curzon had always had a low opinion of spinsters. Of them, he once wrote, "I will say nothing worse than that they represent an imperfect or chrysalis stage of womanhood."

In fact, the most pained letter of the lot came from Mrs. Humphrey Ward. "As to your speech," she wrote, "it seemed more and more impossible that it should not be followed by a vote. If your views were still such, was it conceivable that you should not give effect to them by a vote? . . . Then came the anti-climax. . . . The effect absolutely disastrous."

Surely Curzon might have foreseen that this was what would happen? Yet he still rallied supporters to the Anti-Suffrage League before the debate, and then, having worked them up to a fever-pitch of aggressiveness, deserted them in the moment when the battle was joined.

"I cannot understand why they are so pained," he said.

CHAPTER ELEVEN

Grace Curzon

Curzon's life with his new wife had begun, too, with not a fleck of cloud in the sky and not a hint of barometric pressure.

"I am sure she will have told you, and I hope from what you have seen of me," he wrote to his mother-in-law, Mrs. Monroe Hinds, "that this is a love match on the part of both of us. . . . It has not been a resolution lightly arrived at on either side, and it represents the firm conviction both of our heads and our hearts. I am well aware that Grace is doing me a great honour in consenting to share the life of a man a good deal older than herself, and I feel keenly the responsibility that lies upon me to try and bring true happiness to one who has not always found it, and who deserves from life more than it has hitherto given her. But I will try to do this, and to deserve her trust, while to me she will bring a light and joy that I had never looked forward to find again, in a life that is at times very solitary, and would have become more so as time goes on."

He added, diplomatically: "May I add that I have often told her that she cannot set before herself a better model of goodness, simplicity and dignity than her mother?"

To Grace herself he had written: "I love and adore my beautiful, true and faithful girl with all my heart and soul. . . . We have sifted and tested each other, darling, for more than a year, and the gold has come forth purified from the fire. We know that we are suited to each other, that we can make each other happy, and that hand in hand we can accomplish the remainder of life's journey and maybe do something worthy on the way."

And Grace had written back: "Believe me, my darling, my great man, I think I must have been waiting for you always. You call me a flower. Dear heart, I do feel a wide-open, full-blown rose with every petal open to you, my sun."

It was, indeed, a union which promised happiness and fulfilment for both of them, even though there was a difference of twenty years in their ages.

Grace Curzon was the daughter of an American diplomat, Alfred Monroe Hinds, who had served his country in several South American states, notably Brazil and the Argentine. It was in the Argentine that she met her first husband, Alfred Duggan. She was of Southern stock, almost a child of the plantation, brought up in the tradition of black Mammy nurses and compliant Negro serving-men. He was an Anglo-Argentine whose family's holdings were so vast that "we have our own railway, a hundred miles in length, and you can ride for days without reaching our frontiers."

From her marriage to Alfred Duggan she gained three children, two sons and a daughter, but not much happiness. When he died in 1915 there is no reason to believe that she was deeply unhappy. She was beautiful. She was thirty-six. She was certainly rich (though once more, as in Mary Curzon's case, her estate was entangled in trusts).

"It is curious how seldom you and I have talked about money matters," Curzon wrote to her just before their marriage. "I don't think either of us has ever asked a question of the other. Of course wealth is a great help to those who wish to do big things, and after the war so many people will be poor that those who have money will be able to make good use of it. In time, too, as my daughters marry and go, I shall become poorer, as the fortune is theirs, not mine, and I merely enjoy a portion of it temporarily as guardian."

He added that he hoped and prayed that she would help him to restore Kedleston—"and, oh, I pray, to hand it on."

For Lord Scarsdale had died. His own elevation to an earldom meant that his title of Curzon of Kedleston superseded that of his father, but the estate was his; and, as fervidly as he pursued his political ambitions, he longed for the son and heir to inhabit the estate and continue the name.

To further this aim, Grace Curzon was more than willing. "Keep your Gracie true, clean and worthy," she wrote to him, "to mother your children. I shall always keep the thought of your dear love"—she was referring here to his dead wife Mary—"and the wish to please her, especially with the care of her daughters. This to me will be a sacred charge. I feel that God will reward me for trying to do all my duty by giving us a child —my beloved boy's child. Darling, this thought is already my biggest wish and my most earnest care. I am taking great care of myself. If ever we are blessed, he must be strong and all that your son should be. I thought of this yesterday when I was tempted to move the furniture."

Grace Curzon had always been a great lover of social life, and her marriage to Curzon meant that she automatically became one of the most important hostesses in the land. Perhaps the most important of all. Mrs. Lloyd George was taking a progressively diminishing role in her husband's public (as well as his private) affairs. For Grace Curzon, the urge to become the Coalition's social focal point must have been tempting indeed; for luncheons, dinners, and parties were bound to go on in spite of the stringencies of war.

Nevertheless, in the first year of her marriage, she deliberately cut out most of her social activities and retired to a quiet life at Hackwood, firmly determined not to come back into the round of social activities until she had produced for George an heir. Not that she remained ignorant of what was going on in London. Curzon saw to that. Each day he sent back a copious letter of his daily doings and the latest gossip.

"Haig comes over today to be examined by the War Committee," he wrote her on June 14, 1917, when the forthcoming offensive in France was being planned. And, a few days later: "A week of exceptional strain. Today is the third day on which I have had to make difficult speeches. Tuesday I had to get Crawford out of his mess about the Welsh Church Act. Yesterday, I was called upon to defend the appointment of Northcliffe [as Britain's chief propagandist spokesman in America], of which you know I entirely disapproved. And in 20 minutes I go down to deal with two rather technical questions about the position of the House. This on top of our very important War Committee which has been sitting once, and sometimes twice, a day and makes life very exacting. We have now had Haig and [General] Robertson before us for two days, and we have to take decisions for the autumn and winter which may affect, must indeed affect, the whole future and perhaps the ultimate issue of the war. Last night my dinner for the War Committee (Lloyd George, Bonar, Milner, Smuts, Hankey and myself) went off very well. The P. M. under the influence of two or three glasses of champagne became quite hilarious. After dinner we adjourned to the terrace [this is written from 1, Carlton House Terrace] for the great discussions, but after three-quarters of an hour the wind drove us in and we adjourned to your boudoir, where the guests showed a complimentary but uninstructed interest in the pictures."

He added: "The pow-wow lasted until 12:30 A.M. and sent me to bed quite worn out. I am not sleeping very well owing to fatigue and heat. I often think of my darling girl in her mauve dress with the dark blue ribbon round her shapely waist. . . .

Why did not Gracie wire her boy and tell him if she is going on free from pain and distress? Is no news good news, or is girlie passing through the trouble?"

But the fulfilment of their desires was not so easily come by as they both imagined. Medical advisers were called in and Curzon arranged for Grace to have "just a little operation, it will be quite painless, and very soon all will be all right." But it was not painless, and it was not all right. And Curzon was profoundly disappointed and intensely puzzled. They had each produced three children from their previous marriages. Why could not they produce a son and heir between them? As the months went by, he came to regard the fruitlessness of their marriage almost as a conspiracy organised against him by the same dark forces which gave him the pain in his back. In his letters to Grace he was careful not to express any resentment at her failure. He still called her "my Egyptian," still called himself "your loving Husbin," and still slept with "the sweet-smelling lock of your webby hair beneath my pillow," but the constant refrain now began to run through them: "Surely, surely, we cannot be disappointed again?" But they were.

It was not perhaps unnatural that Grace Curzon's nerves should become frayed as a result of these frustrations, and her husband began to make the chastening discovery that she was not, as he had once imagined, like his first wife, Mary, complacent, uncomplaining, compliant, and adoring. She could not only be wilful, but she was also extremely jealous. She had said very little to him about Elinor Glyn before their marriage—when there had been good reason for her jealousy—but now—when there was none—she broke out into a spate of accusations. Lying in bed at Hackwood, she had received a letter from a mischievous friend telling her that Curzon and Mrs. Glyn had been meeting again. In fact, they had seen each other only once, at a theatre, and had ignored each other; but Grace showed herself more than willing to believe the worst.

In hurt surprise, for this was their first major quarrel, he wrote to her on House of Lords notepaper:

"Why do you quarrel with me and make me miserable? Try and be generous and be the loving wife of your adoring husbin. . . . Please believe that I long to make you happy and to bring about the fulfilment of our desires. My darling, all that I ask you to do is to start with the presumption that I love you and am true. . . . If you start the other way, in the presumption that I am untrue, everything easily becomes coloured and distorted in the effort to make it correspond with the theory. Anyhow, I do love you, and am as incapable of treachery or faithlessness to you as I believe you to me. Now I must run back, my sweet, adorable wife, and make a speech."

But she was not appeased and her suspicions were not allayed. Not long afterwards, he was writing again:

"Why do you say 'as you of course know Mrs. G. is in London'? Really Girlie you are incorrigible. I have not now and I have never had any communication with Mrs. G. since we married. I have kept my word. I have not the slightest idea whether she is in London or in Paris neither do I care. . . . *do begin to believe,* oh Girlie, *please.*"

His experience as the husband of Mary Curzon had given him an idyllic view of marriage, but he was quickly discovering from Grace that there were other kinds of marriage and very different types of women. For three months after the wedding, he was still able to believe that from this union he would gain all the treasures of happy domesticity—a rich and beautiful wife, a companion in his triumphs and a solace in his setbacks, a mother of his children. He could not have guessed what disappointment, frustration, and loneliness were in store for him.

BUT THESE TRAGEDIES were for the future. For the moment, Curzon was not unduly troubled by them, and in both his private and his public life he remained persistently, if not always serenely, optimistic. So long as the war was on, he was content to remain what Beaverbrook has called "Lloyd George's carthorse." His eye was on the Foreign Office, as the logical step to the premiership, but for this he could wait, until such time as foreign affairs once more took precedence over the conduct of the war. Balfour, holding that office, was not even a member of the War Cabinet, and as such did not have as much say in the affairs of the nation as Curzon, who was. Curzon was content to bide his time. He still believed he enjoyed Lloyd George's confidence, if neither his affection nor his admiration; and this was, indeed, the case. The Prime Minister considered Curzon an indispensable member of the Coalition, though no longer for the same reasons as before; it was not so much Curzon's ability and talents which he needed now, but his power, prestige, and influence among the Establishment of the Tory Party at the Carlton Club. In fact, the Carlton Club members were no longer as fervid in their loyalty to Curzon as they once had been, for his aboutturns over the Indian reforms and the Suffrage question, and his attitude towards the Irish problem, had disillusioned them, and they were beginning to suspect that he would give way—or change his mind—on any subject rather than sacrifice office. But Lloyd George does not appear to have been aware of this emerging scepticism.

It was not the busiest time of Curzon's life, but he was still cramming into his days and nights more activities than most men find time for in a week. He attended Cabinet meetings: "Today I presided over the War Cabinet," he wrote to Grace on October 9, 1918. "Ll. G. and Bonar do not return until tomorrow. Our Army in France is making the most eventful push of all towards Le Cateau—8,000 German prisoners yesterday and the advance continuing today." He made speeches: "Cunningham has just been in to say that Lansdowne made a nasty speech, and that the House of Lords were talking at a loose end and that I have got to be there to pull it together." He gave parties at Hackwood, and, of course, supervised all the arrangements: "The Queen of the Belgians rang up. . . . I suppose she wants to stay the weekend. I suggest you ring P. M. and try to bag him for at least one night. (Later) P. M. telephoned today to say he is in bed with a chill (I know these Downing Street chills) and cannot come tomorrow. I don't think we ever expected him. I am bringing down claret, cigars, cigarettes; jam, bottled fruit and six lbs. of butter were dispatched from Kedleston in early part of the week. [He enclosed a seating plan for the dinner table.] I hope my diagram helped you to a solution of how to get a quart into a fruit bottle!"

Every spare moment of his time he spent in passionate pursuit of his favourite hobby, replanning houses or restoring castles. At Hackwood, though the house was only on lease, he was engaged in removing a large hillock which obstructed the view from the ground-floor windows. This he did at his own expense, and it cost a pretty penny, though he conducted a long and protesting correspondence with the agent when he refused to pay for the repair of the coalshed. At Kedleston, he was personally supervising the replanning of the house and its gardens. He helped to dig the ground, saw down the trees, and superintend the fitting of new bathrooms and plumbing. ("He climbs fully clothed into all the baths, to test their length, first lining them with newspaper," his plumber commented.) Curzon had hoped to persuade Grace to move to Kedleston, now that his father was dead, but she complained of its lack of warmth, its lack of toilets, and its lack of telephones. In truth, she never cared for Kedleston, and for all Curzon's efforts, she never went to live there. She was inclined to agree with Dr. Johnson's description of it: "It would do excellently well as a town hall," and she wrote later: "Much as I admired it, I never felt the affection for it that I did for Hackwood or Montacute. I always thought it needed a warm sun to bring its frozen beauties to life. If only it could have been built at Genoa or Naples." Or, for that matter, near enough to London to keep her close to her relatives and friends.

In addition to this, he had bought himself a new castle—the lovely old fortified manor of Bodiam, in Sussex—and was directing its restoration. And he was engaged in writing the history of all his houses, poring over old documents, writing letters in search of information.

Small wonder that he complained of exhaustion. "I have been very unwell all day. I could not sleep last night," he wrote. "I think I am very tired and over-strained. I shudder at the week that lies before me. . . . But I suppose I must struggle out." His back was bad, and a new harness with which he had been fitted did not improve matters. "Poor tummy aches. It is a terrible experience for a man to be in the family way!"

But he would not stop. Pain and incipient exhaustion only seemed to galvanise him into further activity. He worked all through the day and far into the night. What little sleep he did get was that induced by laudanum and other drugs. And they took their toll of him, mentally and physically. His smooth, ruddy face became lined and drawn. He raged at the servants, and when a servant-girl at Carlton House Terrace one day broke a vase, he bundled her down the steps into the street and shouted: "Go, girl, go!" (and then ran after her, tears starting in his eyes, and brought her back). He bickered in the Cabinet and often seemed on the point of tears; and indeed when he got home he often collapsed on his bed, and his servants in the corridor outside could hear him heaving with sobs. Moody, fractious, always looking out now for snubs, though never for the kind of fight he would have relished in the old days, Curzon seemed a flaccid giant compared with the titan who had once ruled over India's millions. His voice still boomed out in rich, port-wine tones, but the wit, playfulness, and sense of fun had all but disappeared. He looked around the Cabinet Room now as if in search of pistols hidden in the pockets of his colleagues, and almost challenged them to shoot him down. Indeed, one of them needed little encouragement. When Curzon was acquitted by Bonar Law of misusing state-owned cars, Lord Derby sat down in a fury and wrote a telltale letter full of spite and venom, citing instances of Curzon's misappropriation of his office landaulette to carry Grace and himself to weekend parties at Hackwood. The full text of this letter is printed in Lord Beaverbrook's *Men and Power*, but Lord Derby's heirs have since forbidden its republication.

It is small wonder that Curzon detested Derby from that moment on.

But his increasing personal resentment against Churchill—in addition to his political antipathy—can only have been due to the emotional suspicion with which he now viewed his colleagues. For Churchill always fought fair. He said what he had to say in the open, and often followed up his remarks with a scribbled note which he passed to Curzon across the Cabinet table. Curzon always carefully gathered up these notes afterwards and put them in his personal file, and one of them from Churchill says:

"Please pardon these few words from one who though a critic is no enemy."

But Curzon was not appeased. Another note, from Curzon to the Prime Minister, says:

"C: It seems to me entirely wrong that W. Ch. should air his independent views on a F. O. occasion. Ll. G.: I quite agree. I have done my best to stopper his fizzing."

And another, from Austen Chamberlain:

"I think you are right to show Winston that you profoundly resent his constant and persistent interference. It goes far beyond anything that I at least have ever known in Cabinet, even from the most important members of a Govt. Unless you make him feel that it is a matter which you feel personally, I despair of doing anything with him. To a *personal* appeal I think he is nearly always open (I mean to an appeal on personal grounds)."

Curzon, however, preferred to nurse and nourish his resentment, and he was overjoyed and wrote exultantly to Grace when Churchill received a rebuff in Cabinet from Bonar Law.

"This morning I have had a Cabinet," he wrote, "at which Winston was most annoying, to such an extent that Bonar for the first time in my experience lost his temper and told him straight out that if he did not know how to behave, he had one course open to him, which was to leave the Government. Bonar subsequently apologised for his heat, but it had not been unprovoked."

Such was his mood in 1918. Everywhere he saw enemies. The only man who seemed (for the moment) not to be against him was Lloyd George. He moiled, sweated, and brooded. It was a time when he should have been conserving his strength, for the war was almost over, and his "carthorse" days too. The generals had done their best (and often their worst), and the turn of the politicians was coming. Curzon had no doubt in his own mind that in the winning of the peace, he, with his wide knowledge and vast experience of the world, would have a vital part to play.

But there were already those among his Cabinet colleagues who wondered whether he would have the physical stamina or the mental stability for the tremendous tasks ahead.

THE COMING OF PEACE gave George Nathaniel Curzon all the opportunities he loved for gathering unto himself the pomp and panoply of official celebration. He was called upon to move, in the House of Lords, an address of congratulation to the Crown on the victorious outcome of the war, and even his worst enemies had to admit that he more than matched up to the majesty of the occasion. As a misty darkness fell over London on the afternoon of November 18, 1918, and the lights came on in the Chamber, he rose to his feet, erect in his harness, his eyes shining, his face glowing, and from his lips the triumphant, imperial phrases rolled across the House. While his audience sat back, like transfixed pebbles, the waves of splendid sound crashed on their ears with ever-mounting fervour, until he reached his peroration with the words:

"A little more than one hundred years ago, the great romantic poet of our land, looking on the birth of a new Hellas, wrote these prophetic words:

> 'The World's great age begins anew,
>   The golden years return;
> The earth doth like a snake renew
>   Her winter weeds outworn.
> Heaven smiles and faiths and Empires gleam
>   Like wrecks of a dissolving dream.'

"A similar vision now rises above a far wider horizon. May we see it, under the guidance of Providence, assume form and substance before our eyes."

It may have been overoptimistic, but it was great oratory, just the same, and there were plenty of damp eyes in the House (including, of course, Lord Curzon's) when it was over.

There were other triumphs. He helped to organise the reception accorded to the French Premier and Marshal Foch when they visited London a fortnight later. He was chairman of the Cabinet committee which planned the official peace celebrations. And when President Wilson, who was shortly coming to Europe for the Peace Conference, refused an invitation to London to stay with the King and Queen—for he was suspicious of the intrigues in which Lloyd George might try to entangle him—Curzon thought up the solution. He remembered that he was Chancellor of Oxford University, and he wrote to Lloyd George:

"I think I helped to solve the problem of getting Wilson to come to England on his way to Paris. For, a little before leaving London I had got my University of Oxford to vote him an honorary degree and to ask him to deliver the Romanes Lecture. As soon as I told [Colonel] House this he said it was the one thing the President would love and that it would bring him to England without fail—giving him an academic rather than a political excuse for his visit. He accordingly wired at once to Wilson and has no doubt of his acceptance."

Through all these events he moved in serene majesty, sublimely aware and proud of his role, to such an extent that the American ambassador privately dubbed him: "His Royal Pomp."

But there was a rather less glorious attitude which he adopted just about this time, and that concerned the fate of the defeated Emperor of Germany. It is difficult to understand why Curzon felt so malevolent towards the Kaiser. There is no reason, of course, why he should not, like a vast number of British subjects at this time, have hated him for the war he had done so much to cause and the devastations, killings, and sufferings which had followed in its train. But when the mob is screaming for blood is just the time when a statesman should be expected to keep his emotions in check; and that is just what Curzon did not do. Two days after the Armistice he wrote to Lloyd George, on November 13, 1918:

". . . I suggested the possibility of creating—as the first step to a League of Nations—an international tribunal of jurists of the highest eminence (they might or might not include neutrals, probably Yes) for the express purpose of trying the Kaiser, his son and the other offenders. They might be cited before it. I do not know enough about international law to be sure whether Holland having interned them, if she has, could or would give them up for trial. But what would that matter in the case of the Kaiser and his son? The charges could be sent to them and their replies invited. Either these would be just and considered, or they would be refused. In either case, the Tribunal could consider the evidence and eventually pronounce its verdict. If the sentence was that of outlawry from the principal countries of the world, it would be a punishment signal, crushing, unheard of in history. . . . I pray you to consider it seriously. Public opinion will not willingly consent to let this arch-criminal escape by a final act of cowardice. The supreme and colossal nature of his crime seems to call for some supreme and unprecedented condemnation. Execution, imprisonment, these are not, or may not be, necessary. But continued life, an inglorious and ignoble exile, under the weight of such a sentence as has never before been given in the history of mankind would be a fate worse than death."

Lloyd George seized upon Curzon's letter as just the right backing for the campaign with which he meant to win his forthcoming election. He had already found the rallying slogans: "Hang the Kaiser" and "Make Germany Pay." Curzon had provided the right sort of fuel for his electoral machine, and he used it. He had the decision to try the Emperor incorporated in the peace treaty, and invited Holland, which had given him refuge, to deliver up the German monarch from asylum.

For the first time, Churchill could not hide the detestation he felt for Curzon in participating in such obvious appeals to the blood-lusts of the masses (though he may have understood them better, a generation hence, when the Nuremberg trials of Hitler's aides took place), and his comment on Curzon's letter to the Prime Minister was: "This was in Oscar Wilde's phrase the pursuit by the inexpressible of the uneatable."

But did Curzon really want to see the Kaiser hanged?

He was certainly not alarmed at the prospect until the King got in touch with him and showed him a memorial he had received from a number of German princes warning him that if the Emperor of Germany were brought to trial now, a British monarch might not be exempt from such dire punishment in the future. Curzon professed not to be impressed. But his lust for revenge noticeably cooled, and when Lloyd George subsequently proposed (with all his Gallic relish for a spicy occasion) that

Wilhelm should be brought to London and put on trial there, Curzon back-pedalled in panic and alarm.

"My dear Prime Minister," he wrote, on July 7, 1919, "I venture, for what they are worth, to put before you some views about the contemplated trial of the Kaiser in England. I have always been in favour of his trial. Indeed, I was the first to raise the subject in the Imperial War Cabinet last year. On the whole, I adhere to the views I then expressed, though perhaps less strongly than at the time when the subject was first raised. But I confess that I had never contemplated, and am a good deal staggered at, the idea of the trial taking place in England; and, the more I reflect upon it, the more I am inclined to think that we may be on the verge of committing a great mistake."

He then set out his reasons—that prejudice against the Kaiser might preclude him from having a fair trial; that the King, as his relative, might be embarrassed; and that unseemly disturbances would probably take place. He was, he said, still in favour of the trial—so long as it took place outside England. But the whole tone of his letter suggested that he wished he had never written his original exhortation to vengeance.

And, of course, Lloyd George was aware of this. He wrote back:

"The arguments you advance against trying the Kaiser in England I had already heard from the King—every one of them. I therefore presume it was the result of a conversation you had with H. M. . . . All the reasons which you assign are really arguments against trying the Kaiser at all. You tell me that Churchill and Milner agreed with you. Of course they did; they were firmly opposed to a trial. They are, therefore, quite consistent in their attitude. You, on the other hand, took the initiative in proposing this trial. The proposal you made was ultimately adopted by the Cabinet, pressed on their behalf on our Allies, and ultimately adopted by them after a full investigation by a very able Commission representing the leading Allies, including Belgium. To go back on it now would indeed be not only to make the representatives of this country at the Paris Conference look silly, but to make Britain, France, Belgium and all the other Allies look extremely foolish."

Curzon swallowed the rebuke. The Kaiser was, of course, never brought to trial because the Dutch refused to give him up. And Curzon now had much more important things to think about.

CHAPTER TWELVE

The Pains of Office

Yet it was upon the slogans of "Hang the Kaiser" and "Make Germany Pay" that Lloyd George won the 1918 General Election and carried George Nathaniel Curzon back to office with him.

It may seem, at this distance, that he need not have made this appeal to the British public's hunger for revenge in order to re-establish himself at the head of the nation. For in spite of all the internecine struggles and intrigues, the quarrels and the upsets—and in spite of the hatred his Celtic temperament aroused among his enemies—Lloyd George had been a great Prime Minister. Once again in her hour of need Britain had not failed to produce the man best capable of leading her to victory. It seems tragic that he had to appeal to the worst prejudices and murkier emotions of the people in order to get back. (Though who, in view of Churchill's experience in 1945, will dare to say that he was not right?)

It is a measure of the way in which Curzon's character was shaping now that he found himself in Lloyd George's postwar Cabinet at all. Earlier in the year he had shown himself determined to support, once peace came, nothing less than a return to the old party lines in politics. He was dead against a continuation of the Coalition, with, he suspected, its gradual creation of a Centre Party that would cut across the old division between the Tories and the Liberals. He had written to Bonar Law (February, 1918):

"I should like to say at once that the movement [towards a continuance of the Coalition] is one which not only can I not support, but which I think would be entirely mistaken. As matters stand, I agree that if there were to be a General Election in the near future, it would be the duty of our party to give the fullest support to the Prime Minister for the prosecution of the war to the end—the object, indeed the sole object, for which the Coalition was formed and still exists. But, from the idea that our party should merge its identity in some new party, or should pledge its allegiance after peace has returned, I entirely dissent and I hope that you as our Leader will give no encouragement to it."

But with the coming of peace, and perhaps because he felt it certain that Lloyd George would be bound to win the coming election, he changed his mind.

If others appeared to have their doubts about Curzon's future prowess as a statesman, Lloyd George did not at this time count himself among them. On the contrary, he made it quite clear to his Lord President of the Council that he needed him, and that, if only the Coalition could continue, there would be no limit to the power and responsibility he might achieve. The golden apples of perpetual political happiness, Lloyd George hinted, were glowing just over the horizon, ready for Curzon to pluck. But only by sticking to the well-trodden Coalition road would he reach them.

It at once seemed to Curzon that a continuation of the Coalition was an urgent national necessity, and in November, 1918, he wrote to Bonar Law in a very different strain.

"I had a few words with the Prime Minister about the Gen-

eral Election this afternoon. I told him that I was in favour of as
early a General Election as can be managed. I think the Government (I am assuming that they go to the country as a Coalition Government asking for a renewal of support) require a fresh
national mandate if they are either to conduct the war to an end
—should the Armistice break down—or if they are to undertake
the even more difficult labours of the Peace Conference."

And his letter concluded: "One thing is certain, viz., that the
old party programmes are obsolete. Asquith's attempt to serve
up the stale dishes of his—and the reception it has met with—
are sufficient proof of this."

In a statesman who made less of a parade of his political
rectitude, this about face might have been received by his colleagues with a cynical smile. In Curzon's case, they accepted it
as one more nail which they would hammer into his political
coffin.

He followed his letter to Bonar Law with one to Lloyd
George in which he said:

"I wrote to Bonar as you suggested about General Election."

The Coalition Government was swept back into power in the
winter of 1918. On January 3, 1919, Curzon was in bed at
1 Carlton House Terrace when Lord Robert Cecil came round
with a message from the Prime Minister. He and Balfour, the
Foreign Secretary, were about to leave for Paris to take part in
the protracted and difficult negotiations with the Allies to draw
up the peace treaty. Would Curzon, in their absence, take over
as Acting Foreign Secretary, it being understood that when
Balfour returned at the end of the year he would resign and
Curzon be appointed Foreign Secretary in his place?

It was Curzon's reward for faithful service to Lloyd George,
and he accepted with alacrity.

On Monday, January 6, 1919, he imperiously ordered the
removal of the "brass and glass" inkstand, waved aside his
minions, and sat down for the first time behind the desk of His

Majesty's Minister for Foreign Affairs. On Thursday of that same week he celebrated his sixtieth birthday, and he had good reason to feel pleased with himself. It was forty-one years since his admiring friends had talked about the "brief interval" between his departure from Eton and his arrival at the Foreign Office, but he had made it at last.

Now to set the world to rights—and then march on to the premiership.

THERE WAS some strange poison in Curzon's hands, as will have been realised by now, that seemed to put a tarnish on everything he touched. He held the golden apples in his fingers, and even as he gazed at their bright and promising gleam, they started to go rotten.

It was a blight that did not confine itself to his political dreams and ambitions, but permeated his private life too.

He was by this time only too well aware that the idyll of his new marriage was over. There had been tiffs during their courtship and quarrels during the first year of marriage, most of them caused by Curzon's intense preoccupation with his official duties and Grace's suspicion (almost certainly false) that he was neglecting her for other women. Curzon had always hoped that Grace would be like his first wife, Mary, content to wait upon the wishes and attendance of her lord in loving patience.

Grace Curzon was not that kind of woman. She needed attention, she needed distraction, and when she did not get them she sulked or fumed. To punish Curzon, she determined to stay away from him. As early as 1918, she began what was to become the habit of separation (which she grew to like and Curzon increasingly to hate). The pattern of their relationship is indicated by a letter which Curzon sent to Grace at Hackwood on December 31, 1918:

"My darling wife,—I was so hurt at your letter this morning

that I wrote you a reply which however I will not send. Your telegram has decided me against that. After all I am coming down tomorrow to spend the first anniversary of our wedding day with you. I shall come with love in my heart and all the memory of one year of married life. Has that not been enough, my darling, to prove to us both that we can both be happy and keep us both happy. Life is a momentous thing and we can meet it safely if we are not always reverting to the past which has perished and gone. If we trust instead to our own experience together and to the better virtues of our nature we will find in our mutual confidence a firm guarantee of the future. I will come down by the 3-25 tomorrow."

This was followed by a letter dated January 3, 1919, saying:

"Darling Grace,—I was sorry you would not let me come down to Hackwood for our wedding day. I felt it very deeply."

In the course of the next few years, he was to pour out a copious stream of letters to Grace. He did so because, at all the moments when he most needed her, when he was sick or depressed or in pain and desperately longing for her comforting presence, Grace Curzon was rarely with him. She had begun to find all sorts of excuses for being away. One of them was her brother, Trillia, who had been gassed on the Western Front during the war and was slowly dying of tuberculosis. He was well provided with pretty nurses, and the devoted attendance of his mother and another sister, but when it was decided to send him to Switzerland, Grace announced that her presence was necessary, and she went with him, staying in Paris for a long period on her way back.

What she and Curzon still shared was the desire for a son and heir, but he was beginning to suspect that even in this he was doomed to be disappointed; though he never, even up to the last, really lost hope.

"I do hope my darling is NOT ill," he wrote, in April, 1919, "though I have fears. We have been so often disappointed."

On the advice of their friend, the Queen of the Belgians, who had tried them successfully before the war, Grace decided to undergo a course of mudbaths at the German spa of Langen-schwalbach, and her letters are filled with complaints about the rigours of the experience.

"The mud sounds very disgusting," he wrote to her, but added: "God grant that your pilgrimage may have the consequences we both pray for and desire."

The doctors' reports were encouraging, but the eventual results were not.

When Grace wrote to him in terms of love and affection, then he was overjoyed. "My darling sweet girlie," he wrote, "This morning I received the precious loving letter from my Girl in which she said that she loved her Boy and would like to put her arms around his neck. So indeed would he, and you may be sure that all the time, in the midst of my own work, I am thinking of my beloved wife suffering distress and inconvenience and sometimes pain for me, and for what is yet to be. It will be worthwhile —later on, darling, and we shall bless the days and hours of the trial you are going through."

But more often he was writing in this strain:

"I have got your nasty letter. Rather too bad, girlie, considering my 38 loving letters to you."

He was beginning to learn that when Grace was displeased with him she had an even more practical way of showing it than just writing him bad-tempered or accusing letters. She withheld his allowance (she was giving him £5,000 a year) and, on at least two occasions, stopped her cheques after she had sent them to him. In a letter from Spa, in Belgium, where he was leading the British delegation at the renewed peace negotiations, he breaks off a long description of his arguments with the French and Italian delegations to say:

"Today the bank returned to me your two cheques of June 6 and July 6. Perhaps you will let me know when they can be presented. I kept them back for over a month but there must have been some contretemps. . . . Meanwhile, I have a faint idea that Lady Curzon of Kedleston (whom I thought to have been in Scotland) is kicking up her heels and probably having a quite agreeable time in the unfortunate (?) absence of her husband."

IT IS NOT SURPRISING that, when his back was bad or when things were going badly in the Cabinet, Curzon's temper was short. His subordinates in the Foreign Office soon learned that he could be both imperious and insulting. He had as little time for most of them (and gave them as little consideration) as he had extended to his aides in India. And only too often his minions, Vansittart, Leeper, Nicolson, even the chief of them, Tyrrell, felt the lash of his words and the frost of his contempt. But they were Civil Servants and had to put up with him. His domestic servants did not. Curzon still insisted on hiring all his servants personally, and each morning he held a parade of his butler, footmen, and housemaids to inspect their uniform and dress and examine the state of their nails. Backstairs gossip soon spread the rumour among London's domestics that he was a terror to work for, and he found it increasingly difficult to get servants or keep them.

"Of course the doctor is right when he says I should not worry," he wrote to Grace, "but who can guarantee that with Chope [the butler] and our particular class of servants? . . . I told you yesterday that the long lout of a footman was willing to stay for a few more days, to help us pending the news of the man we engaged and who has run away on the manufactured excuse of a sick aunt in Reading. The latter we have not heard a word from since, and it is only too evident that he has broken his engagement. That is bad enough. But when I returned at 8.30 last night for dinner, I learned that the big man had also run away in the afternoon. So we were left with a new valet, three footmen, and odd man!"

Finding a suitable valet was the bane of Curzon's existence. They had to see him, and dress him, at his worst moments and they quickly emulated the cooks in the old story; they may have been good valets as valets go; but as valets go, they went.

"Yesterday morning, I spent one and a half hours going through all my clothes with the new valet," he wrote. "He walked in at twelve today and said he could not stay. He found that his health would not stand it. He had varicose veins which caused him intense pain and made it impossible for him to run up and down stairs. He also had bad gastritis (hence his foul breath) and realised he must have an outdoor life. I pointed out that he might have told me all this before entering my service. He admitted all this and had no reply. So he goes at the end of the month, after being in the home one day. What on earth am I to do? I am in absolute despair. And now I have to go down and make a big speech on Ireland, about which I know practically nothing. Pity me, my darling girl."

Curzon's most extraordinary experience with his valets occurred later on, when he hired one at short notice just before leaving London for the Lausanne Conference. As Sir Harold Nicolson reveals in his delicious book of sketches, *Some People,* most of the Foreign Secretary's aides quickly realised that the man—Nicolson called him Arketall—was a dedicated devotee of the bottle. He boarded the train at Victoria Station half-tipsy, and he never thereafter retreated from this condition. But Curzon himself, his mind soaring through the lofty stratosphere of high diplomacy, did not at first notice this. In fact, Curzon rather liked him, since, unlike his predecessors, he never seemed to take offence when rebuked. No one warned Curzon of his servant's alcoholic proclivities. Instead, his aides stood aside and watched him in fascinated amusement, waiting for the crash to come. It took quite a time. Arketall had thought up a wonderful wheeze for getting his hands on the alcohol he needed. He announced to the management of the hotel where the British delegation was staying that his master, being the apostle of peace, was the enemy of all the dark forces who wished to throw Europe back into the abyss of war. The Secret Service had warned him that attempts would be made to poison the Foreign Secretary's drink, and therefore Arketall had been delegated to test them first. Each evening the management sent up two or three new bottles of brandy or liqueurs (he was particularly devoted to Green Chartreuse) and each night Arketall retired to bed and swigged them.

He might well have gone on swigging them, too, if he had not, one night, become so emboldened by drink and his belief in his own immunity, that he dressed himself up in Curzon's evening clothes and went down to join the guests at a dance below. Mingling with the world of high diplomacy, his ambitions soared, and soon he was dancing with the delegates' wives.

Then at last, his aides felt it necessary to break the horrid truth to Curzon. Arketall had gone too far. Curzon ordered the man not only to be dismissed on the spot but to be put on the first train back to England. He was sent to his room to pack his clothes and go.

It was only after he had been safely seen on to the train that the awful discovery was made that all Curzon's trousers were missing. The dreadful drunken valet had stolen the great man's pants. While Curzon stormed, trouserless, up and down his room, his aides telephoned the authorities to arrest Arketall at the frontier. But in the meantime, one of them decided to have a look at Arketall's room. Under the bed, he found several dozen empty bottles of Green Chartreuse. Under the mattress, he discovered the Foreign Secretary's missing trousers.

As a sidelight on the unpredictableness of George Nathaniel Curzon, it must be recorded that over this particular domestic disaster his rage soon turned to laughter. "I rather liked that man," he said. But he also wrote to Grace Curzon to tell her to pay him nothing more than the week's wages that were due to him.

Trouble with his wife. Trouble with his domestics. And trouble, too, over money.

Curzon had never believed in living meanly. As a member of the governing classes, he considered it a necessary duty to keep up the standard by not only owning great houses but also using them to entertain his colleagues in a manner to which they could have seldom elsewhere become accustomed. In his papers is a letter (August 29, 1923) which begins: "I hear that snake Lord Derby is near to you. He is always intriguing against me, Grace. I have evidence." He then goes on:

"I spent a vile day yesterday paying bills, making up accounts. I made a summary of the exact total expenditure which *I* have had to meet in 1922. You might like to see it so I send you a copy. Although we do next to no entertaining, we are living on a scale which seems incredible. The wage bill alone, which used to be £90 a month, is always £200."

The list appended shows the following record:

1922.	1. Carlton House Terrace and Hackwood rent, rates, living, repairs, wages, entertainment	£20,389–15–3
	plus	209– 8–0
	(Chope's wage book: £9,415)	
	2. Hackwood, rents, rates, taxes, gardeners	2,496
	3. Montacute ditto	1,589
	4. Naldera	299
	5. Income Tax and Supertax	6,067
	6. Sandra [his daughter, Alexandra]	1,025
	7. Personal gifts	294
TOTAL	(excluding all expenditure at Kedleston, Bodiam, Oxford)	£32,371.

The total may not exactly match the figures, but it certainly gives a glimpse of the scale upon which Curzon was wont to live. Yet he worried about every item in his bills, which he never failed to supervise personally.

"Darling, I have had a horrid row with Chope over bills. Girlie, we must draw in on flowers. I found that Stevens' minimum charge for flowers, even at a lunch, is £22, and every time he puts a basket in the stand on the staircase he charges two guineas. His bill for three occasions only is £75. With my reduced income, I cannot manage it. Mrs. Moon sends me an account for simply fooling about at Hackwood for seven months for £105. How can I go on paying these sums? Oh, dear!"

Just before this he had written: "Do you realise that your Eton dance [for her son] cost you £300, and that the household expenses for June and July, which I have just been asked to pay, amounted to £2,150?"

And he added: "Here I am, still on my back. It is a very persistent attack this time, and I mend but slowly. I also lie awake at night worrying about money matters, for I have nothing in the bank and I don't know how to go on. I hope you will soon, Gracie, help me with those debts of £2,400, October to April? Now the lawyer is bombarding me for £2,000 for Irene's surtax. I have not got it. My daughters will be the death of me."

For what he had long had to bear in mind had come to pass, and his children were coming of age and going out into the world, thus reducing his income.

Irene had already departed. Now it was his second daughter's turn. Cynthia wanted to get married.

"She had come to ask my permission to marry young Oswald Mosley," he wrote to Grace. "He is M.P. for Harrow and one of the youngest members of the House, where, I believe, he has made something of a mark. . . . I asked her he if he was gay or sedate. She replied that he had begun by flirting a bit with married women, but had now (at the age of 23!) given that up and was full of ambition and devoted to a political career where every sort of prize awaits him. I said of course if she had made her choice and it was a wise one, no one would welcome it more than myself, but that I ought to see him before I gave my assent. . . . I asked if he had any means. She did not know. As he had a motor and a flat, she thought yes! Was he marrying her for love, or was he thinking of her money? Oh, no, such an idea had not crossed his mind. They were going to have a great career together and he was going to climb to the very top—with her aid."

He saw Oswald Mosley the following day: "Very young, tall, slim, dark, rather a big nose, little black moustache, rather a Jewish appearance," and he gave his consent. But he told Grace: "It will make it easier for all of us if it is all right, though I suppose that financially it will hit me rather hard."

It was in this happy atmosphere that the engagement of his daughter to Oswald Mosley was announced. In a rush of gratitude for his willingness, Cynthia told Curzon that (unlike her elder sister) she would not insist on taking her allowance away from her father, but would be satisfied with the provision of a substantial marriage settlement. But she was soon to regret this. She and her husband were involved in some financial losses over the failure of a political newspaper in which they were interested, and she was soon back, demanding her portion. She got it, but not before the lawyers had been consulted. Curzon had tried to alter the provisions of the will of Levi Leiter, Cynthia Mosley's grandfather. To Grace he wrote:

"The excellent Tom Mosley has been to see Humbert [the legal adviser] and, in the same breath, talks about the value he and Cim [Cynthia] attach to paternal and filial relations, and their serious thoughts of going to law! The latter is a mere bluff. Of course, one thing is certain—they mean to take the whole money, and I think the best thing to do is to say: Take it. I cannot stand this perpetual torrent of threats and abuse and insinuation. But I am going to write an account of my administration of what *they* call *their* money since their mother died, and of what they have done to me. They shall have this. And there I will leave it."

It was against this background of domestic upheaval, dissatisfaction, disappointment, mental and financial worry, and physical distress, that George Nathaniel Curzon had to face the problems of His Majesty's Minister for Foreign Affairs in one of the most difficult periods in the history of Western civilisation.

CHAPTER THIRTEEN

"Lord Alabaster"

F OR A TIME everything went splendidly—as it always did at
first. With Lloyd George away in Paris, Curzon was often
called upon to preside over the Cabinet, and this never
failed to exhilarate him; a proconsular urbanity came into his
voice, and from his position at the head of the table he was able
to look at his colleagues with the cool patronage of a leader
instead of the suspicious acerbity of an equal. "George Curzon
is rehearsing for premier again," whispered Austen Chamberlain.

Since Balfour was also in Paris, Curzon had the run of the
Foreign Office, too, and he kept his subordinates constantly on
the jump. In came the ambassadors of foreign nations, to be
gently lectured on Britain's place in the new-won world. Out
went the peremptory instructions to Britain's representatives
abroad. And each evening a Foreign Office messenger carried
across to Carlton House Terrace the boxes of diplomatic telegrams over which Curzon loved to pore, in a kind of joyful
misery, through the long night hours.

"Last night I had my solitary dinner and then 27 boxes—the
record to date," he wrote to Grace. The routine was always the

same. He picked glumly and complainingly at his food—for he hated the "soggy messes" the fashionable French chef served up for him—and then retired to his study, where the valet of the moment stacked his boxes, opened a bottle of champagne, and helped his master tighten his harness. Then he would read and sip and make notes until three or four in the morning, after which he would climb upstairs to bed and read on until his nightly dose of sleeping drug had taken effect.

This was a solitary labour about which he often complained. "Your letter brings a little tear to my eye," he wrote to Grace while she was away in Paris. "For I contrast your social and gay enjoyment with my ceaseless and tireless routine." But when things were going well he enjoyed his bouts with his boxes, for they contained the tangible evidence of his position and power. One scribbled note from him, and an ambassador in a faraway place must dance to his tune.

And yet, after all these years, nothing gave him quite as much pleasure as making a speech and basking in the praise or applause which followed it. "My dinner at St. Stephen's Club on Tuesday night went off very well," he wrote. "Jim Salisbury was in the chair, and I chaffed him for the first 5-10 minutes, and then gave them about forty-five minutes of foreign affairs, chatting to them in confidence and without preparation." And on a later occasion, after the Premier's return, he wrote: "Last night at Ll. G.'s dinner, he made a speech and then Bonar [Law]. I thought the whole thing was over when there were loud calls for me, and I had to get up and make an impromptu oration of a quasi-chaffing character, which was much applauded. Then F. E. [F. E. Smith, later Lord Birkenhead] followed with what I thought was a very ill-timed harangue about the House of Lords. And then, when dim and incredible females began to arrive, I slipped off to my boxes."

Lloyd George was settling the fate of Europe in Paris, and

this gave Curzon the opportunity of playing in his favourite diplomatic backyard, Asia. All the time the Premier and Balfour were away, he worked with patient enthusiasm on a pet project, the formulation of a new Anglo-Persian Treaty, which, he believed, would stabilize relations with that country and strengthen the defensive boundaries of India against Russian ambitions. On August 16, 1919, the treaty was signed and Curzon was joyful and triumphant. He was less so, a year later, when the treaty collapsed, but meanwhile he wrote to Grace:

"The papers give a good reception to my Persian Treaty, which I have been negotiating for the past year, and which is a great triumph as I have done it all alone. But not a single paper as much as mentions my name, or has the dimmest perception that, had I not been at the F. O., it would never have been done at all. I only wonder that they do not attribute it to the superhuman skill and genius of Ll. G."

He was never very fond of the Press. They rarely reported his speeches at the length he considered they deserved. They criticised his actions. He was always to regard them as the paid spokesmen for his opponents' intrigues.

This period of euphoria lasted for about six months, during which even the absence of Grace did not overmuch perturb him. He could write to her in a playful mood, saying: "Please don't come back from Paris with dresses showing your beautiful legs. I concede much to modern fashion, but not *that*." But swiftly his suspicions of his colleagues—and his contempt for their incompetence—returned, and the period was approaching when he would begin to think that the world (or at least the Cabinet) was against him more virulently than ever.

"This morning," he wrote on August 20, 1919, "at the end of our third Cabinet—it lasted three and a half hours—in the last twenty-four hours, the conclusion was reached which I have always predicted must come. The Cabinet, led by the P. M., asked me to go over to Paris and take in hand the Eastern question and *gave me authority for any settlement that I might like to effect.*"

Curzon would normally have jumped at this opportunity to demonstrate his ability to pluck success from other men's failures. But now he hesitated. Turkey and the Middle East were in ferment, and the Allies could not make up their minds what to do about them. He was still only Acting Foreign Secretary, and he suspected that if he did achieve a success, Lloyd George and Balfour would get the credit for it, and if he failed, he would get the blame. It was a period of his life, he decided, when at all costs—if he was to reinforce his prestige with the public and with his own Party—he must avoid a setback.

So he wavered. "I said at once that I could not go out now. I was tired and needed my holiday as much as A. J. B. [Balfour] and must insist on taking it." And, for the first time, his resentment against Lloyd George broke the surface and was never to be submerged again. "Now that things in Paris are in an inextricable mess, the P. M. says that nothing will induce him to go back. He got the glory of the peace with Germany and does not mean to have the discredit of the failure elsewhere. A. J. B. wants to clear out. So I am left, as usual, to clear up the mess."

He procrastinated and complained all through the next few weeks. "I am heartily sick of this indeterminate position," he wrote, "possessing full powers in one set of things, but powerless in others, pursuing a definite policy here which may be thrown over any day in Paris. You can realise the unsatisfactory and almost humiliating position in being, at the same time, Secretary of State and yet only a substitute. Actually, A. J. B. has never yet answered my letter about going to Paris written nearly three weeks ago."

Lloyd George terminated that avenue of objection by persuading Balfour to change places with Curzon, who was now confirmed as titular, as well as actual, Foreign Secretary. Now at last he could be master in his own house.

But he soon discovered that he was not.

IN THE CRITICISM which Curzon was afterwards to express over A. J. Balfour's tenure of office as Foreign Secretary there is much truth. For rarely can there have been a man in the history of British statesmanship who cared less about the eventual results of the aims and objects of the policies he espoused. In him, the whole system by which politicians reached power and wielded it in Curzon's day was indicted. He had brains and talents, but he had come to office not because of them, but by inheritance. He was a typical product of the Eton incubator. The clan-loyalty of the Salisburys was behind him from the moment he entered politics, and it gave him everything he needed—security, political *droit de seigneur*—everything except the sense of mission and responsibility for the future which is the gift of the politician-turned-statesman. He could look upon his colleagues in the Lloyd George Cabinet and sneer at them as a bunch of careerists; and it was true. "It is no use worrying about Lloyd George," he once told Curzon. "He is not a gentleman, and never will be." But Lloyd George was like many another upstart in the politics of the day—a careerist who had entered politics not, like Balfour, because it was expected of him by his elegant and admiring contemporaries, but because it offered opportunities of advancement. But once he had won his place, the position rather than the man took over; and despite all the selfishness and intrigue in which he indulged, it could never be said of Lloyd George that he was not conscious, as he legislated, of the future consequences of his legislation.

With Balfour, the position could not make the man because he was supremely aware from the start that the man was already made. He almost literally did not care what future historians

thought of him, being satisfied in himself with his *raison-d'être*.
He had touched the heights as Prime Minister (though a bad
one), and he did not care whether he was a good Foreign Minister or not. He did not care or protest when Lloyd George
usurped his functions at the Paris Conference. What did it matter what the little upstart did? He was only appealing to *hoi-
polloi*, the voters, the mass-millions out of which he had come.
Balfour did not have to rely upon the vagaries of the people;
breeding and background, rather than achievement, was his
insurance.

Curzon had seen, in his first nine months as Acting Foreign
Minister, how far Balfour, in this complacent mood, had let
things slide. As Foreign Minister during the war, he had, of
course, not unnaturally taken a back seat. He had not even been
a member of the War Cabinet, and the Prime Minister and his
service chiefs had always been in full control of affairs. But with
the coming of peace, why had not Balfour brought the position
and responsibility of his office back into the forefront of affairs?

Curzon indicted him for this failure in these devastating
words:

"In December, 1918, after the Armistice, Balfour went to
Paris with the British delegation, and I acted for him at the
Foreign Office in London. It was during that period that the
fatal ascendancy and interference of [Lloyd George] in Foreign
Affairs was allowed to establish itself so firmly that they could
only be ultimately uprooted by [Lloyd George's] disappearance;
and the chief culprit was undoubtedly Balfour. From an early
stage, he—a former Prime Minister and the Foreign Minister of
the British Empire—allowed himself to be displaced in Paris and
pushed aside."

This was indeed true. Lloyd George created a system of high-
powered political meetings which have since become familiar
in this age, and in order to get the peace discussions down to
bedrock, reduced the composition of the policy-making commit-

tee to the four heads of State: himself, Wilson for America, Clemenceau for France, and Orlando for Italy. But it might have been expected that Balfour would have kept in touch with what was going on. Curzon insisted (and it has never been denied) that he did not.

"Though he was living on the floor immediately below Ll. G.'s rooms," Curzon wrote, "he did not know, was not told, and was as a rule too careless to inquire, what was going on. I can speak of this from my own knowledge since, on the few occasions when I was summoned to Paris during that year, Balfour freely admitted it, and in his half-cynical, half-nonchalant way, expressed his astonishment and his ignorance of what the little man was doing."

The ferment in the Middle East came to a head when the Greek armies swarmed ashore, twenty thousand strong, at Smyrna. They killed the Turkish troops who opposed them. They ravaged the Turkish population. And they did it with the consent of Lloyd George (always violently pro-Greek), Clemenceau, and Wilson.

Curzon was not the only member of the British Cabinet to consider this a fatal mistake. "I well remember the bewilderment and alarm [writes Winston Churchill in *The World Crisis*] with which I heard on a lovely afternoon in Paris of this fatal mistake. . . . All the half-raked fires of Pan-Turkism began to glow again. That Greeks should conquer Turks was not a decree of Fate which any Turk would recognise."

The Turks had been ready to accept their defeat at the hands of the British in the war. But now, with the hated Greeks upon their backs, they began to fight again, and they produced their man of the hour, Kemal Pasha, to restore their independence, their nationality, and their pride.

"I cannot understand to this day," writes Churchill, "how the eminent statesmen in Paris, Wilson, Lloyd George, Clemenceau and Venizelos [the Greek Premier] whose wisdom, pride and address had raised them under the severest tests so much above their fellows, could have been betrayed into so rash and fatal a step."

But, Curzon pointed out, Balfour was not aware of and was never consulted over "the calamitous invitation of the Greeks to Smyrna. He was equally ignorant and indifferent to what was going on behind the curtain. He played lawn tennis and attended concerts and presided with exquisite courtesy over the British Delegation, and charmed everybody by his manners, and steadily, day by day, pulled the extinguisher more firmly down on the head of his own Department until it almost ceased to have a separate existence."

In case the point he was making had not become sufficiently clear, Curzon went on:

"The above remarks may be held to constitute an attack upon the conduct and capacities of Balfour as Foreign Minister. They do. I regard him as the worst and most dangerous of the British Foreign Ministers with whom I have been brought into contact in my political life. His charm of manner, his extraordinary intellectual distinction, his seeming indifference to petty matters, his power of dialectic, his long and honourable career of public service, blinded all but those who knew him from the inside to the lamentable ignorance, indifference and levity of his regime. He never studied his papers, he never knew the facts, at the Cabinet he had seldom read the morning's Foreign Office telegrams, and he never looked ahead. He trusted to his unequalled powers of improvisation to take him through any trouble and enable him to leap lightly from one crisis to another."

And he added:

"So the drama went on throughout the fatal year. Lloyd George was supposed to be upholding the flag of Britain, and Balfour that of the Foreign Office with sustained and vigorous brilliance in Paris. In reality, Ll. G. was sowing the seeds of European disaster. Balfour was signing the abdication of the

Foreign Office. When I succeeded him in October, 1919, the mischief was already done."

It may well be asked why, in that case, Curzon ever consented to take on the job at all. Anticipating that someone would ask just this question, he left behind several "Notes for my Biographer" in which he eloquently argues his justification.

"It is not in a spirit of egotism but with truth that I add the following reflection. I thought it my duty in the interests both of the Foreign Office and of the Conservative Party to remain in the Government—of the Foreign Office because both they and I felt the greatest apprehension at the possible or probable appointment that might be made in my place; of my party because I was one of the few representatives in the Government of the older Conservatives and of the older traditions and ideals of public life, which under the hectic influence of the Lloyd George regime were in danger of fast disappearing. The Foreign Office staff and the principal ambassadors abroad, if they heard of my likely resignation, implored me not to carry it out. My Conservative colleagues in the Cabinet abounded in the same advice. I think that they and I were right, for it was only by staying on that I was enabled to defeat the war scare in the autumn of 1922, and twice to save the country from the imminent peril of war."

Curzon's colleagues were to express rather more cynical explanations of his conduct, as will be seen.

Now it was undoubtedly true that Lloyd George was inclined to keep as close a control upon foreign affairs in the postwar period as he had exercised during the war itself. He did so because he distrusted the type of mind which prevailed in the Foreign Office and suspected that the superiority of breeding, background, and tradition which the officials of that department affected were but cloaks to conceal incompetence, rigidity, and lack of foresight. He believed that the Foreign Office regarded him as an upstart, and what was worse, as an amateur who must, at all costs, be kept ignorant of the manoeuvres of an essentially

professional game; and he was determined that so long as he
was Prime Minister, he would never fail to demonstrate that he
was the captain of the team. The exercise of a little of that Celtic
charm and tact, which he could muster in such abundance when
he was inclined, might easily have won the loyalty and support
of the Foreign Office. Curzon came to them from their own class
and tradition, but it would be stretching a point to say that the
Foreign Office personnel really liked him. He hectored and
bullied them. "He always made one aware that one was subordinate, and never that one was necessary," Vansittart afterwards
said.

But Lloyd George, pliant in so many things, did not realise
this and would not temper his class-consciousness to the extent
of making use of the formidable Foreign Office tradition of duty,
service, and experience. Whenever possible, he used nondiplo-
matic emissaries to carry out his missions. One of his favourites
was Field Marshal Smuts. And, starting during the war, he gradually built up a secretariat of which Philip Kerr (later Lord
Lothian) was the head, and Edward Grigg (later Lord Grigg)
was an occasional go-between. They conducted what Curzon
was afterwards to describe, bitterly, as "the Second Foreign
Office."

Though Curzon complained about this division of power,
there is no doubt that so long as it suited him, he accepted it.
"Foreign policy being for the time being synonymous with the
execution of the Treaties," he wrote, "he [Lloyd George] could
not be denied a predominant voice in the execution of his own
handiwork." He raged about the difficulty of establishing contact
with the Premier—for Lloyd George could sleep, and Curzon
could not. "He rarely answered or even acknowledged a letter.
During the six years I served under him as one of his principal
ministers, I think that his letters to me (in response to many
from me) were less than six in number. If I marked a file to him
from the Foreign Office, with a query for his assent or opinion,

it would not be returned for days, or not at all. In the mornings
he was usually absorbed with conferences or meetings, with
his cronies such as Churchill. In the afternoon, he had the habit
of going to bed and to sleep and refusing to be disturbed. He
was commonly pleasant to meet and easy and friendly in private conversation. But the close intercourse which ought to
exist between the Prime Minister and his Foreign Secretary
did not exist."

What did not occur to Curzon, not unnaturally, was that
the Prime Minister considered him as the tag end of the old-
established gang of hereditary rulers whose automatic assumption of the positions of power he was determined to challenge.
He had appointed Curzon as his Foreign Minister, but he placed
no reliance in him. Once he had admired his skill and foresight.
Now he had begun to be bored by his verbosity, had become
suspicious of his loyalty, and was tolerating him only because
he believed—and continued believing to the end—that Curzon
commanded the influence of the Tory Party. He needed not a
strong Foreign Minister but a weak and amenable one. He
believed that in Curzon, anxious to keep office at all costs, he
had got one. What he did not realise was the anger, frustration,
and hatred that would grow in Curzon's breast as he began to
realise why he had been chosen. It was, in Curzon's view
(though perhaps Lloyd George had not intended it that way),
the final humiliation—and when the opportunity came for revenge,
Curzon did not miss it.

The first year of office was a succession of conferences in
which the Allies vainly tried to find a formula for the resolution
of the problems which had been thrown up by the war. The
delegations moved from Paris to San Remo, from San Remo to
Spa, and from Spa to Cannes. They covered miles of ground
and acres of typescript, but came no nearer to settling their
antagonisms. And all the time, they were dogged by the delegations from the small nations of Europe and Asia pleading for

a voice in the eventual settlement. "Crowds of people from every land under the sun," wrote Curzon, "Syrians, Zionists, Armenians, Poles, Ukrainians, Chaldeans, everyone who wants to influence the conference. They take rooms in the same hotels as we are, and they dog our footsteps wherever we go."

And meanwhile, Curzon's resentment against Lloyd George grew. He wrote to Grace: "Darling, I am getting very tired of trying to work with that man. He wants his Foreign Secretary to be a valet and a drudge, and he has no regard for the convenience or civilities of official life."

The Prime Minister was, in fact, beginning to be tired of his Foreign Secretary. He considered that Curzon talked too much, and had got into the habit of cutting him short in midflight. Curzon had never got over his contempt for the French, of whom he once remarked that "they are not the sort of people one would go tiger-shooting with;" and Lloyd George found that he got on better with Briand (at that time French Premier and Foreign Secretary) when Curzon was not there. Over one such meeting, held at Sir Philip Sassoon's house at Lympne, Curzon considered that he had been deliberately snubbed. "I am also in trouble," he wrote to Grace, "over the extraordinary tactics of the P. M. over Lympne. He has been trying by every manner of means to keep me from going, on the grounds that it ought to be a conference between Briand and himself alone. When, moreover, it transpired that the former insisted on bringing Berthelot, as there were other Foreign Office affairs to be discussed, I sent Vansittart [his chief assistant] over to enquire whether I should be expected to go as well. He returned no answer, but telephoned to Vansittart without even consulting me ordering him to go to Lympne tomorrow in my stead. Being quite ignorant whether this is merely one of his slapdash movements or whether it masks, as it appears to do, a deliberate affront, I asked A. J. B. [Balfour] to come round and see me, which he did before lunch. He was very much perturbed and thought the action deplorable. He promised to find out what it meant."

Lloyd George on this occasion sent round a note of apology, saying he had been told that Curzon was ill and could not come; but, in fact, the Premier just did not want his Foreign Secretary around.

From this incident, Curzon added one more name to the list of those he considered his enemies. Vansittart, having gone to the meeting, was now considered a member of the hostile camp. Once he had called him "my tower of strength." Now he described him as "hesitant. I fear he will be no use to me." He rebuked him for getting too much notice in the newspapers when he was married, telling him it was his job to get publicity for the Foreign Secretary and not for himself. "He appeared to believe I had the Press in my pocket," remarked Vansittart, "and blamed me when a critical story about him was published."

In fact, Vansittart was extremely loyal to his chief, and even refused the offer of the post as Lloyd George's political adviser on the grounds that it would offend the Foreign Secretary "and put me among the enemy." But Curzon would not believe this. "I declined in favour despite all endeavours to serve," wrote Vansittart. "When informed by telephone at Kedleston that a foreign statesman of the first rank and second order was dead, he snorted: 'Do you realise that to convey to me this trivial information, you have brought me the length of a mansion not far removed from the dimensions of Windsor Castle?'"

His temper was getting shorter, his manner with his subordinates increasingly testy. "Clerks paled in the presence," recalled Vansittart, "door-keepers fled, when, imperiously driving our primitive lift, he embedded himself waist-deep in the basement. There was lightness in the mornings, for he spent them at Christie's, well-versed in all works of art, having telephoned at ten to make sure I was punctual. Harold Nicolson laughed as, trained to the minute, I spurted across the Horse Guards' Parade."

Curzon came to believe that it was as a result of his opposition to Lloyd George's policies that the Premier held back for a year the marquisate which, he maintained, was the reward he deserved for his services in the War Cabinet.

"It was in November, 1920," he wrote, "that first A. Bonar Law and afterwards the Prime Minister (David Lloyd George) spoke to me about the intention of the latter to propose my elevation to a Marquisate (after being Leader of the House of Lords for 4 years, a member of the War Cabinet, and subsequently Foreign Secretary)."

But the reward did not come, and having waited impatiently for a few weeks, and waited in vain, he decided to tackle the Prime Minister about it. Lloyd George told him that Lord Stamfordham had objected on behalf of the King, on the ground that such advances in the ranks of the peerage were never given except on leaving office. (Whether he conveyed this remark with a slight note of hope in his voice, Curzon does not mention.)

"I knew this to be so entirely contrary to the facts," Curzon wrote, "that I at once gave a list of over a dozen names to the P. M. proving to the contrary. He declared that he would not be put off by so absurd a plea, and that my name should appear in the New Year's Day list on January 1, 1921. However, I heard no more about it. My name was not in the list, and I never mentioned the subject again to the P. M., conceiving that he had either changed his mind or found the objections insurmountable."

A few months later, however, Curzon received a letter from Lord Birkenhead, the Lord Chancellor, asking for "my support to his elevation to a Viscountcy. . . . I thereupon told him my story, and added that I did not mean to mention the matter again, a course which he also decided to adopt. I heard no more until just before the King's Birthday the P. M., meeting me at dinner, told me that I should presently receive a letter containing the pleasure of the King. This letter came on May 28, 1921. When the list appeared, I found that the Lord Chancellor had been similarly honoured."

He always believed afterwards that he got his marquisate only because he might otherwise have made trouble over the elevation of Birkenhead, Lloyd George's crony.

"On this occasion," he added, "there was less trouble about my titles than before, for I only desired to keep the name Curzon of Kedleston in connection with the Marquisate, and to substitute the Earldom of Kedleston for my existing Earldom of Curzon of Kedleston."

He was content, though not completely so. It was some return for his labours, but was it enough? "Even radical newspapers, ordinarily none too friendly, actually complained that I had not received a Dukedom, in order to lend distinction to that somewhat tarnished order."

The congratulations rolled in from his friends, and among those he most treasured was one from Sir Arthur Hardinge, saying: "You ought to have got it when you left India, but no doubt our old friend St. John Brodrick was not then in a very kindly mood." For he had had his revenge at last upon St. John Brodrick. He wrote to Lord Midleton (as Brodrick now was) asking him to take a seat on the Government Front Bench in the Lords, and was able thereafter—for Midleton accepted—to patronise him as one of his subordinates.

THE SITUATION IN TURKEY was growing serious. Lloyd George had always been pro-Greek, and he hated the Turks. He wanted Greece to become the great power in the eastern Mediterranean, and there is no doubt that he encouraged them, against all advice, to pursue their ambitions in Smyrna and Asia Minor.

Churchill was against him in this. So was the War Office. And so, after some preliminary hesitations, was Curzon. He had begun by advocating the expulsion of Turkey from Europe, but he had accepted the majority decision of the Cabinet to allow the Turks to remain there. Now, as he watched the Prime Minister's perfervid pursuit of the pro-Greek idea, he began to have his doubts and to oppose him.

When the Greeks sent Gounaris to London to ask for aid in money and arms, Curzon told him that England could do nothing and that he should rely upon the good offices of the Allies to extricate the Greeks from their position in Asia Minor— where they were about to be overrun by the resurgent Turkish armies under the command of Mustapha Kemal. (The French, having meanwhile decided which side was going to win, had sent an envoy to the Turks and had begun supplying them with money and guns.)

The ill-fated Gounaris (he was subsequently executed for his failure) flitted to and fro between Athens and London begging for money and arms to carry on the war and, in Churchill's words, "still more for help to get out of it. He was confronted by Lord Curzon, who soused him in sonorous correctitudes. At these interviews the main effort of Gounaris was to throw the agonised fortunes of Greece into the sole hands of Great Britain; the main object of Lord Curzon was to avoid incurring in any form or sense this ugly responsibility."

This was wise politics and policy. If only he had fought for it more forthrightly. It was about this time that Curzon became aware that Lloyd George, acting in secret, was pursuing a policy exactly opposite to that of the Foreign Office. He used as his intermediary his private secretary, Philip Kerr, who was later to be characterised by Curzon as "most unsafe and insidious" and "full both of ability and guile." Kerr went to the Greeks and gave them advice diametrically opposed to that which Curzon, with the full weight of the Foreign Office and the War Office, had given them. He encouraged them to go on fighting. He promised Gounaris the loan which Curzon had refused him, and the Greek ambassador was soon cabling a coded message to his Government to tell them that everything was fine. They should refuse any settlement, even on the terms which Lloyd George (in public) had urged them to accept. He would be behind them. If Gounaris would only stay on in London, the Prime Minister would arrange for him to negotiate with the Treasury for the money that Greece so badly needed.

The Greek ambassador emphasised that no one, particularly Curzon and the Foreign Office, should know what had been taking place between the Greeks and Lloyd George's emissary, Philip Kerr. "I beg that it may not be known," he telegraphed, "that M. Gounaris is remaining here as a result of this discussion in order to regulate the financial position. The Press should merely be informed that as M. Calogeropoulos [the other Greek delegate] is proceeding to Brussels to meet his daughter, M. Gounaris has postponed for a couple of days his crossing to Paris. Finally, Mr. Lloyd George informed us that Great Britain has consecrated a warm corner in her heart for Greece, and proposes to assist her to return to her pristine glory. We expressed to the Prime Minister our deep gratitude."

The British Parliament and people were by no means so heartily behind the Greeks as this message would indicate, but the unfortunate Greeks were not to know this. Instead, they were encouraged to pursue their suicidal policy, and they were eventually ruined by it.

Now Curzon was not by any means ignorant of the clandestine negotiations in which the Prime Minister was engaged. He had learned from his experience in India, when he fought Kitchener, that it is sometimes useful to know what your opponent is telegraphing. He sent for the Foreign Office experts, who, he knew, had broken the Greek diplomatic code, and got

from them transcripts of all the telegrams the Greek ambassador
was sending home.

Why did he not go at once to the Prime Minister, flourish
the offending telegrams, and demand an explanation? He did
not do so—not at this moment, anyway. And the only explanation possible is that such a confrontation would have meant
an open break with the Prime Minister—and his own resignation.
And since he believed the Coalition Government had some time
to run, he was not ready to resign—yet.

Instead, he put the intercepted telegrams into his personal
file for future use.

The intrigues of "the Second Foreign Office" went on. Curzon
continued to break the telegraphic codes, to read the evidence,
and though he seethed with furious indignation, to hold his hand.

CHURCHILL DID NOT KNOW about the ammunition that Curzon
was accumulating in his locker, or else he might have been
even more scathing about the Foreign Secretary's attitude at
this time. He put Curzon's grumbling and unhappy inaction
down to lack of energy and conviction, and to his unwillingness
to cause trouble for himself. He was growing steadily more
convinced that Curzon had reached a stage in his development
when he would compromise over anything rather than resign
his office. When the Foreign Secretary backed down over a
new agreement with the Egyptians—in which he made a remarkable retreat from his old Imperialist attitude—Churchill scribbled a note and passed it across the Cabinet table to the Foreign
Secretary, who afterwards put it in his file.

It read:

"Surely you cannot but realise how very seriously an Egyptian surrender will be attached to your own great reputation in
the British Empire. It leaves me absolutely baffled to compre-

hend why you should be on this side or why you should have insisted on keeping Egyptian affairs in your hands, only to lead us to this melancholy conclusion. It grieves me to see what is unfolding."

Curzon scribbled back: "My dear Winston, I wonder what you would say if on a Colonial subject [Churchill was Minister for Colonies] I felt myself at liberty to make a speech—quite independent of the Colonial Office and critical of the attitude adopted by its chief."

To which Churchill replied: "You may say anything you like about the *Colonial* Office that is *sincerely* meant. But there is no comparison between these vital foreign matters which affect the whole future of the world and the mere departmental topics with which the Colonial Office is concerned. For these great matters, we must be allowed opinions."

Curzon commented, in a letter to Grace: "Rather a long and worrying controversy between Winston and myself over the Middle East. He wants to grab everything and to be a sort of Asiatic Foreign Minister. I absolutely declined to agree to this."

As he watched Curzon's attitude towards the mounting drama and disaster in Turkey, Churchill's contempt for Curzon came out into the open. The clash was not far off. His indictment of the Foreign Secretary's lack of vigor might have been even more bitter had he guessed how much Curzon knew of Lloyd George's intrigues, and how little he was combatting them. But even so, his attitude was sour enough when he wrote, in *The World Crisis*:

"It was Lord Curzon's failing . . . that he loved to state a case, and lost interest in it once it had flowed from his lips and his pen. He realised and deplored the plight of Greece; he hated the Turks and deplored their growing strength. He was scandalised by the suddenness with which the French had not only washed their hands of all Greek obligations, but had actually thrown their weight upon the Turkish side; but he was not often capable of producing real action in any sense. In deeds he rarely dented the surface of events. . . . He could not be reproached . . . because he had never at any time done anything in this theatre either good or bad which deflected the march of events."

Very soon now Curzon would be referring to Lloyd George, Churchill, Birkenhead, and Chamberlain as "the Camarilla." And they were already calling Curzon "Lord Alabaster."

CURZON HAD HELD ON to his secret telegrams for almost a year now, and had not used them—though Lloyd George's intrigues with the Greeks and his utilisation of "The Second Foreign Office" went on apace.

Early in 1922, however, rumours began to circulate through political circles in London that the Prime Minister's star was on the wane. In January of that year, when several of his friends and Ministers (though not, of course, Curzon) had gathered at Cannes, he had been strongly urged to go to the people and ask for a new mandate. The warmest advocate of this course was Beaverbrook, no less fervidly because one of the main planks in the platform was a proposal for an Empire Commercial Union. There was also present in the room a parrot in a cage.

"Sir Laming Worthington-Evans, the Secretary for War, spoke brilliantly in favour of an election [writes Beaverbrook in *Men and Power*]. He had a splendid voice. It seemed that he was carrying everything before him. When he concluded his argument, a hush fell upon the company. The opponents of the election were silenced. Then suddenly from that cage, the shriek of the English-speaking parrot cried: 'You bloody fool. You bloody fool.' Evans' argument was lost in laughter. The parrot had decided the issue. There was no election."

It was a fatal error for Lloyd George. Thereafter, his position progressively weakened.

And seeing the now hated Prime Minister beginning to fade, Curzon decided that the time had come to make his position clear. If Lloyd George fell, Curzon must be able to demonstrate that the policies the Prime Minister had pursued had been undertaken independently of his Foreign Secretary, who had been kept deliberately ignorant of many of them.

He chose as the occasion of his protest the dispatch of Lord Derby to Paris by Lloyd George to confer with the French Premier, M. Poincaré. The Prime Minister had not told him about it, but he discovered it through a leak in the French Press. He at once sat down and wrote three letters: to Lloyd George, to Derby, and to the French ambassador, St. Aulaire, who had taken part in the negotiations. His letters to Derby and the French envoy were strong, forthright, and pained. To Derby he wrote:

"I have had brought to my notice the passage in the *Echo de Paris* of February 24 describing in some detail the part alleged to have been played by you in the recent secret negotiations between the Prime Minister, Poincaré and St. Aulaire. . . . I confess that what shocked me was that you, who had served with me as a colleague and a friend and were an ex-ambassador, should have been willing to act in this way, without any communication to me. But for the disclosure I might never have learned what happened. I want you to consider what would be your feelings if you were in my place—as the writer in the *Echo de Paris* clearly expects you to be—and you heard that a negotiation had been conducted behind your back."

He was curt and cutting with St. Aulaire. "My dear Ambassador, I have now seen the passage in the *Echo de Paris* giving in full details the secret negotiations in which Your Excellency, the Prime Minister and Lord Derby recently took part. It more than confirms the impressions which I confessed to Your Excellency on Thursday last, and I have only to add that while I hold my present office I trust that such an incident may never recur."

It might have been expected that his letter to Lloyd George would be equally strong. Instead, he wrote:

". . . If it be so [that] you preferred to communicate confidentially with Poincaré through Lord Derby, instead of through the French ambassador or myself, I think that I might have been told instead of being left to ascertain the fact (if such it was) by accident. This is only one of a series of incidents extending over a long period of time which has led me to think that as Foreign Secretary I either do not possess your confidence or that I am intentionally excluded from a knowledge which I ought to share."

This is the sort of paragraph which usually is followed by the words: "I have no alternative, therefore, but to offer . . ." But Curzon went on:

"No one recognises more fully than I the commanding position in Foreign Affairs which your great experience and authority, as well as your position in all the meetings of the Supreme Council since the War, have compelled you to occupy, and no Foreign Secretary can ever, I think, have been more anxious to co-operate loyally with the ideas or plans of his Chief. But it has resulted in the fact that there have grown up, and there exist side by side, two Foreign Offices, one on either side of Downing Street. I submit to you all that passes on my side . . . but I only gather what passes in Downing Street by accident or by papers which are sent to me when the incident is over, or by references in intercepted telegrams to meetings of which I only hear for the first time."

He ended: "I daresay that for many of these meetings there is very good reason. Nor would I make the exaggerated claim that I ought to be invited. My only claim is that I ought to hear. I will give you from memory only—*for I have never been so querulous as to keep a list* [author's italics]—a number of cases come to my mind."

It was a lame letter indeed from one who was, later on, to describe himself as "profoundly humiliated" by these events. But he had written it. He had hit back at last at the intrigues of the Prime Minister.

He reached for the envelope, and began to write Lloyd George's name across it; and then he paused. Perhaps, after all, the Prime Minister was not on the point of departure. What if he interpreted the letter as a resignation—and decided to continue in office *without* Curzon's services?

Reluctantly, Curzon made up his mind. He took the letters to Derby, St. Aulaire, and Lloyd George, and instead of posting them, put them back in his file for future use.

CHAPTER FOURTEEN

Curzon versus "The Camarilla"

TROUBLE NOW CAME AT CURZON from all directions, and the belief grew in him, almost to a point of obsession, that the whole world was bent on crushing him, politically, mentally, financially, and physically.

His dream of producing a son was beginning to fade now, for none of the complicated operations, adjustments, or cures which Grace had undergone had produced the so desperately desired result. It began to look as if the marquisate would die with him, and he was black with jealousy when he learned that one of his relatives was about to produce a likely heir to the Scarsdale title.

In many of his letters now, he introduced pained or indignant references to his daughters, particularly Cynthia. "Cim's letter which I mentioned to you yesterday," he wrote to Grace, "is a most outrageous letter from a daughter to her father. You will remember that when, a little while ago, it was decided that the cheques from Washington [from the Levi Leiter trust] should go to her, she hotly resented the idea that she would not, according to her promise, pass them on to me. She then said she was a woman of honour. Now her letter contains the

words 'I can no longer undertake to hand over to you the
cheques from the marriage settlement fund. I give you ample
warning.' I think I must sell Broadstairs if I can get a good
offer; and it will not be very long, I suspect, before the Romney
will have to go. I must also cut down the garden at Hackwood. . . . What a curse money is. However, I will not bother
my poor girl with more. At least I can play about with the
insurance money, and by painting the wings instead of facing
them with stone [at Kedleston] have more for other things.
The men are already at work moving the summer house."

He pleaded with Grace to come to him for a spell at Kedleston. "Bring your mother," he wrote, "and you will not hate it
quite so much." But Grace did not go. Relations between them
had begun to be more strained than ever.

He had not been sleeping well, and when the drugs did
take effect he had bad dreams. "I had a most troubled night.
First I had a horrid dream. I had come to join you in London.
We were in rooms, presumably in some hotel. You were very
angry, though I have no idea about what, and eventually stalked
out of the room and rushed down the street, abusing me at the
top of your voice. All this was very agitating."

His back was bad. His relations with Lloyd George were
growing steadily worse. And then, early in 1922, he was struck
by a new affliction—a terrible pain and swelling in his right leg.

"Poor me. I have had a miserable morning," he told Grace,
"back aching, involuntary bursts of tears. The chef gets worse.
He has given us one ice three times in five days, and a second
in two."

He followed this twenty-four hours later with: "I have sent you
a wire to say that I had a rather better night, with much more
(artificial) sleep than I have had for a fortnight. . . . The
Danish doctor, Knutsen, came this morning and I enquired
exactly what I had in my leg, and the reply was thrombosis,
phlebitis and lymphangitis! . . . The right leg is more than two

inches longer than the left leg halfway up the groin. It is now
elevated on a pillow, but this seems to make it tingle and
prickle more than when it is flat."

It might have been expected, seriously ill as he was, that
Grace would rush to him, but she was busy preparing her
Lansdowne House Ball and did not come. She wrote instead
to say that her presence would only irritate him.

"The pain in my back has flown to a new place," he replied,
"and my poor leg is just as swollen and prickly as ever. . . . In
spite of your assurance that I must be so much better for your
absence (which you don't for a moment believe) I was nevertheless so tired and unwell yesterday evening that I had to
refuse to let Sandra dine with me."

His illness had prevented his accompanying the Prime Minister to Genoa, where one last attempt was being made to come
to some accommodation with the victorious Turks, and its failure provided him with his only joy. "Genoa has now finally
collapsed," he wrote, "and the P. M. is coming back with nothing—entirely his own fault. I hope it will be the last of these
fantastic gatherings, which are really only designed as a platform on which he is to perform."

Otherwise, he lay in bed, surrounded by his Foreign Office
boxes—for he still continued to work like a demon—racked with
pain, and a prey to dark suspicions. Churchill came to see him,
and, at first, he was pleased by his colleague's sympathy and
cheery chatter.

"Winston has just been in," he wrote, "very fat, conciliatory,
pleasant and amusing. He says Clemmy is going to have a baby
in September and they are looking out for a place on the sea,
at Frinton or elsewhere. Shall I offer them Naldera?"

But after Churchill had gone, suspicions began to crowd
into his mind, and from this moment he saw the shadows of
conspirators in every corner of his room.

In the "Notes for my Biographer" which he left behind after

his death, Curzon claims that he only became aware of a move to get rid of him long after the scheme had been frustrated. He wrote:

"During the last months, Birkenhead and Churchill were his (Lloyd George's) evil geniuses. The former egged him on in all his plots and plans. The latter, running in front harness with F.E. [Lord Birkenhead], exhibited his notorious lack of judgment and failed, as usual, to bring his audacious schemes to fruition. Only afterwards did I learn of the deep-seated plot to get rid of me in the summer of 1922. My illness was the excuse. Winston Churchill suddenly evinced the most affectionate interest in my welfare and twice came to see me in bed in London—in order to report how I was getting on. Though I was doing the entire daily work of the Foreign Office from my bedroom (as I had often to do my work in India when Viceroy) Lloyd George startled me one day by coming to see me himself—a thing he had never done before. I wondered what it could be for. Before he left he came out with the suggestion that Balfour should take my place at the Foreign Office for the remainder of the session. This was at the end of May. I accepted. Balfour had not the least intention of supplanting me, and only consented as an act of kindness. But when the session ended, and the Foreign Office and the public had become used to my absence, and its cause, Balfour was to retire and either Birkenhead or Churchill or perhaps even Derby was to take my place."

And in another note, he stated:

"I may add the following to the above notes, in order to complete the record of the treachery of Birkenhead, Churchill and company. Bonar Law told me at the Crillon in Paris, on the occasion of my visit to him in January, 1923, that Derby had told him that in the early part of 1922 (after the abortive Cannes Conference), when the question of the possible retirement of Lloyd George was raised, Birkenhead and Churchill had both approached him (Derby) and asked him if he would accept the premiership with Churchill leading in the Commons and Birkenhead in the Lords—Lloyd George, Chamberlain and myself all being kicked out. And failing this, whether he would serve as Foreign Secretary under either of them. These amazing suggestions Derby declared he had declined. But I do not know which was the greater—the absurdity or the perfidy of the offer."

All this (Curzon wrote) he became aware of only afterwards. In fact, however, the nightmares and dire imaginings troubled him all through his illness. The newspapers had, not unnaturally, begun to speculate about him, for they suspected that he was more seriously ill than he would admit—and it was no moment in history for an incapacitated Foreign Minister. Curzon, however, chose to regard it as all part of the deep-laid plot.

"I dare not put anything in the papers," he wrote to Grace, "or the *Daily Express* (Beaverbrook) will continue his clamour for me to resign. I wonder why I am pursued by that little brute, unless he wants to get F.E. [Lord Birkenhead] into my place. Winston yesterday brought me a message from Derby that he would call and have a talk. They all seem desperately anxious to know how near I am to resigning—it is very transparent."

He followed this with: "The *Daily Express*-Beaverbrook (for obvious reasons) announces that I am seriously ill, and that my friends are very anxious about me. I have told the Foreign Office to contradict."

It all depended, obviously, on how the words "seriously ill" were interpreted. No one reading Curzon's letters at this period can fail to be aware that they were written by a man sorely distressed in body and in mind, and hardly in a condition to face the problems of His Majesty's Minister for Foreign Affairs. It is hardly to be wondered at that his colleagues and the Press were worried about him.

Churchill and Walter Long, in fact, recommended a hypnotist as someone who might help him to cure his chronic insomnia, which was now worse than ever. But, coming from that source, it was hardly to be expected that Curzon would respond to such unorthodox treatment—though he did indeed send for the doctor they mentioned.

"Yesterday was a woeful night," he wrote afterwards. "I had in the wonderful Doctor Leahy about whose treatment of insomnia Walter Long and Winston Churchill told such wonderful tales. He came at five, a rather pleasant, not over-educated army surgeon. . . . He discoursed for the best part of an hour about his method, the conscious self, the sub-conscious self and heaven knows what. . . . He stood at the end of the bed, made me look at a gold ring on his finger, and talked all the time about the certainty that I would have a quiet night, a tranquil night, restful sleep, no more worry, the sub-conscious self fulfilling itself, then told me to close my eyes, went on chattering, declared I could not open them (which I found not the slightest difficulty in doing), announced that in half a minute, one minute, two minutes, I should be fast asleep—and finally after half an hour of this foolish chatter left me far more awake than when he first came. Then I took, under his instruction, my drug which failed to operate. At 3-30 A.M. I was desperate—I spent over half an hour ringing for nurse, who never came. I felt that I had the worst night for weeks."

Grace did not come either.

"No letter from Gracie," he wrote. "I think she must have been too busy, or have forgotten poor old Husbin. . . . (Later). I knew it. Didn't I tell you, Gracie, that you would never come back on Sunday? Nurse has said to me every day: 'Never mind, her Ladyship will be back on Sunday.' And I have replied each day: 'Wait and see.' And so it is. And I lie here day after day, in solitude and misery, with no one to see or talk to except the children. . . . When that sharp little daughter of yours, Marcella, came in I said: 'I have something to tell you about Mummy. Guess what it is.' 'She's not coming back on Sunday,' she said. 'I never thought she would.' "

IN JUNE, 1922, Austen Chamberlain came to tell him that the Resolutions for the new Session would be announced in Parliament towards the end of July, and that Curzon would be expected to introduce them. "That gives me exactly four weeks from today," he wrote. He had moved to Hackwood by this time (Grace had meanwhile gone to London) and had sufficiently recovered to take his first steps out of bed, though he was bandaged from groin to foot, and had grown so plump that his harness gripped him as in a vice. He received with fury and indignation the news that his old friend, Sir Henry Wilson, had been assassinated by Irish terrorists, but when it was announced that he would be buried in St. Paul's Curzon could not resist remarking to Grace:

"Murder has very curious consequences, for it transforms a good man into a great man and a fine fellow into a hero. Had he not been assassinated, Henry Wilson, for all his services and qualities, would never have lain in St. Paul's."

The Press was still anxiously discussing Curzon's fitness for service, and it was Northcliffe now who was clamouring for his resignation. "This morning I was thrown back by reading two vile paragraphs in *The Times* and *Daily Mail*, part of their ceaseless vendetta against me. I might have thought that Downing Street was somewhere in the background, were it not that these are the last two places with whom they would communicate! I accordingly telephoned at once to Vansittart and suggested a form of denial [that he was to resign] for the press tomorrow. . . . I am indeed ill-treated, for the Northcliffe people will not spare me even in my illness, and seem bent on getting me out, alive or dead."

He decided to utilise the four weeks before he reappeared in Parliament by going to Orleans, in France, where he had been recommended to try the services of a doctor who specialised in the cure of phlebitis. "Will you go with me, Gracie?" But Grace was involved in the dinners and balls of the Season and could not leave London. Swathed in bandages, gripped in his harness, in a sweat of pain and mental distress, he somehow got through the appalling journey. He was treated as a V. I. P. all the way, but that did not help.

"Hillel [the valet] got out at the wrong station and was not at Orleans when I arrived shortly before six p.m.," he wrote to Grace. "I was met by the Prefect—a polite gentleman—and his son, and he took me in his car to this hotel, which is only about 100 yards distant. When I came here I was carried upstairs by two men, and shown the most appalling set of rooms. The hotel is a commercial travellers' hotel, with the smallest comfort or luxury. Room with the most atrocious paper, only one electric light, light thin curtains, only a commonplace chaise-longue, and the most appalling din."

He could not sleep. The trams rattled outside. He roused the management to eject a client who stamped around the room upstairs. He had his valet search frantically around to discover a mouse which was scratching in the wainscotting. He even telephoned the Prefect to ask him to ban traffic from the region of his hotel in the night hours. The Prefect responded by putting his own house and servants at Curzon's disposal.

He sent long and loving messages to Grace, envying her the dances and dinners she was enjoying, and saying: "You would pity me if you saw me in this horrible place." But he added: "The only good thing is the doctor's confidence in my cure, which he says will easily be accomplished in a fortnight."

As, indeed, it was. He was by no means a well man, but by August, Curzon was fit to travel back to England again, insisting that he was ready to take on his duties at the Foreign

Office once more. He was on the verge of events of great
importance and drama.

CURZON HAS MAINTAINED, as has been mentioned earlier in
this story, that in September and October, 1922, he personally—
and almost unaided—saved Great Britain from a disastrous war
with Turkey. Several of those concerned in the dramatic events
of this momentous autumn have already given their versions of
what happened—Churchill, Lloyd George, Chamberlain, and
Bonar Law among them—and none of them agree that his role
was anything like as heroic as he afterwards claimed. But he
has left his versions behind (for he wrote several "Notes for
my Biographer"), and it is right that they should be examined.
    About the situation which confronted the British Govern-
ment at this time the facts are not in dispute. The Greeks, having been persuaded by Lloyd George to go into Asia Minor,
had been encouraged by him not only to remain there but to
annihilate the resurgent Turkish forces of Mustapha Kemal.
Right until the last, the Prime Minister continued to promise
them moral support and physical aid, if necessary, convinced
that their troops would wipe out the Turkish rabble. He had
done this behind Curzon's back but not without his knowledge,
for the Foreign Secretary had gone on perusing the decoded
telegrams. But though he scornfully remarked that an Army
which could not maintain order twenty miles outside Athens
could hardly be expected to conquer Asia, and though he had
forecast that disaster faced them, Curzon continually put off
making his own position an issue, and allowed himself to be
voted down in Cabinet. A resignation, followed by an open
attack upon the Prime Minister's suicidal pro-Greek policy, might
not have prevented the tragedy that was coming but would at
least have warned the nation of what was going on.
    Instead, he held on. Afterwards he was to complain bitterly

that his critics coupled his name with Lloyd George's in condemnation of what had been allowed to happen to the Greeks. But believing what he did, and still remaining in the Government, how can he be entirely dissociated from blame?

What happened to the Greeks was exactly what he had forecast. The Turks put them to the sword. Lloyd George was still optimistic. After Curzon voiced an objection to his policy at a Cabinet meeting, the Prime Minister scribbled a note and passed it over:

"We are really taking sides *against* Greece, whilst pretending to be neutral, and when the Greeks win—as they will—for Kemal cannot drive them out of Smyrna, they will resent for ever our futile attempt——"

But the Greeks did not win. With high patriotic fervour and ferocious savagery, the Turks drove the Greek Army before them into the sea, and then slaughtered the Christians in Smyrna and set fire to the city.

The jubilant and victorious Kemal, having done his worst with the Greeks, next turned his attention to Constantinople. The city had been occupied by token forces of the Allies under the Treaty of Sèvres, but Kemal now regarded this "shameful document," as he called it, as a dead letter. He wanted the city and the Straits, and was planning to send his hordes sweeping back into Europe.

The main British forces in the area were stationed on Chanak, where they were under the command of General Sir Charles Harington. There were also (at the moment, anyway) token forces from the French and Italian armies. But the forces were thin on the ground. Their situation looked grim. The Turks had already begun riding into their lines, and, in the language of the Second World War, were "making faces" at the British troops.

The Prime Minister, supported strongly by Churchill, Birkenhead, and Chamberlain, decided that the time had come to make a stand against the Turks. If Churchill had been against Lloyd George's philhellenism before, he was certainly with him now, and foreboding pictures rose in his mind of the brutal and savage Turks once more bringing slaughter, loot, and rapine back into the Balkans. The Cabinet met in Downing Street on Saturday morning, September 16, 1922. Curzon was not there. He made it a policy never to miss a weekend in the country, and he had departed for Hackwood. In his absence, Churchill drew up a manifesto which rallied the country in the face of grave crisis, and asked for the aid of the armies of the Dominions in preparation for the military operations which seemed imminent if Kemal was to be halted. (The appeal to the Empire was printed in the newspapers before the Governments concerned had decoded it, and they were embarrassed and furious.)

Curzon expressed anger and indignation at the action which had been taken in his absence. He believed the Churchill manifesto (especially since Churchill had written it) was alarmist and unnecessary and dangerously provoking.

"The General Staff (military and naval) lost their heads," he wrote, "and insisted that British lives were about to be sacrificed, British troops hurled into the Dardanelles, the freedom of the Straits gone forever, Thrace over-run, Constantinople handed over to massacre. I believe the bulk of this to have been a gross and ridiculous exaggeration. But it was made the excuse for Churchill's flamboyant manifesto, for the fantastic rumours in the Dominions, for the equally silly appeal to the Balkan States, for the rushing of troops and ships from far and wide to the Hellespont, and for the expenditure of the best part of £3,000,000."

In fact, it now seems probable that it was the Churchill manifesto which did the trick, and persuaded Kemal to hesitate and hold up his advance. If Lloyd George and his colleagues had only stopped there, they would have been able to claim truthfully—they claimed it anyway—that their forthrightness had saved Europe from a Turkish invasion. But from then on, a warmongering element seems to have got into their blood—and their subsequent actions (against Curzon's advice) were reckless indeed.

Curzon maintains, with some substance of evidence, that Lloyd George and his colleagues, convinced that they could outfight the Turks, were determined to provoke them to the point of war. But first, because he was against them, they had to get rid of Curzon.

"The country having been thrown into confusion, and the Alliance threatened, by the warlike attachment of a section of the Cabinet (Ll.G., Churchill, Birkenhead, Chamberlain, Horne and the myrmidons)," he wrote, "and by Churchill's famous manifesto of September 16, 1922, and my hostility both to the attack and the manifesto being well-known, the Cabal in question attempted to get rid of me by two successful strokes."

The first move in the plot (words like "the Cabal" and "the Camarilla" are freely sprinkled over his notes about this episode) took place on the Sunday morning following the Cabinet meeting at which the manifesto had been drawn up.

Says Curzon: "Chamberlain rang me up from Chequers with the famous rebuke (dictated by Ll.G., Birkenhead and Churchill, who were also there) for my absence from London the previous day, and with the order to return—*which I was expected on the score of illness to refuse (but did not)*. Secondly, having defeated this ruse, and having insisted at the Cabinet on Monday, September 18 on going to Paris myself to put matters right with M. Poincaré and the French, I was confronted half an hour before the Cabinet met with a letter from the P. M. suggesting that Birkenhead should accompany me. When I declined this suggestion, the P. M. actually brought it before the whole Cabinet and tried to force it upon me in the presence of F. E. [Birkenhead]. I still firmly declined in spite of the utmost pressure (Churchill describing my action as 'a deplorable error'), and said I would go alone or not at all. From that moment my star rose and theirs waned."

Curzon became convinced later that the reason Lloyd George wanted Birkenhead to accompany him to Paris was because the Lord Chancellor had secret instructions to force the issue, and not arrange a settlement with the French.

"I was a barrier strong enough to resist and defeat their perfidious design. His (Lloyd George's) Private Secretary subsequently told the French journalist, Pertinax, after Ll. G. had fallen, that the one fatal mistake they had made was to allow me to go to Paris in place of, or without, Birkenhead, who had been instructed to bring matters to an issue even at the cost of war."

Lloyd George was to maintain, on the other hand, that he had wanted Birkenhead along because the Foreign Secretary was still recovering from phlebitis and was tired and far from fit. This was certainly true. He was touchy, petulant, and highly emotional, and certainly in no condition to deal calmly with the French Premier. Poincaré, who was implacably determined that no French soldier would lift a hand against the Turks, had, twenty-four hours after the publication of the Churchill manifesto, "welshed" on Lloyd George by withdrawing his token army from General Harington's command.

Vansittart, who accompanied Curzon to Paris, wrote: "Curzon would have fared better supported by F. E.'s unique power of repartee, for, so soon as he upbraided Poincaré with desertion, he received a broadside which dissolved him." He did indeed. The Frenchman lashed him without mercy, with such effect that at one point he stalked out of the conference room, collapsed on a couch, and burst into tears. "The meeting adjourned," Vansittart recalled, "while he was revived by a secretarial flask."

For three more days, the British Foreign Secretary and Poincaré argued, wrangled, and beat the table, shouting at each other. But eventually a formula was found, and the French agreed to join with the British in making another approach to the Turks that would stabilise the situation. Shattered and exhausted, Curzon returned to London, convinced that he had saved the situation and prevented war. For a brief moment, it seemed as if he and his colleagues were reconciled. The Cabinet congratulated him on the success of his mission. Churchill passed a note across the Cabinet table which said:

"As I was one of the gloomiest about Paris, let me offer you *proportionate* congratulations."

Curzon, for his part, chose to forget the quarrels and intrigues, and made a statement saying: "At no point did the Prime Minister and his colleagues fail to give complete support going even beyond what I had asked for. The trust and wide latitude given me have contributed materially towards the result of the conference."*

Peace at last? Peace on Chanak? Peace in the Cabinet?

It certainly seemed like it. Curzon and his colleagues beamed at each other like one great happy family. But their lips soon curled back into the accustomed snarls of anger and suspicion.

In Greece a revolt broke out. King Constantine was toppled from his throne. M. Venizelos, who had been in exile, hurried to London as the emissary of the new Government, convinced that Lloyd George, who had always been his friend and admirer, would renew his backing of the Greek armies. Kemal seemed to have reached the same conclusion, and instead of responding to the invitation to an Anglo-French conference, he sent his troops back again into the no-man's-land which separated them from the British troops, where they made menacing gestures through the wire.

The hopes of the pro-Greeks in the Cabinet rose once more. Under the new regime, Greece would be resurrected. Venizelos was given promises of aid and support. And on September 29,

---

* The biographer is tempted to add an exclamation mark to this sentence.

1922, the Cabinet decided by a majority, with Curzon voting against (for he still believed that peace could be secured by negotiation), and they dispatched a message to General Harington. He was to hand an ultimatum to Kemal telling him to withdraw from Chanak or face attack. It looked like war, and very soon, for the time-limit the Cabinet had told Harington to give was dangerously short.

"In the Cabinet discussion of these events," wrote Curzon, "Ll.G., Churchill and Birkenhead excelled themselves in jingo extravagance and fury. Chamberlain followed in their wake. . . . Finally, on the advice of [Earl] Cavan and [Lord] Beatty, who found themselves once more in the congenial atmosphere of war, the famous ultimatum was drawn up and sent off to Sir Charles Harington. It was couched originally in even more bloodthirsty terms, but I insisted on softening [it]. I felt confident that Harington, who had shown conspicuous commonsense and judgment throughout, would not allow the nation to be rushed into war by this violent and incendiary order."

The Cabinet met in continuous session, and now, where there had only a few days before been nothing but the murmur of contented bees, came the high-pitched buzz of angry wasps. Curzon pleaded for a delay of twenty-four hours in the presentation of the ultimatum. He was voted down.

"Matters came to a head on Saturday (or was it Sunday) night," he wrote. "The Cabinet met at 11 P.M. to receive the expected reply of Harington about the ultimatum, and to hear (as the majority hoped) that the first shot had been fired and the first bomb thrown. No reply was received from the general, though a telegram from Constantinople reached me. Then the warmongers ran amok. Birkenhead wanted to censure Harington at once. The plan of a Mudania Conference (with the Turks) was to be cancelled, and *conte que conte* we were to be drawn into hostilities. This attitude was warmly supported by Lloyd George and Churchill."

While the Cabinet ministers wallowed in rancour and spleen, Harington—with the calm confidence of the man who knew the situation on the spot—had meanwhile been ignoring the orders of the enfevered politicians at home. He never presented the ultimatum. Nor did the Turks make any further advances beyond the demarcation line on Chanak. The situation was saved.

But Curzon had no doubt that it was he personally who had saved the day. "I fought the battle alone, or almost alone," he wrote, "until at last the meeting was adjourned without any action being taken. It was at the end that Baldwin, Boscawen and Peel [three other Tory members of the Cabinet] told me they were prepared to act with me throughout and to resign with me if I felt compelled to do so. . . . The next day the above mentioned Conservative Ministers, with one or two others, asked to meet in my house, and offered to continue to do so, until we either defeated the plot or resigned in common. On the morrow came the news that Harington had refrained from acting on the ultimatum, and had saved the situation."

It was thus, Curzon maintained, that he had rescued Britain from war with Turkey. When Harington returned to London, and was given a lunch at which Curzon spoke, he (Curzon) wrote to Grace:

"He is a fine fellow, but I did not let out that he had cold feet about once a fortnight at Constantinople, and that I was always applying footwarmers to his lower extremities."

Never had Curzon felt more triumphant. He had bested his traducers. He had saved his country from the horror of war. Even the hated newspapers had begun to hail him as the peacemaker in a Cabinet of warmongers. "It has been a Homeric struggle," he wrote to Grace; but he had won.

Now, for the first time, he began to consider seriously the question of his resignation. Was the time ripe at last? The Tories were growing increasingly restive and were clamouring for an end of the Coalition. Austen Chamberlain was the elected Tory leader, but his actions over Chanak had put him among the pro-Lloyd George faction, and he had lost ground among the influential members of the Party. If the Government fell, and the Tories came to power instead, who else could they choose but Curzon himself—Curzon the saviour of his country? There was no one else to choose.

It was at this moment that Bonar Law (who had previously retired from the Tory leadership on the grounds of health) came back on to the scene.

CHAPTER FIFTEEN

Breach with Lloyd George

O NE OF THE GREAT SKILLS of democratic government, which few politicians learn and even great statesmen rarely sense instinctively, is to know when to resign. George Nathaniel Curzon never acquired the art at all because he could not—even when high principle was involved—relinquish office and the perquisites and trappings that went with it.

Not even the gesture which ended his glorious reign as Viceroy of India was a genuine one, for he had not meant it to be accepted. He regarded resignation as a blackmail letter rather than as a genuine expression of his deeply held beliefs, and by the time the great political crisis of October, 1922, came along even Curzon himself seems to have lost faith in its efficacy as a weapon. That can be the only explanation of the fantastic twistings and turnings in which he indulged during the last days of Lloyd George's Coalition Government.

He was afterwards to insist that he had endured the Prime Minister's intrigues, insults, and humiliations only because he believed that, by staying on as Foreign Secretary, he was obeying the wishes of his Party and because his high sense of duty had convinced him that he would thus save his country from the horrors of another war. In that case, why did he not immediately resign after the crisis over Chanak was successfully resolved? That the inclination to do so was in his mind is indicated by the notes he wrote afterwards about these events. Commenting on the heated Cabinet meeting which had taken place while the Government waited for the result of the ultimatum to the Turks (the ultimatum General Harington never delivered), he writes:

"Next day, the above mentioned Conservative Ministers [Baldwin, Boscawen, and Peel] asked to meet in my house, and offered to continue to do so until we either defeated the plot or resigned in common. . . . I regard that evening as the beginning of the break-up of the Coalition Government. When a group of Cabinet ministers begin to meet separately and to discuss independent action, the death tick is audible in the rafters."

He also took from his files "a formal letter that I had more than once drawn up for presentation to the P. M., threatening my resignation unless these indefensible tactics were stopped." This was the letter he had withheld earlier in the year. Now he re-drafted it in rather stronger terms, and sent a copy of it to Austen Chamberlain for his comments. (Chamberlain replied suggesting that he should shorten it.) But still he did not send it to Lloyd George, later excusing himself on the grounds that "the latest edition of the letter I had only withheld a few days earlier because, on the day which I had proposed to deliver it, I was sent by the Cabinet to Paris."

It is difficult to avoid the conviction that throughout this period Curzon was in a dither. He had lost his grip and did not know what to do.

He knew that the Tories were in revolt and wanted an end to the Coalition Government. He knew that Austen Chamberlain, Churchill, and Birkenhead were determined to stand loyally behind Lloyd George, and were prepared to fight both the Carlton Club and the Tory rank and file on the issue. If they were voted down, that would mean the end of Chamberlain as leader of the Tory Party. And, since there was no other leader in sight, that would mean the long-dreamed-of apotheosis of Curzon to the mastery of the Party and the inevitable premiership that would follow when they came, as they surely would, to power.

Yet he still hesitated. He was in no condition, mentally or physically, to make up his mind. He had waited for this opportunity for so long; but now, when it presented itself, he was afraid to take a risk. What if the Chamberlain–Churchill–Birkenhead Cabal won the day, and the Coalition continued? Curzon would be cast out. He would be back in the political desert—and the thought of it was more than he could bear.

The door to freedom and power was open, but he could not summon up the courage to go through it. Instead, he thrashed in a fever of indecision round and round his gilded cage. It was a time for boldness; and boldness had gone out of him.

It was during this period of frustration, while Curzon anxiously searched his mind and furiously chased his own tail, that Chamberlain, Churchill, and the pro-Coalition Tories in the Cabinet decided on a bold stroke of their own. The time was approaching when the Conservative Associations would be having their annual meeting, and it was certain that one demand emerging from it would be one to end the Lloyd George administration and put a Tory in his place. The group proposed to anticipate this agitation.

They proposed to have an immediate General Election on a Coalition platform, with the backing of the Carlton Club hierarchy. It would seem that the intention of the group was to propose that, *after* the election, Lloyd George would give way to a Tory premier, for one of the leading Tories afterwards wrote to Curzon about a conversation he had had with Churchill.

"I told him," wrote Sir G. Boscawen, "that much of the criticism of LL. G. was unjust, but that the average Conservative distrusted him profoundly and wanted a Conservative P. M. He

[Churchill] said that we could have one after a General Election and advocated an election at once at which we should go to the country as a united government."

Curzon was approached. He was asked to come to a dinner at Churchill's house to discuss the situation. He accepted the invitation. Of what happened at the dinner Churchill wrote an account in a private letter to Lord Ronaldshay (now the Marquis of Zetland) on November 29, 1927:

"There were present, besides Curzon, at this first dinner: Austen [Chamberlain], Birkenhead, Worthington-Evans and Horne, representing the Conservatives, and Ll. G. and I, representing the Liberals. The object was to discuss the question 'whether it was fair to the Conservative Party, and straightforward, to bring on a General Election before the meeting of the National Union [of Conservatives].' This was discussed exhaustively for nearly two hours after we had left the dining room, all the Conservative ministers taking part. Ll. G. and I said very little, as the subject was domestic to the Conservatives."

In the end, Churchill goes on, the decision was in favour of an election before the meeting of the Conservative Associations.

"George Curzon, who was sitting in an armchair," writes Churchill, "got up and said, with great spirit, 'All right. I'm game.' As we were going downstairs (I was conducting my guests to the door), Birkenhead said to me, 'How fine of old Curzon to do that. What a good sportsman he is.' (It must be remembered that there had been a good deal of friction between Curzon and L. G. on Foreign Office matters in regard both to the French and the Turks; and it is this which gives significance to the remark)."

But having thrown in his lot with the hated Cabal, Curzon almost immediately regretted it. He was in a ferment of uncertainty once more. Had he done right? Had he backed the right side?

His state of mind was certainly not calmed by yet another

example of Lloyd George's intrigues behind his back. Shortly after the dinner at Churchill's, a certain M. Giannini arrived in London as a private emissary of the Italian Government. Lloyd George did not inform Curzon or the Foreign Office of this fact. Instead, he arranged for Giannini to be seen by Sir Edward Grigg, who acted as his go-between on this occasion, and they discussed a deal whereby the Italians and the British should co-ordinate their policy towards the forthcoming discussions for a final settlement of the peace negotiations.

After he had had a number of talks with Giannini, and reported back to the Prime Minister, Grigg had a fit of conscience and decided to tell Vansittart about what was going on. Vansittart asked him to draw up a memorandum on the secret talks, and passed it on to Lord Crowe, his colleague in the Foreign Office. Crowe decided that Curzon should be informed. He sent him a letter which said:

"The attached notes have been communicated by Sir Edward Grigg to Mr. Vansittart privately and in strict confidence as a friend. He does not wish to see them made official, but asks Vansittart to deal with them as he thinks fit. Vansittart has handed them to me, adding that he is most anxious not to get Grigg in trouble, because he and I feel sure he is merely acting on the standing directions given him by the P.M. It is, however, clear you must see these papers, and I cannot conceive that Grigg can really suppose that they could be kept from you. I gather that he merely does not wish to appear as the party communicating them."

Here was yet another example of the perfidy of the Prime Minister. But what could he do now? He had already told the Chamberlain–Churchill–Birkenhead combination that he was with them. They informed him that they proposed to hold another meeting at Churchill's house, at which the plans for a General Election would be co-ordinated.

Was it at this moment that Curzon decided to perform another of his by now notorious pirouettes, and finish by facing, politically, the other way?

Not quite. His mind was still not absolutely made up. He needed yet another strong arm to spin him around, and he got it from Bonar Law. Bonar Law had, the year before, retired from the forefront of Tory politics because of ill-health. But now he re-appeared on the political scene. Beaverbrook and his newspapers were boosting him as the only man who could save the Tory Party (and, incidentally, in their view, the country) from chaos. He had already made it clear, in a letter to *The Times*, that he disapproved of the policy towards Turkey of the Lloyd George–Chamberlain–Churchill faction. He soon found that both the hierarchy of the Carlton Club and the rank and file of the Tory Party were behind him in his objections.

He decided to intervene. But it was, for the moment, no more than the objection of a leading Tory who thought the affairs of the country were going the wrong way and felt the need to say so. He had no thought of resuming official political activity, but only of warning and guiding his colleagues. When he talked to Curzon, he did so (Curzon believed) only as an *eminence grise* giving counsel from the antechamber. It was as such that Curzon accepted him, and it was in the light of this belief that Curzon finally made up his mind. He became convinced that Bonar Law's views would carry weight against Chamberlain in any argument against the continuation of the Coalition.

There was, however, the question of his pledge to the Cabal. How was he going to wriggle out of that? Churchill had arranged a dinner party for Sunday night, October 15, and it had been assumed that Curzon would be there with the others to formulate the programme and tactics of the group. What excuse could he find for not going? He could hardly plead illness, for his colleagues all knew that George Curzon always came to a meeting when he wanted to, sick or not. Yet if he went, he would have to make his change of front clear to the others, and he was not anxious to come fully out into the open yet.

It was Lloyd George who provided him with his excuse, and unwittingly signed the death warrant of his Administration. The Prime Minister was due in Manchester on Saturday, October 14, to make an important speech on foreign affairs. It might have been expected that he would consult his Foreign Secretary beforehand—and there are two versions of why he did not.

Curzon writes:

"On Friday morning October 12 [he obviously means October 13], the P. M., fresh from an interview with the King, came for a few minutes into the Cabinet Room, where, after a meeting, a few of his colleagues were still assembled. He was in the highest spirits and in his most bellicose mood, and indicated in a few sentences some of the things that he proposed to say at Manchester tomorrow. Among these, in passing, he mentioned the subject of Turkish massacres, upon which I said to him that I hoped he would not take up that ground, since in recent cases the Greeks had been pretty well as bad—although the Turkish record over the whole war was, of course, appalling. On Sunday morning I read his speech with dismay. On the evening of a conference at which I should probably be charged with the task of making peace with a victorious Turkish Army and an exultant Turkish nation, he based his entire defence of the recent action of H. M. G. [His Majesty's Government] upon the desire to save Constantinople and Thrace from the bloody shambles of a Turkish massacre. He openly flouted the Turkish people. He once again flouted the French. . . ."

The inference of this is that the Prime Minister (in what was indeed an injudiciously timed harangue) had once more deliberately gone behind the back of his Foreign Secretary. But there is a different account, written by Sir Maurice (afterwards Lord) Hankey in a private note to the Prime Minister, Stanley Baldwin, on November 4, 1927. Hankey was Secretary to the Cabinet in 1922, and he writes:

"The ostensible reason on which Curzon seems to have based his breach with Lloyd George was a speech made by the P. M. on Saturday October 14. It is clearly stated in my diary that the P.M. had intended to consult Lord Curzon about the speech, but an unfortunate contretemps prevented this. Mr. Lloyd George had been to Churt to prepare the speech, and on Friday October 13 came to London, saw the King at noon, and, as Lord Curzon told me himself, had an appointment with him at 12-45 P.M. Owing to some question of emergency having arisen, however, a Conference of Ministers had been meeting, under Lord Balfour's presidency, at 10, Downing Street, and when Mr. Lloyd George arrived from his meeting with the King, instead of finding Lord Curzon alone he found a number of Ministers gossiping after their meeting, who all stayed on to talk matters over with the P. M. The result was that Mr. Lloyd George never had his heart to heart talk with Lord Curzon, and only gave him and his colleagues a general outline of what he meant to say."

Hankey adds in a margin-note: "As a matter of fact, before going to Churt, Mr. Lloyd George had given the Cabinet an outline of what he meant to say, and the particulars are on record in the Cabinet Minutes."

Whichever version is nearer to the whole truth, the fact remains that the speech provided just the avenue of escape Curzon had been seeking. He decided to take the plunge—though only in the shallow end for the moment.

"I came to the conclusion," wrote Curzon later, "that I could not by my presence at the Sunday dinner at Churchill's acquiesce in the sudden announcement of a General Election, whereby the Coalition, including myself, were to go on as a happy and united party. I saw that an irreparable and final split in the Conservative Party was imminent, and I saw the chances of a successful conference and an honourable peace imperilled if not destroyed. I therefore telephoned to Austen Chamberlain, who was at his country place in Surrey, asking him to come to see me sufficiently early on the Sunday afternoon to admit of a long conversation with me before the dinner. He did so, arriving at 5 o'clock, when I put before him the reasons for my abstention, which I asked him to explain to the meeting."

Chamberlain came, listened, and took a note with Curzon's excuses to the Churchill dinner.

That night Curzon sat down and wrote yet another letter of resignation. It was a new version of the old complaints. But this time it began by saying: "I write to beg you to ask H. M.'s permission to resign the office of Foreign Secretary in your Government." But even this one was never presented. It lies among his papers in an envelope across which he has written:

"Draft letter to P. M. written by me on Sunday October 14 [it should be October 15] after my interview with A. Chamberlain (prior to the decision at Churchill's) and only withheld because the situation developed so rapidly that its presentation was unnecessary—on October 18 Lloyd George fell."

On the morning after the Churchill dinner, Curzon went round to see Austen Chamberlain at 11 Downing Street to hear what had passed on the previous night. The pro-Lloyd George ministers had, in fact, decided to summon an immediate meeting of Conservative M. P.'s at the Carlton Club for Thursday, October 19, to place a programme before the Party, and to invite an expression of confidence in Austen Chamberlain's leadership.

Chamberlain was convinced that he could still swing the Tories around to his pro-Coalition viewpoint. Curzon, certain that he could not, did not tell his colleague that he had his letter of resignation in his pocket.

"While I was talking with Chamberlain," Curzon wrote, "the P. M. phoned and asked to see me as soon as I left No. 11. My feelings were such that I asked to be excused, but offered to call later in the day. The P. M., who was going to the country to play golf (!) subsequently wrote asking me to come at 12 on the morrow, October 17, 1922."

What the note from Lloyd George actually said was:

"My dear Foreign Secretary, I have promised to go to the country this afternoon. Would tomorrow at 11 suit you? Whatever befalls politically, I am anxious there should be no personal misunderstandings among men who have worked together for the nation in great days."

For the Prime Minister by now knew what was in Curzon's mind. He divined that his Foreign Secretary had decided to throw off the chains at last.

Of the meeting which took place between the two men the following morning, only Curzon has left a record. He went back and wrote out an account of it "for my Biographer." It must indeed have been a fascinating encounter. At long last, Curzon felt sure enough of himself to speak out about all the resentments, frustrations, and humiliations which had been for so long curdling in his mind. It was not so much a meeting, or even a confrontation, as a psychological purge of all the rancours and resentments of twenty-five years' standing. For there is little doubt that gradually through their association, Curzon had begun to see Lloyd George as yet another Kitchener endeavouring by trick, guile, and stratagem, to trip him up on the path to power; and by the commanding position which he occupied now, he was able to savour not only a victory over the Prime Minister but a symbolic wiping-out of the stain of defeat which he had carried with him on his departure from India. He had waited a long time—but the bullies, the braggarts, the small-minded upstarts had been bested at last. Curzon had come through in the end.

Not, it must be hastily added, that Curzon (even by his own account) can have had it all his own way.

He writes of the meeting:

"Our conversation, which lasted for one hour and twenty minutes, was one of the most curious in which I have ever taken part, illustrating as it did so many aspects and methods of this extraordinary man (Lloyd George). On scores of occasions, at Cabinets and elsewhere, I had listened almost with stupefaction to his amazing faculty of confusing the issues, of a calculated and overpowering irrelevance in argument, of attempts to frighten his opponent by sudden and menacing attacks; also, when required, of gracious flattery and compliment and cooing apology, and of the most moving and sentimental appeals. All these tactics he employed at one time or another in our conversation, and had there been anyone to preserve the record a more complete conspectus of his talents could not have been given to the world."

Curzon, "meaning at last to have it out," had furnished himself with a list of the principal occasions during the preceding year "in which he had made my task either difficult or impossible."

But Lloyd George was not easily daunted.

"To every one," Curzon wrote, "he had a reply. If I quoted from secret sources of information, known both to him and me, which disclosed the underground movements both of himself and his secretariat, they were immediately denied. If I referred to the actual performances of his private secretaries (of which I had their written evidence in my pocket) he asked how I could believe such things of men of honour. If I reproached 10 Downing Street with having betrayed the Foreign Office, how often had not the Foreign Office misled 10 Downing Street. If I spoke of Giannini as an envoy, he was represented as a casual friend dropping into Downing Street to have a few words with Grigg. If the P. M. had recently summoned Venizelos to England without telling the Foreign Office, this was an act of prescience of which the Foreign Office was not capable, and which had saved the situation. When I retold the tale of the intrigue with Lord

Derby and the French Ambassador to get into touch with M. Poincaré behind my back some months ago, Derby was represented as the villain of the piece."

The two men wrangled on, both of them undoubtedly unburdening themselves of the spleen and resentments of years.

"In the course of this astonishing travesty of facts and evidence," Curzon went on, "the Prime Minister had at one moment offered a frank apology for any injustice to the Foreign Office of which he might have been guilty. He explained on the one hand that he had been led on by the expediency of war, which he had been entrusted with a mission to terminate, and of the subsequent peace which he had equally received a mandate to conduct—to interfere more in foreign affairs than would otherwise have been the case. On the one hand, he admitted he was a very irregular person who could not pursue ordinary methods, but who, somehow or other, arrived at his goal. He reached the climax, however, when in moving sentences, and with a voice charged with emotion, he asked me not to forget the great scenes in which we had taken part, and the common comradeship of the war, and thanked me for the loyalty which I had consistently shown both in speech and in action to him."

Curzon added: "I could not, or at least did not, question the sincerity of these utterances, sharply as they contrasted with the treatment I had so often received at his hands, and they enabled us to part in the most friendly fashion."

Did he, then, hand in his resignation at long last? What he wrote is this:

"I said that he was aware that my resignation was in his hands, and that he could act upon it when he chose, to which he replied, with unconscious gift of prophecy, 'As I shall probably be resigning myself on Thursday, we had better postpone a decision until then.'"

It was all over. Curzon was free at last. The years of bondage were over.

Birkenhead commented: "So the pro-Consul has ratted on us at last."

Churchill, rather more calmly, for he was writing years afterwards (to Lord Ronaldshay) said:

"I considered at the time that we had great reason to complain of a sudden and surprising change of front on G. N. C.'s part, after the definite agreement signified at the first dinner, and that no new fact, except the gathering feeling against the Coalition and his constant irritation against Ll. G.'s interference in the Foreign Office, existed to justify such a change."

Curzon records that, from this moment, he was not invited to any meetings of his principal colleagues, "being regarded either as a base deserter or as a lost soul. I made up my mind, however, that until after [the Conservative meeting on] Thursday I would not say a public word to embarrass or even to dissent from them. I did not wish to be unfaithful to the memories of my long association, or to be in any way personally responsible for the crisis which I knew to be gathering."

But he kept in touch—indeed, he kept in touch. There were constant conversations with his Conservative colleagues. "I consulted Bonar Law," he wrote, "who had not made up his mind as to the attitude he proposed to take."

But Bonar Law was definitely against the Coalition, and Curzon was more than ever certain that Chamberlain's pro-Lloyd George attitude would be voted down. The hours ticked by slowly as the vital Thursday meeting of the Tories loomed closer. And each hour seemed to bring Curzon's triumph nearer. For who else could the Tories choose?

"On Wednesday morning," he wrote, "when I saw Bonar Law he said that though his doctor had not vetoed his reappearance as a party leader, he himself had not the inclination nor the moral resilience to undertake the task. He knew from sad experience what the strain and burden of high office were. He had now been free from them for a year and a half, and he had pretty well made up his mind that he was not the man for a fresh undertaking. He knew well, from information and appeals that had reached him, that if he came out against Chamberlain at the Carlton meeting next day, the latter would be beaten and that the responsibility of forming a new Government would probably devolve upon him. But he had not the appetite for the task. . . ."

It must, therefore, be Curzon, for he was the leader next in line.

But, to quote Curzon's own words, *"upon what vicissitudes great events may turn."*

On Wednesday morning, the premiership seemed within his grasp. Twelve hours later, it had slipped once more through his fingers.

"In the evening, when I saw him [Bonar Law] again," Curzon wrote, "all had been changed. His mind had been made up. He had resolved—or been persuaded—to assume the lead, and he even gave me the substance of the speech which he proposed to make on the morrow."*

* It is about this meeting between Bonar Law and Curzon at Onslow Gardens that one of the more famous and sardonic stories of the crisis has been told. Sir Archibald Salvidge, the Tory leader from Liverpool, describes in his diary how, on this evening before the Carlton Club meeting, he went to see Bonar Law to plead with him not to split the Tory Party by coming out against the Coalition. He maintained vehemently to Bonar Law that he would be playing a lone game, and that not one of his Tory colleagues in the Coalition Cabinet would be with him. "Bonar puffed at his pipe for a few moments," Salvidge wrote. "At last he said, almost regretfully, without the slightest note of triumph in his voice, 'I may as well tell you that Lord Curzon is here. He is waiting in another room.' It was an absolute bombshell. So the much-vaunted loyalty of the Cabinet towards Lloyd George was a myth! Already the Coalition's Foreign Minister had a foot in the other camp." And Salvidge goes on to say that he carried the news of Curzon's desertion to Lloyd George and his colleagues at 10 Downing Street "and when I reached the news about Lord Curzon there was a gasp of consternation all around." Now this is a good story, but it is hard to believe that the other members of the Coalition were so naive as not to know that Curzon was in process of deserting them. They may not

Curzon's state of mind at the news of Bonar Law's decision to bid for the leadership can only be imagined, for he does not describe his feelings. But he at once decided that he would not attend the Carlton Club meeting.

"We discussed whether I ought to be present or not," he wrote. "In any case, I said I would not speak against my colleagues, and should insist on maintaining silence. But when he [Bonar Law] declared that this would be impossible, and that I could not escape being called upon, I decided, with his concurrence, that out of loyalty to Chamberlain I had better stay away. . . ."

The Carlton Club meeting voted down Chamberlain and hailed Bonar Law as their leader. Lloyd George resigned (never to rule again). The Coalition Government, which had won the war and lost the peace, which had touched the heights of inspired achievement and plumbed the depths of scummy discord, collapsed in a whimpering heap of rancour and malevolence.

"That afternoon," recorded Curzon, "Bonar Law came to my house after his audience with the King and asked me to continue in my office as Foreign Secretary, and to give him all the help I could in forming a Government and supporting his administration. This I willingly undertook to do."

In a way, it had been a victory. Curzon could at last look

---

have known the truth for certain, but they would have been bad politicians, and very dull people, had they not already suspected it. For this was Wednesday night. On the previous Sunday Curzon had wriggled out of the Churchill dinner. On Monday he had evaded an interview with Lloyd George. On Tuesday, he had talked with him for an hour and a half and made it clear that they had come to the parting of the ways—and that Lloyd George knew this is proved by the letter which he had written to Curzon on the Monday. On Wednesday morning they all knew that he had been to see Bonar Law. They must have been simple indeed if Curzon's defection came to them, on the Wednesday night, as a dramatic and confounding surprise. But perhaps they were merely putting on a show for Sir Archibald Salvidge.

forward to being his own Foreign Secretary, free from interference and intrigue. But it was a victory not in fortissimo, as he had hoped, but in diminuendo.

Still, as he got back to Foreign Affairs that winter of 1922, Curzon could comfort himself with the thought that there was yet time. After all, it could not be said that Bonar Law was a physically fit Prime Minister—or even a *willing* one.

THERE ARE TWO sour, but not unfascinating footnotes to the political crisis which ended the Coalition.

Chamberlain, Churchill, and Birkenhead, particularly, found it hard to forgive Curzon for the manner in which he had deserted them. They attacked him trenchantly, even bitterly, whenever the opportunity came along—and one appeared to do so, in December, 1922, while Curzon was at the Lausanne Conference.

The Greek Prime Minister, Gounaris, had been dragged from his sickbed, court-martialled, and shot in peculiarly savage circumstances—he was given a heart stimulant to keep him upright before the firing squad—for his part in the failure of the Greek armies in Turkey. At his trial in Athens in November, 1922, he produced letters which he had received from Curzon—letters which, he maintained, had promised him British help and encouraged him to pursue the Anatolian adventure. These letters were published in part in the *Daily Express,* and were immediately seized upon by Birkenhead and his friends as a weapon with which to attack Curzon.

"It was while I was at Lausanne in December 1922," wrote Curzon, "that my late colleagues, incensed at their defeat and at my triumph, organised the plot against me. . . . Birkenhead in the Lords and Grigg (LL. G.'s Private Secretary) in the Commons started the hare that the two letters . . . had never been circulated to the Cabinet, were unknown to Ll. G. and his colleagues, represented a display of autocratic independence on my part, and were responsible for the final collapse of the Greeks in Anatolia. . . ."

When the letters were subsequently examined, however, it was discovered that a number of Ministers had not only read them but also initialled them. Birkenhead was forced to get up in the Lords and make an apology. Curzon savoured his triumph.

"Had I been at home I could even more effectively have pulverised the enemy," he wrote, and added virtuously: "I declined, however, while fighting the battles of my country at Lausanne to take part in the ignoble affray at home."

But he never forgave Birkenhead for "the dastardly attempt," and Lloyd George, Chamberlain and Company henceforth became known in his letters to Grace as "the Dirty Dogs." Grace herself enthusiastically entered into the feud which Curzon now waged against Birkenhead, and wrote about a first night which she attended with Lady Cunard:

"Maud had the Royal Box, and the box opposite was occupied by Lord Birkenhead, who, to my horror, came in to visit our box!! I heard Maud say hallo to F. E. [Birkenhead] so I took great care not to look round. He then leant his two arms on the back of my chair and remained there, in full view of the whole theatre (which was crowded with friends) for the entire act. His wife was watching the proceedings from the box opposite with opera glasses, laughing the whole time. I felt sure he did the whole thing out of bravado. Maud was told next day by Locker Lampson, who was in Birkenhead's box, that when he returned to his wife he burst into tears, saying 'Lady Curzon cut me!!!' I fear however they were only drunken tears. Sir Frederick told me he thought he was blind drunk."

But if others could be vindictive, so could Curzon. During the last days of the Coalition Government he had, among all his other duties, been called upon to mediate in a farcical squabble in the royal household between the Lord Chamberlain and the

Lord Steward. The Lord Steward believed that the Lord Chamberlain was trying to usurp his precedence and functions, and had even gone to the extent of elbowing the Lord Chamberlain out of the way at royal levees, much to the embarrassment of the King.

Curzon eventually found a satisfactory resolution to the quarrel. The Lord Chamberlain was suitably grateful and wrote him a warm letter of thanks.

Now the Lord Chamberlain was the Duke of Atholl, who was extremely proud of his job at the Palace. When the Government changed, he presumed (as a Tory) that he would be confirmed in his post. Judge then his astonishment when, on the morning after the Conservative Party's announcement of the new Cabinet, he saw in the morning papers that he had been superseded. Not only that. It was Curzon who, as Leader in the House of Lords, had the say over Palace appointments, and he sent the new Lord Chamberlain (Lord Cromer) to Atholl to tell him to hand over his insignia at thirty minutes' notice.

Atholl was heartbroken and wrote a long, anguished letter pleading for a reconsideration and asking for an explanation. Curzon replied that he had read in a paper that Atholl had spoken on a Liberal platform, and therefore had thought he was against them, and that though it seemed that he (Curzon) had been mistaken, it was now too late to alter the appointments. Nor would he be budged by an appeal "from an old friend, for old time's sake" which followed from the Duchess of Atholl.

But a hint of the real reason why Curzon so curtly dismissed the Duke is given in the Duchess' letter, for she wrote:

"Is it because Bardie [Atholl] attended the Churchill dinner?"

He was always afterwards to consider the guests on that occasion as his mortal enemies.

CHAPTER SIXTEEN

The Conspirators Triumph

THE LAUSANNE CONFERENCE was different from all the others in which the Allies participated after the war. Hitherto, it had merely been a question of the victors handing out terms to the vanquished, who waited in the antechamber to hear their fate. Now the situation was changed. The Turks were in no mood to accept dictation. They had won the war in Asia Minor and wanted recognition, as well as the spoils, of their victory; and there was no question of imposing a settlement upon them, but rather of persuading them to accept an arrangement which would ensure that the Allies themselves should not be humiliated.

It was a conference which lasted for nearly twelve weeks, and they were long, exhausting, and quarrelsome weeks. There is no point in retelling the story of how they were spent, in wrangling, intrigue, and a prevailing atmosphere of crisis. For the purpose of this biography, the importance of the Lausanne Conference is the manner in which it demonstrated two things: the superb qualities of George Nathaniel Curzon as a negotiator, when he was on top of his form; and the personal relationship produced between himself and his new chief, Bonar Law.

In the first few weeks of 1923, Curzon was at his best. Freed from the restraints and frustrations of the Lloyd George regime, he felt the reins of power and prestige back in his hands, and he rode his horses well. The Turks were arrogant. The French and Italians were tricky, evasive, and untrustworthy.

Curzon was sure, at first, that he had a failure on his hands. "Today we came to close grips with the Turks," he wrote to Grace. "They were exceptionally rude and dilatory, behaving at the conference as no people would." He added: "I don't think poor Husbin will ever be Prime Minister, or indeed is fitted for it. The chances of a success here are so great that my shares will go down."

He was once more sleeping badly, and the failure of his valet (the Green Chartreuse-drinking alcoholic to whom reference has already been made) did not improve his temper. "He was blind drunk yesterday night, and tonight was found dancing downstairs with the lady visitors. I must dismiss him tomorrow and must now do without. This is the third drunkard running with which Chope [his butler] has provided me. It is awful hard luck on me. I shall have to dress myself."

The conferences with the Turks were nothing but "wrangle, wrangle, wrangle." He despised his French and Italian colleagues: "This evening I had a long talk with Barrere and Garroni, and Ismet Pasha [the Turkish delegate] about outstanding points. The way my two colleagues fawned upon him filled me with disgust. They are like old roues courting some youthful courtesan. It filled me with disgust and is the last way in which to approach an Oriental."

Of Ismet, he wrote later: "He came to see me this evening, and *stank* like a polecat."

But after this bad start, things improved, and they improved mainly due to Curzon's untiring efforts. He held constant meetings. He displayed a firm and unshakeable hand in face of Turkish arrogance and Franco-Italian hesitations. "My main difficulty," he wrote, "is that all my stands have to be made alone. These old buffers shudder with terror and are always imploring me to hang back. If they had been conducting negotiations we should not have had peace in a twelve-month, and even now they may wreck by their servility what I am on the verge of winning by firmness."

Slowly, however, his firmness won, and with it his spirits and his confidence rose. "I wonder if you read the wonderful tributes to me in the English newspapers, the Daily Telegraph, the Daily Mail, the Evening Standard and many others," he asked Grace. "I have suddenly been discovered at the age of 63. I was discovered when I was Viceroy of India from 39-46, then I was forgotten, traduced, buried, ignored. Now I have been dug up again and people seem to find life and even merit in the corpse."

Even so, he still had his moods of despondency and pessimism, especially after Grace, who came to stay with him at Lausanne, became bored and returned to London within ten days. "I have often thought of you during the day," he wrote, "and realised that politics is a poor (even when it is not a dirty) game."

But he plugged on. He was both convinced and determined that he could produce a settlement from the Conference, and he did not spare himself. Over Christmas, while all the other delegates disappeared to their homes or to winter sports, he stayed on alone in his Lausanne hotel, writing notes and memoranda. When the meetings were resumed, he pleaded, he wheedled, he threatened, he spurted gushers of words over their cringing or reluctant shoulders.

This was a time in his life when he was buoyant with hope and expectation again, and, at least in those moments when the conference was going well, he relaxed into his old boyish good spirits. He would invite his juniors to dinner and preside over them like an amiable uncle, regaling them with stories of his youthful adventures in distant places, his deep voice rolling over them in waves of oratory theatrically broken by pregnant pauses, whispered asides, and Rabelaisian chuckles. Only an occasional spasm across his leonine face or a faint sigh would betray the fact that his back was giving him pain. And as a special reward (as on the occasion when they had recovered his trousers from his erring valet), he would end the evening with his famous imitation of Tennyson reciting "Tears, idle tears."

But, of course, the conference did not always go well, and then Curzon's voice took on a hectoring tone, and aides marched around with hunted looks on their faces.

It was almost entirely due to his indefatigable efforts that anything at all (for no agreement was signed while he was there; it was sabotaged by the French) emerged from Lausanne. He became convinced, while he struggled on, that his Prime Minister was not giving him the support and encouragement he needed and deserved. Bonar Law was, in fact, wrestling with the French over Germany and was desperately anxious not to get Britain involved in war with the Turks; he repeatedly sent messages to Curzon urging caution.

These Curzon took badly. For all the loyal support he had publicly expressed towards Bonar Law, it cannot be said that in his heart he admired his Prime Minister. From his point of view, Bonar Law was, in any case, only an interim Premier keeping the seat warm until the more rightful occupant, himself, was called upon to occupy it.

Even in his letters to Bonar Law, his attitude was inclined to be that of a touchy schoolmaster to a not entirely trustworthy prefect.

"Before you fill the Regius Professorship at Oxford," he wrote to him, "I hope you will consult me as Chancellor of the University. Ll. G. usually did so with these appointments."

Bonar Law replied mildly that he had no objection; and he was equally soothing and unruffled when Curzon protested to him over the fact that he had had a "courtesy visit" from the French ambassador without giving him a full account of their conversation. But he cannot have been entirely pleased when he received letters from Curzon couched in these terms:

"I have been fighting here a battle the magnitude and difficulty of which you hardly realise at home. I am more than grateful for the free hand you have given me. But I have sometimes felt a little hurt that from start to finish I cannot recall a word of encouragement of my labours, while I am continually being told to beware of situations of which I am just as conscious as anyone at home and am perhaps able to apprise more accurately."

It may well be that the innate contempt which Curzon felt for him communicated itself to Bonar Law, even though he could not guess what Curzon was saying about him privately in his letters to Grace. She had written to him:

"Poor Bonar looks as if he has not shaved for days. He looks more like a Labour M. P. than a Tory one. . . . Sir George told me the whole truth, that if Bonar's health gave out you would be the only possible Prime Minister."

To which Curzon replied:

"I can well see that he could be quite dangerous if left alone."

Just before the abortive Conference of the Allied Prime Ministers began in Paris at the beginning of January, 1923, Bonar Law summoned his Foreign Secretary to Paris. Curzon went with great reluctance. He had travelled for ten hours in a day-train "because my health is such that I dare not travel by night," and he arrived irritable, suspicious, and unwell.

"I went to the Crillon, where, in Lloyd George's old familiar rooms," Curzon wrote, "I stayed talking to him until 1.30. when lunch supervened, and I did not get away until 3.30. . . . I found Bonar in a great panic, willing to give up anything and everything sooner than have a row, astonished at the responsibility I have assumed at Lausanne, and prepared for me to back down everywhere. He has not the least grasp of Foreign Affairs, no instinct for Oriental diplomacy. I have ascertained too that the various foolish telegrams I have received from the Foreign

Office lately have all been sent by him. I was really very much
staggered at his flabbiness and lack of grip, but I endeavoured
to give him some spirit and courage. . . . I do not think he will
ever be a great, though he may be a cautious and popular, Prime
Minister."

The Lausanne Conference dragged on. "Tonight I received
one of the usual carping telegrams from Bonar Law," wrote
Curzon. "I have written back to tell him what I think. From start
to finish, he has never sent me one word of encouragement, but
is always telling me to mind this and to mind that, of which he
is wholly ignorant. I hear he has been defeated by a unanimous
Cabinet about the American Debt, at which I rejoice."

These were the private remarks of Curzon to his wife. But
Bonar Law can surely not have been ignorant of what was going
on in his Foreign Secretary's mind. Nor was he unaware that, if
his health was in bad condition, so was that of his Foreign
Secretary.

Curzon came back to England in February. He came without
a treaty having been signed, but that was not his fault. His
labours had been great and good, and it was as a result of his
efforts that a treaty was signed later in the year. He was hailed
as a triumphant negotiator—and it was his due, for amid all the
squalid intrigues and underhand plots, he had never flagged.

He returned resolved to plunge into domestic politics. The
talk in the political world was all about Bonar Law's health.

"He continued to have trouble with his throat [writes Robert Blake in *The Unknown Prime Minister*]. Off and on, this
complaint had bothered him ever since the Election. It grew no
better, and on the last day of the session his voice was temporarily so weak that he had to delegate Baldwin to answer for
the Government on foreign policy. However, the Easter recess
was now at hand. It was hoped that Bonar Law would be fit
again when Parliament met in the middle of April."

He was not. And meanwhile, Curzon made his plans, aware

that his moment was approaching once more. He could not believe that there were any rivals who could best him this time. In fact, Bonar Law, determined in any case to retire in the autumn, had made an approach to Austen Chamberlain. He was anxious to heal the breach in the Tory Party and bring back Chamberlain and Birkenhead into the fold. He sent Beaverbrook to Chamberlain with the offer of Lord Privy Seal in the Government—and the premiership when he stepped down. Chamberlain, still smarting over the rupture, refused.

But Curzon was not to know this. Grace wrote him of a conversation she had had with Sir George Younger, Chairman of the Conservative Party organisation. "I asked him what about Austen [Chamberlain] getting back," she wrote. "He nearly jumped out of his skin, and said Austen would *never* get into this Government, and that the country would not stand him at any price. He said Curzon must get known in the country on his return."

That he determined to do. This time he was resolved that no one should cheat him of the rightful reward for his life of service.

He was sixty-four.

HE WAS SIXTY-FOUR and aware now that time was growing short for him. Into his letters and into his demeanour crept an attitude of alternating urgency and defeatism, bubbling optimism and black despair; every little triumph was precious to him, every little setback yet another blow from a cruel and misunderstanding world.

He came into the Foreign Office one day, beaming with happiness, and went over to Vansittart and almost (but not quite) slapped him over the shoulders as he exclaimed: "It is an absolute triumph. I have shown the dirty dogs at last." Vansittart, thinking that he had scored some great diplomatic victory over Poincaré, asked him to elucidate.

"My wife went into Hatchards today," Curzon replied, "and asked the little man how my new book *Tales of Travel* was doing. He said it was selling better than Churchill's or Asquith's!"

But a few days later, he was sulky and thunderous. His daughter Cynthia had written to him another letter about the Leiter will, asking for money. The King's Counsel he had consulted in an attempt to alter its terms had informed him that he could not withhold it from her. The alterations at Kedleston were costing more than he had calculated, the restorations at Bodiam Castle had gone wrong owing to the stupidity of the workmen, yet another of Grace's cheques had been sent back from the bank —and he had found the footman at Carlton House Terrace in bed with the upstairs maid. He read in the newspapers that the Ilford murderers (Mrs. Thompson and Bywaters) were to be executed and he exclaimed: "Good!" And he looked around at those Foreign Office officials who had not succeeded in running for cover and exclaimed, in his most contemptuous tones:

"What ghastly people one has to live among!"

It was less than a year before that Grace had been writing to him:

"I am feeling so well, and still full of hope—and so much love, waiting for the future Earl of Kedleston, as well as his beloved Daddy!"

And Curzon had written back, referring to the birth of another child among his relatives: "Never mind. We shall knock them out yet!"

But now the references to an heir fade from their correspondence at last, and a new asperity creeps in. Increasingly, Grace refers to "your Curzon-like manner" and ceases to sympathise with him even about his relationship with his daughters.

"Fatherhood is not your strong quality," she remarked.

While Curzon worked at his Foreign Office boxes, or dashed up to Kedleston and down to Bodiam, or wrote his magnum opus about the great houses in which he had lived, or squabbled with the butler about the household expenses, or lay in bed, writhing with a new pain in his back, Grace lived her separate life as society hostess and kept him up to date on the political gossip.

"Maud Cunard went to the Duchess of Atholl's reception, which she tells me was more like a funeral than anything else," she wrote. "She also told me she dined with Winston and he had said that the one position he longed for was the Foreign Office. We must not let him have it."

If Curzon was eager for the premiership, so was she, for that would fulfil her ambition to become the first hostess in the land; and she made a point of keeping in close social contact with the Conservative leaders, particularly Sir George Younger. Each letter contained a little suggestion about tactics in dealing with his political opponents. Sir George had referred to the fact that everyone seemed to be afraid of Birkenhead's "sharp tongue." She wrote: "He said the only way to treat F. E. [Birkenhead] is with studied politeness, as it was the only thing he did not understand, and was completely disarmed and could not make his rude retorts. . . . The [Lord] Buckmasters think that F. E. will soon give up and he talks of going to America to lecture. I said 'How good for England!' "

Amid the whirl of her social round, Grace had been having her portrait painted by Sir John Lavery. It got good notices from the more discriminating critics, but some of the acerbities and irritations which had characterised the sittings seem to have crept into the finished portrait, and Grace decided that she did not like it.

Curzon hastened to agree. "I spent a long time looking at it from every angle," he wrote. "I think you are quite right in condemning it. It is not a good picture. It is not like you. It does you no sort of justice, and could never be hung in the State room at Kedleston, being all wrong in colour and tone. I think you should let Maud [Cunard] buy it from us, if she is so disposed, as I am convinced that it will never give us satisfaction, much less pleasure. I think also if we can dispose of it to Maud, we should at once give the sittings for a full-length portrait to Laszlo."

But Maud Cunard did not buy. Sir John Lavery soon heard rumours of his clients' dissatisfaction, though they had never conveyed their criticism to him, and he wrote to Curzon asking "whether the rumours were correct, and in the event of its being so, I suggested that I should have the picture back and endeavour to sell it—of course, not under Lady Curzon's name."

In the meantime, however, the Curzons, disliking the portrait or not, had been flattered enough to accept when the Liverpool and Glasgow Art Galleries asked permission to display it. Only after these exhibitions were over did Curzon send it back to Lavery, asking him to get rid of it, and also demanding a reduction in the fee of £1,200 which he had arranged to pay. Lavery reluctantly agreed to accept £800 ("providing you do not reveal this to anyone"); and when Curzon then wrote asking for the frame back, he sent a curt letter of refusal and angrily painted out the by now distasteful portrait.

THE TIME FOR A DECISION was drawing close. During the Easter recess, Bonar Law's health had not improved as much as he had hoped. He had taken a holiday at Torquay and had seemed to be fit and well; but the hoarseness in his throat still troubled him, and he had begun to be subjected to pain. Not even he knew for certain yet that he had cancer of the throat, but he was now longing for his retirement in the autumn; and the thought of who was to be his successor can rarely have been absent from his mind. He knew only too well that when he handed back his office to the King, he would be asked, as was customary of a retiring Premier, to name his successor. But who, who, who?

Meanwhile, in the political world, rumours had begun to circulate about Bonar Law's retirement. "There was general perturbation at the prospect," writes Robert Blake. "It was widely felt that Bonar Law, through his popularity in the House and his experience of office, was the lynch pin of the Government. What would happen if he were to resign?"

Curzon had no doubt about what *should* happen—the summoning of himself to Buckingham Palace.

But he was suddenly panicked by rumours that Stanley Baldwin, the Leader in the House of Commons, was in the running for the succession. He at once resolved to scotch it and on April 22, 1923, he sent a letter, marked "Private and Confidential," to Bonar Law. It said:

"My dear Bonar, I have been asked three times within the last three weeks whether it is true that you are about to resign and recommend that Baldwin be appointed in your place. I have replied that there is not the smallest foundation for this canard, and I need hardly add that in my view your retirement would be a national calamity which should not be permitted to occur. I have never thought to push myself and my claims, and have done what work was allotted to me, and I am your senior colleague. I have been leader of the House of Lords for over six years. I am the sole member of the Cabinet who has served continually since 1915. I have a certain record and a certain reputation. Having filled high offices of State for over thirty years, I think I assisted materially to form your administration."

And here he reached the point of his letter:

"If, then, a successor to you were at any time a matter for consideration—and I devoutly hope it never will be—I could not surrender such claims as I may have, or consent to serve under any of my present colleagues. *As to this I am quite clear* [author's italics]. I am well aware that the appointment of the Head of

Government rests with the Crown, and depends on a number of factors which have to be considered in continuation. I also recollect that I am a member of the House of Lords. But when the newspapers have been talking cheerfully for over a year about the possibilities of Derby or Birkenhead as Prime Minister, I decline to admit that it is impossible for a peer ever again to preside over a British administration."

And he ended:

"Please do not understand me to make any suggestion or to prefer my request. The situation, I confidently hope, will never arise. But I thought I ought, in friendship, to let you know what are my personal feelings in this matter, since they are formed not in a hurry but after due reflection. I am, yours, Curzon."

Bonar Law replied to this letter:

"Your rumour is without foundation. I have not been up to the mark for a month or six weeks, but I have no intention of resigning unless my health should make it impossible to continue."

Curzon was not deceived by its noncommittal tone. "His caution in replying on that occasion," he wrote later, only ". . . made me doubt whether I should receive any support from him."

It would seem, however, that Bonar Law at this time, though he had his personal doubts as to Curzon's suitability as Premier, still saw him as the only possibility. Austen Chamberlain had indicated that he did not wish to be in the running. The only alternative, Stanley Baldwin, though Bonar Law liked him personally, was hardly stout or experienced enough material for Premier.

Who else, then, but Curzon?

Yet it is not difficult to perceive Bonar Law's hesitation as he contemplated the decision facing him. There were the political reasons against Curzon which gave him pause: Bonar Law considered him such an implacable enemy of the Chamberlain–Birkenhead group that he would never willingly heal the breach in the Party, which had always remained one of Bonar Law's aims (he was wrong about this, as will be seen). He knew Curzon to be temperamental, unstable, and autocratic, bad qualities in a democratic leader. He was not only unpopular with his colleagues, but to some he had become a figure of fun. There were also the personal reasons: the two men were antipathetic. Bonar Law would not have been human had he not taken into consideration the fact that, by handing on the Government to this haughty aristocrat, he would be giving the highest office in the land to a man he secretly suspected of despising him.

These feelings were exacerbated—indeed, according to his intimates, they were decisively affected—by an exchange of letters which took place between the two on April 25, 1923. The Prime Minister had written to his Foreign Secretary purely as a matter of courtesy to ask him to dot the "i's" and cross the "t's" of a decision he had already made.

Bonar Law wrote:

"Lord —— called to say that he had been invited to form a syndicate to develop Turkey in various ways including a loan, and wished to know if there was any objection on the part of the Government to his doing this before peace was declared. I see none, but would be glad to have your confirmation before writing him definitely."

What the Prime Minister got back was, instead of a polite agreement, a flea in his ear.

"If I may say so," Curzon wrote back, "I think that the right thing would be for your private secretary to say that Lord —— should address himself to the F.O. and not to No. 10. As a matter of fact, I know all about Lord —— who was Lord Lieut. of my present county, Hants, and whom I have known for 30 years. He ran away from his wife—a most charming lady—with another woman: he had to resign the Lord Lieutenancy: he became involved in some very shady financial transactions: he had to sell his place and is wholly discredited. That anyone should offer a loan to Turkey before a peace is concluded would be very doubtful policy. But that that person should be Lord —— renders it quite out of the question. I am sure that you did not know all this. When these persons go to No. 10 instead of here they are really reproducing one of the least admirable features of the L.G. regime."

It was an offensive letter. It hurt Bonar Law deeply. He never told Curzon how much it had hurt him; but it seems to have been the final act of petulance which convinced him that, so far as he was concerned, Curzon was not a future Premier whom he could bring himself to recommend as his successor to the King.

Two days after he received this letter, Bonar Law had an audience of the King and told him that, on the advice of his physician, Sir Thomas (later Lord) Horder, he was going on a sea voyage. In his absence, Curzon would preside over Cabinet meetings. Baldwin would lead in the House of Commons. From that moment on, the drama (or, rather, the melodrama, for such it became) marched on to its sordid climax.

Early in May, Bonar Law disembarked from the Dutch liner *Juliana* in which he had been cruising and went to Aix-les-Bains, where Rudyard Kipling saw him. Kipling was so struck by his dolorous condition that he telephoned Beaverbrook, who came at once. The Prime Minister was taking ten aspirins a day to kill the pain in his face. Beaverbrook summoned Horder at once to Paris, and got his friend aboard a train and saw him comfortably into the Crillon. There Horder examined Bonar Law once more and reached his sad verdict—though he did not tell his patient. The Prime Minister, he revealed to Beaverbrook,

was indeed suffering from cancer of the throat of such malig-
nancy that he did not think he would have much more than
six months to live.

All through the earlier phases of Bonar Law's indisposition,
Beaverbrook had encouraged him to hold on to office. It was
the encouragement of friendship; but not entirely so. As he sur-
veyed the political scene, Beaverbrook too had gloomily wondered who might be the Prime Minister's successor, and was cast
down at the prospects. Curzon? He thought less of him than
did Bonar Law. Baldwin? He was a blundering tyro who had
made a mess of the American Debt Settlement. *And there was
no one else.*

If humanly possible, then, Bonar Law should be rallied and
persuaded to continue in office until such time as the breaches
in the Tory Party could be healed, and new, forthright, and
capable men could emerge.

Now, however, his sense of political responsibility was over-
borne by compassion for his friend. He could not tell him that
he was about to die. But he could at least ease his final months
of life by acquiescing in his desperate eagerness to give up the
agonising worries of office. Without revealing the reason, he
conveyed to Bonar Law that he had changed his mind and
was now with him in his will to resign. Such a fortification of
his own desire, coming as it did from such a trusted and beloved
quarter, had such an inspiriting effect upon the Prime Minister
that the clouds of doubt and despair lifted temporarily from
his mind—only, however, to settle again when he remembered
that, even in resignation, he had a duty to perform: to nominate
his successor. From every point of view, the only possible
inheritor of his position was Curzon. And Bonar Law did not
want Curzon to fill his shoes.

But how could he get out of the responsibility of nominat-
ing him?

Beaverbrook it was who provided him with the escape route

he was seeking. While they were in Paris, he had a conversation with Lord Crewe, the British ambassador, and mentioned what was troubling Bonar Law. Crewe replied that it was not an insoluble problem. It was not necessary for the Prime Minister to give any advice, unless he wished to do so, about the choice of his successor. He cited the precedent of his own father-in-law, Lord Rosebery, who was chosen to succeed Gladstone by Queen Victoria, even though Gladstone, if asked, would have nominated someone else. He mentioned Asquith, who had been made Premier by King Edward VII in 1908, without the advice of his predecessor, Sir Henry Campbell-Bannerman.

These precedents were, in fact, specious ones. Queen Victoria did not consult Gladstone because she was his enemy and deliberately went against his wishes. Asquith got the job because he was the obvious choice, and no consultation was necessary. It would obviously be a different case if the King was in doubt about the succession—and needed advice.

To Beaverbrook, however, this was not so much important as easing the mind of his friend. He sped away to Bonar Law and told him that he need not worry any more. It was not necessary for him to nominate his successor.

Bonar Law, convinced that by his seniority and prestige Curzon would get the office anyway, relaxed. At least he would not have to go down in history as the man who had chosen him.

AT WHICH POINT the conspirators enter.

Curzon was always afterwards to believe that he was not deprived but *cheated* out of the office of Prime Minister of Great Britain, his lifelong ambition; and there are plenty of indications that he was not far wrong.

By this time, he was well in the picture so far as Bonar Law's condition was concerned. Grace was in Paris, and Grace had been picking up the gossip. Lord Crewe had told his wife about

Horder's verdict on the Prime Minister, and Lady Crewe had passed on the information to Grace. (She also suggested that Grace should hurry round to see Beaverbrook and rally him to Curzon's cause, but this Grace decided not to do.) But Grace did telephone her husband and pass on the information, and also told him that she was coming back to England to be with him in the moment of triumph which was now certainly imminent.

Curzon was equally certain. Bonar Law returned to London and retired to his house in Onslow Gardens, and there began to write his letter of resignation to the King. He was not fit enough to present it personally. Curzon and Grace went down to Montacute, their house in Somerset, for the Whitsuntide weekend, there to await the summons which would soon be coming. He did not realise it then, but his habit of taking country weekends even in moments of crisis (it had once, it will be remembered, got him into trouble with Lloyd George) proved, in this case, to be fatal to his ambitions. For Montacute had no telephone and was remote from London. He was out of touch at a vital moment. While he rested serenely in his ivory tower, the knives and the truncheons were coming out from under the cloaks of his enemies.

Baldwin, for one, had decided that this was the time of now-or-never for him. He refused to be reconciled either to the apotheosis of Curzon or to the wrecking of his own ambitions. One day soon the rebel Tories would come back in line, and that would mean his supersession. He resolved to make a fight now for the premiership before it was too late, and he was in no mood to look askance at any weapon which might come in handy.

Whom did he have on his side? He knew he did not have Bonar Law. Over the Whitsuntide weekend, the Prime Minister summoned him to Onslow Gardens and told him frankly that although he was making no recommendation as to a successor, he was convinced that Curzon would inevitably be summoned.

Baldwin appeared to have accepted this dismissal of his hopes, and when he left, Bonar Law felt easy in his mind, convinced that he had persuaded Baldwin to work amicably in a Curzon administration.

In fact, however, Baldwin had already decided upon his tactics, and these certainly did not include a submission to Curzon. He had approached Lord Derby, whom he knew to be an old enemy of the Foreign Secretary, and got from him a pledge that he would refuse to serve under Curzon's premiership. He then went into colloquy with his friend and supporter, Lord Davidson. Davidson drew up a memorandum which was afterwards used, with devastating effect, in the negotiations of the next few days. This is what it said:

"The resignation of the Prime Minister makes it necessary for the Crown to exercise its prerogative in the choice of Mr. Bonar Law's successor. There appear to be only two possible alternatives—Mr. Stanley Baldwin and Lord Curzon.

"The case for each is very strong.

"Lord Curzon has, during a long life, held high office almost continuously and is therefore possessed of wide experience of government. His industry and mental equipment are of the highest order. His grasp of the international situation is great.

"Mr. Stanley Baldwin has had a very rapid promotion and has, by his gathering strength, exceeded the expectation of his most fervent friends. He is much liked by all shades of political opinion in the House of Commons and has the complete confidence of the City and the commercial world generally. He, in fact, typifies both the spirit of the Government which the people of this country elected last autumn and also the same characteristics which won the people's confidence for Mr. Bonar Law, i.e., honesty, simplicity and balance. There is, however, the disadvantage that compared to many of his colleagues his official life is short. On the other hand, there can be no doubt that Lord Curzon, temperamentally, does not inspire complete confidence in his colleagues, either as to his judgment or as to his ultimate strength of purpose in a crisis. His methods, too, are inappropriate to harmony. The prospect of his receiving deputations as Prime Minister from the Miners' Federation or the Triple Alliance, for example, is capable of causing alarm for the future relations between the Government and Labour—between moderate and less moderate opinion.

"The choice, in fact, seems to be recognising in an individual those services which, in Lord Curzon's case, enabled him to act as Deputy Minister but which, as is so often the case when larger issues are involved, might not qualify him in the permanent post. The time, in the opinion of many members of the House of Commons, has passed when the direction of domestic policy can be placed outside the House of Commons, and it is submitted that altho' foreign and imperial affairs are of vital importance stability at home must be the basic consideration. There is also the fact that Lord Curzon is regarded in the public eye as representing that section of privileged Conservatism which has its value but which in this democratic age cannot be too assiduously exploited.

"The number of Peers holding the highest offices in the Government, that is, four out of the five Secretaries of State, has already produced comment even among Conservatives. The situation in this respect would be accentuated by placing the direction of Government policy in the Upper House, for any further subordination of the House of Commons would be most strongly resented, not only by the Conservative Party as a whole but by every shade of democratic opinion in the country. It is thought that the truth of this view finds support in the fact that, whereas it would be most unlikely that Lord Curzon could form a Government without the inclusion of the present Chancellor of the Exchequer [Baldwin], on the other hand it would clearly be possible for Mr. Baldwin to form a Government even tho' Lord Curzon should find himself unable to join it.

"It is believed that Lord Derby would be willing, if necessary, to serve under Mr. Baldwin, but not under Lord Curzon.

"If the King should decide to call upon the Chancellor of the Exchequer he would, no doubt, urge upon Lord Curzon the reasons for his choice and appeal to him to continue his service."

Now this is, indeed, a well-argued document. A case of special pleading, no doubt, on behalf of the very man, Baldwin, who inspired it—but no less valuable for that, provided that it was presented to the King and his advisers with all the evidences of its origin.

"Here is a document from Baldwin's friends, arguing his case," the King could then have said, and proceeded to view it from this angle, match it against the arguments of equally partial advisers, and come to his decision.

But it was not so presented. No evidence was given to the King that Davidson, a close friend of Baldwin, had written it.

Instead, the memorandum was quietly passed over to Colonel Sir Charles Waterhouse, personal private secretary to Bonar Law. Waterhouse was known to be violently anti-Curzon—to such an extent that when he volunteered to carry Bonar Law's resignation to the King, the Prime Minister's relatives insisted that General Sir Frederick Sykes, a relative and a more trusted emissary, should go with him.

Sir Frederick never saw the Davidson memorandum, but Waterhouse had it with him, and he handed it over to Lord Stamfordham, the King's private secretary. Not only that. The evidence appears to show that he misrepresented the document. Far from saying who had written it, he attributed its sentiments to Bonar Law.

The memorandum, which now rests in the Windsor Archives, has the following note appended to it by Lord Stamfordham:

"This is the Memorandum handed to the King on Sunday, May the 20th, and which Colonel Waterhouse stated, practically expressed the views of Mr. Bonar Law."

No mention of Davidson. The inference which Waterhouse obviously intended should be gathered from the document was that *here were the views of Bonar Law on the succession which he would have made had he been asked by the King.* There is no doubt that the King, in his decision, was decisively affected by the memorandum. But there is evidence that Bonar Law was completely unaware of its existence. Beaverbrook was with him all during this time; he did not see it. His relatives were there; they did not see it.

That was one stab in the back for Curzon. There were others.

First, however, came a sally in his favour. The King called in Lord Salisbury to give his advice. Salisbury, coming in from his country retreat by milk train, made it clear that he was in favour of Curzon's accession to power. (He also made it clear, from a conversation he had had with Bonar Law, that the retiring Prime Minister was definitely not backing either of the two contenders.)

There followed a series of pinpricks from the smaller of Curzon's enemies, Leopold Amery particularly, who buttonholed Lord Stamfordham during a morning walk and inveighed against Curzon; not, to judge from the records, to much effect.

And then came a particularly poisonous thrust. The King decided to consult Lord Balfour. It must have become apparent from this story that Balfour and Curzon, though they came out of the same sort of egg and looked like birds of a feather, were in fact peacocks who simply could not bear to see each other strutting over the same lawn. Each was contemptuous of the other. Twice in Curzon's career, Balfour had—in Curzon's opinion—let him down; while he was Viceroy in India, and while he was a Minister under Lloyd George. Now came the third occasion.

Balfour was in the country, and sick in bed, but once he knew what was afoot he rose and journeyed to London. And there, with the dialectical mastery of which Curzon had so often bitterly complained, he made the case against the Foreign Secretary. He was careful not to bring personalities into it. There was no question of George Curzon's capabilities—it was just that, well, was it really the moment in history to have a Prime Minister in the House of Lords. He thought not, and decisively said so (and no offence to George, of course).

Such were the stealthy moves of the anti-Curzon forces over that pregnant Whitsuntide weekend. (There were others, of course; rather more legitimate moves—from Labour Party leaders, for instance, pointing to their growing strength in the Commons and the necessity of having an Opposition Premier in a place where they could get at him.) And all the time the manoeuvres were going on, Curzon stayed on in blissful ignorance at Montacute.

IN A LETTER which George Nathaniel Curzon once wrote to his brother-in-law, he said:

"Someone once told me that the world is composed of 1) Fools; 2) Damned fools, and 3) Bloody fools. The least one can do is try to stick to the first class."

Over the weekend of Whitsuntide, 1923, Curzon seems to have placed himself definitely in Category Three.

On Whit Monday morning there came a letter in the post from Bonar Law to tell him that the resignation was at last taking place. It said:

"I am sorry to say that I find it necessary to resign. . . . I understand that it is not customary for the King to ask the Prime Minister to recommend his successor in circumstances like the present and I presume that he will not do so; but if, as I hope, he accepts my resignation at once, he will have to take immediate steps about my successor."

Here, surely, was a warning that the road to the premiership was not going to be quite as smooth as he had imagined.

Curzon wrote later: "In the singularly curt and ungracious letter on May 20—and to which I replied, I hope, in a very

310 THE GLORIOUS FAULT

different spirit—he said not a word about myself or the succession, and it was accordingly with no surprise that I heard from Lord Stamfordham that, on the score of illness, he had evaded giving any advice on the subject to the King. Had Bonar Law lifted a little finger on my behalf, I should certainly have been Prime Minister. I bear him no grudge, since he may, after all, have been right. I record the fact."

But why did not the warning bells ring in his ears when he got the letter? And why did he not immediately catch the first train to London and find out what was going on?

Instead, he stayed on at Montacute and waited. "Not being on the telephone, I could not communicate with anyone in London, and I naturally refrained from hurrying back, lest my action should be misinterpreted," he wrote.

How else could his return have been interpreted than in the obvious way—that he was an elder statesman of the Administration, vitally interested in the negotiations which were in progress? Why did he not go back and fight for what he rightfully believed should be his? Was it because he was so sure that he wanted to play the childish, reluctant game of "Come on, coax me, persuade me into taking over"?

If so, it was the profoundest mistake of his life.

The melodrama, which now begins to take on undertones of farce and pathos, dragged on all through Whit Monday. The conspirators went on conspiring. Curzon went on waiting.

That evening, the village post office at Montacute was roused to take an important telegram from London. The village policeman was called to take it immediately to Montacute House. It was signed by Lord Stamfordham, the King's private secretary, and summoned Curzon urgently to London.

The tears of gratification welled into Curzon's eyes. To Grace he said: "The summons. It has come."

The long years of waiting were over.

THE JOURNEY TO LONDON from Montacute on Tuesday morning, May 22, 1923, was something in the nature of a triumphal procession. Crowds cheered their departure. Photographers swarmed the platform at Yeovil, and Grace, whose left cheek was swollen with toothache, had some difficulty in keeping her veil over it in front of the cameras. They chatted happily about plans for the glorious future. Grace told Curzon that she had decided to cancel a forthcoming journey to the Argentine (where she was going to look into the affairs of her estate) as she felt Her Boy would need her at home; there would be receptions, dinner parties, and balls to be given. They decided to use 10 Downing Street for official purposes only, and to do all their entertaining at 1 Carlton House Terrace. It was wonderful, it was exciting, it was the fulfilment of a great dream.

As he listened to his wife's prattle, Curzon read the newspapers. A less confident man might have noticed that, though most of them still seemed confident of his elevation, a note of doubt had crept into the political prognostications of some of them. He does not seem to have been aware of it at the time.

"On my journey to London," he wrote, "I had found in the morning Press an almost unanimous opinion that, the choice lying between Baldwin and myself, there was no question as to the immense superiority of my claims and little doubt as to the intentions of the King. The crowd of Press photographers at Paddington and my house—deceptive and even worthless as these phenomena are—at least indicated that popular belief."

It was not until he was established in his chair in his study, a cushion behind his head, his feet comfortably lying on his footrest, that the warning bell rang in his ears at last. And then it was still only a faint tinkle.

"Upon my arrival," he wrote, "I received a message from Lord Stamfordham that he would call at 2.30 P.M. I scented danger in the delay. But my wife, in her sweet enthusiasm, could not admit that if the King chose to pass me over, he would merely send his secretary to apologise."

Just before lunch, Oliver Locker-Lampson, M.P., was announced and was shown into the study and given a sherry. He brought a message from Austen Chamberlain "that he and his friends earnestly hoped for my appointment, and that some of them, including Chamberlain himself, would willingly consent to serve under me but could not do so under Baldwin." (This cannot have been a completely accurate assessment of Chamberlain's position, for he subsequently wrote to Curzon: "I was prepared for my own exclusion, and am only sorry that Stanley Baldwin did not think it worth while to see me earlier. It would have been a natural courtesy, and I think I might have helped him with my friends." Letter dated May 28, 1923.)

Curzon received this olive branch from the rebels with the magnanimity of a proconsul in a commanding position, and told Locker-Lampson to convey to Chamberlain that one of his first acts as Prime Minister would be to end the breach in the Tory Party and ask him to rejoin the Government. He then went in to lunch, and this time had no criticism to make of the quality of the food with which the chef had provided them.

Of what happened next, perhaps only Curzon's own account can convey the true quality. Promptly at 2.30 P.M. the King's private Secretary was shown in, and he noticed at once that Stamfordham was unhappy and uneasy. He wrote:

"Lord Stamfordham began by explaining, with obvious embarrassment, and in faltering language, the great difficulty in which the King had been placed. H. M. had been much offended at not being apprised of Bonar Law's hasty return to England, nor of his intention to resign, nor of his resignation itself, which he had first seen in the papers at Aldershot before the P. M.'s letter had been placed in his hands. He had further failed to receive, though he had sought it, any advice from Bonar Law as to his successor. In these circumstances, the King had to consult such opinion as he could, and Lord Stamfordham had been sent to London on the previous day for the purpose, and had seen Lord Salisbury and some other, unnamed, politicians.

"Next Lord Stamfordham went on to explain that the King fully recognized my pre-eminent claims—immeasurably superior, as he expressed it, to those of any other candidate. These claims were, he said, such as to entitle me to expect the succession, for which the King regarded me as in every way qualified.

"Nevertheless—and now the blow fell—the King had convinced himself that, inasmuch as the largest section of the Opposition to the present Government was a Labour Opposition, and as that party was not represented in the House of Lords, the future Leader of the Government must be in the House of Commons, where he could answer the Labour leader with full authority. Accordingly, the King had decided to pass me over and appoint Stanley Baldwin instead."

The news was such a shock to Curzon that he refused at first to believe it. This simply could not be. He looked at Grace, who was in the room during the interview, and then back to the embarrassed Stamfordham, and tears came into his eyes. He wiped them away; for this was nonsense.

He replied by thanking the King gravely for the honour he had done him in sending a personal explanation, and then said he presumed that he would be allowed to express his views about it. Stamfordham gave a hesitant nod. At once Curzon remarked that since the King had expressed such high compliments as to his career and service, surely he must realise that the slur involved in supersession would be all the greater. He then went on to point out that the King's decision was tantamount to laying down the doctrine, for the first time in British history, that a peer could never again be Prime Minister.

"I earnestly protest against the new doctrine," he said. "It involves an additional and perpetual and cruel disability upon the order of the House to which I belong."

Lord Stamfordham could only say that circumstances might alter. He was, by this time, looking at the door. But Curzon was determined that he should not go yet. He had only just begun to realise that the premiership might not, after all, be his, and he decided to fight, at last.

"I then went on to say," he wrote, "that the decision of the King would render my position in the Government difficult, if not impossible, and that my retirement at this juncture would not strengthen the Government at home or abroad, where so many important negotiations were in my hands. For this result, Lord Stamfordham said, the King must, of course, take full responsibility, though His Majesty expressed a desire that my services might be retained.

"Lastly, I put before Lord Stamfordham the following consideration. Only an hour before his arrival, there had called upon me a representative from Austen Chamberlain with a message that he and his friends earnestly hoped for my appointment and that some of them, including Chamberlain himself, would willingly consent to serve under me but could not do so under Baldwin. Had I been chosen by the King, I should certainly, in the interests of both the Government and the country have made party reunion the object, if not the condition, of my appointment, and I still thought that I was more likely to be able to achieve it than any other candidate."

By this time it is possible to imagine the position in which Lord Stamfordham found himself.

He knew (though Curzon did not) that as they talked, Stanley Baldwin was on his way to the Palace. He must have been hard put to it not to glance at his watch. He behaved throughout this painful and poignant interview with impeccable *sang-froid*. The only criticism that could possibly have been levelled at him is that, so far as the timing of events was concerned, he was not as completely frank as he might have been.

Curzon thought that there was still time for him to go on

fighting the hopeless battle; and Stamfordham did not disabuse him.

"I wondered whether all these considerations had been present in the mind of the King when he came to his decision," Curzon wrote, "and I asked Stamfordham respectfully to place them before the latter before he finally acted."

Stamfordham knew that it was already too late. Yet, according to Curzon, he undertook to tell the King. He then rose to take his leave. The time was 3.15. Curzon asked Stamfordham at what time the King proposed to send for Baldwin, and he told him, with a vague gesture, "in the course of the afternoon, before he returned to Aldershot in the evening."

It was enough to give Curzon the impression that there was indeed still time, and that his views might still carry weight with the Sovereign. After Stamfordham had gone, he sat back in his chair and he began to sob. But even now he still believed that out of humiliation and defeat, recognition and victory could yet be plucked.

"And now comes the point which causes me the bitterest feeling," he wrote. "Stamfordham's visit to me had been delayed to an hour when all protest or appeal from me was futile. For at that very hour—3.15 P.M.—Baldwin was already at the Palace, receiving his mission at the hands of the King. In other words, the decision had been taken and acted upon without any chance being given to me, the Acting-premier and the Leader of the other House of Parliament and the Senior Cabinet Minister, of even expressing an opinion.

"Such was the reward received for nearly forty years of public service in the highest offices. Such was the manner in which it was intimated to me that the cup of honourable ambition had been dashed from my lips, and that I could never aspire to fill the highest office in the service of the Crown."

Curzon may be excused, in these circumstances, the tears he shed. To one of a younger generation, looking back on the

manoeuvres and intrigues of those days in May, 1923, the resentment he felt at his treatment seems abundantly justified. His
own blind folly—plus his lack of political facility and his over-
weening vanity—may well have contributed to his defeat. But
conspiracy did more. One sympathises with him when he says:

"It is not for me to explain or find reasons for the King's
action. Doubtless he acted for the best. But I think he acted
with insufficient consideration of an old public servant. . . ."

But, of course, the King was not to blame. A new Premier
had been elected not because the King wanted him, but because
other forces had insisted. One is driven to the conclusion that
those who advised the Crown on this occasion were motivated
less by a desire to hand the reins of Government on to a worthy
successor to Bonar Law than by the desire to prevent the proud,
pompous, infuriating Curzon from getting them. Did patriotism
move them? Did high motives beat in their breast as they
counselled the King? Or was it spite and petty malevolence?

We will never know. All we do know is that Curzon was
tumbled and humiliated at a moment when he believed the
climax of his life-dream was about to be reached.

The conspirators got, instead of him, Stanley Baldwin, the
Prime Minister they preferred. And that might have been possible to bear, had it not been for the fact that the people—
who had played no part in this squalid comedy—got Stanley
Baldwin too.

CHAPTER SEVENTEEN

Life with Baldwin

IT MUST BY NOW have become clear that George Nathaniel Curzon had one great strength. In victory he may well have been insufferable, but (after the initial shock had been absorbed) he always proved to be invincible in defeat. The melancholy events which have been recounted in the last pages might well have ended the career of a lesser man. He had seen the supreme ambition of his life denied him in the very moment of his triumph. It was not only his failure, but the manner of it, which hurt him. He had been humbled and humiliated; and not only that. In the setbacks of his earlier life, he had always been able to buoy himself up by the thought that he would, one day, fight his way back to the top. But not this time. He was too old and too ill; the moment had passed, and he knew it would not come again.

Had he reacted as his enemies desired, he would have taken himself off to sulk in retirement, leaving the affairs of Government to the tender mercies of these puny, lesser men. In fact, however, he allowed himself only forty-eight hours for licking his wounds; and then, with no sign of blood showing, he lumbered like a great old bull elephant back among the political herd. His recovery was undoubtedly stimulated by the hundreds of letters, from men and women in all walks of life, who wrote him, inveighing against the decision, sympathising with him in his supersession.

That he remained bitter and resentful goes without saying. He blamed three men for his abasement—the King, Balfour, and Bonar Law. He made his displeasure over His Majesty's part in the affair clear by ostentatiously failing to turn up at a dinner which the King was attending on the evening of the day after the defeat. Grace went alone. "I suppose Curzon wouldn't come tonight because he didn't want to meet me," the King said to her. She replied: "He really is not very well, Sir—and he *is* very hurt and disappointed."

He hit back at Balfour by writing a long and devastating indictment of his outlook, attitude, and career.

So far as Bonar Law was concerned, Curzon insisted that he bore him no grudge. But when the ex-Premier died later in the year, it cannot be said that Curzon's tears flowed. On the contrary, when Bonar Law was buried in Westminster Abbey, Curzon wrote a letter to Grace in which he did not bother to conceal his true feelings.

"My darling Girl," he wrote, on November 23, 1923, "I have just come back from the Abbey funeral of Bonar. It was rather a sombre performance; and one could not help thinking that many of the congregation were wondering how poor old Bonar ever got there. I met [Lord] Burnham afterwards and asked him what the general sentiment on the subject was. He said that everyone knew it to be absurd; but that the Press had been stampeded by Beaverbrook who as soon as the breath was out of poor Bonar's body, turned on the blast of the Rothermere cum Beaverbrook furnace and practically forced the entire Press into line. He concurred in thinking that in a month or two Bonar would be completely forgotten, and that in days to come people would ask who he was and how he ever got there.

When we marched down the Choir to the Nave—where a little casket containing his ashes (for he had been cremated) was let down into a small hole in the pavement, shaped like this I found myself near the Prince of Wales. He fidgetted and looked about; never once turned a glance to the grave or the coffin, and showed himself profoundly bored with the whole performance. Of course cremation had the advantage of saving a great deal of space and thereby admitting of many future interments. But it has its ridiculous side. For a sham coffin was carried under a great white pall and deposited on a catafalque before the Sanctuary in the earlier part of the service and subsequently borne to the grave, where it was put on one side and disappeared, everyone knowing that there was no body in it at all."

For Baldwin, the new Prime Minister, he felt little more than contempt. Baldwin wrote him immediately after his elevation, on May 22, 1923:

"My dear Curzon,—I hope on personal and public grounds that you will feel able to continue your great work at the Foreign Office under the new administration. There never was a time when foreign affairs caused more concern than they do at present and your unrivalled experience is today one of the great assets of the Empire. Yours very sincerely, Stanley Baldwin."

He did not reply to it immediately. In the meantime, Curzon received a letter from Lord Salisbury which undoubtedly had a good deal of influence on his decision. Salisbury too saw the broader significance of the passing over of Curzon; in rejecting him, on the grounds that he was a member of the House of Lords, a precedent had been created. Like Curzon, he asked: "Does this mean that a peer can never again become Premier?" And for him the whole episode spelled the doom, in politics, of the class which he and Curzon represented. It was a time to hold on to one's rights and privileges. He sent a letter round by hand to Curzon on May 23, 1923, which said:

"My dear George,—Before you take an irretrievable step will you let me be so importunate as to sum up the arguments against it. As Foreign Secretary, your own success places a very heavy responsibility upon you. What will happen at Lausanne and at Constantinople? In the Cabinet, on whatever side of the table you sit, your personality will assert itself and have a weighty influence on affairs. These things are not only in the interest of the country but, unless they weigh with you, your own reputation and usefulness may be gravely injured. Just as you will be praised for your public spirit if you stay, so correlatively the party and country will resent your resignation as unpatriotic. The greater your claims, the greater they will think, *ought* to be your sacrifice."

And then he came to the crux of the matter:

"If the Government should turn out to be gravely injured by your loss, this resentment may turn out to have a permanent character. It is hard that there should be a disability attaching to the peerage, but it is in a measure true. More than this, our necessary detachment from the Commons and people reacts upon ourselves, and I think we often become unsympathetic with popular susceptibilities. At any rate, we are often thought to be so. This is so in your case. But if you make a mistake, it will make the judgment all the more severe. You have a great opportunity. Think of it. Yrs. evr, Salisbury."

It was after the receipt of this letter that Curzon accepted an invitation to lunch with Baldwin. From it, Baldwin emerged rubbing his hand over his stomach in a characteristic gesture of victory. Curzon had decided to go on flying the somewhat tattered flag of his class, and that night a letter from him to the new Prime Minister was issued:

"My dear Baldwin,—Allow me to congratulate you warmly upon your appointment to be Prime Minister. . . . I have seriously considered your kind invitation to me to continue in the office which I recently filled. I have every desire to retire. But, as there are several things which in the national interest I ought to endeavour to carry through, and as my retirement at this moment might be thought to involve distrust in your administration, which would be a quite unfounded suspicion, I will for the present continue at the Foreign Office. Yours, Curzon."

He took up the cudgels again with M. Poincaré over the perennial question of a settlement with Germany. For weeks on end he fought and wheedled and persisted until some sort of formula for a European way of life emerged from the divergent jealousies and antipathies of the Powers.

But his health, ever since the crisis of May, 1923, had been going downhill. His back hurt. His phlebitis had begun to trouble him again. He was overweight. He went that summer for a cure at Bagnolles, in France, but even if it reduced him around the waist it did not dissipate his temper. He could not sleep. "On one side of me," he wrote, "is an Englishman who snores badly. Above me—the floors being very thin—is an elderly Greek whose snores reverberate through the whole building and almost shake the floors. What with both, I did not sleep a second last night. I hammered at the wall to stop F——— and heard his wife expostulating with him. I then went upstairs and banged on the bedroom door of C———. He neither awoke nor stopped for an instant. It was like the discharge of artillery and went on without pause until 8 A.M."

He returned to England a slightly slimmer but no more happy man. Was everything going to pieces in his personal as well as his political life?

"I feel very much disheartened in writing to you," he wrote to Grace on September 20, 1923, "because you do not take the slightest interest in what I say or do. I have been back from France for a fortnight. You have never once asked me how was my leg. I told you that I had crushed my nail in a door, just

like Marcella. You have never enquired how it was getting on.
I told you that after prolonged trouble and correspondence I
had found the secret of your tapestry at Montacute. You never
even alluded to it. I enquired whether I could write about a
tutor for [your son] Hubert. You took no notice. Not one word
have you ever said about my office or Foreign Affairs. You
who once reproached me for not keeping you au fait with
everything that passed. . . . If I could reproach myself with
any conscious lack of affection or devotion I should not feel it
so badly. But I have not the slightest idea what I am supposed
to have done or not done. You shower affection upon everyone
else, until I feel that I am the person who comes latest and
counts least. But after all, I am your husband, and to me, since
we are married, you have been, as you know perfectly well,
everything in the world. I beg you, Gracie, to consider these
things, whether you wish to wound me or destroy me."

To which Grace replied:

"I am afraid no good will come of writing disagreeable letters to each other, as neither will in the least convince the other.
As our feelings are what they are, the only possible thing is
that we should lead our separate lives as much as possible, I
shall always play my part where I am needed, and do all I
can to help your public position. I don't mind your calling me
selfish, as it is utterly ridiculous. I am full of worries about
money matters and my affairs in Buenos Aires. . . ."

She departed for the Argentine on the trip which she would
have cancelled had Curzon been made Prime Minister. And it
is while she was away that he seems, at last, to have lost all
heart for the struggle. He had now convinced himself (with
some reason) that his only *raison d'être* in the Baldwin Cabinet
was to fight the battles which the Prime Minister would otherwise have been incapable of winning. "Baldwin comes back
next week," he wrote. "I am amused at the papers giving him

all the credit, where they give any, for the steady and upright policy we have pursued, considering that I have sent off every telegram and that he has never read one of them until it has been sent."

It was a time when Baldwin, increasingly aware that not everyone in the country considered him big enough for the boots into which he had been slipped, suddenly decided to go to the polls. He told his Cabinet and the Party that he wanted a General Election. Curzon came out at once and called it a disastrous decision. It was one more proof, if any were needed, that the man who had superseded him was a fool.

"Burnham said to me," he wrote to Grace, "'As you know, we backed you (in the *Daily Telegraph*) for the premiership against Baldwin, and every day is tending to show we were right.' . . . Smuts came to see me this afternoon . . . to implore me on no account to leave the Government or retire from the Foreign Office. He said that he and all his [Dominion] colleagues had been profoundly impressed by the feebleness of the P. M., who evidently knows nothing about anything except business and finance. They all realise that the only effective force, so far as the Home Government was concerned, had been myself, and that I was the Prime Minister in everything but name."

But Baldwin wanted the election as an endorsement of his administration, and no warnings would stop him. In his opposition to this project, Curzon even made temporary truce with his old enemy, Lord Derby.

"I think the Cabinet were profoundly incensed and shocked," Curzon wrote, "by the way they have been treated and the recklessness with which the Government and the country— entirely contrary to the wishes of either—has been plunged into a general election by the arbitrary fiat of a single weak and ignorant man. Jim Salisbury is talking of resigning and I think

I will. Derby is furious and says Europe is dominated by two madmen, Poincaré and Mussolini, and England is ruled by a damned idiot, Baldwin."

But Curzon added, sourly:

"This is the man he assisted to put into power in May last, and for whom he helped to turn me down. I wonder what all the men who clamoured for Baldwin will think now."

Whatever they thought, they thought it even more when the General Election was over, with—as Curzon had predicted—a disastrous setback for the Tories. The Labour Party came into Government, if not into real power (for the Liberals held the balance in the Commons). Curzon retired to Kedleston to supervise his rebuilding projects and the rehabilitation of his gardens.

When the Labour Party fell from office, he had a sporadic moment of hope, which was soon extinguished, that he might even yet achieve his goal of the premiership. But Baldwin was re-elected leader of the Party, and became Prime Minister once more. This time, Curzon was not even asked to fill the post of Foreign Secretary—it was given to Austen Chamberlain instead—and he was fobbed off with the office of Lord President of the Council. His instinct was to refuse, and retire for good and all. He was tired and ill and unhappy. But Grace, who had learned to like the prestige (and the diplomatic passport*) of a Cabinet Minister, persuaded him to accept. His demotion was not made more pleasant by the news that his old enemies, Churchill and Birkenhead, were in the new Cabinet, and that Churchill as Chancellor of the Exchequer was now his senior. He wrote to Grace, bitterly:

"While I was at the Foreign Office, up to a year and a half ago, I was the pacifier of Europe, the dominant figure among the Allies at Lausanne, the trusted friend of the ambassadors and ministers here. In May of last year, I was all but made Prime Minister amid the applause of a large section of the Press.

* Baldwin let her keep it after Curzon's death.

Even in January last, when I left the Foreign Office, I cannot
recall anyone but the Rothermere and Beaverbrook Press discovered that I had been a failure. The Foreign Office expressed
the keenest desire for my return. The papers wanted and
expected me to be made a Duke. Nine months have passed,
in which I have not lifted my voice or done anything to provoke notice, and suddenly, with one accord, the papers fall
upon me, denounce me as impossible, and clamour for my
supersession."

He had no doubt as to the identity of those who had con-
spired to strip him of his position and attack him in the Press.

"Yesterday," he wrote, "LL.G. opened fire at me in the *Daily
Chronicle* with a peculiarly malevolent attack. Considering that
I was his colleague for years, and one of his War Cabinet
ministers, the act and the language are those of the unmitigated
little cad that he is. Of course he has never forgiven me for
being instrumental in bringing Bonar Law in, and has at last
given vent to his spleen. I hope neither of us will ever speak
again to him or to his."

He added:

"Of course, at the bottom this is the carefully planned
revenge of the Birkenhead, Churchill, Chamberlain faction (with
Ll.G. in the background) for my action in October, 1922. With
their powerful backing in the Press, they have poisoned the
public mind until I am now depicted as a monster. It is also
the price that Baldwin has had to pay for their adhesion. . . .
Politics, as we have often remarked, are a dirty game, and the
mud which others stir seems to settle with an almost malignant
monotony on me. As you know, I would not have swallowed
what I have done, or consented to take office again, were it
not that you so strongly wished me to do so and that I am
always urged and expected to do 'the big thing.' . . . What a
pity it is that I am never able to agitate and petition and
intrigue, and therefore, in a crisis, I usually go under."

It was, as can be seen from these writings, the twilight of his career, and the darkening sky around him was filled with resentments, regrets, and bitter thoughts.

"There is a Cabinet tomorrow," he wrote, "at which I will preside for the first time, as in 1916, as President, and all the new Ministers will be sworn in. How unlike the last experience, when all was new and promising."

Only occasionally, now, does a shaft of his old sense of humour pierce the surrounding gloom. "As to me," he told Grace, "I look more like a butler than ever, and if I do leave the Government I am sure I can always get myself a good position." He found some compensation in his vast, ever-developing plans for the improvement of Kedleston. In 1926, the lease of Hackwood would be up, and it was his hope and dream that Grace would thenceforward consent to make Kedleston her home. He had Sir Edwin Lutyens, the great architect, make a plan for the reconstruction of the gardens. (He did not carry them through because they proved too expensive.) He waded about in the mud, personally overseeing the workmen, and fuming at their inefficiency and stupidity. He still dashed away to superintend work on his cherished castles of Tattershall and Bodiam. "I had a most successful day at Tattershall yesterday," he wrote to Grace. "Butler accompanied me, and he was ravished with its beauty, and so was I. Everything in perfect order, and beautiful. On our way back, we just had time to rush into Lincoln Cathedral, 5 P.M. nearly dark, but a service going on in the choir, and the glorious voices of the boys ringing down the lofty nave. It was a thing to be remembered."

Kedleston. The castles. After-dinner speeches. Long hours of research for vast histories he was writing of the great houses in which he had lived. The compilation of a vehement document justifying the manner in which he had administered his daughters' inheritance during their minority. The assembly of his papers for the benefit of his biographer—and the weeding out and destruction of those letters that illuminated the corridors of his life which he did not wish a biographer to enter. These were the activities with which he filled his hours.

But they were not enough, and he was at times dismally unhappy.

"I am having a peculiarly bad and lonely time here," he wrote to Grace from Kedleston, "with all these troubles and worries and never any one to turn to or speak to. I think you must try, Girlie, to be a little more with me in future. It is telling on me badly."

But Grace was leading her own separate life—parties at Hackwood; luncheons, dinners, and balls in town; and her newly acquired string of racehorses. She was seeing less and less of her husband. In January, 1925, he went for a short holiday in the south of France, where he stayed at the house of his old friend Consuelo Vanderbilt. Grace was in London having her picture painted by Sargent, but she promised to join him. Of course she did not, for she wired at the last moment and said she was in bed with a temperature. For the first time in his life, Curzon took no work with him, but spent his days driving around the countryside. "The only thing is that I do not sleep very well here," he wrote, "and my room being over the kitchen, the odious smell of cooking rises and comes into the room in the afternoon and evening."

Grace reported a rumour to him that he was, after all, going to be made a Duke for his services to the nation, but he only half-believed it.

"Your dear friend ——— hopes it will be done," he told her. "He does not know our Baldwin, who owes everything in the world to me and has never said one word in my support, either in public or private. But after all, what does it matter, darling?"

He added, in a later letter:

"I fancy it was the King who turned down the idea of a Dukedom, but we shall find out later. I am very glad I never moved a little finger in the matter."

GEORGE NATHANIEL CURZON had grown so used to sickness— for he had been in almost constant pain for forty-eight years— that he did not recognise a physical crisis when one struck him. From the south of France he went straight back to Kedleston, slopping around the garden once more, harrying the workmen; and it was in the garden that he collapsed and was carried to his bedroom. There he lay in his four-poster bed, surmounted by the huge "C" which had been stitched into the canopy by the seamstresses of the Royal School of Needlework. He covered himself with overcoats, for it was damp and cold and he would never have heating in his bedroom, and he lay for forty-eight hours, wretched in mind and body. He was seriously ill, but he did not—or would not—recognise the fact.

At the end of two days, he rose and journeyed south, for he had undertaken to make an important speech at Cambridge. From Carlton House Terrace, where he had stayed the night, Grace drove him to the station. "I am glad to remember that I did a thing which our busy lives seldom permitted," she wrote afterwards, and added:

"That night I was dining with Cecil and Alice Bingham, who had a big dinner party from which we were all to go on to a Ball given by Lord Brassey. Towards the end of the dinner I was called to the telephone to answer an enquiry from the Press—I was asked if George were ill, as there was a rumour that his speech at Cambridge would not be given. I said that I knew nothing of this, and that he had been perfectly well that afternoon. I felt very uneasy after this enquiry, but I did not telephone to Cambridge because I was sure that if George

needed me I should have received a message, and I knew that
if nothing was wrong he would have disliked receiving a fussy
telephone call from me based only on a rumour from the Press.
So I went on with the Binghams to Lord Brassey's Ball."

But Curzon did indeed need her. He had had a haemorrhage
while dressing for dinner, and had lost a great amount of
blood. Even so, he was determined to deliver his speech, and
was only persuaded not to do so by a grave warning from the
doctor who had been called in.

Grace drove him back to London the following morning to
Carlton House Terrace, where two doctors were waiting to
examine him. They advised an operation, but decided to wait
for three days, until he had built up his strength.

He spent those three days in typical Curzonian activity. He
called in his brother, Francis, and set about bringing his will
up to date. He compiled a vast memorandum of some 44 clauses
and 3,500 words, written in his own hand, giving the details
and location of all his papers. It included such paragraphs as:

"My Master Bramah key is on my watch chain. It opens all
or nearly all my despatch boxes and cases."

And:

"When the lease at Hackwood comes to an end, there will
probably be trouble with the owner or agent who has been
consistently disagreeable. I have spent thousands of pounds on
the place inside and out, and he has refused to discharge the
most elementary obligations of the lease. I mean to take *everything* inside and outside that belongs to me. I will not leave
him a single thing."

And:

"If she [Grace] contemplates selling any of the pictures at
Montacute or 1 C. H. T. which I have left to her, she will find a
full description with the prices that I gave for them in the
marble paper memo book in the library at 1 C. H. T. Should

the plea ever be put forward that the pictures were purchased
with the funds that would ultimately fall to my daughters,
the reply is that I bought nearly the whole from funds belong-
ing to me *personally* which I saved up for the purpose; and
that if I had bought them with Leiter money, I had a perfect
right to do so under the orders of the Court out of the allowance
made to me personally by the Court."

For he was determined that not even death should end his
feud with his daughters.

All this he wrote out in his own hand. He also replied personally to all the letters which now began to flow in, as the
country learned that he was gravely ill; and he sent round by
messenger a note of sympathy to the King, who had also been
ill.

He was operated upon on March 10, 1925. For eight days
afterwards, he seemed to be recovering; and then complications
set in. On March 18 his doctor, Sir Thomas (later Lord) Horder,
drew Grace aside and said to her:

"It is right that he should know. He is dying. He is a very
great man, and it would be wrong to deceive him any longer. He
should be told the truth, so that he may prepare his mind in his
own way."

When she went back into the bedroom—he had been moved
from his own upstairs room into Grace's more commodious bed
—Curzon immediately roused himself and asked her:

"What do they say? Am I going to recover?"

Grace told him the bad news.

It would be appropriate to record that he then gave vent to
his favourite Curzonian phrase of distaste: "How ghastly, how
absolutely ghastly!"

But though he could not quite bring himself to that, he did
receive the dolorous news with the calm fortitude and lack of
distress which had so often eluded him in moments of lesser
disaster. He did not even burst into tears.

He repeated the Lord's Prayer to himself. And then he, who had been all his life such a despairing insomniac, suddenly discovered the knack of it—and went off into a deep and peaceful sleep.

It was in his sleep that, on March 20, 1925, George Nathaniel Curzon died.

CHAPTER EIGHTEEN

Kedleston, and Peace at Last

I T WAS THE DEATH of a man, but it was also the end of an epoch.

George Nathaniel Curzon had been the author of many notable achievements in his lifetime. He had been a great Viceroy of India. He was always a devoted and indefatigable public servant, dedicated to the idea of Empire. He fought hard and he laboured long in his country's service.

He left behind him lasting monuments to his love of beauty and tradition: the castles of Tattershall and Bodiam, which he gave to the nation after his death, and the Taj Mahal and scores of other shrines, which he restored to their pristine glory in India during his lifetime.

But in politics, it was more by his disasters than by his triumphs that he left his footprints behind in the sands of time. He came into political life, by way of Kedleston and Eton and Oxford, as the predestined inheritor of an aristocratic tradition— as a statesman shaped by tradition and background to be a ruler of his people. In his lifetime, and in his own person, he saw that tradition shattered by the emergence of new forces. The pattern

of Government and the attitude of the people had been changing since the turn of the century, but Curzon was the catalyst
that quickened the revolution. It would have come anyway. With
the rise of the Labour Party, it was inevitable that the centre of
Government should move more and more away from the House
of Lords into the Commons, more and more out of the hands of
the predestined rulers into the avid fingers of the New Men. But
it was Curzon's failure to get the premiership in 1923—a failure
due more to his own personality than to his position and background—that speeded the change.

After his defeat it was not only obvious that there would
never again be a peer as Prime Minister of Britain, it was also
clear that a decisive crack had been made in the walls of the
hereditary Establishment. And nothing more symbolised the
metamorphosis than the group of men who carried Curzon's
coffin into Westminster Abbey for a burial service prior to his
interment at Kedleston. Two of the pallbearers represented the
Old Order from which he had come—Lord Salisbury and Lord
Oxford. But the weight of the coffin was borne by the New Men
who had taken over—Churchill, Birkenhead, Stanley Baldwin,
and Ramsay MacDonald. As he lay there in his coffin of two-
hundred-year-old Kedleston oak, covered with a pall embroidered
with the Curzon arms, his Garter and his Star of India on top of
him, one suspects that he can hardly have missed either the
irony or the significance of the occasion.

The Archbishop of Canterbury conducted the Service. The
newspapers now discovered all his virtues and achievements, and
lauded him. In life he had never been short of a critic; in death
he suddenly had none.

When the service was over, his body was put aboard the
train and taken north to his beloved Kedleston. There, in the
beautiful little memorial chapel which he had built, he was laid
beside his beloved first wife, Mary, underneath the marble figure
of the adoring angel.

And though his last years of life had not been exactly filled with mirth, he did, in death, have his one little joke.

Some months after his interment, Grace visited his tomb to leave some flowers. The electric light failed and she fumbled around among the shelves upon which lay the remains of the Curzon ancestors. Her fingers encountered a slip of paper on one of the shelves. When the lights went on again, she read it:

"Reserved for the Second Lady Curzon," it said in Curzon's handwriting.